the centenarian

or The Two Beringhelds

THE

WESLEYAN

EARLY CLASSICS OF

SCIENCE FICTION

SERIES

General Editor

Arthur B. Evans

Cosmos Latinos: An Anthology
of Science Fiction from Latin
America and Spain
    Andrea L. Bell and
    Yolanda Molina-Gavilán,
    eds.

Caesar's Column:
A Story of the Twentieth Century
    Ignatius Donnelly

Subterranean Worlds:
A Critical Anthology
    Peter Fitting, ed.

Lumen
    Camille Flammarion

The Last Man
    Jean-Baptiste Cousin
    de Grainville

The Battle of the Sexes
in Science Fiction
    Justine Larbalestier

The Yellow Wave:
A Romance of the Asiatic
Invasion of Australia
    Kenneth Mackay

The Moon Pool
    A. Merritt

The Twentieth Century
    Albert Robida

The World as It Shall Be
    Emile Souvestre

Star Maker
    Olaf Stapleton

The Begum's Millions
    Jules Verne

Invasion of the Sea
    Jules Verne

The Mighty Orinoco
    Jules Verne

The Mysterious Island
    Jules Verne

H. G. Wells: Traversing Time
    W. Warren Wagar

Deluge
    Sydney Fowler Wright

The centenarian

or *The Two Beringhelds*

Horace de saint-Aubin

PSEUDONYM OF

Honoré de Balzac

translated and annotated by

DANIÈLE CHATELAIN *and*

GEORGE SLUSSER

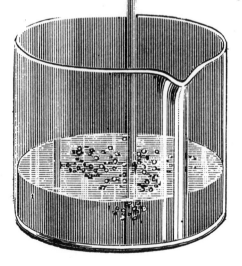

Wesleyan University Press   Middletown, Connecticut

Published by

Wesleyan University Press,

Middletown, CT 06459

www.wesleyan.edu/wespress

© 2005 by George Slusser and Danièle Chatelain

All rights reserved

Printed in the United States of America

5 4 3 2 1

ISBN 0-8195-6797-3

Library of Congress

Cataloging-in-Publication Data

appear on the last printed page of this book

CONTENTS

The novel *Le Centenaire, ou les deux Beringheld* appeared in four volumes, all dated 1822, under the imprint of Pollet, Libraire-Editeur, rue du Temple, no 36, Paris. The work is signed "M. Horace de Saint-Aubin, auteur du *Vicaire des Ardennes*," but the author in fact is the twenty-two-year-old Honoré de Balzac. The contract between Pollet and "M. Honoré de Balzac, homme de lettres" is reproduced in Balzac's *Correspondance* (1:197–198, letter 76 [Paris, August 11, 1822]). Balzac was to receive two thousand francs for the *Vicaire* and *Le Centenaire*, both to be completed in 1822. It is difficult to call these works "juvenilia," as Balzac was already a working professional, grinding out over sixty pages a day to meet his deadline.

"Horace de Saint-Aubin" and the earlier pseudonym "Lord R'Hoone" were the first literary incarnations of young Balzac. Lured by the promise of fame and fortune, Balzac, like many writers of his time, entered the thriving popular fiction market that flourished during the restoration of the monarchy in France (1814–1830). During that period we witness the beginnings of the concept of a "genre" novel, as distinct types of narrative sprang up in imitation of successful and widely read works. Maurice Bardèche (in his *Balzac* [Paris: Julliard, 1980], 52–68) describes the several types of novel then popular: the sentimental novel, the historical novel in the manner of Walter Scott, the novel of adventure, and finally the "roman noir" or gothic novel. Under the nom de plume Lord R'Hoone (an anagram on Honoré that also suggests "runes" and the Ossian vogue), Balzac wrote *L'Héritière de Birague*, a gothic novel à la Anne Radcliffe inspiration, followed by *Clotilde de Lusignan*, a Walter Scott imitation. *Le Centenaire* appears at first glance to be more of the same: an unoriginal imitation of another English-language success, Charles Maturin's *Melmoth the Wanderer*. In the "Avant-propos" to his *Comédie humaine*, written in 1842 toward the end of his career, Balzac in fact formally renounced the parentage of any novel that did not bear his name, including thus *The Centenarian*. This disavowal as well as the stigma that inheres to apprentice fiction and genre fiction alike has led modern critics to ignore these novels. Noncanonical, they are a priori inferior work. In the case of *The Centenarian*, however, nothing is further from the truth.

The Centenarian offers a creative fusion of genres in vogue: the gothic novel, the bildungsroman, the sentimental novel—even, in its Napoleonic episodes, the historical novel. These unite, in the final pages, to form a striking action narrative. Like threads in a tapestry, a genre attaches to each of the three central characters: the Centenarian (the gothic), his son Tullius or General Beringheld (the historical bildungsroman), and Tullius's "fiancée," the beautiful and chaste mountain girl (the sentimental novel). Beringheld, a huge, commanding, yet decrepit figure who claims to use science to produce the elixir of life that has sustained his existence for four hundred years, is a gothic presence. Gothic elements are plentiful in Balzac's novel: there are ancient Indian sages, haunted castles, pictures whose eyes appear to move. And, as in gothic novels (we think of *Frankenstein*), "magical" and alchemical occurrences are set against facts and phenomena drawn from contemporary science. In Balzac's work, however, immediately we see that the science is at once more detailed, more seriously up-to-date, and at times even visionary: for instance, he describes a cesarean birth carried out under hypnosis, using surgical techniques that leave little or no trace, like today's lasers. Equally striking is his description of the Centenarian's laboratory in the catacombs beneath Paris. In contrast to Frankenstein's bare space, Balzac details an array of retorts and beakers and infernal machines, the likes of which would not be seen again in fiction until the end of century with Wells. Visually, Balzac anticipates even further, this time to Rotwang's laboratory in Fritz Lang's *Metropolis*. With Balzac's *Centenarian*, the gothic has already mutated into science fiction.

The Centenarian is the dominant figure, yet much of the actual narrative is devoted to his son, Tullius, the "second Beringheld," who grows up during the French Revolution and comes to manhood in the armies of Napoleon. The novel begins in 1811 as General Tullius Beringheld is returning to Paris from the Spanish Campaign. He stops in Tours and there is involved in an episode involving the Centenarian, the father he has never formally met. The Centenarian has apparently lured the daughter of a popular factory owner to his laboratory and extracted from her being the elixir of life that sustains his existence. He is taken by a mob but escapes. The general, suspicious to local authorities because of his apparent knowledge of the Centenarian, feels obliged to hand them his memoirs, a document that explains his past and involvement with the old man. The narrative is now suspended in a long flashback. This memoir is in fact a detailed novel of education, a bildungsroman that recounts the birth, childhood, and schooling of young Tullius. The final episode in his story, which traces his rise to general in Napoleon's campaigns, is in itself a miniature historical narrative.

A large part of Tullius's education, however, is of the sentimental order. As in the bildungsroman, there are two contrasting female figures. The first, a ravishing marquise, older and worldly wise, introduces the young man to sensual love. The second is her exact opposite, the faithful lover Marianine. Along with Marianine come all the trappings of the sentimental novel: "sublime" high mountain settings, striking sunsets, swoons, purity of heart, and unending devotion. But just as Tullius, through his education in the world that shapes the Restoration France of Balzac's *Comédie humaine*, evolves away from the various genre worlds—the gothic, the sentimental and the heroic world of Napoleon—Marianine too will grow in the course of the novel out of the role of faithful rustic lover into that of strong woman: intelligent and calculating, a formidable adversary.

The climax of *The Centenarian* is a crucible in which these elements unite and from this blending is born the world of Balzac's later fiction. Marianine and her father leave Castle Beringheld for Paris to be near Tullius Beringheld in his glory. Napoleon, however, orders Tullius to the Russian front. During the time of his absence the beautiful Marianine, despairing of her lover, is stalked by the Centenarian who, not knowing she is Tullius's fiancée, sees her as a potential victim. She now appears destined to become, in the hands of the Centenarian, the standard gothic female victim. Yet caught between the Centenarian and her love for Tullius, she develops real strength and personality. In her culminating struggle with the Centenarian in the catacombs, she defeats the old man on his own ground, tricking him into expending the vital energy he needs to survive. In turn, however, her newfound self-reliance bodes ill for future domestic life with the younger Beringheld, as this romantic hero, inexperienced in the ways of post-Napoleonic mercantilism, prepares to enter the new Parisian arena of struggle.

Balzac's novel offers a compelling study of social and cultural conflict, prefigured in the subtitle "The Two Beringhelds." For at the heart of its action we find, in the diverging ways of the two protagonists, a clash not only of generations, but of two worlds at a crossroad—one the past of the ancien régime, the other the future of nascent capitalism. The Centenarian traces his aristocratic lineage back to Charlemagne; it is a line dominated by primogeniture. In terms of normal lineage, Tullius Beringheld would be the old man's great-grandson many times removed. In the immediate physical sense, however, he is the old man's flesh-and-blood son. A few years before the Revolution, the then Count Beringheld proves impotent and the countess sterile. Unwilling to let the male line die out, the Centenarian enters the countess's chambers, fathers an heir, and Tullius is born. Tullius, however, is a "new" man of his times, where careers are open to talent rather than birth. Caught up in the events of his time, Tullius breaks all ties with the past to take on a world where titles are bought and what counts is money and the social intrigue it engenders.

More important, however, this new world of postrevolutionary France is marked by the rise of modern experimental science with its strong influence on all domains of intellectual activity. At the core of the conflict between the two Beringhelds lies the problem of how science is pursued and used. The crux here is clear. Science in Tullius's world is a science of institutions, socially oriented, directed at serving the material dynamics of the emerging nineteenth century. In contrast, the Centenarian's science is ancient and personal. A "lone genius" in the mode of the Renaissance alchemist and overreacher, he puts science at the service of one project: that of keeping himself alive. For the Centenarian, the highest form of science is not one that explores material realms unknown, but instead pursues means of extending the life of the body that contains the mind and allows it to function.

The Centenarian is set in Tullius's world. In this world, the Centenarian must pursue his science in isolation, on its criminal fringes. The old man is set apart from the world of fashion by his uncanny physique—a huge, decrepit frame, dressed in an archaic greatcoat, he is a being not just from the distant past but from legend. In order to maintain the spark of life, the Centenarian must take the "vital fluid" of others. These are always people on the fringes of society. He bargains with the hangman: the Centenarian demands to be given a criminal before the man is fully hanged in exchange for curing the hangman's sick wife. He scours the battlefields of Napoleon to take dying soldiers to his lair. He lures women in despair for their lost lovers. He performs the actions of a vampire, but gets his elixir not by drinking blood but by distillation, making use of the most sophisticated laboratory equipment—"state of the art" technology. Likewise, when he fathers Tullius, he visits Countess Beringheld not as a succubus, but equipped with modern surgical devices and efficient pain-killing medicines.

Balzac's novel is one of the earliest works of science fiction. More than *Frankenstein*, *The Centenarian* focuses on the struggle between the obsessed scientist and social norms that is central to the genre to this day. Written a few years after Mary Shelley's novel—a work to which it owes virtually nothing—this novel offers, every bit as much as its English counterpart, a model or prototype for SF. Balzac's work is SF, not just in its scientific trappings but in the deeper sense that life extension and the questions it raises concerning the scientist's responsibility to community and nature have been a central problematic for SF throughout the twentieth century: witness the writing of Heinlein, Simak, and Haldeman, Dick's *Ubik*, Gibson's *Count Zero*, and the persistence of cryonics as area of scientific investigation. In its themes and motifs Balzac's novel has international appeal. Yet it is also as a novel operating in a particular French context—that of the Cartesian duality of mind and matter—perhaps the first uniquely French work of SF. For all of these reasons, and the fact that the novel is immensely entertaining, *The Centenarian* deserves the extended life given it in this new translation.

Balzac's *Le Centenaire* posed an interesting problem for its translators. It was hastily written and seems to be the work, in its early pages, of several hands. In many places it offers repetition and formulas. Padding is evident. Yet not only is it an important novel for Balzac's development as a writer, but over the course of its pages Balzac visibly grows as a writer, developing many aspects of his future narrative style. At first we were tempted to cut certain excesses. We soon realized, however, that by offering a literal translation, excesses and all, we give the reader an organic sense of the writer's progress as he moves from awkward experiment to mastery of plot and character development.

Some background is needed to depict the conditions under which the work was written. Balzac, throughout his career, was a writer who produced under the pressure of deadlines. His "juvenile" exploits differ only in degree, not in kind. *Le Centenaire* was written for the emerging commercial publishing market. Authors were offered "genres" to imitate and asked to produce novels in little time. The young Balzac wrote a series of these novels under various pseudonyms. Horace de Saint-Aubin was the name he used for one particular publisher, Charles-Alexandre Pollet.

Existing documents give some idea of the speed required of Balzac in producing this novel. In the contract between Balzac and Pollet, signed and dated August 11, 1822 (*Correspondance*, ed. R. Pierrot [Paris: Garnier, 1960], 1.197–199), Balzac promises to deliver two novels, *Le Vicaire des Ardennes* and *Les deux Beringhenn* [sic] *ou le Centenaire*. The former will be four duodecimo volumes, each at least ten folios; the latter three duodecimo volumes, nine to ten folios each. Balzac gets two thousand francs for everything, paid in installments, both novels to be delivered within nine months. In a letter to his sister, Laure Surville, dated August 14, 1822, Balzac complains of this servitude. Balzac had enlisted Laure and her husband to help him write *Le Vicaire*; he seems to have done so for the second novel as well. Driven by what will be the motto of his life and work, "l'infernal besoin de l'or" [the infernal need of money], Balzac informs her that he has two unwritten novels to produce and a deadline of October 1. Laure, he sees, is not up to such a task: "cette suée du travail est impossible pour toi Laure" [such sweat and work are impossible for you, Laure]. As she cannot produce the sixty pages a day of text he thinks he needs, he asks her to send him back the draft that apparently he had sent her to continue and develop. Balzac was ready to use collaborators, provided they could write at breakneck speed. His final comment tells all about the working conditions of a genre writer: "Et vous savez que pour Pollet en un mois on fait un roman" [And you know that for Pollet one writes a novel in a month] (200).

A letter from Balzac's mother to Laure dated slightly later, August 30, 1822, describes the writer frenetically at work: "Le pauvre Honoré est un peu malade . . . Il s'est donné un fier coup de feu; il n'a pas une minute à lui" [Poor Honoré is a bit sick . . . He has given himself a real fever; he hasn't a minute to himself] (206). She describes him working simultaneously on the two Pollet novels and gives precise information about the composition of *Le Centenaire*: "Honoré veut que je te dise qu'il savait bien pourquoi il s'était dégouté du *Centenaire* là-bas, c'est qu'il était fini, et trop grandement fini, car en étalant un peu la fin, il y aura 4 volumes" [Honoré wants me to tell you that he knew why he became disgusted with *The Centenarian* when he was over there; it was because he was finished with it, and glad to be finished, for by spreading out the ending a bit, he was able to get four volumes] (206). Apparently by padding his ending, an exhausted Balzac was able to produce a four-volume novel instead of the three volumes contracted.

A glance at the French text reveals on every page conflicting needs: the author on one hand is seeking complexity of character and story line; on the other, he must fill pages. His instinct as narrator is to write a well-crafted story, but if he moves his action along too fast he cannot meet the contracted length. So he suddenly begins to pad the narrative, often in awkward ways. In a text where every line counts toward the filling out of folios, we find short statements followed by long rows of exclamation marks. Blank spaces between paragraphs are filled in with rows of dots, becoming lines of their own. There is the constant practice of doubling, even tripling, nouns and adjectives with synonyms, which often adds little to comprehension and occasionally obscures meaning. Such punctuation gimmicks would not pass modern editorial practices. Yet Balzac, it seems, was able to turn padding into a functional device in his narrative. As his novel progresses, excessive punctuation takes on an almost expressionist function. Multiplying question or exclamation marks comes to read like musical or stage notation, giving the reader a sense of emotional heightening or urgency that the words alone might not impart. The presence of such devices poses a dilemma to the translator. We did, in certain key scenes keep a hint of such diacritical excesses in order to give today's reader a flavor of this device without creating roadblocks to reading. Balzac may have written this novel "in a month," but that month proved an exciting writer's workshop. Punctuation is one area in which Balzac's talent to turn impediment into asset is visible.

To take into account the problems of translating such a novel and to make it interesting to read, both for the literary scholar and for the general reader, we used the following method. Though *Le Centenaire* claims primary inspiration from the gothic novel, it is in fact a composite of various other generic styles, all current at the time of its writing: the sentimental novel, the novel of education, and the historical novel. In translating the various sections, we took inspiration for each from the prose feel of these same styles among the British novelists: Mrs. Radcliffe, Maturin, Sterne, Scott. The works of these writers in French translation were in fact models both for young Balzac and for the genres in which he chose to write.

It is the energy of Balzac's style that brings these otherwise disparate elements into a fast-paced whole. We tried to give the modern English reader a sense of this complex texture. For example, we give a literal rendition of footnotes and "editorial" devices that other translators might omit. The imperatives of the genres Balzac used as models required an elaborate editorial apparatus and other digressive, sometimes dissonant, elements. We reproduced all of these verbatim in order to give the reader a sense of the heteroglossia of this text. But at the same time we strove to capture a continuity of style that is unmistakably Balzac's. The novel in French, despite its repetitions, formulaic excesses, and intricate editorial apparatus that allowed Balzac to develop the Tullius story line and to pad the ending of the fourth folio, picks up steam as it goes along and becomes a "good read." As we witness Balzac's skill as narrator emerging from what in the hands of a lesser writer would remain a jumble of styles, we gain a sense of the development of Balzac's genius as a storyteller.

The novel was reprinted in 1837. Maurice Bardèche points to numerous places in this text where original material was omitted, notably in notes and certain details that pertain to the Centenarian's scientific activity (*Balzac* [Paris: Julliard, 1980], 67 n. 8). Such details include the mention of a cesarean operation by means of surgery in the case of Tullius's birth. There is also omission of a key note in which Tullius remarks that he has mastered the Centenarian's science. Though the 1822 text has excesses that could have benefited from the editing obviously given to the 1837 edition (Pollet published the text as he got it, errors and all), it is this early text that gives, in all its richness of detail, the true sense of Balzac's understanding of science at the time of its composition. If we are to claim that this is a significant early work of SF, it is crucial we present the 1822 text in its entirety, lest essential details be lost and the historical significance of *The Centenarian* be distorted.

There is, however, one aspect of the original 1822 text that caused us to make changes. From the opening pages of the novel, Balzac frequently switches from past tense to narration in the present tense. We began to see as we translated that Balzac intended this switch as a means of heightening the immediacy and "drama" of his narration. His use of this device early in the novel may be instinctive; by the end of the novel he seems fully conscious of its use and its narrational significance. In a note that appears late in the novel, in the twenty-eighth chapter, a few pages from the end, the "editor" remarks: "I have put the narration in the present, as if the Editor himself were telling the events or was witness to them." This note (also omitted from the 1837 edition) emphasizes the sense of emotional immediacy Balzac associated with the present tense. In the text this device is, now and then, successfully used for sustained effect, as with the telling of the arrival of the Centenarian in Jaffa to cure the soldiers who are sick with the plague. Often, however, the switch from past to present tense is erratic and meaningless. Within a same paragraph the narration will move from past to present and back again. We have kept the present tense in those passages where its use is consistent with an obvious desire on Balzac's part to highlight the immediacy of the telling. In all other places, where the use of the present is inconsistent, we have maintained the past tense.

Danièle Chatelain and George Slusser

BALZAC'S *Centenarian*
AND FRENCH SCIENCE FICTION

Honoré de Balzac's *Centenarian* is more than an "early" work of science fiction; it is a novel that is crucial for our understanding of a specific tradition of SF—the French tradition that parallels in importance the Anglo-American strain of SF. Balzac's novel is roughly contemporary to Mary Shelley's *Frankenstein*, and in its own tradition it is equally significant to our understanding of how the genre evolved. But if *Frankenstein* has had its day with modern critics, *The Centenarian* remains virtually unknown in France, as it is elsewhere. We do not usually associate Balzac with science fiction, yet *The Centenarian* is a fully formed work of SF. Even more interesting is the fact that although the novel had no direct influence on works of postwar SF in France, it is nevertheless a work whose central dynamic is replayed in a large number of these works—to the point that the figure of the Centenarian can serve as interpretive icon for novels by authors from Jules Verne to Michel Jeury and beyond. The novel's lack of direct influence means that in the French tradition it does not represent a beginning. It may, however, be the first significant realization of the fictional potential of a cultural dynamic that emerged over 150 years earlier.

We need a general definition of SF, and Isaac Asimov's may suffice: SF is the "literature that registers the impact of scientific and technological advancement on human beings" (*Asimov on Science Fiction* [Garden City, New York: Doubleday, 1981], 105). But, we ask, at what moment and in what intellectual and cultural conditions does this "impact" take place, allowing for the creation of a "science fiction"? In France, the event that appears to bring interaction between humanist preoccupations and those of developing Western science is René Descartes's famous "method" resulting in the formulation *cogito ergo sum*, a statement of radical separation of thinking mind and material world. As an instrument of science, Cartesian reason proposed, by means of a *mathesis universalis*, to reduce the extended world—which included the physical body of the thinking subject—to quantified geometrical models. This same body however, with Montaigne for example, was already the focus of humanist concern. As the uniquely *human* form, this body became the subject—I live, I think, I feel, I die—of what today we call "fiction." In Descartes's system however, this body, and the ensuing fiction that presents it, is forever impacted by rationalist science. As defined by the Cartesian duality, the body constitutes a third term in a functioning system. It is now the difficult interface between the mind it contains and the world into which it extends. Given this, might not one see Blaise Pascal's later, existential response to the Cartesian duality of mind and matter as an example of the "impact" of scientific advancement on human beings?[1] Pascal produces fascinating miniscenarios but he is not writing fiction. It is only later, in Balzac's *Centenarian* and its context of materialist science, that the Cartesian mind-body problem fully invests a fictional structure. It takes fictional shape perhaps because Balzac, seeking a truly materialist interpretation of man in nature, must refocus the mind-matter problem in a more foreshortened manner. Now we have the intimate struggle between a mind (which, even if conceived in material terms, retains its Cartesian sense of uniqueness) and its own body, whose limits comprise the mind's personal *res extensa*.

This same mind-body antagonism will resonate in later works of French SF. It creates what can be called a Cartesian science fiction, one whose central problematic, in terms of the relation between scientific activity and the world on which it operates, is the opposite of the *Frankenstein* tradition. In order to understand Balzac's work as the first example of this Cartesian tradition, we will examine several significant aspects of the novel. First, *The Centenarian* offers what is essentially a Cartesian transformation of its gothic source—Charles Maturin's *Melmoth the Wanderer*. Second, as a French version of *Melmoth*, *The Centenarian* transforms mythic or religious paradigms (the quest for human immortality and the Promethean overreacher) into a purely scientific quest upon which uniquely Cartesian limits are placed. Third, in contrast with Mary Shelley's *Frankenstein* (1818), to which it is roughly contemporary, Balzac's novel shows science taking a radical inward direction. Here, the privileged realm of scientific activity becomes mind, the mindspace itself, as it is confined, indeed trapped, in the scientist's body. Fourth, the problematic of *The Centenarian* is seen replayed in an uncanny manner in later works of French SF, revealing its mind-body antagonism to be the central thematic and formal problem of this unique form of SF. In this light, we examine in some detail significant reworkings of this Centenarian problem in Verne, Philippe Curval, Kurt Steiner, and Michel Jeury. The conclusion to be drawn is one of an amazingly coherent cultural dynamic, successfully regulating the impact of physical and mental sciences alike on human beings.

Transformation of the Gothic: The French Melmoth

To create a science fiction, Balzac needed a literary form within which he could explore the mind-body relationship bequeathed him in the "philosophical" formulations he devoured in early years of study. He found that form in the gothic novel and in one specific gothic work: Charles Maturin's *Melmoth the Wanderer*. Brian Aldiss in his *Trillion Year Spree: The History of Science Fiction* sees the SF genre deriving from "the dream world of the Gothic novel," specifically from *Frankenstein*. *Melmoth*, however, as a work in a line that includes William Godwin's *St. Leon* (1799), raises the particular problem of the physical extension of life and the relation of extended life to the pursuit of knowledge. Melmoth finds the extension of physical life a curse and seeks to end it, admitting thereby that all the knowledge he has amassed was not worth the search. In contrast, Balzac's Centenarian sees his physical existence as unique and ever desirable, and turns his science to the sole task of giving ever more life to his material body, however old and decrepit. Unlike the world of his Anglo-Saxon precursors, that of Balzac excludes divine intervention. Its boundaries are purely those of the mind-matter duality. In this context, the physical body that contains and vectors the Centenarian's mind must be preserved at all costs in and for itself, beyond any fear of "damnation" or other theological categories.

Melmoth was published in 1820, and its popularity was such that it was almost immediately translated into French. Of the two French versions, it was the freely translated edition of Jean Cohen, *Melmoth ou l'Homme errant par M. Mathurin, auteur de "Bertram,"* appearing in April 1822, that Balzac apparently read.[2] If Balzac takes aspects of his story directly from the English novel, his transformations are highly significant, both in terms of narrative strategy and of the way in which he develops the figure of the long-lived wanderer. Balzac adopts the Gothic "atmosphere" of Maturin's work: isolated castles, paintings with eyes that move, catacombs. His Centenarian, like the Wanderer, is of giant size; like Melmoth, he has both the ability to exceed "the period allotted to mortality" and "a power to pass over space without disturbance or delay, and visit remote regions with the swiftness of thought."[3] Balzac's figure, like Melmoth, is physically decrepit, yet possessed of powerful inner energy; both men have burning eyes, but eyes that become increasingly dull as vital energy leaves them. The Centenarian, like Melmoth, seeks out his victims in moments of extreme misfortune, when they appear ready to give body and soul to their "savior."

Yet the Centenarian's motives for his actions are quite different from Melmoth's. Rather than being driven by some conventionally gothic "touch of evil," he is motivated by a physical necessity that is treated as morally neutral. For example, the following words of Melmoth ring with sinister irony: "I never desert my friends in misfortune. When they are plunged in the lower abyss of human calamity, they are sure to be visited by me" (45). Melmoth weighs his deeds in terms of moral categories: "I have been on earth a terror but not an evil to its inhabitants." The Centenarian, on the other hand, acts out of sheer physical necessity. Some of his acts, such as saving Tullius's life and curing the soldiers of the plague, can be deemed "good"; others, such as seducing poor Fanny, appear to be "evil." Their common denominator, however, is a physical equation in which any energy spent must in turn be restored. For example, the energy the Centenarian expends creating the elixir that cures the Napoleonic soldiers from the plague must subsequently be taken back from the Turks he spirits from the battlefield to a laboratory under the pyramids, where he distills the life force from their dying bodies.

The moral ambiguity of the Centenarian's actions is further revealed in his "framing" of young Lagradna's lover, Butmel, for the murder of the Pollany girl. The latter is clearly a victim of the Centenarian, and Butmel is wrongly convicted of the murder. The night before his execution, however, the old man mysteriously appears in his prison cell. The two subsequently exit through a loose stone in the ceiling, but it is clear that the Centenarian did not enter this way and thus that he has the power to render his material being vaporous enough to pass through walls. Before taking Butmel to safety he explains his motives: "Butmel, you are innocent. I know it! But the one who is truly guilty must protect himself from the punishment human beings reserve for their own kind . . . human justice needed a victim and to your great misfortune I have chosen you!" He claims to be protecting the man who was Count Beringheld at the time. This count, however, is but a façade behind which the Centenarian must operate to give his line an heir. There is a more immediate reason for his actions: the old man needs the Pollany girl's vital energy *in a purely physical sense* if he is to bring his heir, young Tullius, into the world. The material equation is simple: he snuffs out the girl's (and Butmel's) lineage to keep his own alive. Butmel, however, is not to be totally sacrificed. He is taken from his cell to an Indian monastery, where he learns the secrets of the Brahmins. Separated from Lagradna during her procreative years, he is returned to her at the end of their days. By means of such scenes the "curse" of Melmoth is secularized. In Balzac's adaptation of conventional gothic motifs, action increasingly follows the material imperative of exchanges that appear to prefigure the laws of conservation of energy and of entropy, laws themselves prefigured in Mesmer's theory of animal magnetism and more directly in Coulomb's work on electricity, of which the young Balzac was certainly aware.

As the action of *The Centenarian* develops, the protagonist's two necessities—preservation of his individual life force and preservation of his lineage—become increasingly antithetical to each other. The initial suggestion for the "two Beringhelds" of the subtitle may have come from *Melmoth*, for there are two Melmoths: Melmoth the Wanderer and John Melmoth the contemporary figure. In Maturin's work, however, John's main function is that of witness. In his role as reader of manuscript and hearer of tales, he provides the narrative conduit whereby the Wanderer's long story is conveyed to the contemporary reader. Increasingly, however, in Balzac's novel, the main focus of the narrative becomes Tullius and not the Centenarian. In making this shift, Balzac turns the narrative center of interest away from the gothic past toward the contemporary present. The central "plot" of Maturin's novel is the Wanderer's search across past centuries to find someone unhappy enough to take his place: "I have traversed the world in the search, and no one, to gain that world, would lose his soul." There are no souls to lose in Balzac; there are only minds and bodies. And if the Centenarian has a curse, it is twofold—to preserve his physical being and to preserve his lineage—and the drama of his existence comes from their increasing antagonism. On the level of family, conflict arises between blind genetics and changing social ideas of society and succession. On the level of the Centenarian's personal existence, irremediable opposition exists between acts of mind and duration of body.

It also appears that Balzac was inspired by the ending of Maturin's novel. But if this is so, he develops its inconclusiveness in a significantly different direction. The conventional wisdom on Melmoth's destiny assumes a theological frame in which the only possible end can be damnation. The final pages of the novel, however, remain ambiguous as to Melmoth's fate. Does he wrestle with devils? Or is his final battle a solitary one, a struggle between purely material forces, between physical vitality and its termination? Not only is this unclear, but it is also uncertain whether Melmoth's life does indeed end or whether he escapes the forces that beset him, possibly to reappear in some other place and time. Balzac may have been attracted by two aspects of Melmoth's "final" moments. First, there is—in conformity with a secular and "scientific" age—the suggestion of a purely material combat between, on one hand, the search for extended life and, on the other, the sheer wear and tear of this quest for life on the finite resources of one's physical being. Second, there is the possibility that the protagonist might have *won* the battle in this instance. Did Melmoth slip away somewhere? Where did he go? And what might he do with what, in a secular sense, is no permanent triumph over God's tyranny but only a material reprieve? Thoughts like these may have gone through Balzac's head. Indeed, his Centenarian also escapes his pursuers and, apparently surviving a potentially fatal loss of vital energy, seems to disappear into the catacombs beneath Paris. If he does survive, however, he remains doomed to rebuild his laboratory and for ever seek out new sources of vital fluid lest he perish.

The end of Maturin's Wanderer makes allusion to two literary sources, one of which in a sense cancels the other, with its conventional suggestion of divine retribution. The first is Marlowe's *Doctor Faustus*. Melmoth's pact with the devil, of course, promises both a Faustian career and a Faustian outcome. Doctor Faustus is given a vast world in which to exercise fabulous powers but his time is strictly allotted. With Melmoth, Faustus's futility is magnified into a crushing existential weariness by a much greater extension of life. Faustus hardly has time to feel the weight of years before he is dragged screaming from life; Melmoth has centuries of agony, but in the end seems to face the same fate. At the time of his end, however, as no one can be found who will take on his destiny, Maturin conjures as model another Renaissance figure and his destiny: "Have you seen the fate of Don Juan, not as he is pantomimed on your paltry stage, but as he is represented in the real horrors of his destiny by the Spanish writer?" (537). The reference is to Tirso de Molina's *Burlador de Sevilla*.[4] In this play Don Juan Tenorio is a figure of apparently unstoppable energy who runs into the statue of the Comendador. The weight of stone transforms itself into some mysterious force—the don's sword aims at stone and strikes empty air—counterenergy to the don's energy, which physically plummets him into Hell. The Don Juan reference prepares the reader to accept what, in the final moments of *Melmoth*, is a secularized rendering of Faustus's ordeal. The Wanderer enters his apartment, and John and Monçada hear terrifying noises: "They could not distinguish whether they were the shrieks of supplication or the yell of blasphemy—they hoped inwardly they might be the former" (541). They open the room; it is empty, but they find a small door and tracks leading down to the cliff overlooking the sea: "There was a kind of track as if a person had dragged, or been dragged, his way through it—a down-trodden track, over which no footsteps but those of one impelled by force had ever passed" (542).

Marlowe's active devils have been replaced by sheer physical force, and the ambiguity surrounding Melmoth's exit suggests that such a collision of vital energies need not be the end; perhaps some preserving balance can be struck between opposite physical impulsions once theological oversight is out of the way. Either Melmoth was dragged, or he dragged himself. In light of Don Juan, the Faustian pact becomes irrelevant. Melmoth's existence, now measured in years on a physical life-line, ends in that private space where individuals face their material destiny alone. It is but a step from Melmoth's closed chamber, without witnesses, to the solitariness of the Centenarian's "statue-like" body. Balzac in a sense conflates Don Juan and his statue into a single figure. For the Centenarian's body is now both the source of the vital force that consumes it and, in its immobile mass, the final barrier against the dissipation of that force.

The Centenarian as Scientist: Materialist Cartesianism

Balzac, in his earliest writings, displays a romantic fascination with "science," both as a deep understanding of the workings of physical phenomena and as the means of controlling these natural forces. An early project of Balzac's, *Falthurne, manuscript de l'abbé Savonati, traduit de l'italien par M. Matricante, instituteur primaire* (fragments written in 1820), features a strange woman adept in the secret science of the Brahmins.[5] Her science, said to involve a profound knowledge of the correspondences between material things, allows her to perform feats of "magnetism" or action at a distance on physical objects by means of a form of mental energy. Such science—a mix of vitalist magnetism, alchemy, and magic—is suggested by the title Balzac first designated for *The Centenarian*: *Le Savant*. The word "savant" indicates the sort of broad knowledge acquired by the long-lived Melmoth, knowledge that seeks to master the deepest processes of material life. Balzac's Centenarian, as he appears in the novel, is forced by his existential situation to focus these powers (which he gives ample proof of possessing) on one particular specialized task, that of preserving the source of his own vital energy, energy that all such physical acts of magnetism inexorably disseminate and waste. The difference in focus between titles—from *Le Savant* to *The Centenarian*—effectively narrows the scope of the protagonist's activity from general science (the search for an abstract "absolute") to what becomes existential science. Beyond any quest for general knowledge, this selfish science addresses the particular problem of controlling the processes of nature only insofar as they affect the individual's bodily existence. It is possible that Balzac's shift of title and focus between his early speculations on a novel about a scientist to the writing of such a novel in *The Centenarian* again owes a debt to Maturin's novel, which focused the question of "science" on what was ultimately the physical destiny of its titular character.

From the perspective of modern science Balzac's Centenarian offers a curious view of the nature of scientific activity. His science is oriented toward the past. The Centenarian does not seek to discover new knowledge in the present or future. Instead he rediscovers theories or principles formulated earlier by wise men who achieved absolute knowledge of the unity of all things, a knowledge now lost in the fragmented present. Moreover, in a second, corollary sense, science for the Centenarian remains an individual and not a collaborative activity. Both of these views run contrary to how science was actually practiced in his time. But the Centenarian is not concerned with trial-and-error experimentation, a tedious process that requires humility, nor with the institutionalized process that allows an investigation of nature to continue beyond the life of any given scientist. The science he possesses is both absolute and something he must protect from being known by others, lest (in his eyes) it be dissipated and lost. Formulated in the distant past, this knowledge was passed down from age to age via the Rosicrucian order. But no further transmittal appears possible, as the Centenarian claims to be the *last* Rosicrucian. His situation as scientist therefore poses a dilemma. He alone possesses this science, and it gives him the means of acting on the material world. To act, however, is to consume the energy that sustains the unique repository of this science—the body. The primary use of his science, therefore, is to keep his body alive. The science then becomes the condition of the Centenarian's bodily existence. Its "field" of investigation, rather than extended nature, is the narrow confines of a single body that houses the unique secret of a single mind at its contracting core. Melmoth was granted life extension as the condition of a pact with supernatural forces; Balzac's Centenarian has only this science of life extension. His damnation does not come from external powers—it has become the intrinsic condition of his finite physical existence. In the material world of Balzac's novel, science must work ultimately to preserve the means whereby it exists. This strange view of science will pass into Balzac's mature work. There, this fascinating variation on the mind-body problem will be codified into the basic law that regulates his fictional world.

Throughout much of *The Centenarian* we have only glimpses of the scientist at work. In the long narrative episodes focused on Tullius, the reader hears tales of the giant's "magical feats" and occasionally observes acts that appear to involve profound understanding of the physical and life sciences. For example, the Centenarian seems capable of acting on objects at a distance by means of magnetic energy. He performs astonishing medical procedures and cures, in particular a cesarean section, and provides treatments with various (unnamed) potions and vapors. He claims to extract by means of a highly sophisticated (if unexplained) technology an "elixir of life" from living beings. This elixir is described as a material essence that can be transferred from one body to another by being somehow ingested. All these activities remain uncommented upon until late in the novel, when Balzac creates a scene where the old man is obliged to speak as a scientist and expose the sources and nature of his knowledge.

Chapter 25 recounts an evening at the famous Café de Foy in the Palais-Royal. A discussion among several bourgeois on the state of contemporary science is overheard by an old man sitting in the corner: "as he was sitting on an extremely low stool, he concealed his great height and seemed to be at the same level as all the others; his hat fell down over his eyes." This stranger stirs when one of the men attacks Mesmer, presented as simply one more in a line of "magicians of the fifteenth century, with the makers of gold out of water, with the alchemists, with judiciary astrology, and god knows what other so-called science, that rogues abuse in order to dupe honest property holders." But it is disparagement of the Rosicrucians that causes the Centenarian finally to interpose himself. A lifetime of commitment, he states, is needed for any science. But the Rosicrucians have pursued the highest goal of scientific research, "a science whose goal is to make the life of man longer, almost eternal. To seek what is called the *vital fluid*." By means of such a science, he continues, the scientist gains time to go everywhere, do everything, learn all there is to know, rival God's omnipotence. This could be a speech from Melmoth's lips, except for one thing: this most arduous of sciences is also the most ruthlessly selfish. Its search justifies any manner of cruelty and he who finds it will defend his secret to the death: "And if a man discovered this vital fluid, do you think he would be stupid enough to tell about it?" Far from threatening the rights of property holders, this science is a closely guarded property. The Centenarian alone, outside God's ken and against his will, owns and defends it.

The discussion that sparks the Centenarian's speech concerns the state of modern science. The word "modern" in this discussion means something very different to the Centenarian. The people in the café talk about chemistry's "developing in a frightening manner," a phrase that suggests the work of Antoine Lavoisier. But there is a chasm between the Centenarian's concerns and Lavoisier's method, which involves measurement of elements, leading to the formulation of a table of elements based on their atomic weights. Interestingly, Lavoisier's discovery of the role of oxygen in combustion and his subsequent formulation of an oxygen-based system refute the theory of phlogiston, the imaginary fluid supposed to cause combustion. The Centenarian's method is clearly the opposite of Lavoisier's inductive and empirical approach to natural phenomena. And his search is for an entity on the order of phlogiston. His goal remains that of "romantic" science—the search for the *ur*-form, a first principle and common cause to all subsequent proliferation of phenomena. It is not, as with Lavoisier's work, directed toward the advancement of knowledge. Instead, it partakes of the romantic desire to reverse the fall from primary unity, to repair that fatal moment when our knowledge of things fragments, leading to the present "modern" condition. The Centenarian attacks the bourgeois pettiness of his interlocutor because it is a further sign of the degradation of unitary knowledge. Bourgeois "rationalism" in its divisive nature becomes analogous, on the level of "thought," to those processes of physical decay that beset the material body.

The Centenarian, however, does see some use to modern science, but only in the sense that it can develop technologies capable of helping to retard the inevitable breakdown of physical unity. He makes this clear in a final tirade: "The next-to-the-last true Rosicrucian was alive in 1350; he was *Alquefalher the Arab* . . . he found the secret of human life in the caves of Aquila, but he died for not having known how to keep the flame burning in his retort. Since then, what great steps science has made, walking side by side with the science that you scorn, and with the *true* medicine." The two "modern" sciences the Centenarian refers to—magnetism and medicine—are functional sciences. Their purpose is to keep the flame alive in that beaker which is the Centenarian's own physical body. The first science, magnetism, offers a means of conserving vital energy by allowing action at a distance. Indeed, the old man makes use of telepathy and telekinesis in order to shrink time and space, to make them converge on his physical being at a point of rest or stasis. In this way he can roam the physical world, yet barely move from the spot, conserving the maximum of his energy. Medicine, the second science, was in the nineteenth century closer to physiology than what we today call biology, a science of life seen as an evolving system. In the medicine of Balzac's time, one studied the human organism in order to treat disease, not to understand or eliminate what causes it.[6] In terms of what the Centenarian calls *real* medicine, the fundamental disease to treat is the process whereby the organism moves from birth to old age. If he perfects the science of medicine, it is in order to extend the life of his own body. The Centenarian, then, is not an experimental scientist as we understand it today. But he is certainly more than a simple alchemist or the Faustus figure that Maturin presents. His science, drawing upon contemporary speculations on magnetism, joins materialist and vitalist thought with what is a uniquely romantic adaptation of the Cartesian mind-matter duality. In the ideas and destiny of the Centenarian, the old duality reappears as a "material" struggle, a conflict between the mental energy of thought needed to preserve knowledge of the "absolute," and the bodily limits that oppose this expense of vital force.

The Centenarian versus Frankenstein

Unlike *Frankenstein*, *The Centenarian* has not been an influential work. But it is a work that is *representative* both of a unique cultural dynamic—one that defines along the Cartesian axis a particular interrelation of mind, body and natural world — and of a form of narrative that, within the Cartesian tradition, qualifies as a work of science fiction according to Asimov's definition. Where Descartes problematized the relation between rational mind and material body, Balzac's *Centenarian*, 150 years later, presents a romantic refocusing of this problematic. It is romantic in the sense that Balzac, in response to excessive emphasis on the "moi" or "me" in his time, radically foreshortens the extended world, locating it primarily as the material body that constrains the individual subject. Conventional wisdom sees Balzac as a materialist. Yet it is clear in *The Centenarian*, despite its materialist façade, that the Cartesian paradigm operates at the core of the action. Mind is presented as a more subtle and mobile form of the same material substance that forms the body. Yet, in the Centenarian's dilemma, mental activity stands in absolute opposition to the physical functions of the body that contains it. Allen Thiher, in his book *Fiction Rivals Science*, parallels Balzac's work in the 1820s with the publication of scientific papers such as Sadi Carnot's *Réflexions sur la puissance motrice du feu* (1824) and Ampère's work on electromagnetism.[7] These studies in material kinetics were mirrored on the more popular level by discussions of animal "magnetism." Balzac could see mind, in light of these "fluid" sciences, acting as a volatilized form of material energy. However, as soon as he calls this material force *volonté*, or will, he lets Descartes return through the back door. The struggle in *The Centenarian* is expressed as one between fluid and solid. This opposition is simply calqued on the Cartesian pattern. And because he would see both terms of this antithesis as material entities, the mind-body relationship becomes less a duality than an antagonism, a terrible inverse relationship between the expense of spirit and the length of material life. In the grip of this dynamic, the more the Centenarian's scientific activity strives to expand, the more his body contracts in centrifugal manner to an immobile figure of stone. His mind, manifest in material form as his two burning eyes, is in turn trapped in the physical form that hardens around it inexorably. This body, becoming an unyielding "statue," is now his only means of preventing further diminishment of this single, physical life.

The problem posed by *The Centenarian* and the Cartesian nature of its solution remain central to Balzac's vision and the preoccupations of his culture. Thus we note a long string of Balzac's subsequent fictional works (beginning with *La Peau de Chagrin* (1830) and other "études philosophiques" that expound the dynamic "laws" of Balzac's creation) that involve a like contraction of the place of mental activity to the physical space of the body. The Centenarian's eyes, his vital spark, recede farther and farther into his rigid skull. In analogous manner, in Balzac's later works, the location of scientific and other creative activity will retreat deep into the space inside the brain itself, finding there a place where, in paradoxical fashion, the confined mind is free to roam seas of thought. This same Cartesian mindspace, in uncanny fashion, will be the prime field of action for numerous works of postwar French SF. The French writers inherit themes and icons from the more expansive tradition of Anglo-American SF. Yet, as they reshape these themes in their Cartesian crucible, their works come to read like "remakes" of Balzac's novel. They appear as endless dramatizations of the same fatal antagonism between mind and body that marks Balzac's unforgettable character.

Even so, if we are to define the uniqueness of this French SF tradition, we must compare *The Centenarian* and *Frankenstein* as two contemporary reworkings of the same gothic tradition, one in a culture that formulates the problems of science in Cartesian terms, the other in non-Cartesian culture. To the extent that *Frankenstein* marks a beginning for Anglo-American SF, Balzac's novel reveals that, at the same moment in literary history, a thoroughly French version of scientific fiction was moving in very different directions. For both Mary Shelley and Balzac, the gothic functions as the reverse or "night side" of the bourgeois novel of manners. As such, it functions as the place outside normative existence where ancient powers—the larger-than-life "myths" of Doctor Faustus or the Wandering Jew—can encounter the modern forces of science. Yet what is implied by the terms "gothic" and "science," and the trajectory they take in each culture, is radically different and produces radically different works. By examining the type of gothic each culture envisions, and the form of scientific "method" this choice engenders, we gain insight into the differences between the French and Anglo-American SF traditions, differences crucial for defining two significant cultural responses to the advent of science in the realm of literature.

In France, as in England, at the time of *The Centenarian* and *Frankenstein*, experimental science was developing rapidly. The *perception* of science, however, in terms of its methods and limits, was taking very different paths in the two countries. The deductive and reductive nature of science in France becomes clear as the century progresses. Balzac, for example, in his "Avant-propos" to the *Comédie humaine*, written in 1842, places his vast work under the aegis of zoologist Geoffroy Saint Hilaire. The latter's theory of epigenesis, in which embryos develop through successive differentiation from a basic, undifferentiated structure, becomes Balzac's principle of "unity of composition": "Il n'y a qu'un animal. Le créateur ne s'est servi que d'un seul et même patron pour les êtres organisés" [There is only one animal. The creator used one and the same pattern for all organized beings].[8] Bound by such a pattern, scientific inquiry cannot move into new areas of investigation but remains in thrall to this undifferentiated *ur*-form, a metaphysical idea that lies outside experimental verification. Such is the Absolute of Balthasar Claës, the chemist-protagonist of Balzac's novel *La Recherche de l'Absolu* (1834). The Absolute is not a force that exists in space and time. It is described rather as a fulcrum, a point that fixes axes of succession and similitude to form a static coordinate system. It is a force "common" to phenomena only in the sense that it comprises the system by which they relate among themselves. Balzac is not a declared positivist. Yet the idea of science adumbrated by Claës, and the closed spatialized nature of its dynamic, seems very Comtean.[9] John Stuart Mill, in his essay *Auguste Comte and Positivism* (1865), sees the purpose of positivism, which stood in his eyes for French science in general, as the formulation of "an elaborate system for the total suppression of all independent thought."[10] Mill, once infatuated with the intellectual rigor of Comte, now criticizes him in a manner that clearly distinguishes between positivist science and the more empirical British tradition: "[Comte] has an objection to the word *cause* . . . He fails to perceive the real distinction between the laws of succession and coexistence which thinkers call Laws of Phenomena and those they call the action of Causes: the former exemplified by the succession of day and night, the latter by the earth's rotation which causes it" (57).

Extrapolating from these tendencies—theoretical and empirical—we see Dr. Frankenstein, in contrast with the Centenarian, doing science in terms of the action of causes. He works not to sustain a closed system of life as does the Centenarian, who searches within an already differentiated body for some primary, undifferentiated force that would regenerate it forever. Instead, Frankenstein creates a *new* being, a causal action with open-ended consequences, both of danger and of promise. In this sense the two fictional scientists are alike only in the extremes to which they carry their respective traditions. For the Centenarian does not search all nature for his Absolute, but sets the limits of his search at the boundaries of his own organism. Much in the manner of Blaise Pascal's response to Descartes, a metaphysical problem—the existence of mind in relation to matter—is turned into an existential quandary. This occurs as Balzac equates the limits of scientific activity with the limits of the span of life granted the individual observer, a span governed by the inverse relation between mental effort (all acts of the scientific mind) and bodily resistance. The Centenarian is a radical figure because he literally *embodies* a scientific tradition—the French tradition Mill describes as a "mania for regulation." Frankenstein, in an equally radical yet opposite manner, takes the empirical, epistemological tradition of British science and literally *excorporates* it. Rather than seek to preserve an original form of life such as the Centenarian's given body, Frankenstein creates a new form of life, one that arises from a new combination of already dead and dislocated parts.

Both Frankenstein and the Centenarian offer in the gothic manner a vision of the scientist as a monstrous being. The impact of Shelley's novel in the Anglo-American sphere has propagated along lines of monstrosity, generating a moment in the horror film where the scientist and his unsightly creation become indistinguishable, both answering to the same name. Gothic horror of this sort never took on in France, where the vogue of Hoffmann and the "fantastic" essentially took its place. Balzac's novel seems, however, one of the rare examples of the horrific gothic in French literature. We see the Centenarian gathering dying soldiers on Napoleon's battlefields, spiriting them away as they groan and plead to underground laboratories, where he takes their vital fluid by what gruesome means we can only imagine. In the "Fanny" episode, rife with gothic horror, the hangman is preferable to this monstrous old man.

Balzac, in allowing the story of Tullius to take up increasing sections of the narrative, is already seeking (as Mary Shelley in *Frankenstein* does not) to shift emphasis from horror to contemporary manners. Balzac continues to modernize his monstrous figure throughout the *Comédie humaine*. Yet the very fact that the Centenarian's presence, however diluted, continues to be felt reveals that a gothic element, though no longer recognizable by genre trappings, haunts Balzac's mature work. This "submerged" gothic, operating beneath the façade of realism, will continue to be felt in later works of French literature. A later example is the treatment, in Jules Verne, of the scientist's laboratory apparatus first detailed in *The Centenarian*. Robert Lambourne, Michael Shallis, and Michael Shortland, in *Close Encounters: Science and Science Fiction*, claim Frankenstein's laboratory as the source for later proliferation of nineteenth-century scientific apparatus in Anglo-American SF films of the 1950s. For Lambourne et al., this "silicon jungle" of beakers and retorts has come to signify the lone or "mad" scientist who, locked in such cluttered laboratories, pursues dangerous research beyond the consensus world of institutionalized science and society. Mary Shelley describes no such equipment. Indirectly, the source of such iconography may be Balzac. Again, however, the path can only be subliminal. For if the Centenarian's seminal laboratory, which Balzac *did* describe in amazing detail, disappears from French literature, it does resurface in film, specifically in the films of Georges Méliès. But here, all Gothic connotation of such apparatus has disappeared. Its function is now domesticated; it has become the stuff of farce. In fact, looking backward from Méliès, we see a similar transformation taking place, the Gothic mechanism vanishing before the reader's eyes, and taking its place the normative world of social order. The Centenarian gloats over his infernal machinery. And yet, from his description, we see that all these objects have already been neatly classified and ordered. There is not "jungle" of objects. The scrolls and artifacts, such as the piece of Joan of Arc's stake, are arranged in chronological order. The bell and chair of his infernal machine to extract the vital fluid from human victims, occupy here the center of an neatly classical space. It is but a step from here to the comfortable order of Captain Nemo's laboratory in the Nautilus in Verne's *Vingt mille lieux sous les mers*. In such spaces, we witness the triumph of the rational mind over gothic clutter. All sciences and technologies, even infernal ones, are classified and put to the service of general mankind.

It is in a similar domesticated space that later French fiction develops the gothic figure of the overreaching scientist. By the late years of Balzac's *Comédie humaine*, the Centenarian has been completely absorbed in a figure such as the scientist Laurent Ruggieri, who appears in the trilogy *Sur Catherine de Médicis* (1846). Laurent no longer proclaims an individual hubris. He may speak with an arrogance similar to that of the Centenarian, but he couches his overreaching pride in general, socially acceptable terms: "Je pense que cette terre appartient à l'homme, qu'il en est le maître, et peut s'en approprier toutes les forces, toutes les substances" [I believe that this earth belongs to man, that he is its master, and can appropriate all of its substances and energy to his use] (271). The setting of this novel, devoted for the most part to intrigues and love affairs, is the Renaissance; Laurent poses as a scientist on the verge of modernity, not as a gothic alchemist. And yet his discourse, despite its plea for scientific collaboration and the passing on of scientific tasks to future generations, remains centered on, indeed obsessed by, the problem raised by the Centenarian—the fact that science is long and individual life short. What is more, Laurent's lament is ultimately a personal one: God has not given *him*, in his unique *me*, enough time to do his task. The "gothic" precondition to any general statement about reason's ability to appropriate nature remains the ability of an individual mind to master its own personal spatiotemporal "status." If Shelley's *Frankenstein* can be seen, as Aldiss sees it, as the book that launches the scientist of gothic literature on an extroverted search to extend his personal reach to investigation of the general physical limits of human existence, *The Centenarian* points in a very different direction: one clearly suggested in the Cartesian method, whereby mind, in order to locate its uniqueness among things of the extended world, systematically divests itself of all physical appendages, including (in Descartes's thought experiment) the body itself, ultimately severed from mind as another "machine." Balzac, as a romantic "materialist," rediscovered that this same body, however alien and limiting to the existence of mental activity, is at the same time the necessary means by which mind can reach into the world of extension, indeed, perform any act of "will." These respective directions—outward and inward—mark a fundamental difference between Anglophone and Francophone SF.

To see *Frankenstein* as the origin of Anglo-American SF is controversial. The novel does, however, leave a precise legacy. First, if we assume that Frankenstein's purpose in creating his being is to extend the scientist's powers over nature, it is important to note that this creation specifically reaches beyond the sanctity of the human body. Frankenstein does not resurrect a whole body; instead he creates a being from the scattered *parts* of dead bodies, from which soul or Cartesian mind has long departed. Frankenstein has moved boldly beyond the hegemonic idea of the "human form divine," indeed beyond the sense, engrained in the culture and much scientific thought at the time, that the human whole is always greater than the sum of its parts. The alchemist label no longer fits Frankenstein. For even if the alchemist's sublimation of base metals points toward Frankenstein's creative act, there remains in the terms used by the alchemist a sense of restituting something previously fallen, restoring something debased to its "original" form. Frankenstein, in contrast, succeeds in generating a new form from parts that have in their discorporation lost all significant attachment to their primary form—that of a created human being. We seem to glimpse the modern mindset that envisions cloning. For in cloning we reproduce a human form, not from some "homunculus" or other miniaturized form of man, but from a nonmimetic entity, the undifferentiated gene that exists below the threshold of any concept of an individual "self." Even so, it is still the original form that is reproduced. But Frankenstein's creature as it emerges is not meant to be the replica of a preexisting form: it claims to be a new being, brought forth from elements in themselves incapable of regenerating an identifiable human whole.

Frankenstein then is the first fictional scientist to seek his "elixir of life" not in the sanctity of whole forms but in a flux of elements below the threshold of the human gestalt. Steven B. Harris is not correct in seeing *Frankenstein* as another example of "mal-resurrection."[12] Frankenstein, on the contrary, creates his form from parts that have already undergone the process of material dissolution. It is the very same process that Balzac's Laurent Ruggieri, still haunted by the terrors of the Centenarian, so fears: "Si ce monde [le monde de l'âme] existait, les substances dont la magnifique réunion produit notre corps . . . ne se sublimiseraient pas après notre mort pour retourner séparément chacune en sa case, l'eau à l'eau, le feu au feu . . . Si vous prétendez que quelque chose nous survit, ce n'est pas nous, car tout ce qui est le *moi* actuel périt!" [If this world of the soul did exist, those substances whose magnificent coming together produces our bodies . . . would not scatter after one's death, returning each to its domain, water to water, fire to fire . . . If you pretend that something survives this process, whatever survives is not us, for all that comprises the present *me* perishes] (271). If the Centenarian's alchemy transmutes material elements, it always does so above the threshold of the *me*, a bodily whole. When he distills his "donors" into the essential elixir, he may seem to decompose the original shape, creating a life force out of new elements forged in a purely material transfer of energy. Yet in his exact equation of one life taken so another (his own) may live, he continues to see his actions in terms of the human norm, as a form irreducible to mere flux of random matter.

In shaping life out of such randomized elements, Frankenstein takes science in a different direction. Physicist A. S. Eddington describes a human being's relation to nature in open-ended, non-Cartesian terms: "If we continue shuffling a pack of cards we are bound sometime to bring them into their standard order—but not if the conditions are that every morning one more card is added to the pack."[13] Frankenstein works with an apparent understanding of such a relationship between mind and material world. The Centenarian, however, working within the equations of a closed system bounded by his own bodily form, can allow no new card to enter his deck. Were he able to extend his life indefinitely, he might conceivably become a figure like Heinlein's Lazarus Long. This master hero extends his single "life line" across Heinlein's entire opus. Long makes use of new sciences such as genetic engineering and cloning in order to regenerate his own flesh-and-blood in myriad forms, expanding the original body into a vast circumference that becomes coextensive with the known universe. And yet, despite the sweep, the limits of Lazarus's expansion—as with the Centenarian—remain those of his own body, the patriarchal body that refuses to yield its place to any progeny. Significantly, at the end of *Time Enough for Love* (1973), the key text of the Long saga, Lazarus's body is pulverized into particles on a World War I battlefield. But these particles retain the memory of their original form and Lazarus is again resurrected in his own original body. As if sensing the futility of such an expansive course, the Centenarian never takes this route. Instead, as his mind or spirit or "will" retracts within the material confines of his body, he carves out at the core of a bodily universe the only possible place of expansion—his own mindspace. Trapped in a waning body, the Centenarian can only seek worlds without end in some final hour that stretches.

In contrast, Frankenstein not only reconstructs the "frame" (his words) for a new species of life out of randomized elements; he summons the energy to combine and animate these parts from an equally random force—that of electricity. Shelley's text is suggestively vague: "I collected the instruments of life around me that I might infuse a spark of being into the lifeless thing that lay at my feet."[14] Following this lead, later film versions make this force a bolt of lightning, something more randomly elemental. Frankenstein may believe he follows God's model—the epigraph from *Paradise Lost* suggests this. But because he draws on natural elements and forces whose "laws" are governed neither by the human form nor the divinity that made it, he can neither predict nor control the processes he sets in motion. His creature emerges as something both less and more than human, a being in which the degree of these conditions remains indeterminate, capable of evolving in an unknown manner and future. An example is the narrative of the creature's "education." In the forest the creature is thrust in grotesque manner into the role of Rousseau's *sauvage*: "All my past life was now a blot, a blind vacancy in which I distinguished nothing. From my earliest remembrance I had been as I then was in height and proportion. I had never seen a being resembling me" (103). But where Rousseau's figure remains a sort of Cartesian experiment in self-reduction, Frankenstein's figure has no essential humanity to discover. Its "learning" is a mimicking of human speech and manners. Moreover, it finds dialogue only with a blind man as sighted (normal) humans reject its form as monstrous. But as the creature is forced to recognize the anomaly of its condition, it grasps the potential inherent in being a *new* entity: "Of my creation and creator I was absolutely ignorant; but I knew that I possessed no money, no friends, no kind of property." And, unlike Rousseau's savage, the creature from the outset speaks and uses language eloquently, allowing him to articulate the new powers that come from his otherness: "I was . . . endued with a figure hideously deformed and loathsome. I was not even of the same nature as man. I was more agile than they, and could subsist on a coarser diet; I bore the extremes of heat and cold with less injury to my frame; my stature far exceeded theirs" (102). The creature glimpses the possibility of new freedoms beyond the anthropocentrism of the Cartesian vision.

When the creature learns it is an Adam without an Eve, it seizes upon this state of singularity to demand a second act of creation that even more radically violates the limits set by the human body and nature: "You must create a female for me, with whom I can live in the interchange of those sympathies necessary for my being" (123). Frankenstein has the means to do this; but why does he refuse to do so? The creature, though in Frankenstein's eyes a debased copy of the human form, places his demand on the human level of *moral* imperative: "I demand it of you as a *right*." And it is on this same moral level—and not in the name of science and the unpredictability of material consequences—that Frankenstein refuses: "Shall I create another like yourself, whose joint wickedness might desolate the world!" (123). The work said to launch the speculative enterprise of Anglo-American SF is also the work that sets a "Frankenstein barrier" to that tradition.[15] Frankenstein's scientific activity takes us to a point where retreat is inevitable. Where further action risks transforming the balance between human being and material world, the human course of action is to retreat in the name of morality.

A similar limit to scientific expansion is found in J. D. Bernal's *The World, the Flesh and the Devil: An Inquiry into the Future of the Three Enemies of the Rational Soul* (1929). Frankenstein, seeking mastery of "the physical secrets of the world," recognizes Bernal's first category, the need of science to force nature to accommodate humanity. But the step he takes is in Bernal's second category, "flesh." For Bernal, the human body as traditionally defined is a poor machine. In order for humans to access new, physically hostile environments, this machine must be improved by means of prostheses or other mechanical alterations. Frankenstein's creature is by the accident of its making such an enhanced being. The crux here remains, as in *Frankenstein*, the category of "devil." This is again the Frankenstein barrier—that seemingly ineradicable division in the human psyche between the power to transform the human form and destiny beyond all recognition, and the moral imperative that refuses this transformation. "You will never make me base in my own eyes," Frankenstein asserts (103). The scientist creates and then retracts, fearing he might irremediably alter the form of the human body as we know it.

Frankenstein gains the power to transform the world by taking an open-ended evolutionary approach both to external nature and to the human body. What stops him from exercising that power is no natural barrier, but William Blake's "mind forg'd manacles." The residual idea of a soul returns in the form of a moral governor that prevents Frankenstein from taking his second step into the not-yet-known. For the Centenarian, in contrast, the barrier exists not in the mind but in the body; master of mental powers that allow him to range as "magnetic" energy over a vast realm of space and time, the Centenarian remains in thrall to his own body, and the physical process of aging threatens to dispossess these powers of their location. In terms of the Cartesian mind-matter duality, the first and essential point of contact between mind and *res extensa* is the body. In the shadow of this tradition, the Centenarian's search is not like Frankenstein's, to create a new, more adequate form of body for some future generation. Rather, it is to investigate the mysteries of one's own body insofar as that body constitutes the necessary interface between the self and the material world. The Centenarian too has his "creature," young Tullius whom he engenders through magnetism and brings into the world through advanced medical and surgical means. This creation, however, violates no moral sanction; it violates instead the physical sanctity of the Centenarian's body. There is a struggle here as in *Frankenstein* between creator and creature. But in Balzac's world, if it is the creature who wins the struggle and the bride, the result is not the generation of a new form of life or destiny. Tullius, in entering Parisian society, displaces the lone scientist's physical struggle between mind and body to the figurative level of the social "body" of the *Comédie humaine*. The "body" Tullius and all subsequent characters inhabit becomes an analogous closed system where circulation of blood is replaced by circulation of money. Banks and consortia as "organisms" sustained by moving money with the immobile usurer Gobseck at their center have displaced the Centenarian and his body, producing another material circuit that leaves no location for scientific or artistic speculation except the inner realm of the mind. For the scientists and artists of the *Comédie*, creation soars within the isolated space of the creator's mind but is held inexorably to the iron law of the *peau de chagrin* (the wild ass's skin, or the skin of sorrow, the word *chagrin* having both meanings) where once again metaphor has displaced the literal skin of the Centenarian's body. Each of Balzac's subsequent seekers does ultimate battle, not with external nature, but with his or her own bodily condition.

Replaying the Centenarian: French Science Fiction

As we have already noted, the novel *The Centenarian* has remained obscure to this day, forgotten by readers and scholars alike. Balzac's figure did, however, bequeath his personal mind-body struggle to the metaphorical social body of the *Comédie humaine*. What is passed on here is not a story. It is more an existential situation, a dynamic set of conditions that regulate the nature and reach of scientific investigation within the parameters of French Cartesian culture. This problematic in turn sets the preconditions for the development of an SF or literature of scientific speculation in France. Such links must remain highly speculative. And yet the fact remains that any number of works labeled "SF" in France, when read in the light of *The Centenarian* and its central dynamic, appear to be creative replays of, or variations on, Balzac's scenario. The Centenarian, as rediscovered in these pages, is a genuinely iconic figure, for it embodies the contradictions that ensue when mental expansion encounters the physical limits set by contraction of the many containing "bodies" that comprise the landscape of French SF. In fact, in work after work of French SF, the final such container is the walls and synapses of the human brain itself. Here in this Cartesian inner realm of mind, inhabiting its most essential and necessary space, a human being's search to abide and extend its knowledge and physical reach generates endless dramas of entrapment, paranoia, fantasies of escape. These replays are found both in Jules Verne and in postwar French SF writers. We will discuss works by Verne and by three of the other writers: Philippe Curval, Kurt Steiner (André Ruellan), and Michel Jeury.

Arthur Evans signals the importance of vehicles and vehicular motion in Jules Verne.[16] An example is the *Nautilus* that allows Captain Nemo, as avatar of the Centenarian, to escape the boundaries of nations and cultures and move unseen beneath the oceans of the world, gathering knowledge on natural phenomena. Verne's vehicle, whose motto is *Mobilis in mobili*, seems a vast improvement on the Centenarian's statue-like body and his catacomb. But like the catacomb, the *Nautilus*, however mobile, serves the same purpose as storehouse of all knowledge and culture. Its superior mobility seems to extend the scientist's reach to all corners of the natural world. But the Centenarian's body appears equally mobile, for he too can range the world. The expense of energy needed to be mobile, however, takes a tremendous toll on the individual body of the seeker. Such is true for Nemo as well. Indeed, all the vast knowledge stored in the *Nautilus* is but a second skin for Nemo. It must collapse and perish, as his physical body does: "Il semblait qu'il voulût une dernière fois caresser du regard ces chefs-d'oeuvre de l'art et de la nature, auxquelles il avait limité son horizon pendant un séjour de tant d'années dans l'âbime des mers" [It seemed as if he wished one last time to caress with his gaze those treasures of art and nature, which had formed his horizon during so many years spent in the depths of the oceans].[17] As Nemo breathes his last, Cyrus Smith and company execute his wish to bury this trove of knowledge with his body. The scientist in French SF seems destined, in the example of Nemo, to repeat the destiny of Balzac's last alchemist.

The condition of the Centenarian, as replayed in Nemo's story, appears to be the site that French culture has chosen to debate the question of what direction scientific investigation should take. Roland Barthes, in his famous essay "Nautilus ou bateau ivre," speaks for French culture with customary authority.[18] Barthes has reduced these two famous vehicles and their authors, Verne and Rimbaud, to a strict Cartesian duality. With the *Nautilus* the claim is made that mind uses new technology to extend its vehicular reach into the extended world. To the average reader, Verne's hero signifies science exploring, by means of submarines and rockets, ever broader realms of physical nature. Such is the popular claim of science and of science fiction. But for Barthes this is not what Verne is doing, indeed the very opposite is true. As if seeing with the eyes of the Centenarian, Barthes presents Nemo's *Nautilus*, his vehicle of exploration, as his second body. For Barthes, movement in Verne, following the internalizing path of Cartesian method, is centripetal rather than expansive. The result is not discovery, but rather closure: "Verne a construit une sorte de cosmogonie fermée sur elle-même . . . L'imagination du voyage correspond chez

Verne à une exploration de la clôture" [Verne has built a sort of cosmogony closed upon itself . . . In Verne, to imagine the voyage corresponds to an exploration of its closure] (81). Barthes, in effect, exhorts any subsequent SF that might wish to take this externalizing direction to redirect its efforts from the outside world to a world inside the mind of the scientist, into those Freudian depths that lie at the center of the same mindspace that both Nemo and the Centenarian before him carve out within their bodies, bodies that constitute the farthest limit of material necessity for the mind whose vehicle it is.

Barthes instead claims that science should follow the interiorizing model of his other inspiration, Arthur Rimbaud's "Bateau ivre." In this light, scientific exploration must be redirected into realms of "imagination," or "dream."[19] In Verne's work, for Barthes, the great example of such re-direction is *L'Île mystérieuse*. But Barthes's rereading is possible only because he recasts Nemo's adventure in the form of a mind-body dilemma that reminds us of the Centenarian. Moreover, Barthes seeks to resolve the problem of the patriarchal scientist in a manner analogous to Balzac's, whereby the Centenarian is displaced by the bourgeois Tullius. Barthes has Nemo accommodate himself to the limits of his body, thus creating a realm of activity in which he can reinvent the world, all the while sheltered comfortably from the terrors of *res extensa*: "*L'Île mystérieuse*, où l'homme-enfant réinvente le monde . . . s'y enferme, et couronne cet effort encyclopédique par le posture bourgeoise de l'appropriation: pantoufles, pipe et coin du feu, pendant que dehors la tempête, c'est-à-dire l'infini, fait rage inutilement" [*The Mysterious Island*, where the child-man reinvents the world . . . locks himself away, and crowns his encyclopedic effort by a bourgeois posture of appropriation: slippers, pipe and fireside, while outside the tempest, that is to say, the infinite, rages in futile manner] (80). Trapped in his body, the Centenarian is terrified by his fleeting vital energy. Barthes, however, turns Nemo's body into the bourgeois equivalent of Descartes's "stove," in which the *cogito* is born of the act of shedding all material attachments, pure mind declaring itself a child that is now father to the man.

For Barthes, the true science is one that explores this Cartesian psyche within a physical brain. This is now, however, the brain of an armchair bourgeois who passes time tracing infantile fantasies of external exploration to their encapsulated source. For Barthes, "navigation," the means by which the mind claims to explore the external world, is a "myth," indeed, "dans cette mythologie de la navigation, il n'y a qu'un moyen d'exorciser la nature possessive de l'homme sur le navire, c'est de supprimer l'homme et de laisser le navire seul; alors le bateau cesse d'être boîte, habitat, objet possédé; il devient oeil voyageur, frôleur d'infinis" [in this mythology of navigation, there is only one way to exorcise the human impulse to take possession of the boat, and this is to suppress the man entirely, and let the boat go alone; this way, the boat ceases to be a box, a habitat, a thing possessed; it becomes a traveling eye, stalker of infinities] (82). Barthes's formulation accepts the irreducible division of mind and matter and in doing so declares the latter off limits, a place where man neither should nor must go. And yet where death makes Nemo give up *Nautilus* and body alike, the Centenarian has refused this final concession, just as his body remained his only and final vessel. And Barthes seems, like the Centenarian, to adhere to the body (however bourgeois it has become) as external boundary from which the investigative eye turns inward, transposing the physical properties of the external unknown to figurative labyrinths deep inside the folds of the brain. Science is, of necessity, the "appropriation" of this inner mindspace. Barthes has unwittingly tracked the Centenarian's powers to their lair; in doing so he defines the field of scientific investigation which will be that of French SF.

Pascal Thomas, in a survey of French SF of the 1970s and 1980s, concludes the following: "The unifying feature that emerges, from an epistemological or political point of view, is the isolation and claustrophobia of the protagonist; very often he is locked in imaginary universes, or universes whose relation to our own is badly defined . . . There must be something in our national culture that pushes toward those themes."[20] For Thomas this "something" is paranoia. The observation is astute, for given the legacy that runs from Balzac's Centenarian to such artists of the incommunicable as Gambara or Franhofer, the problem of isolation stems less from a split personality than from an alternate one. Furthermore, in cases of paranoia, the mind not only claims it is another world but aggressively seeks to substitute its world for the "real" (i.e., material) one. It is often within such an aggressively proclaimed mental space that the scientists and other protagonists of French SF finally become free to explore phenomena and push back frontiers of knowledge that had either eluded them or proved nonexistent in the external world. Often it is at the limits of this inner space that they encounter the "other." These limits, moreover, are all the more narrow and claustrophobic in that (as with the Centenarian) they are the boundaries of the physical body itself. As with Nemo's *Nautilus*, this body can take a number of metonymic forms: apartments, rooms, subterranean shopping malls, museums, laboratory equipment, test tubes. These however are always surrogates for a protagonist's personal body; as such, they always represent the farthest physical limits of an entrapped mind, a mind thus forced to seek its infinities in some inner hidden world inexorably bounded by the material envelope.

Postwar French SF offers a rich field of writers and texts, and a historical span that reaches from the early 1950s to today. We can only discuss a few of these here and it may seem presumptuous to seek to define an entire literature from these samples. But in a strange way the works discussed are representative of this corpus, for they define the inner-directed realm in which many of these novels and stories operate. In these examples, "plot" and field of action are bounded by the material confines of a single protagonist. In this sense they offer, as with the Centenarian, a curious conflation of the life extension and the live burial scenarios. As with the Centenarian's grotesque attempts to preserve the uniqueness of mind as "self" within the encroachments of his ever shrinking physical body, many works of French SF display an analogous contraction of the protagonist's world to the narrowest and most personal material confines. The result is what we might call scenarios of self-incarceration. These confines may be demarcated by a domestic space à la Barthes, as in Philippe Curval's *Cette chère humanité* (1976), where an entire continent, the Marcom or Marché commun, becomes physically enfolded by means of some (in Barthes's sense) imaginary "interdimensional" physics in the space of the protagonist's bathroom.[21] More restrictive yet, the space of closure may be that of an individual world vision that somehow turns into a material place, trapping a protagonist in the way ideas become "frozen words" in Rabelais. It may ultimately turn out to be the physical space of the mind itself that entraps the thinker. As in Curval's novel, these protagonists are often scientists who, as they strive to extend their visionary reach, find that vision simultaneously hardening and contracting, drawing tighter around them the material prison of their own bodies and skulls. This is even true in cases where scientists, like Balzac's Ruggieri, strive to unite in a collaborative effort. The institutions they create, in a manner analogous to a body closing in on a single mind, in turn become physical oppressions. Where vast social machines (multinational corporations, hospitals, bureaucracies) are constructed in the human image, they take on oppressive "flesh" and turning against their maker(s), entomb and suffocate the mind of their creator, who now must depend on this entity for its continued existence.

A novel where such a social mind reveals itself to be an oppressive "body" is Kurt Steiner's *Le Disque rayé* (*The Scratched Record*, 1970). This work is in a sense a French rewrite of Wells's *The Time Machine*. In Steiner's version, however, the time loop itself becomes a hellish form of life extension. Once in the loop, physicist Matthews Wood is able to prolong his existence indefinitely, perhaps infinitely. Such longevity proves at the same time to be damnation, for by means of the loop Wood's existence is endlessly trapped in the brief interval between the moment of his death (which is a dated certainty) and the endless reliving of a scenario that takes him over and over through a same series of alternate worlds, always back to the place of departure in 1970, from which the journey must begin all over again. The narrative begins with Wood, called here by his nickname Matt, in a world of ruined structures and primeval life forms, much like the land-scape encountered by Wells's Traveler at the far temporal reach of his voyage. Inexplicably, Matt Wood finds a revolver in his hand with one bullet missing. He also finds a strange object in his pocket. Overpowered by monstrous creatures, he fires shots. In-stead of his being killed, the presence of this object in his pocket as the shots are fired propels him into an alternate world. Here again, he is assailed. He fires another shot and is projected into a third temporal dimension. Now, however, he discovers that in the skirmish he has lost the object in his pocket and has sus-tained a leg wound. He also realizes that he has taken with him in his pocket papers containing advanced scientific theorems. He had snatched these up during his ordeal in the second world but does not understand them. The first world was a terminal beach. The second was a highly advanced world but at the same time a totalitarian nightmare. This third world in contrast offers a per-fect utopian society. It is a world whose every function, social and physical, is regulated by a huge central computer—the Plani. The Plani, described as an *être mathématique concrétisé* [a mathematical being made matter], is an artificial intelligence that has become sentient. Indeed, its control of every aspect of existence seems as absolute as it is utopian, for it appears to extend in space and time across all possible worlds, including those Matt has visited. As in all utopias, however, despite perfection, mankind is not happy. Matt joins a rebel movement. Led by his companions to penetrate the Plani, Matt discovers inside this Aleph-like structure a full row of objects exactly like the one he had found in his pocket at the beginning and subsequently lost in the last world. As police enter, he grabs an object from the row. He fires his last bullet, falls, and awakens in 1970.

In 1970, Matthews Wood, the physicist, returns to his apart-ment to find a wounded Matt lying in his bathtub. In the utopian world, Matt had seen a statue inscribed with the name Matthews

Wood, the man whose physics created the Plani, and whose date of death is 1970. Matt now understands that he is the "older" version of this same Matthews, basing his claim of seniority on the biological days passed in his interdimensional voyage, days that (as with Wells's Traveler) leave physical marks on his appearance and a wound in his leg. A dialogue ensues between the two time doubles. Matt (the consciousness the reader has followed throughout the narrative) realizes with horror that what he has lived through is a tautology, and that the vast universe of alternate worlds has somehow shrunk to the confines of his own mind. He sees in turn that this mind is housed in a body whose wound threatens to be fatal, to put an end to mind and universe alike: "La Plani n'existe que si je divulgue son existence, ou, du moins, les connaissances qu'il suppose" [The Plani only exists if I reveal its existence, or, at least, the knowledge that underlies its existence].[22] There are, however, two Woods, even if there are only a few days of physical time that separate them, which is the exact time needed to make another loop. Matthews (the "younger" twin), speaking for the two, takes his double's reasoning to a higher level: "Nous sommes la victime d'un sophisme réalisé" [We are the victims of a sophism made reality] (147). This machine then, created by mankind as a giant simulacrum of the human mindspace, becomes in turn the physical prison of a single human being, whose function is to serve as the "ghost" that preserves and sustains it. Once the dynamic is in motion, Matthews/Matt Wood, in its continuous looping through time, must endlessly repeat the scenario we have just read and thus provide the spatiotemporal structure necessary to sustain the Plani's existence. Matt's time loop is in a sense the Plani's "body." The elixir of long life here is recast as the energy Wood restores as he moves from one time world to another; it is an energy perpetually renewed by the paradox of time travel, by means of which the "older" double returns spent, only to send out the "younger" one to repeat the voyage. And by the dreadful irony of time travel, this process incorporates, indeed uses to its advantage, the desperate attempt of the "two Woods" to spring the loop, to escape the eternal return and thus destroy the Plani that has made them its necessary victim. Matthews (rightfully) reasons that Matt must kill him in order to break the circle. Matt, however, at the same time also reasons: Matthews cannot kill him, for to do so is to kill his earlier self, thus cease to exist. But Matt has little choice, for to remain in 1970 with an incurable wound and bacteria received in some alternate world is just as surely to die. But not only can reason not resolve this quandary, the outcome is "protected" by fatality. Matthews is fresh and without wound. Driven by instinct to survive, he takes the object and empty gun from the sleeping Matt. He loads the gun, then takes the scientific papers and mails them under his name to the Institute of Physics. But the Plani's plan has no loopholes; all the pieces are now in place. Inevitably, there is a scuffle; Matthews holds the gun, Matt turns it on him, a shot is fired, and the "younger" self, now wounded, is sent on its inexorable journey. The Plani has perfected the Centenarian's science to the degree that, in this version of Heinlein's "perpetual motion fur farm," only the barest minimum of negative entropy occurs as Matt, the older wounded version, remains to die in 1970.

The third example of the Cartesian replay, Michel Jeury's *Le Temps incertain* (*Uncertain Time/Weather*, published in English translation as *Chronolysis*, 1973) locates the struggle of two massive intertemporal powers—the Krupp-like conglomerate HKH and the Hospital Garichankar, both neo-Balzacian entities—within the mental space-time of a single protagonist. This spacetime in turn is confined to the final instant of life before the death of this protagonist's physical body. Daniel Diersant, injected with chronolytic drugs at the moment of his death, is plunged into a state of *éternité subjective* [subjective eternity]: "Si vous mourez en chronolyse, il est possible de multiplier par dix puissance douze environ la durée subjective de vos dernières secondes de vie" [If you die in the state of chronolysis, it is possible to multiply more or less by ten to the twelfth power the subjective duration of the last seconds of your life].[23] This would seem a replay of Philip K. Dick's condition of "half-life" in *Ubik* (1968), a novel much admired by Jeury. Yet there are subtle differences that modify the carcereal relation between mind and body. Dick's "half-life" is clearly a material condition, a matter of more or less energy, thus of inevitable entropy. We remember that Balzac's Centenarian, as his body hardened to a rigid shell, confining the spark of life more and more to its frozen depths, increasingly considered life not merely as material energy but as *his* energy, implying that this self is a subjective entity, something that even in this materialist context somehow remains qualitatively different from the physical body that imprisons it. Jeury's ultimate field of play is, by his own naming, a *subjective* eternity. But "Eternity" has now become a single spatiotemporal instant, the smallest possible envelope of mind, now stretching to seemingly unending vistas.

Life extension is again, however, as with Steiner, a living hell: Diersant, within this mindspace, is condemned to relive the instant of his own death—a car crash—again and again, each time from a maze of different angles, creating a labyrinth from which escape seems impossible. In Jeury's novel, the scientist's mind itself has become the space of experiment, conducted by the doctors of Garichankar, who are seeking to discover the "real" condition of his death, a fact of crucial importance for the intertemporal struggle under way. Opposing their search are agents of HKH, for whom the endless disruption of Diersant's time path is (again) the necessary condition upon which the hegemony of their alternate time line depends. Diersant's quest, like that of Wood, is to break free of this infernal iteration within which he comes to realize, as Hamlet foretold, that one can be king of infinite space yet bound in the smallest nutshell. Though a "breakthrough" does occur, Diersant only appears in the end to move to another level of subjective eternity.

It is uncanny how these works of Verne, Curval, Steiner, and Jeury can be read as "remakes" of *The Centenarian* despite the fact that Balzac's novel was unknown to all these writers and has had no direct resonance either in canonical French literature or in SF. As we have suggested, the explanation may be that all these works, insofar as they deal with a relation between science and human existence that is particularly and enduringly French, were written "by" the Cartesian tradition, a tradition in which the rational scientific mind is acutely aware not only of its privileged relation to all other extended things but of its problematic connection to its own body. *The Centenarian*, contemporary to *Frankenstein*, is perhaps the first work in the French tradition to formulate the problematic of the mind-body relationship in the context of modern science. As such, it stands as a key work of French SF and thus deserves to be read and studied by all readers and scholars interested in the formation of this genre.

George Slusser and Danièle Chatelain

the centenarian

or The Two Beringhelds

I have gathered together all that is known about the Centenarian. The information on which this tale is based is taken from secret memoirs, notes, letters, and correspondence, all of which remain in the hands of persons still living, and there are eyewitness accounts of some of the *effects* recorded here.

I have arranged the facts in narrative form and coordinated them so as to produce a consistent story.

Restricted to the passive role of historian, I have abstained from all personal commentary, and I offer this tale to the contemplation of each individual, regretting only that I have so little information about *happenings* so extraordinary.

Nonetheless, I dare to hope that among the number of those who will read this work some will be found willing to admit that *things that appear the most bizarre are in fact very real*, and that those scientists who seek to enlarge the circle of human knowledge will find here the story of something *they witness every day of their lives*.

As for the critics, I admit that theirs is the easier task . . .

Horace Saint-Aubin

Chapter one

THE ROCK OF GRAMMONT — THE GENERAL —
THE YOUNG GIRL — THE OATH

There are certain nights whose sight is majestic, and whose contemplation plunges us into a reverie full of charm; I dare say they
are few who have not felt, in their souls, this Ossianic vagueness,
produced by the nightly appearance of such celestial immensity.[1]

This kind of *soul dream* takes on the hue of the temperament
of the person who experiences it, and causes either pleasure,
or pain, or even a kind of feeling that partakes of these two extremes, without being either one.

No one will ever find, I believe, a site more apt to inspire the
effects of such meditation than the charming landscape one discovers from atop Grammont Hill, nor a night more in harmony
with such thoughts than that of June 15, 181–.[2]

Indeed, a number of strange-shaped clouds were just then forming magic and airy structures, which, when moved on by a brisk
wind, unveiled open spaces in the firmament; and then, though
the night was dark, the moon here and there cast a glow often
eclipsed: such swaths of light, which tinted but the extremi-
ties and outer leaves of trees without penetrating, as does daylight, the entire foliage, produced accidents in harmony with the
phantasmagoria of the sky.

It had rained that morning, and as the ground was still wet footsteps could barely be heard; because the wind was only blowing now
and then, and because its violence was felt only in the high reaches
of the clouds, the night was allowed to retain a majestic calm.

In the midst of these circumstances, the viewer perceived the
cheerful plain of the Touraine and the green meadows that, on
the side of the river Cher, lie before the capital of this province.[3]
The murmuring leaves of the poplar trees that dot the countryside

seemed to speak under the efforts of the breeze, and the funereal owl, the corax, uttered their slow, plaintive cries. The moon cast silvery light over the wide expanse of the Cher; a handful of stars sparkled here and there, piercing the cloudy veil of the heavens with their diamond-like glimmer. Finally all of nature, plunged in sleep, seemed to be dreaming.

At this very moment, an entire division of the army was returning from the Spanish campaign to Paris, to receive their orders from the sovereign of the time.

The troops were about to reach Tours, where their arrival would break the silence of the city. These old, sunburnt veterans were marching day and night, across their homeland, admiring it, shaking off the dust they had gathered in the unconquerable land of Spain. One heard them whistling their favorite songs; the fleeting sound of their marching feet was heard in the distance, just as one could see, from far away, the bayonets of their rifles glinting over the countryside.

General Beringheld (Tullius), allowing his division to go on before him, had halted on the heights of Grammont, and this ambitious young man, recovering from his dreams of glory, contemplated the scene that suddenly opened to his gaze. Wishing to give himself entirely to the charm that overtook him, the General dismounted, dismissed the two aides-de-camp who accompanied him, and retaining only Jacques Butmel alias Lagloire, former member of the consular guard and his devoted servant, he sat down on a mound of grass, seeking a new direction for his future life, and passing in review all the events that had marked his past life. He held his head against his right hand, placing his elbow on his knee, and in this pose, he fixed his gaze on the charming village of Saint-Avertin, occasionally lifting his eyes to the heavens, as if seeking guidance from that silent vault, or as if those feelings that had always led him to great things now made him desire to escape to the stars.

The old soldier had lain down, and, head on the grass, appeared to be thinking of nothing else, except to catch a moment's sleep, without worrying about what motive the General might have had

6

for stopping, in the middle of the night, on the Hill of Grammont. We can sum up this soldier's character perfectly by saying that the least of his master's wishes was for him what a *firman* of the Grand Potentate was for a Muslim.

"Ah, Marianine! Have you remained faithful to me?" Beringheld exclaimed after a moment of meditation; these words issued involuntarily from the saddened heart of the General, then he fell back into a deep reverie that held him in thrall.

Tullius had been looking out over the meadow for about ten minutes, when he spied a young girl dressed entirely in white, advancing with care across the countryside: one moment she hurried forward, the next she slowed her pace, all the while moving toward the base of the hill, on the top of which Beringheld was sitting.

Carefully examining all the movements of this young girl, the General at first thought the cause of her nighttime wanderings must be madness; but, when he saw a feeble light illuminate the face of the rock, he changed his mind; his curiosity was aroused to the utmost because the carriage and manners of the young girl indicated that she belonged to a family that one might rank among what is called *the upper class*. Her carriage, her figure were graceful; she had protected her head from the chill of the night with a shawl that she had arranged with a certain elegance, her red belt stood out against the white of her dress, the moonlight shone upon her steel necklace, finally her solitary errand in the night, her uneven gait and the light that shone upon the base of Grammont rock, formed a set of circumstances destined to justify the curiosity of Beringheld and explain what happened next.

He left the place and started down the hill to meet the young girl who had already reached the bridge over the Cher; his plan was to speak with her before she might reach the base of the hill.

The General had hardly taken three steps, when a ray of moonlight, shining on a small grove of trees that adorned the slope of the hill, made visible to him a square-shaped cloud or rather a mass of whitish vapor, extremely volatile and abundant, that he recognized as thick smoke, issuing from the core of the rock.[4] This circumstance surprised him all the more in that he saw no reason for anyone to use a fire during this season; what is more, the presence of a hearth at the spot toward which the young girl was heading appeared odd, and once again disturbed all his thoughts and conjectures as to the reason for the stranger's promenade.

Beringheld had such energy and will power that it was impossible for him to control his feelings; his heart was full of the same headstrong passion that he put into everything; and so, he began to run, and rushed down the hill more like a wolf swooping down on his prey, than a young man hastening to give advice against rashness, or to protect weakness.

The young girl saw him, and, noticing the shiny decorations on his General's uniform, quite naturally became frightened. Believing she could conceal her action from the piercing eye of Beringheld, she left the *levee*, went more slowly among the trees on the prairie, and sought to hide herself carefully behind the trunks of the elm trees, in the folds of the levee, or under bushes.

Nevertheless, however hard she tried, she found it impossible to give the slip to the General, who soon found himself at a small distance from the mound where she had taken refuge. She stopped, realizing she could not avoid the stranger who was pursuing her. Beringheld, for his part, moved by some vague feeling, stopped as well, and began to examine the young stranger more closely.

There are physiognomies that at once betray the feelings of the soul, through certain signs that are immediately recognizable by anyone who has observed nature. In an instant, the General had guessed the young girl's character: her large eyes, round and shining, indicated by their mobility, a soul easily enraptured; her broad forehead, her somewhat thick lips seemed to speak of a heart that was big, generous, and proud with that pride that excludes neither confidence nor affability. One must not think that, for all of this, the girl was beautiful; yet she had a noteworthy physiognomy, a look of distinction, and what attracted Beringheld even more was an *inspired look*.

This attitude, this manner of being, stood out from an ensemble of details that would be very difficult to explain, but which the mind could easily grasp; in fact, all the gestures and features that constitute rapture, found themselves so reunited in the being of this young solitary, that the General did not hesitate to think that she was either an *artist*, or a young girl driven by some violent passion: her imagination must have been extraordinarily lively, ardent and not frivolous in the least, for the features of her face indicated a strong character, full of energy and steadiness.

All these distinctive features were nonetheless concealed, or rather tarnished, by a veil of sadness and suffering that ran much too deep to have been caused by a feeling of melancholy alone, or by the ravages of a *grand passion*; one even saw that her pain did not have its source in some physical malady inherent to the subject, but that her dark obsession was caused by circumstances that one could call *external*.

The General had no sooner finished his scrutiny than he moved toward the mound, from which the stranger, standing and attentive, was watching Beringheld with mixed feelings of anxiety, fear, and curiosity.

Here I should note that Tullius was wearing his general's hat, in such a way that the jutting angle of its pointed crest cast a shadow on his face.

Thus, it was not until he had actually set foot on the grassy mound, that the young girl could see the General's face. As soon as she saw it, she fell back a few paces, betraying a movement of surprise that Beringheld took for fear.

"I hope, Mademoiselle," the General remarked, "that you will not find it odd that I rushed to offer you my aid, seeing you alone, in the night, in the middle of these fields, with soldiers passing by on the road at every moment. If my presence disturbs you, or if my offer is indiscreet, please say so . . . Nonetheless, when I tell you that I am General Beringheld, I believe you will be convinced you have nothing to fear from me."

At the name of Beringheld, the young girl came closer to the General and, without uttering a word, her eyes ever riveted on the face of the famous warrior, she bowed respectfully; her reverence, however, bore the mark of that same astonishment and uncertainty already stamped on her face; as she arose, she stared at Tullius's features, attentively, like someone in a stupor.

The General, seeing the young stranger's exalted attitude, this time was convinced that she was suffering from mental alienation. He looked at her in a pained manner, and exclaimed:

"Poor unfortunate creature! . . . Although I have no reason to be satisfied with the constancy and the wit of your sex, I cannot keep myself from pitying you . . . At the very least, your state proves that your feelings were not paltry ones, and that you loved with madness!

"Oh! General, what makes you think this way about me? . . . The astonished state in which I find myself is nothing if not most natural, and I can easily explain it to you, without going back on what I promised. I have a rendezvous . . ."

"A rendezvous, Mademoiselle?" . . .

"A rendezvous, General," the young girl replied, with an accent and tone that succeeded in confounding Beringheld, "a rendezvous in which I take great pride; yet the man for whom I am waiting resembles you so much, that the sight of your face filled me with deep astonishment."

Barely had the girl spoke these words, that the astonishment that possessed her invaded the intrepid soul of the General: he paled, he staggered, and in turn stared at the stranger with haggard eyes.

A moment of silence ensued during which the stranger studied the alterations in the General's face, and it was she who spoke first:

"Might I in turn inquire how it is that my words seem to perplex General Beringheld?"

The General, prey to a flood of memories, which it was easy to interpret as being painful, exclaimed:

"Is it a young man?"

"General, I cannot answer your question."

"If my suspicions are correct, Mademoiselle, you are now in the gravest danger, and I don't know by which means to make you realize it."

"Monsieur," she answered, with a faint smile, "I am in no danger whatsoever, this is not the first time that I have come to this rendezvous."

The General made the gesture of a man who feels relieved of a great burden.

"My child," he said in a paternal tone, "I will probably take up residence in Tours for a time; no doubt I will see you in society. Your manners, your way of speaking, reveal a young girl who is the pride and joy of a distinguished family; for the sake of your honor, will you take my arm . . . and return to town? . . . A secret foreboding tells me that you are the plaything of the person who awaits you, and . . . that sooner or later you will come to harm . . . There is still time, will you come? . . ."

The young girl made a haughty movement that revealed that these suspicions were hurting her.

"Oh! Please forgive me, Mademoiselle," Tullius continued, "if I had no interest in your well-being, I would not speak to you in this manner! And . . . even if this rendezvous of yours is motivated by deep feeling, you see me ready to serve you with the same zeal as I would an old friend."

As he finished speaking these words, eleven o'clock tolled at the Cathedral Saint-Gatien. The tollings, carried by the wind, were scrupulously counted by the stranger.

"General," she said, "I came somewhat ahead of time tonight, thus I have time to explain to you how it is that a young girl of my age, bearing, and birth happens to be here, on the meadow of the Cher, in the middle of the night, waiting for a bizarre signal to be given, while my family thinks that I am sleeping quietly . . . I owe it to myself to dispel those doubts in your mind which, tomorrow, must make of me the talk of the town, for surely you will not be able to keep this matter silent." She accompanied these last words with a gently ironic smile, which lent her physiognomy a piquant charm.

"Alas! Mademoiselle, I beg you in the name of all you hold most dear, for your mother's sake, for your sake, tell me if the man who summoned you at this hour to this out-of-the-way place, is young or old! . . . If it is true that he looks like me . . . I tremble, for I, a General accustomed to the horrors of combat, shudder for your sake . . . If *it were he!* . . . Poor child! . . .

"General," she replied, assuming an attitude of sternness, which the pale moonlight turned into something apt to stir the imagination. "General, are you going to stop questioning me? . . . There is more, and when I will have finished my simple tale, and hear the signal, do not follow me, do not retain me. Do you swear it? . . ."

"I swear it," the General said gravely.

"On your honor?" she said, with a look of fear.

"On my honor," the General repeated.

At that instant, Beringheld glanced at the hill; he saw the smoke, now blacker and more abundant, shape itself into a thick cloud. The young girl, visibly anxious, turned her eyes in that direction, posing her gaze on the feeble and flickering light that was coming from the base of the mountain.

She and Beringheld scrutinized each other after having stared together a while at the rock, and they remained a moment plunged deep in thoughts that seemed to blend as one, to judge from the expressions on their faces. Finally, the girl said to the General:

"Swear you will not go to the *Cave of Grammont*,[5] that is, to the spot where that light is shining; swear it to me, General!"

This request was accompanied by a look of supplication and fear that revealed how much the young girl was afraid this would be refused.

"I promise it," said the General.

The innocent joy the stranger then manifested was proof of the virginal candor of her soul. She sat down, spreading her shawl on the grass, and, pointing out to the General a stone where he could sit. She waited until some soldiers had gone by, as well as a doctor who, returning on horseback from some urgent call, had stopped on the road, trying to recognize the people he vaguely perceived; he seemed to look at the General and the young girl with astonishment, but soon he rode off at full gallop. Then the pretty *Tourangelle* spoke in more or less the following terms.

Chapter two

"There is nothing less natural than this nocturnal errand I am on; thus, you must be thinking that only a matter of the great importance could bring me to undertake such a thing, and above all, you must imagine that I have no power to free myself from this obligation.

"My father is one of the richest manufacturers of the city; he employs a great number of workers, so that his well-being is dear to a large number of families who depend completely on him. His great charity, his goodness, have earned him the esteem of the entire city, the love of many people, and great popularity.

"I am his only daughter, he loves me dearly, and I, Monsieur, love him as much as daughterly love is permitted." With these words, a tear came forth from the girl's eye, the tear rolled down her cheek and fell in the grass, where it must have produced the effect of a dewdrop; it was as pure as she was, and, if there are divine spirits whose task it is to keep track of those sentiments which do honor to mankind, then that tear was no doubt gathered up to heaven. The accents this child lent to her simple words moved the General.

"I have done, she continued, "all I could to meet his every need; I have sought to give him all the moral joys that a child's perfections can offer; I had the good fortune to be given talents, therefore every day I thank God for having made me a musician, for my fingers, as they play upon the keys of my instrument, ease the sufferings of my father."

The young girl could not hold back her tears.

"Ah! Monsieur," she continued, "one has never suffered until one has witnessed the heartrending spectacle of the mortal illness of a father one cherishes."

She paused briefly, and after wiping the tears from her pretty dark eyes, she went on:

"Three years ago my father, needing to hire more workers,

was obliged to go to Lyon to find some. He brought back with him from this city an old man very skilled in the art of silk dying; it was thanks to the brilliant colors this worker knew how to prepare that my father's products earned the fame and reputation they now enjoy. This worker died a year afterward; my father had provided him with assiduous care, as he does always with any of his workers who fall sick.

"Since that moment, my father fell prey to the cruelest sickness that ever afflicted a living being, if such suffering can be said to exist at all. It is far from me to accuse anyone, but the onset of his illness coincided almost exactly with the moment that this man breathed his last.

"Is he really dead?" Beringheld demanded.

"Oh, yes! Monsieur, for the doctors opened him up . . . But it seems that his parting breath bequeathed his suffering to my father.

"At first, he felt a total weakening which kept him from appearing before his workers, and it was from his bed that he directed their work: I it was who served as his interpreter, and, in trying to imitate his goodness, I earned for myself a benevolence and a love that belonged to him alone.

"His ever increasing weakness was accompanied by a pain that wracked all the bones of his body; the seat of this mortal pain lay in the brain; an awful stabbing in this part of his head announces an attack, the pain then recurs throughout his entire machine. Then the least noise, a slight draft, doubles his suffering; it seems, he says, as if some unknown force were pulling his eyes back into his head, by a slow, cruel movement, which sometimes reveals itself in the form of visible convulsions.

"He cannot eat! The lightest of foods, the purest water, so overburden his too fragile stomach, that he feels a horrible fatigue: at times his pulse stops, his heart sinks into an extreme agony, and he seems ready to expire. A cloud comes over him, and . . . he complains he no longer can see me.

"The finest linen, the softest material cause him unimaginable suffering; the satin on which he lies is never soft enough . . . his deep stabbings of pain penetrate all the fibers of his body; indeed, his hair, his skin, his eyelashes, all pain him; his teeth seem to be rotting out of his head, his blood carries all the corrosive substances of arsenic through his veins; his burning palate dries out; drops of icy sweat ooze painfully from his pores, and streak his forehead; it seems as if death is about to seize him, and he accuses it of coming too slowly. Often I hear his delirious words accusing his Fanny; often his eyes perceive formless monsters that torment him.

"He then describes to me large shadows, whose colors arranged lengthwise darken by degrees, turn white all of a sudden, then white, red, green, and finally become dazzlingly bright: or there are serpents with the heads of women, monkeys that laugh the way Satan must laugh, and in the midst of such delirium, his pain become more acute, his members stiffen, everything about him takes on the cadaverous look of a man who has expired: his eyes are dry, fixed, his lashes bristling . . . he froths at the mouth, does not speak anymore, . . . and, Monsieur, the person who suffers all of this is my very father . . . I feel his sufferings, I see them, I cannot do a thing to lessen them. O my father!!! What purpose does your daughter serve?

"What purpose!!!" exclaimed Fanny in a kind of frenzy, "but don't you say that your food has more taste when it is I who serves it to you? Am I not the only one who knows how to wipe your brow? Are not my hands the only ones you can endure?

"During his seizures, gentle music sometimes calms him. Oh! Monsieur, with what trepidation do my fingers caress the keys of my piano! It seems as if the pedal can never dampen the sound enough; composers never create pieces of music ethereal enough for his ears. I wish the sounds would be as gentle as they are in my imagination, I would like to be able to write music in order to gather together the weakest notes, the lightest, those that use the minimum sound necessary to be heard . . . I would wish there were clouds of music, of sounds and harmonies, indeed, the music of the Sylphs . . . whenever I sing, I strive to make my voice so pure that nothing jars or offends the ear. I practice for a long time beforehand, before singing him a ballad. If I read, I draw the softest sounds from the *middle* of my vocal organ . . . I would like someone to teach me something capable of pleasing my father, of charming his ears and eyes without fatiguing them in the least. How happy I am when, after having played, read, or sung a piece of music, I see my father's eyelids close; how happy when after a moment of sleep his eyes open and meet the moist eyes of his daughter, when his hand seeks mine and squeezes it, and he says to me: "Fanny, it is good . . . I slept . . . '"

Fanny, believing she really was holding her father's hand and hearing his plaintive voice, paused; her tender eye swelled with tears that she fought back. Letting go of the General's hand, she continued:

"All the most skilled physicians in France and abroad were summoned, they all came, their remedies were of no avail, my father was not helped in the least, his sufferings became worse from day to day.

"These have reached the highest degree of pain a man can bear short of death. He draws upon his resignation; he needs his fortitude, the knowledge that he is useful to so many unfortunates who regard him as their providence (and his daughter's love must count for something as well), without which he would have killed himself long ago. Many times this thought has come to him; but then, General . . . I would forcefully remind him all these considerations, and . . . he would resign himself to go on living.

"For a long time I have witnessed the heartrending spectacle of his illness, each day it confronts me; each day my heart bleeds: alas, I have never once served my father his food or drink without seeing my hands tremble! . . . Oh! If only I could share in his suffering, as cruel as it is, then perhaps I would have the strength and even the courage to imitate him in his noble silence.

"No king on earth will ever receive from someone proofs of love so powerful: the workmen have paid a watchman to prevent any vehicle from passing near his house. All the work in the factory is now done manually; it is a catastrophe in the factory whenever a thunderstorm occurs, and each one is grieved thinking how impossible it is to prevent the sound of thunder from reaching my father's ears.

"They wait anxiously for me each morning to learn how he spent the night; there is not one single worker who does not, each evening after work, offer a prayer to *Our Lady of Bonsecours*, the church of whom stands opposite the factory; finally, we obtained from the parish priest the favor that the bells never be rung, and on Sunday it is the workmen themselves who go around to the houses and announce the hour of the services.

"Furthermore, whenever my father has a couple of hours free of suffering, I rush to tell the men, and some of them kiss my dress for joy! They have set money aside from their salaries to pay a very large sum to whatever man can cure their father! . . . But I fear the one who will ultimately cure him will not accept it!"

As she said this, Fanny seemed gripped by a supernatural feeling, a sort of frenzy lit up her gaze; her dark eyes, fixed on the heavens, caused the General to believe that only a divine hand could cure the girl's father, and that if he were to die, she would follow him to the grave.

At this moment, a faint sound was heard, it came from the *Cave of Grammont*, and Fanny turned her head in curious haste toward the hill. She stared at it attentively for a moment, then returned to her story:

"You see, General, a daughter's love is the only kind that moves me; if nothing afflicted me, I have the frankness to admit that I would not be, at this moment, so pure of heart, but the sole sight of my dear father's misfortune makes all the strings of my heart tremble, and you can judge that this interest alone for the well-being of such a cherished being could guide me through these meadows in the dark of night.

"About fifteen days ago, a workman called me aside and told me he had recently met in the region, a *being* (permit me, General, to use such a term to designate him; the promise I made I must keep: my father's life and the end of his ills depend on it; but even if they did not depend on it," she said with dignity, "I would still be every bit as faithful to my word) . . . a *being*, I say, whom

17

he had a while ago seen perform a most extraordinary cure, and as grave as my father's malady seems, he assured me that if this being wished it, my father would be cured.

"The workman took me to this avenue, and told me that it would not be long before we would see this individual pass by. Indeed, after three evenings during which I waited for him in vain, I saw him come walking along slowly; and so, General, I went up to that angel, and my prayers softened his heart. He promised to cure my father, while acknowledging to me that certain unfortunate circumstances obliged him to remain in hiding, and that . . . . in short, *I promised to do everything that he wanted.*"

The young girl uttered these words with an air of such mystery that it made one suspect that she gave even more importance to what she was not saying.

"Every night," she continued, "I come here to get the healing balms that lessen my father's pain: without having seen my father, this being has guessed everything, and in ten days' time all suffering has gradually ceased: nights are no more than simply twelve hours for my father, and he spends them sleeping; he is beginning to eat; he is no longer delirious. I have however inherited this from him, for I now have fallen prey to a rapture of joy and happiness. Today was a holiday for half the city; my father got out of bed, saw his workmen again, and his factory, . . . he cried for joy when he saw his looms, and, seeing this touching spectacle, each and every person was moved to tears. Tomorrow, General, my father will be completely out of danger . . . for according to what this being told me yesterday, *tonight is my last errand* (Beringheld shuddered); indeed, I rush with joy to get the potion which will efface the last signs of that terrible illness . . . And yet," she added, "I still cannot be sure that he is cured, so much do I desire to be certain that he will never suffer again."

Fanny said nothing more. She looked at the General with surprise, for terror was written on his face, the girl's story had plunged him into a deep meditation and it was only after a long silence that he exclaimed:

"And this man looks like me?"

"I told you that."

"Oh, young Fanny, you are risking your life . . . If my hunch is correct, your father is cured . . . I know the *old man*! . . ."

Hearing this word, the astonished young girl looked at the General with curiosity, but he continued to speak:

"Go back to town, you are going to die!" The General spoke these words with such a tone of conviction that anyone but Fanny would have fallen to trembling.

At that instant, a sound like that of a rattle was heard, and Fanny, quick as a flash, leapt forward . . . Then Beringheld, faster yet, caught her in his arms as he exclaimed: "No, you shall not go! . . ."

"General," young Fanny said, with a sublime cry of despair, and with that feminine rage that distorts and contracts the features of beauty; "General, you are going back on your word . . ." Her voice was stifled with fury; . . . "General, you do not have the right to hold me back . . . General, you are abusing . . . you . . . Oh, my father," she said, summoning all the power of her voice, and sobbing, "Oh, father dear! If you die, blame only him! General, I shall kill myself—on the spot! . . . General . . ."

Certainly, Beringheld must have had extremely great and compelling reasons to break his oath in this manner.

Young Fanny fainted from anger. Frightened, Tullius laid her down on the grass and ran to the river to fetch water in order to revive her; then, he reproached himself a thousand times over for his conduct. Indeed, if his conjectures turn out to be wrong, he would be most blameworthy, for he could bring about the death of Fanny's father. Nonetheless, his premonitions were of such force that they counterbalanced in his mind any sense of wrongness and violence in his actions. He came rushing back holding in his two hands his hat filled with water. Imagine his surprise! The place was empty! Fanny had disappeared, and, when he looked in the direction of the rock, he saw, in the light of the moon, the large red shawl, which as it flew betrayed the rapid flight of the young girl. A deathly tremor ran through the General's body, he froze with astonishment, he pondered Fanny's flight; the shawl showed her jumping over a ditch. Then, a bush hid her from view, he saw her again, she disappeared, returned, and finally entered the *Cave of Grammont*.

Beringheld, judging that it was futile to run after the young girl, climbed back on the levee and went off slowly to seek his faithful Lagloire, who was probably still sleeping on the heights of Grammont. As he walked along, the General could not take his eyes off of the *Cave of Grammont* . . .

"If she does not perish there tonight, I will warn her father, insofar as I then will have no oath to keep! Anyway, it's possible I could be wrong" . . .

Such were the General's thoughts, reduced to their simplest expression. When it became impossible to see the cave, he contented himself with the presence of that feeble light that tinted the base of the rock . . .

He was approaching that spot of light, when dull moans reached his ears, plaintive moans like those of a child, or even like those of someone who is dying a violent death, echoed in the General's heart, with all the more force that the silence of the night was so deep, his suspicions so real for him, and Fanny so intriguing. He remained frozen to the spot, his gaze fixed on this glimmer that now seemed to wander about, and that soon went out . . .

A mechanical movement causing him to glance up at the crest of the hill, his eyes no longer were able to perceive the cloud of smoke. At that very moment, one last protracted cry was heard, and soon nothing more disturbed the silence of the night.

The General was stunned: it seemed to him that he was the agent of the girl's death; he thought he could still hear this last plaintive cry cut off by the nocturnal silence that served as its funeral elegy.

"General," exclaimed old Lagloire, "what in blazes is going on in that hole? . . . Nothing, not even the final handshake of a comrade cashing in on the field of battle, has ever moved me like the cry that just awakened me."

"Let's run, Lagloire! I want to be sure of what has happened," Tullius exclaimed.

Immediately the General and his soldier rush through the

bushes, across the irregular terrain of the levee and through the trees of the grove. They double their efforts in order to reach the spot where the light had been shining; nevertheless, the General takes a thousand precautions to ensure that his steps and those of his soldier aide make as little noise as possible. Lagloire had noticed the change that had come over the General's features; he concluded from this that something must have happened, something most extraordinary, capable of astonishing this impassive warrior.

Chapter three

THE OLD MAN — HIS FEATURES — THE SACRIFICE — THE
RESEMBLANCE — THE GENERAL'S SORROW — THE STORY OF
A WORKMAN

Beringheld and his soldier soon came to the place called the *Cave of Grammont*: they approached cautiously, and upon the order of his General, Lagloire crouched down behind a tree trunk; Tullius did the same. They listened carefully for the least noise, keeping a sharp eye on that part of the rock that protruded. And, thus suspended over the cave, they soon witnessed a scene that its perpetrator no doubt never intended for mortal eyes.

From the depths of that hiding place, an old man sprang forth!
. . . And Beringheld shuddered when, in the pale light of the moon, he thought he recognized him.

This extraordinary being was of gigantic height; he had hair only on the back of his head, and its whiteness cast a strange glow, for it looked more like silver threads than the pure snow that usually adorns the bald heads of old men. His back, though not bent, suggested a surprising decrepitude. His bony limbs were all out of proportion with his tall size, and this ossification seemed covered by only the thinnest layer of flesh, compared to what it should have been for bones of such an enormous mass.

Once outside the cave, he took a few steps, rose up on tiptoe, and turned around in order to investigate the rock on which it was possible that he had heard a noise; thus was Beringheld able to confirm his suspicions, for he recognized the stranger. As for Lagloire, as soon as he saw the old man face to face, though accustomed to strange sights, he shuddered with horror.

The man's skull seemed to have no skin on it, so much had this part of his body become one with the rest: his ancient forehead seemed to belong to the mineral rather than the animal order: therefore the first idea that came to mind, on seeing this skull which appeared to be *petrified*, was that the Almighty had shaped it from the hardest granite. Its grayish color confirmed this, and a lively imagination would have believed it saw, covering this frontal bone, the very same moss that grew upon marble ruins. Nothing in the world expressed impenetrability in the same way as this severe forehead did; indeed, were one commissioned to make a statue of Destiny, this forehead would render its inflexibility in a marvelous manner.

Nothing however could give any sense of what the eyes of this strange being were like: their eyebrows, void of human color, were like the fruit of some force-grown vegetation; and the hand of time that sought to uproot them, had clearly been stayed by some superior force. Beneath this bizarre forest of bristling hairs, below the forehead, two dark and deep cavities extended far inward; from their depths a residue of light, a thread of flame, lit up two black eyes, that rolled slowly in orbits that were too vast for them.

The parts of the eye, that is, the eyelid, the eyelashes, the cornea, the tear ducts, were all dead and dull: *the quickness of life* had abandoned them; alone the pupil burned in solitary manner with its thread of ardent flame, dry and yet ablaze. The uniqueness of this individual amazed one more than anything else; it stamped on the soul a sort of involuntary terror.

The old man's cheeks, having lost all their vital colors, belonged more to a cadaver than to a living man, yet they were firm although excessively wrinkled, and the huge size of the maxillary bones contributed in no small manner to the roughness of his skin. His long beard, white and sparse, barely served to give the stranger a venerable look; on the contrary it added, by its disorder and bizarre disposition, to the supernatural look of this head. The old man had a large nose, whose flattened nostrils gave him the vague look of a bull: finally, this resemblance was bolstered by his mouth, large beyond all measure, remarkable, not only by the bizarre disposition of the lips, but also by a black spot located exactly in their center.

This black spot seemed to be caused by cauterization. At this spot the two burned lips exactly traced the shape of a coal, and the lip itself had the consistency thereof; moreover, this deformity was neatly confined, and one could only give a idea of its size by applying a pencil to the place on the lip to reproduce this effect.

The stranger's massive legs revealed a muscular strength such that, when he was standing up, it seemed as if there was no force in the world powerful enough to shake those two immovable pillars.

Nonetheless, this breadth of shoulder, this girth, came, as I already said, from the bone structure. This old man was lean, his belly showed no protuberance; to judge from his movements, one could believe that blood barely flowed in his veins; there was little sign of life in this cadaverous mass: in sum, he offered a perfect resemblance to those two-hundred-year-old oak trees, whose knotted trunk is hollow, continuing to stand for a long time without life, seeming to witness the spectacle of young trees, for now timidly developing, but who one day will witness the death of these kings of the forest.

The totality of this old man's countenance offered a large and handsome mass, and in its contours, its form, its fullness, it offered a striking resemblance to the face of young Beringheld; one recognized there *a family likeness*, if such an expression is possible.

Whatever the case, the look of this old man impressed on the soul a succession of very strange thoughts: one would wish never to have seen it, and yet one's imagination felt a certain pleasure in the seeing. The light of the moon, the silence and the location, the stirrings of the wind, the *solemnity* of this bizarre creature's movements—all made him similar to the original and fleeting figure of a dream, and if one began to meditate, the imagination, as it pondered, would make of him a pyramid of Egypt, for there was something *monumental* about his presence. Those painters who, till now, have depicted Time, have never given us anything so capable of expressing the idea of this divinity, as the spectacle of this old man. His movements seemed to belong more to the tomb than to life, more to centuries stretching into the past rather than to the present. Finally, should the dead return to life, were the shades to walk and take on the semblance of life, this old man would belong to that pale company.

His simple dress bore no resemblance to any known style; yet without being too strange and removed from the manner of dress of the day, it appeared to belong to no particular age. A vast overcoat of Carmelite brown, which he cast on the ground as he emerged from the *Cave of Grammont*, revealed from the fine nature of its fabric that the old man, whenever he draped it around his huge form, could make it blend with the styles of all nations.

Had the imagination the power to envision this old man standing astride ruined worlds, it would see him as the eternal prototype of *Man* abandoned by his Divinity, or perhaps even that of Time, of Death, or of a god. The ancients would have deified him; modern man would have burned him at the stake, and the novelist would be horrified to see before him the creature he would call *The Wandering Jew*, or a *vampire*, the objects of so many mad imaginings.

Finally, a scientist would imagine that some new Pascal, uniting the talents of Boërhave,[6] Agrippa, and Prometheus, had created an artificial man.

Once the tall old man had come out of the cave and cast a rapid look at the grove of trees that dominated the rock, he advanced into the meadow; he took a look around the countryside. He returned only after he had assured himself he was completely alone, for he had climbed up to the levee and ventured far enough to see if some pedestrians might not be traveling the Bordeaux road that formed an elbow above the *Cave of Grammont* . . . Finally, after all these preliminaries, and after all this searching done with the careful prudence of old age, he went back deep into the cave.

"Well, General?" Lagloire asked Beringheld.

The General, immobile and dumbfounded, made a sign with his finger for his old soldier not to speak. The old Sergeant, imitating the General, tried to tell him, using signs, that the old man looked like him; but a faint noise interrupted Lagloire, who went back behind the trunk of his tree, from which he had moved slightly away.

The rustling of leaves and undergrowth made the stranger tremble slightly. He returned to the cave for a moment, as if to set down what he held, but he came back out at once and lifted up his enormous head. He fixed his gaze for a long moment on the spot where the rustling of leaves suggested the presence of a living being. The General and Lagloire huddled up as best they could, and turned around the trunk ever so slightly as the old man moved from place to place, seeking to convince himself that the noise was not caused by human beings.

He advanced as if he was about to climb the rock, but stopped, seemed to ponder, and, thinking perhaps, as one can presume from the movements he made, that some animals caused this slight rustling, went back to the cave, and soon reappeared, carrying a sack on his shoulders that contained a load that had a rather large volume without seeming heavy, for when he put it on the ground, it made only a slight noise, similar to that which pieces of wood might make, or rather charcoal. The eye was horrified by the forms betrayed by the folds of the cloth, and, certainly, the first thing that these long shapes with rounded ends suggested was that the sack contained the remains of a cadaver.

With his finger, the old soldier showed the General that the sack was tied with the red belt of the young girl who had been walking earlier in the field; Beringheld shuddered, and tears, drawn from him by Fanny's misfortune, streamed down his face.

Once the burden had been set down, the old man again disappeared; he returned with the young girl's shawl, put it on top of the bag, and, drawing from his bosom a whitish substance, he placed it on the red cashmere: in an instant, without explosion, without flame, effortlessly, the sack, the belt, the shawl, and everything inside the canvas, all were annihilated, in such a way that no trace or odor remained; only a small wisp of smoke evaporating in the air. The old man seemed to examine carefully the direction from which the wind was blowing, so as to move away from the malignant influence of that bluish smoke, which he avoided as if it were deadly.

"I'd rather face a battery of twelve-pounders than this!" whispered Lagloire.

"So would I," answered Beringheld, wiping away his tears.

"Could that be the body of the young girl?" the old soldier asked.

"Silence!" . . . the General said, putting his finger to his lips.

Indeed, the old man had turned around. He gathered up his overcoat, wrapped himself in it and went off down the Avenue de Grammont. What most struck Lagloire is that this gigantic old man, before he headed off in the direction of the levee, cast a glance at the spot where he had destroyed his burden, and that tears fell from his lifeless eyes. For a moment his attitude was one of melancholy and regret, yet an inexplicable gesture put an end to his brief reverie.

The occasion served to push to the maximum that sense of the *extraordinary* that appeared to be the mark of this old man. Everything about him surpassed that which was familiar: finally, one would have said that this being came from a region situated beyond those pillars of the ideal upon which the human spirit has engraved: *nec plus ultra*.

Beringheld, unable any longer to bear the idea of Fanny's death, fainted, and Lagloire remained dumbstruck seeing his General felled by the spectacle. The old soldier helped Tullius to his feet, and supporting him with the care of a father, led him up to the crest of the hill. From there, they could see the old man walking at a steady pace toward the city of Tours. The General pointed him out to his faithful servant, with a gesture that expressed with energy the horror that possessed Beringheld.

"We'll settle his account, General!"

Beringheld nodded his head slowly, as if to say that he doubted this, and that mortal hands could do nothing against the old man.

"Is the girl dead then?" asked Lagloire, looking at his General with that somber, pensive bearing characteristic of old soldiers, when they are deeply moved.

Tullius contemplated his soldier with a pained expression: there was silence for a moment, and Lagloire, feeling his eyes become wet with tears, exclaimed:

"Come on, General, I have never cried before, not even when I saw old Lenseigne fall in battle! Let's leave this place."

At this moment, the sound of several approaching carriages was heard: Lagloire, seeing wagons and Beringheld's coach, ran to order the soldier driving it to halt at the slope of the hill; when he returned, he led his dejected master toward the levee.

The General walked slowly, watching the old man who advanced at a slow pace down the majestic avenue that led to the Iron Gates of the city of Tours.[7] On arriving at the spot where he was to meet his carriage, he cast a glance at the knoll on which Fanny had told him her tale; he noticed an object shining there that he could not identify; and so, he made a hurried rush toward the meadow, and when he was near the knoll, he recognized the metal necklace that the unfortunate young girl had been wearing; he snatched it up, then casting one last glance at the landscape of the meadows of the Cher, at the Cher itself, the rock of Grammont, the cave, the brush lands and the knoll, he walked on, deep in thought, and re-joined his carriage: the driver whipped the fiery steeds, and the carriage shot forward, hooves resounding on the pavement. Soon the coach caught up with the old man, who was walking so slowly that one could barely tell that he had moved; his gait was stiff and solemn, it seemed that the path this bizarre being was tracing moved along an immortal line, from which he could not deviate. When the carriage came up behind him, he did not move, did not even turn his head; the wheels brushed lightly against his coat, and he did not seem to be touched: to him, the resounding noise of the carriage was as if it were nothing.

At the moment the General and his soldier passed next to this stranger, they looked at him once again and were again struck by the oddities of the old man. But something extraordinary that they had not noticed plunged them into a new state of astonishment.

When they saw the stranger emerge from the Cave of Grammont, the flame in his eyes, although bright, nevertheless had something reddish about it, like the somber glow cast by a dying fire; but now, that flame appeared bright to them, sparkling, piercing, and full of a terrible mobility. The General and Lagloire looked at each other in silence, and when they had gone fifty feet beyond the spot where they again had seen the stranger, Lagloire said to his master:

"But, General, isn't that the *spirit* that my Aunt Lagradna and my Uncle Butmel were always talking about at Beringheld, and who made such a stir in the village?"

The General, in prey to a violent agitation, answered nothing, for Lagloire stopped talking and Beringheld lapsed into a reverie that his old soldier respected. It was while absorbed in this meditation that the General arrived almost to Tours, without having spoken a word.

This city is closed, at its south side, by two splendid gates of iron: they replace the drawbridge that was there formerly, when Tours had been fortified. Large trenches spread out from each side of the grille that divided the ramparts, and the pavilions of the municipal customs agency have replaced the towers that must have been there before.

When the noise of the carriage became audible at this location, two men of the people, coarsely dressed, stepped out onto the roadway, and stopped the carriage from going further. The gestures these two men were making to each other, the extraordinary look on their mysterious faces, disturbed Lagloire, who, though he saw the gate was only a few paces away, still leapt to the ground; and, putting his hand on his saber, and curling up the ends of his mustache, he turned around them as if making a reconnaissance.

The driver, at the sight of Lagloire twirling his mustache, and of the two men he was sizing up, held back his horses: this sudden stopping of the fast-moving carriage drew the General from his reverie, and he stuck his head out the door to see what was causing this interruption.

One of the men had already grabbed the horses by their bits before the driver could stop them, but Lagloire, taking this stranger by his coat collar, had already energetically begun his interrogation with a loud curse.

"Sergeant," said the man's companion, "we are simple folk, workmen in Monsieur Lamanel's factory. We are concerned about a person whom you must have seen, if you are coming from Grammont, and we should like to ask if you have any news about her."

Hearing these peaceful words, the Sergeant let go of the worker's coat, and said: "Who is it you're talking about, for we come from the top of that hill."

"Did you," the other workman asked, "encounter a young girl clad in a percale dress with a red belt; she was wearing a shawl on her head in the form of a coiffure, and . . ."

"Yes," Lagloire abruptly interjected.

With this reply, the anxious countenance of each workman was animated by a heavenly joy and they looked at each other as if to give congratulations on some happy news.

The General, having overheard this exchange, called Lagloire. The latter led the two men to the carriage door where Beringheld was sitting: all the answers of the first workman convinced the General that, at this moment, he had before his eyes the very worker that Fanny had told him about; the one who had introduced the young girl to the existence, the power, and the presence of the old man.

Then Beringheld gave the order to draw his carriage up against the breastwork of the rampart, so as leave the passage open, and he said in a sinister tone that struck terror in the workman:

"I did see the girl you speak of; I know what has just happened to her; she told me the reason for her nocturnal wandering; but you who brought her to consult the old man, where did you know him from? . . . Tell me all the circumstances that led you to meet with him, hide nothing from me, you are speaking to General

Beringheld . . . I swear to you on my honor, that even if you are guilty of a crime, your secrets would be so deeply buried in my heart, that no oath, no other obligation could force me to reveal them. Speak! And then I will tell you what has become of poor Fanny."

Despite these words, the workman hesitated, glanced at the General, the road, his companion, and Lagloire with uneasiness and a sort of shame, which manifested itself in his sudden blushing.

This silence beginning to stir the General's curiosity; he said to the workman:

"Take a good look at me, and see how closely I resemble the old man."

The workman shuddered.

"I have," the General continued, "had so many dealings with this stranger, that the most insignificant details interest me greatly. You will be truly guilty if you do not tell me about your adventure."

The workman took the General's hand, squeezed it; and moving close to his ear, he whispered: "General, are you above all prejudice?"

"Certainly!" Beringheld replied, with that scornful smile that is so persuasive.

The workman then told his companion to move away. Lagloire remained, because the General vouched for his silence and fidelity; the workman had no difficulty believing this, at the sight of the thoroughly Roman face of Jacques Butmel, alias Lagloire.

The Workman's Tale

Leaning thus against the panel of the coach door Beringheld had opened, the stranger, speaking in a low voice and in a manner that could not to be heard by anyone except the two persons he was addressing, expressed himself in the following terms:

"General, I am from Angers, where I was a butcher long before the Revolution.

"The executioner had just died and left no heir, and as bad luck had it, fate designated me to succeed him!"

Upon these words, which the storyteller had just uttered with visible repugnance, Lagloire made a half-turn to the right, and began to whistle so as to hear nothing more: seeing the soldier's maneuver, the man's eyes filled with tears, which he fought back; then the General urged him to continue, in a benevolent tone that made convincing the reasons he used to console him.

"General," the workman continued, all distraught, "no one in this city, except my wife, knows of the gruesome function I used to exercise."

He spoke these words with passion and then went on:

"We were in 1780 more or less, I had been married for some time; my wife fell dangerously ill: a cancer and a mortal fever complicated and compounded her sufferings. No doctor would set foot in my house.

"One evening, my wife was on the verge of giving up the ghost. I was sitting beside her bed, my back turned toward the door; all at once I heard the hinges creak; my wife awoke, raised her eyes, uttered a horrible scream, and fainted. I turned around; I was struck dumb! . . . I seemed to see the ghost of the first criminal I had executed.

"This shade came forward slowly, and the fire from the eyes of this tall, old man, as he approached, made me well aware that he was alive. Though trembling, I arose in order to question him and to put myself in a defensive position, when he ordered me, with a sign of his hand, to sit down at my place.

"He took a seat, and felt the hands of my wife. After this examination, he turned to me, and made me the most horrible proposition."

At this instant, the workman halted, but urged on by the General, continued finally in a low voice: "He asked me for the body of a living man!"

Beringheld shuddered, the executioner watched the expression on the General's face with curious anxiety; judging nonetheless that the movement of horror he had just witnessed was not directed at him, he hastened to add: "I accepted!" . . .

"But," he continued after a moment of silence, "it was only after much struggle and after several more visits from this strange person whose arguments, or rather my fierce love for my wife, convinced me that I must to do his bidding.

"At each visit, the old man, with cruel subtlety, stayed the sufferings of my wife and halted the advance of her illness, promising me her cure as soon as I fully agreed to his terrible proposition. I adored Marianne and her cries of pain broke my heart!

"And so, one evening, I promised that, at the next execution, I would cut the criminal down from the gallows before the cord killed him, and that I would deliver him to the old man.

"And I did it, General!" the workman exclaimed. "How many men have committed worse crimes for their mistresses! . . . What more can I tell you? My wife was cured, she is still alive today, and she will always ignore what price I paid for her existence."

These last words filled the General with unimaginable terror; it was as if the words spoken concerned him personally, as if they invoked memories in him so painful, that they resembled, in their effect, a burning remorse.

"Due to the events of the Revolution," the workman continued, "the circumstances that surrounded the visits of this bizarre being have been nearly erased from my memory: the same is true for the details of what exactly he did to achieve the cure of my dear Marianne. All I remember is that he used no instruments, only his two hands and some liquors that he brought hidden beneath his overcoat, in such a way that I was never able to see them. My wife was almost always *asleep* when he left; he forbade anyone, even me, to go near her: on awakening, she remembered nothing; in vain I questioned her about the drugs the old man had her take; she would not answer me and stared at me with amazement.

"For thirty-two or thirty-three years since these strange events happened, I have never seen this old doctor again; I did not dare ask him what he did with the criminal, who, in any case, deserved ten deaths rather than just one! All that I know is that he disappeared without a trace.

"Finally, General, two weeks ago, I was on my way to Grammont, I spotted a beggar covered with the vilest rags. I don't know what feeling impelled me to look closely at this wretch; I recognized the old man! I froze in astonishment before him, and, after a moment of silence, reminded him I was the executioner of Angers . . . He began to smile. Then I told him that there was a sick person in town beloved by all, and that he ought to save him.

"I told him of our master and his young daughter . . . He asked me many questions about the character of Mademoiselle Fanny, the distinguishing features of her face. My answers seemed strangely satisfying to him, and he finally told me that if I wanted to see my master cured, I simply needed to inform his daughter; for it was with her alone that he would speak and communicate, because very important considerations obliged him to remain in hiding.

"I did not tell Mademoiselle Fanny all the circumstances that concerned me alone; but, General, her father is doing better, and she goes every night . . ."

"She *went every night!*" the General exclaimed, drawn from his reverie by Fanny's name.

With this exclamation, the workman noticed in the General's hands the metal necklace that Fanny had been wearing, and that Beringheld moved it about, gazing at it with tenderness. The man remained motionless, as if lightning had struck him.

"Poor wretch!" the General uttered, "you could not have known where you were taking your master's daughter."

The former executioner, his eyes dazed and stunned, was unable to utter a single word; the most frightening thoughts overwhelmed all his senses.

"You haven't changed trades at all," said Lagloire with a chilling tone, "the young girl is dead, and you are the cause . . ."

The poor man, coming close to the General's hands, bent over Fanny's metal necklace, he gave it a respectful kiss, and, after this mute homage, he collapsed in pain.

Seeing him lying on the ground, his companion rushed hurriedly to him, and hastened to raise him up, but the workman pressed his hand to his heart, as if to show that here was the place of his suffering, and that he felt he was dying: he summoned all his strength and said to his comrade:

"I killed Mademoiselle . . . Fa . . . a . . . anny!"

The difficulty he had in uttering this simple sentence revealed a rapid decline, his pallor became mortal, and the clear light of the sky allowed one to see his eyes as they fought against the blows of death: soon, in a final effort, he pressed the hand of his comrade, his eye remained fixed . . . and degree by degree all warmth abandoned his body, a body now deprived of life.

The other workman and Lagloire hoisted him on their shoulders and carried him over against a stone breastwork located next to the rampart, at the entrance to the city. The companion, once he laid his comrade down, closed his eyes, knelt piously at his side and recited a prayer. Lagloire, moved by innate feelings in the heart of man, fell to his knees as well, and joined his sorrow with that of the workman who was imploring heaven.

This lugubrious scene was witnessed by the people at the gate and by the General, who never ceased thinking of Fanny.

Finally, Beringheld, leaving Lagloire at this scene of woe, gave the order to enter the city and to be taken to the house that had been assigned to him. The General soon arrived there. He went to bed, but in vain; sleep could not close his eyes: he never ceased thinking of Fanny and of all the memories that this adventure, as well as the encounter with the *Centenarian*,* must have awakened in him.

However, near morning, he was finally able to fall asleep. He was soon awakened from this salutary rest by the terrible scenes that will be recounted in the following chapters.

Lagloire had had his reasons for remaining at the city gates, with the dead workman's companion. He wanted to wait for the old man he suspected of being Fanny's assassin, to follow him, and denounce him to the mob and its justice.

The old man, walking at an incredibly slow pace, was not long in appearing, and the soldier pointed him out to the workman, who trembled with fright at the sight of this bizarre machine . . .

[*Editor's Note: We will learn later why this name was given to the old man.]

34

Chapter four

LAMANEL — THE WORKERS' MUTINY — THE OLD MAN
TREMBLES — THEY WANT TO AVENGE FANNY

At break of day, Fanny's father awakes and glances at the spot where his daughter always was. He does not see her at all. So he turns over on the side that seems the least painful, and impatiently awaits the arrival of his dear daughter. He seeks to prolong that pleasant state of half-sleep, which always follows an awakening; he makes no movement to reach the bell cord in order to call Fanny, for he assumes she is resting, and respects the sleep of a person who has sat up with him so many nights.

In the meantime the workers are arriving on time at the huge factory: all, quite astonished, contemplate as they enter the comrade of the dead worker who, pale and downcast, seated next to Lagloire, casts furtive looks at each person who entered; he seems to be waiting until all the workers were reunited in order to speak.

The tense spectacle offered by the sorrow of the worker and the old soldier acted so powerfully on the mind of each, that no one went to work; the foremen themselves approached this sorrowing group, and dared not speak.

Once the workman had surveyed the assembly, and acknowledged all his comrades, he rose, and this simple movement, announcing something sinister, struck terror in every heart!

"Mademoiselle Fanny," he said, "is dead!"

"Dead!" cried the assembly.

"She is dead, and murdered!"

The silence of death is not deeper that that which reigned in this vast workshop, where two hundred persons, transfixed with grief, remained motionless and their eyes riveted on the worker and the old soldier.

"No trace of Mademoiselle Fanny remains! The only trace of her is in our memories . . ."

At these words, a few tears flowed.

"It is impossible to prove that she was murdered. The comrade you see here led me to the place where she perished; no proof exists.

"But her assassin is in the city, in the Place Saint-Etienne, where we followed him."[8]

The grief impressed on these minds by the death of this so dearly beloved young girl was still too pervasive to allow any idea of vengeance to take hold in their hearts, and if it is possible to represent their stupor by the idea of sleep, one could say that this assembly was not awake.

"Just yesterday she was here . . ." a worker exclaimed.

"Here, she spoke to me here!" another exclaimed.

"Poor young thing!! How did this happen anyway?" one of the foremen asked.

"I don't know," said the workman, "and even if I knew, Mademoiselle Fanny would be no less dead! . . ."

At that moment, a dull but growing murmuring began to make itself heard; it was then that Lagloire, who had not yet said a word, arose, and surveying the assembly with eyes full of expression, cried out in a thunderous voice:

"What? Will you not avenge her?"

These words succeeded in igniting the fury that took hold of this crowd. They all rushed out, moved by a rage kindled by that spirit of justice that grips the multitudes.

The news of Fanny's death spread in the factory, in the neighborhood, in the city, with terrifying rapidity.

While the workers moved through the streets disseminating the fatal news, Fanny's father, hearing his clock strike an hour at which it was impossible his daughter had not gotten up, pulled his bell cord.

The sick man waited patiently: seeing no one come, he rang a second time, and another time again; nobody came running at the sound of that bell, which always before had sufficed to bring an eager servant.

There was an important order to be shipped that morning; the sick man did not see either his secretary or his factory manager appear.

Then a vague anxiety takes hold of Fanny's father: he tries his forces and manages to get up. When he realizes that he could walk in his bedroom with a fairly steady step, he goes toward Fanny's apartment; out of precaution, he opens the bedroom door avoiding making noise, he goes toward his daughter's bed and trembles with joy when he sees it perfectly in order, for he imagines that Fanny might be sick. He ventures onto the staircase, the silence of the house fills him with terror; he sees no one in the courtyards; his legs shake beneath him . . . nonetheless, he continues on toward the workshops; he approaches, but does not hear any noise. He enters and finds them empty.

Alone and abandoned, in his own house, unable to have any idea of the misfortune that awaits him, he heads toward the entrance to his vast enterprise, from which is coming the dull murmur of a several voices. He reaches the entrance, his ears are struck by these words pronounced by a voice full of surprise:

"Mademoiselle Fanny has been murdered?"

"O dear God, yes!"

The poor father, overwhelmed, fell down in the sand of the courtyard, crying out: "My daughter! O my daughter!"

Fanny's chambermaid, the only person who had remained in the house, hearing these doleful words and the sound of the man's fall, rushed in precipitously, and dragged Fanny's father to a step, sat him down, supported his head on a pillow she made out of her shawl, and lavished aid on him.

Another scene, even more terrible, was taking place at that very moment in the Place Saint-Etienne. The workmen, two hundred strong, had marched across the city, swelling their ranks as they went with friends, their relatives, and a frightening horde of people outraged at hearing of Fanny's death. Along the way, tales of circumstances increasingly fantastical passed from mouth to mouth and fired the imagination of this crowd drunk with vengeance. The soldiers who had arrived the day before joined the throng, attracted by the novelty of the situation and through idleness. This crowd, when it arrived in the main street, was already so large, that the street—too small to contain the torrent—in all its length resembled a theater pit, made black by the mass of people that had crowded into its confines.

This mob of people, made up of faces in rage, all of which showed different expressions, converged upon the Place Saint-Etienne and completely invaded it: it awoke the tall old man, and also General Beringheld who by chance happened to be staying at the Archbishop's palace, with the most frightening tumult that any people drunk and aroused by anger has ever produced.

"Justice . . . Justice . . . Arrest Fanny's murderer . . . Justice . . . Lay hands on the murderer . . . Put him to death . . . In prison, put the murderer in prison . . . He murdered Fanny—Fanny . . . Let him be punished . . . Justice . . . Drag him out . . . We demand it . . . The murderer . . . The scoundrel . . . Avenge a father robbed of his daughter . . . Vengeance . . . Vengeance . . . Bring on the guard . . . Put him in prison . . . Tear down the doors . . . Drag him out here . . . Justice . . . Get the guard . . . Where are the police . . . Justice . . . Justice . . . Arrest the murderer . . . Put him to death on the scaffold . . . We won't harm him, but bring him out . . . Turn him over to justice . . . Go fetch the Imperial Prosecutor . . . To court with him . . . No, cut his throat instead . . . Smash his windows . . . Drag him out of there . . . To the dung heap with him . . . Throw his body on the dung heap . . . Let's do to him as he has done . . . Let's kill him . . . Give him the same . . . Avenge Fanny . . . He didn't stop at blood . . . Fanny's blood . . . Imprison him . . . He killed an innocent person . . . Vengeance . . . The dung heap . . . Tear him limb from limb . . . Give him over to us . . . We will give ourselves justice . . . The old man . . . Give us the old man . . . Seize the culprit . . . He must die . . . He killed Fanny . . . Let him die . . . The old man . . . The old man . . . Give him up . . . At once."

For a moment, the crowd stopped its yelling, but this silence was all the more dreadful, and a multitude of hoarse voices again erupted from parched throats:

"Break down the doors . . . The old man . . . The old man . . . Turn him over to the law . . . In prison! . . . We'll try him ourselves! . . . Death to him . . . Strangle him . . . To the dung heap! . . . Give us justice! . . . Fanny! Fanny! . . . Let's avenge Fanny! . . . Burn the house down! . . . Give up the old man! . . . Turn the murderer over to us! . . . Turn over the assassin! . . . To the scaffold with the criminal! . . . Vengeance! . . . Avenge our father! . . . The old man to the dung heap! . . . Put him to death! . . . Bring the weapons! . . . Let's take up stones, stone him! . . . Let's drag him! . . . Be on your guard . . . Where is the law! . . . Arrest him! . . . He killed Fanny! . . . He killed Fanny! . . . He must die!"

A fierce struggle was taking place at the door of the house: those who lived there had barricaded it; but the crowd, pushing forward in wavelike manner against the house, produced a situation such that those who found themselves closest to the dwelling were in danger of being crushed; thus, for their own safety, they sought to break in the doors, and to climb up toward the windows; but as the forward movement was growing with the curses, these latter were forced, in order not to be crushed, to repel the effort. Thus the Place Saint-Etienne presented the image of a flux and reflux of heads, truly terrifying for the many spectators who were looking out the windows.

These movements stopped the shouting: there were only the outer fringes of the crowd and a few isolated voices in the middle that continued to cry out: "Arrest the assassin . . . Avenge Fanny . . . Put him in prison . . . Drag him out . . . Justice," when other shouts of joy were heard from the side of the Rue de l'Archevêché: "Here comes the Mayor . . . Here comes the Imperial Prosecutor . . . Here comes the Guard . . . Make room . . . Let's move aside . . . They are coming to arrest him . . . Make room . . ."

At the same time General Beringheld and his staff emerged from the Cloister Saint-Gatien;[9] and drums heralded the arrival of this armed force.

"Avenge Fanny . . . arrest the killer . . . put him to death . . . give him up . . . ," people were still shouting as they made way for the

Mayor, the Commissioner, and the Imperial Prosecutor and the Police Commissioner, wearing their formal dress, for they had wisely decided that the circumstances necessitated it.

While the civil authorities were toiling with difficulty to clear a narrow path through the angry mob, which filled in immediately after their passage, General Beringheld, at the head of his staff, ordered the soldiers from his division who were in the crowd to leave and return to their barracks or face stiff penalties.

Once he arrived in front of the house that lodged the tall old man, the General, acquiescing to the pleas of the Mayor and Prefect, positioned his soldiers, who joined with the Departmental Guard, and an impressive force was deployed: it was just in time, for the door of the house, the old man's sanctuary, was ready to give way, and the Substitute for the Imperial Prosecutor, accompanied by the Mayor, a Police Commissioner, and a squad of gendarmes, entered the house.[10]

The house was empty; all the lodgers had abandoned it, taking their money with them. The crowd, surrounding the house on all sides, helped the inhabitants leave by the windows; for this wild multitude was after only the old man: thus, it was only after each lodger identified himself that they let him flee.

The Substitute went through the entire house; Beringheld, the Mayor, and the others accompanied him. When the Secretary informed the crowd that the old man was not found there, the shouting recommenced: "Burn the house down . . . We'll rebuild it . . . We'll pay for it . . . Justice . . . He was in there . . . We saw him there."

Finally, the General and the group of persons who were visiting the house came to the largest room that opened onto the street, and a gendarme, glancing into the chimney, saw the old man hanging by his hands, in the middle of the chimney pipe.

The old man, seeing himself discovered, came down, and the people, attentive to what was happening in that bedroom, whose windows were open, let forth cries of joy at the sight of the old man.

"He's been arrested . . . Victory . . . Long live the Mayor . . . Long live the Substitute . . . Victory . . . Long live our mayor . . . Give us the murderer . . . To prison with him . . . We'll drag him there . . . Down with the soldiers . . . We don't need them . . . We'll take him to prison ourselves . . . Give us the murderer . . . Long live our Mayor . . . Victory . . . Let him give us the murderer . . . Throw the scoundrel on the dung heap . . . Tear him limb from limb."

The tall old man was trembling with all his limbs; his face expressed a puerile fear, that terrible fright that seizes all the faculties. He sat down on an armchair without saying a word.

The Substitute, the Mayor, and the Police Commissioner sat down around a table; General Beringheld stood leaning against one of the windows, commanding the crowd to be quiet with a movement of his hand. The multitude fell silent, and its final cry was: "Justice! . . . Justice!"

When silence reigned in the place, the old man regained courage; he went over to the window and, seeing the armed force that protected him, his fear vanished. He went directly up to Beringheld, made a sign to him with his head, which he accompanied with a sardonic smile; the General, frightened, answered only with a gesture, the result of a deep terror.

The tall old man went toward the table around which the Substitute and the other functionaries were talking, while a Secretary was making ready to record the statements. It was a matter of issuing an arrest warrant, and it was realized that a magistrate was needed. A gendarme was dispatched to fetch one.

Having arrived near the table, the old man watched these preparations with a look of irony, which would have frozen the hand of the Secretary had he perceived it; then he said to the functionaries:

"Do you have any idea, Sirs, against whom you are instituting proceedings?"

"No, Monsieur," the Mayor interrupted. "We begin with the usual protocol, and in a moment we will proceed to interrogate you . . . You realize that we are brought to do what we do by duty, and that it is very likely that you are innocent of that which the popular voice accuses you. Once you are vindicated, if there is insufficient evidence to indict you, we will still be obliged, I think, to keep you in prison in order to protect your life from that mob, to whom it will be very difficult to explain your innocence, and no one here will be safe from its fury; for the soldiers who are under the windows do not have bullets; and if the mob did take you, I see no precaution we can humanly take to avoid the danger."

All that time, the old man had remained absolutely motionless; those present were dumbstruck by his attitude and by those peculiarities we have described: it was only after a moment of silence that the Mayor asked the old man for his passport and identity papers.

Chapter five

THE OLD MAN IS IN DANGER — DEPOSITIONS —

THE GENERAL IS COMPROMISED — FURY OF THE MOB —

LAMANEL PROTECTS THE CENTENARIAN

At the Mayor's request, the huge old man, drawing forth a wallet of ancient form, handed him a simple letter.

Once he had read it, the Mayor, astonished, passed it to the Imperial Prosecutor.[11] The letter was an order issued by the Minister of Police himself, signed by the Emperor, and countersigned by the Minister. This order enjoined all concerned *to grant safe conduct, to assist, and not to bother in any way, citizen Beringheld.* His description, written on the back and signed by the Minister, fit the man exactly, as this description was, as we well know, easy to make and the man easy to recognize

At the name of Beringheld, the Substitute and Mayor turned spontaneously toward the General and were struck with surprise at the same time, as they recognized the resemblance that existed between the old man under indictment and the illustrious warrior.

The Prosecutor, rising up, went over to the General, and asked him in a low voice:

"General, would he be your father?"

"No, Monsieur," Beringheld answered.

"Is he as least a relative of yours?"

"I don't know."

"Monsieur," the Substitute of the Imperial Prosecutor said to the huge old man, "this order from Your Majesty is not sufficient to prevent you from being arrested, if the aggravating circumstances warrant it; this paper does not mention the situation in which you find yourself, in no way is it sufficient to stop the course of justice."

At this moment, the Magistrate entered the room. The order was given to the Police Commissioner to seek among the crowd any persons who might have a statement to make concerning this affair, and after a half hour, Lagloire appeared, the workman at the gate, the wife of the dead worker, the assistant customs clerk, the doctor who had crossed the Avenue de Grammont in the night, and the driver of the General's wagon.

The crowd, with that constant energy deployed by masses of people animated by violent feelings, still remained in the Place Saint-Etienne, and was getting larger rather than smaller. Here and there the workers from the factory were whipping up the general fury with their stories and speeches.

"Do you have any other papers?" the Magistrate asked the huge old man.

"No, Monsieur."

"No birth certificate?"

"No, Monsieur."

"How old are you?"

At this question, the old man began to smile slightly, and did not answer. All present looked at him in astonishment, and none could suppress an impulse of terror on seeing his *monument-like aspect*, cold like a tombstone.

As he questioned him, the Mayor averted his eyes so as not to see the thread of light that burned with a red and clear fire as it escaped from the depths of the accused man's eyes.

"Your age?" the Judge repeated.

"I have no age!" the old man said in a broken voice that produced only detached and disjointed sounds.

"Where were you born?"

"At Beringheld Castle, in the Greater Alps," he answered.

The General shuddered involuntarily on hearing the name of his own birthplace spoken; the castle of his father, finally, the domain that belonged to him still.

"In what year?" asked the Judge, with an indifferent air and not seeming to attach any importance to his question.

"*In one thousand* . . ." The old man halted as if he were walking on the edge of an abyss; he cried out in anger: "Children of a day, the *Centenarian* knows much! I will answer nothing more except before my judges, at the High Court, if one drags me before them! . . . There and only there must I answer."

"As you wish," said the Judge.

The various depositions were then heard: the doctor-midwife declared having seen at about eleven o'clock on the previous evening Mademoiselle Fanny Lamanel seated on the meadow located opposite the bridge over the Cher; he had recognized her by her hairdo, by her belt and her shawl. But he said that he also saw a soldier near her, he added that he was not sure if it was General Beringheld, although the person had his height and the same decorations.

At the last words of this deposition, all eyes turned to the General, who blushed.

The examining judge, addressing General Beringheld, asked him if it was true that it was he . . . Beringheld said that it was true.

The workman stated that one of his comrades, who had died from pain upon learning of Fanny's death, had accompanied Fanny as far as the Iron Gates of the city, and that she had not come back.

The dead man's wife declared that her husband had told her, in strictest secrecy, that he had recommended the accused to Fanny as one able to save her father, because this was the same man who had saved her, herself, from a mortal sickness; and that Mademoiselle Fanny went every evening to the Cave of Grammont, and so on.

The wagon driver testified that he had driven the old man from the bridge on the Cher to the Iron Gates, between midnight and one o'clock, the previous night.

Lagloire declared that he had heard, at eleven-thirty, heart-rending screams coming from the *Cave of Grammont*; that before that he saw a young girl on the meadow; that his General and himself had been witness to the flight of the old man; he told of the disappearance of the load, then called upon the testimony of his General.

Now the interest of the magistrates doubled, the entire assembly turned toward General Beringheld with the most ardent curiosity, and the Magistrate ordered him to tell all that he knew.

The General, hearing this order delivered with all the magisterial authority of the members of the judiciary, let a gesture of haughtiness be seen, and seemed little inclined to answer; he even remained silent, and this circumstance astonished the group of magistrates, who, looking at each other, confirmed by their frequent glances that a single thought ran through all their minds: the thought that the General might be an accomplice to the crime, and that one must conclude that the General's attitude, his pallor, his looks, his anxiety, all bolstered this conjecture; especially when one compared his criminal air with the assurance of the huge old man, who tranquilly played with his great overcoat, frightening those who dared to look at him with a movement of his eye.

Old Lagloire went up to the General and said to him beseechingly: "Does my General wish to dishonor his old soldier by making one believe, through his silence, that I have lied! . . . I realize that old crow over there," he said pointing to the Judge, "asked his question in a hardly decent manner . . . but, General . . . what is more, you are the master, and my honor, my life, belong to you."

The Judge pardoned the old soldier's expression, hoping that the General would speak, but the latter still remained silent, obeying motives only he alone knew. Such difficulties however, created by the honor and integrity of the General, were soon annulled by the old man.

"General," he said, holding out his hand to him and clutching his, "don't let the favors I have done you, or our acquaintanceship, prevent you from telling everything! . . . I even wish you to tell it! . . ."

The old man uttered these last words with a smile worthy of Satan; he seemed to be that King of Hell, as Milton had depicted him, rising up in Pandemonium and scoffing at angels.

The General came forward and, looking now and then at the old man, recounted in a concise manner what is the substance of the first chapters of this book. During this account, the old man, not moving and with calm face, remained in the same position; his pallid, corpse-like visage was absolutely immobile; his dry, blazing eyes were fastened on the Mayor; and it seemed as of one were looking at a dead man, or a statue.

When the General had finished, the Substitute made his indictment, the Judge signed the arrest warrant, while informing the old man that the implicating circumstances seemed too compelling not to necessitate his arrest.

Lagloire and the other witnesses now went outside; they announced to the curious crowd that the huge old man, the murderer of beautiful Fanny, was to pass through them. At this news, the cries we have already reported were heard again, this time with a strange violence.

Hearing this uproar, the old man trembled; the terrible fright that had taken hold of him when they discovered him in the chimney returned to shake him: his terror brought him closer to the rest of humanity. This spectacle of the old man in fear of death, and fearing it in an ignoble manner, brought to the soul a disgust, a fright, that is difficult to depict.

"Do you believe," he said trembling to the Mayor and the Judge, "that it will be an easy matter for me to pass through this furious crowd without the least danger? . . . your duty is to protect me, and you must do it for yourselves as much as for me, for they will not distinguish you from me in their fanatical rage. *Come, I know*

46

the excesses of the people! . . . I have experience, and there is not a hair
of difference between this crowd of people and the one that cut throats
at the Saint-Bartholomew's Day Massacre, on August 10, in September,
during the League, and so on. . . ."[12]

The old man's tone of conviction and his voice struck terror in the soul, and the Mayor, listening to the vociferations of the crowd, was convinced that Beringheld ran a real risk of being torn to pieces, because they were shouting with unequaled fierceness: "To the dung heap . . . give the assassin up to us . . . let him die, etc."

The Magistrate, stepping to the window, demanded silence with his hand and harangued the crowd that, unable to hear his words, met him with cries of: "Long live our Mayor! . . . He will hand over the old man! . . . Death to the assassin! . . ."

A terrifying cry of joy arose into the air and set to trembling the old man, who saw his death sworn to by this wild multitude.

"General," cried Beringheld in a sepulchral and half-extinguished voice, "arm your troops in order to protect my leaving and my passage to the prison."

"Old man, I ask nothing better, but it's hopeless! My soldiers will not open fire on the people for your sake; besides, they have no bullets, and the crowd would soon break their ranks."

"Let us try," said the mayor.

The old man was placed between the General, the Mayor, the Judge, the Substitute, the Secretary, the Commissioner, and the squad of gendarmes, but when the crowd saw the preparations for departure, without looking out for those up front, it hurled itself at the house, having the appearance of one of those huge sea waves, and with such a fury that the battalion posted by General Beringheld was scattered like the debris of a ship by an angry sea.

They retreated at once, and barricaded the doors. The crowd began to yell all the louder: their hoarse voices, their twisted faces, expressed more than ever the rage and fanatical energy of a mob of people in anger.

In order to save these blind people from a bloody catastrophe and from the woe of an action that would cost the life of many a victim of this frenzy, were they able to enter and tear loose a man who was now in preventive custody, the Mayor had an idea that was certain to be totally successful.

He sent a gendarme and the Secretary to fetch the unfortunate father of Fanny. The Secretary was ordered to inform him of the situation in which they found themselves, and of the great service that he could render to the people. He was to give him the order to come to the Place Saint-Etienne in order to protect the old man accused of having killed his daughter.

Fanny's father was found in a wretched state; his reason, without having abandoned him, had succumbed to the woe that had afflicted him, his dry eyes, having not yet cried a single tear, remained fixed on that same chair where Fanny had the habit of sitting. Nothing had the least effect on him.

The Secretary carried out the Mayor's orders. He told his story, and yet Fanny's father appeared to have heard nothing. Then, the Secretary, horrified by the danger that menaced the assembled crowd and those who would soon be its victims, depicted to the unfortunate father, with all the energy that such circumstances demand, how great a service he could render to the city and to this misguided crowd. Could he accept that Fanny's assassin be torn to pieces by the mob? Wasn't it necessary that this latter perish on the scaffold instead? . . . Otherwise it would be said that the father had taken justice into his own hands! Should he not restrain his workers? . . .

Lamanel, as if moved by an inspiration that came from outside himself, arose. "I'll go," he said . . . And at once, with a firm step, he went forward, followed the Secretary and the gendarme, appeared to obey some supernatural force.

In the meantime the crowd continued its uproar, its determination; growing by the minute, it had now reached its peak: fear reigned inside the old man's house, the situation became more and more precarious, and it is impossible to describe the agitations in the souls of those who must play a role in such a scene! What terror gripped the magistrates as they listened to those cries, repeated incessantly since morning with the obstinacy of a people in revolt.

"They must all die!" they screamed. "Or hand over the old man! . . . You will not get away! . . . Break down the doors! . . . Death to the killer! . . . Avenge Fanny! . . . Tear the murderer limb from limb! . . . Let the murderer die! . . . Turn him over! . . . To the dung heap! . . . To the scaffold! . . . Cut his throat! . . . Death to him! . . . Down with the soldiers! . . . The old man, the old man, give him to us! . . . Let him die!"

All at once, at the far end of the crowd, an august and solemn silence begins; it spreads imperceptibly and by degrees through this entire multitude; the crowd of its own doing forms a respectful path in front of a single man, whose downcast face, pain and suffering, dampen the passions in the souls of the onlookers: to the gesture of his hand, everything yields, all subsides; at his glance, the workers retreat, and this magic moment strikes the heart all the more in that it follows a scene of such terrifying tumult; the contrast was as absolute as the most poetic of imaginations could have wished it.

The unfortunate father moves in the midst of this silent line and arrives at the house. He climbs the stairs; he enters into the room that held the alleged murderer of his daughter. At the sight of him, he shudders, sits down in an armchair, for the thoughts that troubled his heart came too rapidly and violently. A torrent of tears escapes from his eyes and he exclaims: "Fanny! . . . Fanny! My daughter?"

General Beringheld, going up to Lamanel, draws from his bosom the metal necklace that had adorned Fanny's neck, offers it to the disconsolate father, saying to him:

"Here is the last thing your daughter wore."

Lamanel looks at the General, takes his hand, and presses it against his heart without saying a word! But what a gesture! What a look! What eloquence! . . . What silent pain, and what gratitude! . . .

"I would like your permission to keep a link of this chain," said the General.

Lamanel looked at the necklace with regret, with regret he un-
fastened a link and offered it to the General.

"Such weaknesses! . . ." exclaimed in his tomb-like voice the
huge old man, whose forehead of brass proclaimed that feeling
no longer lived beneath his left breast.

The group started out: the General helped along Fanny's father
who, by his presence, protected the one accused of the murder of
his daughter; the magistrates followed.

When the crowd perceived the huge old man, his gigantic
proportions, as well as the supernatural circumstances that set
him apart from the rest of men, a dull murmur arose which was
swelling apace, already cries were issuing from the midst of the
crowd, already the old man was taking refuge behind the body
of Fanny's father, showing all the marks of a truly hideous fear,
when Lamanel, turning around, made a sign with his hand and
looked upon those assembled with the same air of painful supplication that once before had calmed them. The noise ceased. A
woeful and ferocious silence fell, similar to that which reigned in
Rome, when the ashes of Germanicus passed through it;[13] the old
man was taken to his prison without any further incident; before
entering, the gigantic stranger said to the grieving father: "Your
daughter exists! . . ."

These words were spoken with a tone that nullified their truthfulness: this old man seemed like one of those doctors who try to
make a dying man believe that health is at his bedside.

Thus, despite such an ironic consolation, poor Lamanel suffered a stroke so violent, that he died that night, uttering over and
over the name of his dear Fanny.

A huge crowd of people surrounded the prison until nighttime. The jailer told that when he had locked the door of the old
man's cell, he heard him whisper in his sepulchral voice: "I'm
saved!"

Chapter six

The events of that day found themselves so bound up with the entire life of General Tullius Beringheld that it was impossible for him not to be gravely affected by them. The form of moral sickness that afflicted him subsided a bit, and, curiosity taking hold of his soul, he decided to remain in Tours, to get to know in depth the extraordinary being that, up to now, he had seen but in passing, and as this new Proteus was now fast in chains, to penetrate the mystery that surrounded his existence.

He summoned his brigadier general, turned the command of the division over to him, gave him the order to travel shorter distances each day, because the Emperor would not reach Paris until long after the arrival of the troops. Then he resolved to travel to Paris by mail coach, after having remained in Tours long enough to satisfy his curiosity. The troops left the city the next day.

The next evening, the General spent the evening at the Prefect's house; he found there the Judge who presided over the old man's case, as well as the Imperial Substitute and the Mayor. Toward the end of the evening, these magistrates remaining alone with the General, asked him to come to the Prefect's chambers. There, this latter said to him: "General, it seems certain to us that you are acquainted with the individual who at this moment is the subject of all the conversations in the city: our curiosity has reached its highest peak, and we would indeed like to know . . ."

The Prefect was at this point in his discourse when his private secretary opened the door of the chamber and announced himself:

"Monsieur le Comte," he said, "I come to inform you, and the Mayor as well, of a new incident which is not the least extraordinary in the Beringheld affair, and this is that the old man has disappeared. The jailer did not leave the prison, he was constantly surrounded by people of good faith, the sentinels saw nothing, and when the jailer entered the prison to take the prisoner his evening meal, he found the cell empty, without the least mark of escape, without the least trace, nothing broken . . ."

Everyone remained dumbstruck, with the exception of the General. The functionaries looked at each other and the Substitute exclaimed:

"Indeed, Messieurs, I am far from being superstitious and gullible, but I assure you that this man had so terrified me with his aspect, that I dared not look at him, and I tell you also that I am obsessed by an idea that I cannot prevent from running through my imagination; which is that this man is in possession of an unnatural power . . ."

"I am most inclined to believe it," the Mayor observed, "yet it is the horrible terror that took hold of him, when he saw the fury of the mob, that alone disturbs my thoughts: this fear of death strips him in my eyes of the supernatural aspect you ascribe to him . . . Nevertheless, I admit that if I had him before my eyes, I would be unable to prevent myself from being persuaded as you are . . ."

"We will make," the Prefect interrupted, "a detailed report of these happenings; we will send it to the Minister of the National Police . . . and if we do not discover the place where the old man is hiding, if the search reveals that he is no longer within the confines of the empire, we will abandon there, I believe, messieurs, an investigation that is rendered useless from lack of proof or facts."

"Indeed," said the Judge; "it is impossible to build an indictment on these facts."

"And it would be difficult to argue it," added the Substitute.

"General," the Prefect continued, "you realize we have no legal right to demand that you satisfy our curiosity: once we have testified to our desire to learn what you might know about this bizarre being, you will be free either to instruct us about him or to refuse us this satisfaction; in the case that you would be willing to enlighten us about these matters, we all swear to you that all that you say will remain buried in our consciences."

"Messieurs," said the General, "if the old man has escaped, I can assure you that you will never see him again in this region! . . . On the other hand, his escape bothers me as much as it does you, although it does not surprise me; I admit to you that I had hoped here to penetrate the mystery that surrounds this extraordinary being, and I entertained the vague idea that it would be difficult for him to get out of the ugly situation he was in. Because he has escaped, my stay in Tours becomes useless; I will leave tomorrow. But if you propose to write a report to the Emperor and to the National Police, I feel I ought to give you all the information that is in my power to give: my entire life is linked to these explanations, and for a long time now I have been putting down, in writing, a series of bizarre happenings, from which it would be impossible to separate out the circumstances that concern only this old man. I will send you the manuscript before my departure: I put it in your hands, Monsieur le Prefet, and I count upon your kindness to send it to me in Paris, along with a faithful account of these latest events. I will scrupulously forward the entire document to His Majesty, and to the Minister of National Police."

Then the gathering broke up, the magistrates bid the General good-bye. The next day, one can imagine the consternation that befell the entire city, upon learning of the old man's escape. There were as many different opinions as there were persons, and conjectures were not lacking.

General Beringheld left, but, a half hour before climbing into his coach, Lagloire went to take to the Prefect a sealed package that contained the memoirs of the General's life written in his own hand.

That same evening, the magistrates who had been involved in the affair of the old man, gathered at the Prefect's house; the latter broke the seal on the manuscript's envelope, and the following was read in different installments:

The Story of General Beringheld[*]

Before beginning the General's story, it is necessary to give an account of the bizarre circumstances that preceded his birth: one will find there, by some remarkable oddity, more information about the old man than is contained in the account of the General's life that follows; this is true however only up until that moment when we will rejoin him on the road to Paris.

His father, the Count of Beringheld, was the last scion of a family famous in the annals of France, and one of the noblest: the line descended from one *Tullius Beringheld*, famous among the ancient Germanic peoples and mentioned by Roman historians.

Before France became a kingdom, the Counts of Beringheld lived in the region of Brabant,[14] where they possessed a small principality: they suffered a marked decline. Finally, during the time of Charlemagne they settled in France. The services they rendered to the Emperor won the friendship of this great prince, who purchased their county, whose castle had been pillaged and destroyed by the Saxons. In exchange, Charlemagne granted the Beringhelds another county, situated at the foot of the Alps: he

[Editor's Note: It would have been most tedious for the reader to have to read the memoirs of General Beringheld in their entirety; we have thus been obliged to extract from them those passages that most particularly pertain to the subject and to make these into a consistent narrative, all the while cutting the text so as to create necessary gaps. Thus one may perhaps lose the detailed and conscientious manner in which the General recounts the smallest details concerning the old man and the events of his youth; one can reply however that, by doing so, one gains a precious rapidity that sustains interest.

By not publishing the letters, the memoirs, and other information that form the basis for this entire tale, I sense that at each step I owe the reader explanations. I wish to advise that the details already given about the old man were found in a letter that General Beringheld had written, at that time, to a distinguished scientist in the capital; in addition, one needs to note that the detailed description of the old Ber-

even gave this county the name of Beringheld; it was only much later however that its former name fully died out, and was replaced by the Teutonic name Beringheld.

For a long time the Counts of Beringheld were occupied in transplanting their fortune to France. Though putting all their effort into making themselves respectable by means of their many possessions, their large number of vassals, and fortified castle, which was huge and well situated, they soon lapsed, in terms of fame and military renown, into obscurity: it was only during the reign of Philippe-le-Bel that they reappeared at court, returning to the pages of history, and annals of warfare, with a brilliance that made them famous. They were counted among the greatest vassals, and the head of this family found himself mentioned often in history as one of the great officers in the service of the French crown.

We pass over in silence the great deeds and circumstances that concern this family. It arrived at the height of its fame and prosperity during the reign of Henri III, Henri IV, and Louis XIII; but with the reign of Louis XIV, it waned considerably in the eyes of those who consider only honors and awards, without however losing any of its vast riches: it seemed as if some *genius*, in the midst of the great upheavals that shook France, during the reign

---

ingheld did not issue from the rigorous pen of any author: we deemed it interesting enough to present it in its entirety; it will be the same for other pieces of this story, whose unique character we respect and which we will take and reproduce verbatim from the letters and memoirs. We make this observation, once and for all, in order to avoid criticisms that may be addressed to us, either for lack of plausibility, or for difference in styles.

Despite our desire to let the General speak for himself, we have arranged the narrative as if it were written by the Editor, for the sake of constancy in the manner, the genre, and articulation of the story once adopted. finally, we must make clear that if we have excised some parts, everything that remains has a function; we assert as well that the story of the General is totally relevant to this adventure.]

of Charles IX to that of Louis XV, were protecting this family.[15] Its lands, its goods, its reputation, in a word *the material things of life*, were scrupulously preserved and constantly increased. Nothing that is in the power of man degenerated, there was only the mind and the moral qualities of the soul that grew old; for the races of men cannot maintain themselves forever, and families are like plants that lose their vigor if they remain in the same soil.

Tullius' father, inheriting the sort of bastardization that had seized upon the moral nature of the counts Beringheld, was the weakest and most superstitious being imaginable, one of those men the sight of whom arouses only feelings of pity. Good by nature, he was never able to enjoy the love of his vassals, because the people who ruled him committed in his name extortions and acts of violence.

The sort of moral infirmity perceptible in the character of Count Beringheld augmented in singular manner with the death of one of his uncles, a Commander of the Order of Malta. This uncle, before he died, summoned his nephew; they had a long talk together, the subject of which had a visible effect on the mind of the Count. It was since this time that the power of Beringheld's confessor became much broader, and his ascendancy over the mind of the Count was a mystery to no one.

In 1770, the Beringheld family was reduced, through the death of the old Commander, to this sole Count Etienne de Beringheld, who now uniting the property of all the various extinct family lines, became one of the richest lords of France, and the least known. He married the heiress of the house of Welleyn-Tilna, who, for her part, was also the last offspring of that family and who, like Beringheld, also had no character at all. It seemed that some malicious spirit had amused itself by uniting these two crippled products of two dying races, in order to create out of them such an assemblage of weakness.

The Count and Countess Beringheld lived together for ten years without having children, and the most scurrilous rumors circulated concerning the Count's confessor, Father André de Lunada.

We shall try to take account of the cries uttered by Rumor and her hundred mouths.

It was said that the Commander had told his nephew extraordinary secrets that concerned the entire existence of the Beringhelds, their fortune that was said to be illegal, and so on.

Thus was revived, as a result of this deathbed confession, all the gossip that circulated about the Commander and his family.

This Commander had always been accused of witchcraft, of dealing in white and black magic; the sale of his soul to the devil was no less forgotten than his predilection for chemistry, and physics, nor than the research he engaged in for the sake of one of his family members. We will explain this matter more clearly.

The Beringheld family, like all families, had for a long time been divided into a multitude of branches. It was in 1430 that Georges Beringheld had, for the first time since the beginnings of the family, *two sons,* both of whom lived; the eldest was named Georges, and the youngest Maxime: the result of this was that in 1470, under Louis XI, the family divided for the first time into two separate branches, for Maxime had a son.

Thus Maxime, as he had descendants, received the title of count, and added the name *Sculdans* to his own name, in order to distinguish the junior branch of the family from the senior.

This *junior* branch formed others, and this assemblage of *junior* branches of the Beringhelds became another powerful house, as it inherited the fortunes that its members acquired when there was no direct heir. It was the Commander Beringheld-*Sculdans*, who gathered on his head the vast riches of that *junior* branch, and who, with his death, brought them back into the senior line, represented by Count Etienne, the father of the general in question.

Let us return to the son of this first Count Maxime Beringheld-*Sculdans*, founder of the house of *Sculdans*, as it is around this son that the whole story revolves.

This son of the first Count Maxime Beringheld-Sculdans was the subject of a frightening legend. This Beringheld, the second Count *Sculdans*, devoted himself to the Grand Sciences; he lived in close contact with the savants of his time, visited in the course of his long existence India and China; he participated in the discovery of the New World, circumnavigated the globe, and lived from 1470 until 1572, when he disappeared, the very day of the Saint Bartholomew Massacre.

This long existence caused him to be given the name *The Centenarian*: it was claimed that his spirit came back to earth; and people told of all the times that his spirit had returned to earth. The fact is that the last time he came to Beringheld Castle was in 1550, and he made a present of his portrait: there was astonishment at finding in the Centenarian a vigor and a force that did not usually belong to old age. He had not been seen again since that time; but tradition claimed that the Centenarian had reappeared, and that it was he whose magic power protected the family.

We now understand the relationship of this confusing story to Commander *Sculdans*: it was said that this old Commander, as the result of a vision he had had in Spain, had gone searching for the Centenarian. Because of a report presented to the Spanish Ministry concerning an incident that took place in Peru, the Commander, once he made the voyage, became convinced of the existence of the Centenarian; it was said that this *Sculdans* died suddenly because he set eyes on him.

He revealed all of this to his nephew Count Etienne before he died, and this secret, carried by Count Beringheld into the confessional, was the source of the power held by Father André de Lunada, ex-Jesuit. With this knowledge, this latter would have the means of ruining the Count, whose possessions were thus seen to be the fruit of sorcery, and this Father André, taking advantage of the weakness of his penitent, cherished the idea of gaining control of the family's wealth by preventing the Count, through bizarre means, from having heirs.

Such was, in 1780, the state of the Beringheld family, and such were the rumors that abounded concerning this illustrious house. This preamble is indispensable in avoiding any later confusion.

Beringheld Castle[16] was one of the largest and most Romantic that existed to the eye. Situated amidst the picturesque mountains at the foot of the majestic and beautiful chain of the Alps, it vied, in its boldness and its expanse, with the haughty peaks that surrounded it. It looked itself like a mountain. Its mixture of different architectures from different centuries, made it like a museum of art, and testified to how many centuries and destructions it had endured.

There was a multitude of constructions, a chapel, living quarters, magnificent stables, greenhouses—all buildings that bore the mark of a truly royal grandeur and formed an ensemble that was fully *Romantic* in nature.

Vast gardens blended at their farthest limits with the Alps, and the most beautiful vistas, the most beautiful valleys that nature itself had created embellished this imposing residence. Before the castle there was a large courtyard, at the other end of this was an iron gate, from which an immense meadow dotted with trees spread forth: beyond this meadow was left standing a building people called a "turning house." This turning house was the structure in which the main caretaker of the castle lived; the building was adjacent to the village, of which it constituted the first house, and the caretaker had eventually obtained the right to sell oats, fodder, and wine.

Thus voyagers stopped at this makeshift inn, kept by the caretaker, and it was here that the servants of the castle along with the richest villagers gathered. From their nightly confabulations those rumors arose which we have just set forth in succinct manner, so as to spare the reader from having to hear them again from the mouth of Babiche, the caretaker's wife, who was the natural-born presider over the turning house circle.

On February 28, 1780, a meeting took place at this turning house, which we shall permit the reader to witness so as to make him aware of the particular event that prevented the Beringheld family from becoming extinct.

It was nine o'clock in the evening; a cold north wind harried the old dismantled door of the turning house with such vigor, that at each moment one thought that it would be blown down. Each of the persons present huddled closer and closer to the pinewood fire, which cast so much light that there was no need of candles.

The portly caretaker, well used to hearing on a regular basis the gabbling voices of the companions of his wife Babiche, was sleeping at one corner of the hearth; at the other corner was the village midwife, an old witch who along with her *obstetrical* functions had gained the right to tell fortunes, to cast spells, put the hex on marriages, and cure by means of magic incantations and carefully chosen simples. She was going on ninety years old, and her withered face, her rasping voice, her small green eyes, her white hair that tumbled out from under a shabby bonnet, all contributed in no small manner to bolster the ideas that one entertained on her behalf.

Having been present at the birth of nearly everyone in the village, knowing the genealogy of each and every person, the mysteries of each birth and history of each family, it was impossible that she not be an authority, and a formidable force in the village of Beringheld, especially when fathers described her to their children, at a young age, as a sorceress, or at least as a woman to be revered.

Beside her there was Babiche, a plump, sweet, pretty woman; opposite Babiche was the most powerful grocer in the village, whose name was Lancel. Three or four eighty-year-old crones occupied the center.

The portly caretaker had at his left the head forester of the crown, a pleasant and cultivated man, a musician, married but a short time and who, not having access to the castle, came occasionally to hear the news that made the rounds in the caretaker's circle. He handled business matters for several families who had property in the vicinity; his wife, who was extremely pretty, and with a character gracious enough to shine in more elegant circles, rarely came to such a gathering, where her dignity would have been compromised.

"This morning Father de Lunada had the young man dismissed that Madame had taken a fancy to," said the caretaker's wife. "If this continues, he will not allow a single other person of the masculine kind to remain; I'm always afraid when he passes by that gate and casts his big sly eye on this house, that he might see my poor Lusni."

"Here I am!" . . . cried the sleeping caretaker who, hearing his name pronounced by his wife, thought his despotic other half was calling him.

"The fact is that he is taking drastic precautions in order to keep the pie for himself," said one of the old crones.

"Isn't it a shame to see one of the noblest families dying out, the ancestral guardians of all the village."

"Don't slander the saintly man," exclaimed the prudent caretaker. "Who knows if he's not lurking around here?"

"But what good would it do for Father de Lunada to acquire the immense fortune of the Beringhelds," answered the forester. "He has no heirs, he now enjoys all the luxury he could ever want; his order has been abolished; I for one see no ulterior motive for such conduct, and if the Countess has no children, it's because she's sterile."

"If the Count and his wife were to die, there will not be much left for the Reverend Father . . ." Babiche exclaimed. "It's true, he enjoys, but he doesn't own!" . . .

At these words the old midwife shook her head from right to left, which caused her white hair to tumble down over her black and wrinkled neck. She lifted her emaciated hands toward the heavens, all fell silent, as such a preamble announced that Marguerite Lagradna wished to speak; everyone drew closer, one against the other, and all eyes were fixed on the midwife, whose shining eyes darted about in lively fashion; it seemed as if a demon possessed her, and as if, like a poet, she were touched by some inspiration, the force of which was seeking to escape from her like a flame, or a torrent.

Chapter seven

"Woe to Lunada!" . . . cried Lagradna. "Woe to him, if he would touch the fortune of the Beringhelds! It is sacred . . . all those who have sought to take it have *died in an ugly manner!* . . ."

Lagradna had a way of shaping and hurling forth her words that plunged the soul into a state of terror; she appeared so imbued with what she uttered that she imparted her conviction to others. People were moved by her gestures alone.

"Furthermore," she went on after a moment of silence, looking at the crossbeams of the ceiling, "the race of the Beringhelds must not die out, it will last as long as the world! . . . as this world here!" . . . and Lagradna struck the ground with the long cane she always carried.

"I have known this for a long time, as well as the prophecy of *Beringheld the Centenarian*," and she sang in a hoarse and broken voice:

My race will never perish
Till down on us will crash
A mighty mountain
On the flat terrain
Of Vallinara shire;[17]
Only then will we expire,
The last of my race,
Which nothing, nothing can efface.

Singing this doggerel in a quivering voice, Lagradna held the attention of her audience in singular fashion.

"How can a mountain fall on someone here on the plain of Vallinara? You heard the prophecy," . . . she continued in a booming voice, and standing up in this thatched cottage that now seemed too small to hold her. "Well? . . . This morning I saw the one who made this prediction! . . . Yes, I saw him! And saw him for the second time in my life. The first time it was in 1704. Listen! . . . Count Beringheld, the seventy-second Count Beringheld, had been accused of the death of the young Pollany girl, whose skeleton was found in the caverns under the square tower. The death sentence was to be carried out the next morning, his property to be confiscated: it was pitch-black night and I was coming back from the mountains across the Vallinara; the wind was howling and the forests were rumbling like thunder. I was afraid, and I went along singing the ballad of Beringheld the Centenarian . . . On coming to the middle of the Vallinara, I saw a large black shape moving in the dark, and lit up by two tiny yet quite distinct lights. As I was then heading toward Beringheld Castle, and this dark mass was moving toward the mountains, we were bound to meet . . . At first I thought it was Butmel coming to meet me on horseback . . ."

At these words, the midwife collapsed back into her chair, remained motionless, and tears, flowing from her eyes, rolled down the furrows caused by the wrinkles on her face. This outburst of passion, in one so old, made all present shudder, for they knew that Lagradna had never been married; that she had loved but once in her life; that Butmel, the dear lover of Lagradna, was the man on whom later the blame fell, in an inconceivable manner and by some invisible thread, for the murder of Pollany; that he had been taken to Lyon where he was condemned to death; finally, that he died accused of having killed Pollany; that every time that the name Butmel came from Lagradna's lips, she fell into a reverie that one must not interrupt, under threat of seeing her yield to an access of madness. Soon, Lagradna continued:

"I seemed to see him already with his smile! . . . His hat over the ear, a bouquet in his hand, and joy painted on his face . . . Poor Butmel! . . . You smile no more," she said glancing down at the ground, "and what is that infernal power that had you drawn and quartered for a crime you didn't commit? . . . You, commit a crime? . . . You, the most honest soul! . . . And Pollany was my friend! . . . Your friend! . . . Ah, you smile no more, but," and she spoke with an accent that rends the heart, "you are in heaven, with the angels!"

This thought, that she expressed with eyes raised to the heavens, made her wrinkles vanish for an instant, her visage looked as if she were seeing Butmel, and she ran her fingers over a chain composed of glass beads that her lover had given her. Her ecstasy, during which all present strove not to breathe, subsided by degrees; she came back to herself, saying: "It was not he that I thought I saw on the Vallinara! . . . I kept walking . . . I kept going! . . . I went on! I saw that the two lights were two eyes, the mass, a man; and that man, a cadaver."

An indefinable horror gripped the audience, at these words spoken with such pauses, with accents and gestures that gave Lagradna the appearance of a Sybil in a cave. All thought they saw before them the thing she was describing: the fire cast but a feeble glow and barely lit the room; Marguerite thus found herself framed in a reddish glow, which made her appearance more apt to produce a profound effect on the imagination, especially as she told a story of this sort to this audience.

"This cadaver! . . ." she continued in a voice that would have caused even the strongest of hearts to tremble. "It was the spirit of Beringheld the Centenarian! . . . I recognized him!" . . .

"How," asked the forester, "if this was the first time that you saw him?"

"How? . . ." Lagradna responded in a voluble manner. "Didn't my father see him in September of 1652, when Jacques Lehal was abducted from his chalet without ever being seen again, and when Count Beringheld LXX learned the death of the man with whom he was to fight a duel the following day? Count Beringheld's adversary was a certain Count Vervil. For both, it was to be a fight to the death, and Vervil had the reputation of being the best swordsman of his day. Beringheld's end seemed therefore certain. But this formidable adversary perished two miles from here, in the pass of Namval; a huge boulder fell on his carriage . . . My father saw *the spirit* loosen the stone! . . . After that, he told me how he had heard it told, to his grandfather, that the spirit never appeared, except when misfortunes threatened the Beringhelds, and that a gruesome death always befell someone whenever the Centenarian passed through the region.

"My father, at that time, had already given me all the details, and when I encountered the *spirit* of the Centenarian, as I told you a while ago, I at once recognized his voice, which had nothing *human* about it, a voice that speaks like that of the winds and tempests; I was therefore unable to bear the light of his eyes; when he had passed by, I perceived the massive white head that *reeked of the tomb*; his steps made no sound on the sand, he was light like the morning wind; and, as my head peered outside the ditch where I was hiding, I saw, when he lifted his foot, I saw his dried bones with no flesh on them . . .

"And so, the arrest warrant was annulled, the affair of Count Beringheld transferred to Paris, where he was acquitted, and Butmel became the victim! . . ."

More tears flowed and the old woman fell silent. No one dared interrupt her silence; moreover, the venerable sight of love's misery in this woman inspired a deep feeling of compassion. She waved her emaciated hand, held it out, and exposing its bones, she uttered:

"This arm was young once, covered by soft skin, and Butmel held it often! . . . But now, I see, my arm is wrinkled, and Butmel is dead! . . . I am dead also . . . My heart is dead . . . People only think that I am alive! . . .

"Know," she continued in a firm and sonorous voice, "know that I saw the *Spirit* again this morning . . . Woe to Father Lunada, if he covets the possessions of the Beringhelds! . . . The *Spirit* is afoot in the region, I saw the snow on his head, the bones of his feet; he was on the summit of the *Peritoun*: sitting at the base of the mountain; I thought I would faint, when I saw that the impetuous wind did not move his great brown coat, and that he held steady on his feet; I thought that he was announcing my death; I asked in the village if anyone had disappeared . . . The Centenarian was casting his eye of fire on the old walls of our castle . . . Ah, our countess will indeed have a child . . . Yes, it is Lagradna who tells you so, remember it well! . . . And you, Monsieur Veryno, take care for your wife, she is pretty like Pollany! . . . (the forester shuddered with fear); and you, Babiche, look out for Lusni! . . . He resembles, in size, Jacques Lehal! (the caretaker made the sign of the cross and uttered a *pater*) The *Spirit* is moving about the land! . . .It is rare to see him twice in a century . . . Something dire will surely happen! . . . For, if this *spirit* does not carry someone off with him, he will raise the dead instead!"

The fire had gone out without anyone daring to get up and put on some pine wood; some ashes escaped from the hearth, and a bluish flame that, now and then, lit up Lagradna's visage: this light flickered about the room as did the words of the midwife in the imaginations of the listeners: she had cast them forth one by one, and the paucity of ideas they contained allowed them to impart to the soul a sort of vagueness, a ponderous reverie. One was dumbfounded on hearing her speak, on listening to her diffuse words, and yet she succeeded in troubling her audience. The moment she sat down, a violent gust of wind was heard and the doorbell of the turning house rang.

No one got up to go and open the door, for they supposed that it was the wind alone that had rung the bell; but all of a sudden, when no one thought further about it and when the wind had died down, the bell was again rung with such vigor and persistence that it was clear some flesh and blood being was pulling the deer's foot attached to the end of the chain; then the dog began to bark in a manner that seemed sinister.

No one appeared ready to get up.

"Well, Lusni, my friend," Babiche exclaimed.

"Let's all go. . ." Lusni responded to the measured call of his wife.

At these words, Lusni threw into the hearth a handful of pine branches, a sudden glow lit up the room, and, courage returning to the souls of each, the forester lit a candle, and with Babiche, Lagradna, and Lusni behind him, serving as rearguard, he moved toward the door.

"Are you coming?" cried out a hoarse voice, powerful, strong, and glacial in tone.

"It's he! . . ." said Lagradna. "What does he want here?"

"Who do you mean, he?" . . . Veryno asked.

"Beringheld the Centenarian."

The group remained frozen with fear, halfway to the door, and the candle revealed, in the trembling of its light, the terror of good Lusni, who regretted having listened to Lagradna.

"Are you coming, children of a day?" reiterated the terrible voice, uttering this order with the tone of a master.

"Come on, are you coming?" cried out the voice, gentle now, closer to the supple organ of human speech.

Lagradna, taking the light from the two hands of the caretaker, went slowly toward the door; Babiche, driven by curiosity, followed her; Veryno, ashamed to see himself surpassed in courage by two women, followed closely behind their steps; Lusni as well made efforts in that direction, but remained an honest distance behind; as for the three gossips, they grouped together on the steps of the turning house.

"Since when does this door not open on the first sound of the bell?" said again the terrible voice as Lagradna was rattling the lock.

"Since Butmel died unjustly! . . ." the midwife responded, who was not quite right in the head; indeed, at the age of ninety it often happens.

Hardly had Lagradna uttered the final syllable of the last word, when a horrible burst of laughter resounded in the air and reached as far as the walls of the castle that echoed the sound. All present were frozen with horror.

"*Butmel lives still!* . . ." the voice went on, laughing with infernal laughter. A moment of silence followed this sentence, and bitter tears flowed down the face of Lagradna.

"You are at Beringheld! . . ." the voice went on . . . It came from the throat of a man of gigantic stature. He was speaking, at this moment, to another man in uniform, who ever since he had arrived, had not stopped looking at his valise, brushing his clothes with his sleeves, and looking to see that nothing was missing. The man was interested only in himself and in his horse. The giant, having indicated the direction of the castle, cast a glance at the group, and to all present this glance appeared to make pale the light of the candle. The officer's guide disappeared with a frightening rapidity; even so, one heard the galloping of a horse.

"Did you see him?" . . . Lagradna said to the caretaker, to his wife, to the gamekeeper and the three other old women; "what an eye! . . . Don't think for a minute that that was a horse galloping! . . . The *Spirit* is having fun. You can be certain that he no more has a horse than that there are hairs in the palm of my hand."

The group remained motionless, looking, or rather fearing to look, at no one.

"What in the blazes is wrong with you?" the officer asked them after taking inventory of himself; he enjoyed seeing the fright painted on their faces. He got off his horse, placed his arm carefully in the bridle and continued: "I assure you that my guide is riding a real horse, and a good one to boot! . . . I have never has so much pleasure conversing with a man . . . he asked me nothing for the service he has rendered me; that is being very polite, for he was in his right to require something of me."

"Your guide, a man?" said Lagradna. "You have traveled with a *Spirit*! . . ."

"What is this crazy woman talking about a *Spirit*? . . ." the officer went on, frowning. "Come on, take me to the castle!"

"Did you get a look at him?" Lagradna asked.

"Me, not at all! it is as black as in an oven out there! And when one has a valise to look out for! . . ." he said, looking at the hindquarters of his horse. "Let's go," the officer continued, seeing all eyes turned toward his valise, "let's go. Take me to the castle."

The caretaker took up his light, placed his hand on the windward side to keep it from going out and guided the stranger across the avenue; Lagradna and Babiche accompanied the stranger, in order to open the second gate that most likely would be closed.

The stranger's dress was marked by a regularity, an appearance that gave the sense of a precise and fastidious character. The features of his physiognomy confirmed this opinion: one would have taken him instead for a shrewd merchant, who calculated everything, even his life, rather than for a soldier, who was generally seen as a person determined and adventuresome.

"If it is not indiscreet to ask, might I inquire of you where you took on this guide?" the midwife asked the stranger.

"I got lost," he responded; "just as I was crossing the mountains that lie before the Val . . . Ven . . ."

"Vallinara," the midwife interjected.

"Exactly," the stranger went on, "then I heard the galloping of a horse that was following me, I waited until the rider had caught up with me; I asked him the way to Beringheld; he took me there most obligingly, and along the way, he spoke to me of a horde of little known things, telling curious anecdotes."

"That have nothing to do, certainly, with the present day and age! . . ." Lagradna replied.

"That is true," said the officer, astonished by this remark.

"You didn't get a look at his eyes of fire then."

"There was a light," the officer said.

"A light! . . . It was his eye," exclaimed Lagradna.

At this remark, the stranger remained motionless with astonishment and he muttered in a low voice: "Might this be my doctor? . . . An eye of fire? . . . Why didn't I examine it?"

"And the voice?" the midwife continued.

"*It was his!*" the officer exclaimed, dumbfounded.

As the officer was moving toward the castle, a scene took place the mere telling of which will suffice to give a portrait of the persons who occur in it.

In an ancient dining room, around a well-furnished table, we find the Count, his wife, and Father de Lunada. In front of the Reverend Father are the remains of a number of the most exquisite foods, which attest to the fact that the flower and bloom of his face, the freshness of his complexion, were carefully tended to by the attentions of the masters of the castle. The most tasty wines and a thousand delicacies had already been lavished on Father de

Lunada, when, turning to the Countess, he remarked to her that a feather mattress had not yet been added to his bedding.

"It is not, my dear, out of sensuality that I make this request."

"I am well persuaded of that," answered the young woman seated in a chair the back of which was of an enormous size, and in which she seemed dwarfed.

"But why not," Lunada continued, "profit, in this life, from those commodities that can make it pleasurable. The Lord has allowed them to exist only in order to reward his servants for their struggles with the devil. My son, pass me that cordial in the bottle that is right in front of you; I believe that if my digestion were not quite in tune, I would not be able to pray with all the fervor that one needs to put in one's prayers." The Count handed the bottle to a servant.

"Your prayers have not yet succeeded in allowing us to have children," Count Beringheld said.

"My son, God is wise, and does nothing in vain: if He has allowed the disbanding of our Society, it was in order to punish the earth; and, if you do not yet have any posterity, you can only attribute it to your sins! You must double your acts of penance, your rigors, your fasts; I will add my prayers to them."

"Father," the Countess observed, "could we not consult some practitioners of the art, in order to find out if there might not be ways to . . ."

At these words, fear was seen in the face of the ex-Jesuit: "Can you imagine that such men might be more powerful than God? . . ."

At this exclamation, the Countess fell silent; her face regained the cold passivity that comes from extreme devoutness. Her husband, mouth agape, eyes wide open with astonishment, watched the face of his confessor, whose expression was the real barometer for the entire household.

"There is nothing to hope for except from God!" Father de Lunada continued. Nonetheless, one must admit that the motives of Father de Lunada were not as criminal as they might appear. The Reverend Father used to be a member of the famous Society of Jesus. When this order was abolished, he took refuge in Italy and, returning to France some time afterward, he was taken in by Count Beringheld.

Father de Lunada was very learned, but he was profoundly ignorant of certain matters: convinced of the truth of religion, but even more convinced of the grandeur of his profession as Jesuit, his character offered a unique mixture of simplicity and wit, of goodness and craftiness, of ambition and desires; finally, to sum it all up, the spirit of the Society of Jesus had not been able to corrupt his fundamental nature . . . and, without turning Father de Lunada into a fanatic, a genius, or a man of ambition, the Society of Loyola had inculcated in him its principles and its unique form of religion, which, at every instant, seemed to run counter to the natural ideas of the Reverend Father. What resulted was a unique combat that revealed itself in the Reverend Father's conduct, beliefs, and character.

Thus Father de Lunada wished that, if Count Beringheld was not to have children, the family fortune might come to him rather than to the State; but he would not have taken the least action requiring energy in order to make himself master of that fortune, nor to prevent the Count and his wife from having heirs. One can be sure that the authority that the Reverend Father exercised over the masters of the castle had nothing despotic about it; it merely resulted from the bizarre circumstances that brought three such weak beings together, among whom Father Lunada was simply the stronger of the three.

Thus, the castle was dominated by the dreary aspect of these three beings following their paths in life, having to lead them nothing but the torch of the ex-Jesuit, a torch composed of all the decisions of the church, which the Reverend Father applied according to his interests; and, as all who govern, he was jealous of his authority, which made for the fact that, as he was not totally the master, he was obliged to struggle with people who, without his giving them real motives to do so, made him out to be odious. And so, in Beringheld Castle, one wandered through a labyrinth of domestic intrigues, little vexations, and such like, which the weakness of the masters and the boldness of the servants kept alive at every minute; and in a castle inhabited by such a small number of persons, one can imagine the degree to which these nothings were magnified by gossip and the continuous presence of the same individuals. In a word, let us imagine the Palace of *Foolishness*, which now, the goddess absent, is given over to her subordinates.

[End of Volume One]

Chapter eight

THE OFFICER FROM ANJOU — HIS TERROR —

BERINGHELD THE CENTENARIAN IS IN THE CASTLE —

A HASTY DEPARTURE

We left the officer, escorted by Lagradna, Babiche, and the caretaker, on his way to the stately manor house of Count Beringheld, to whom the Reverend Father de Lunada had just uttered his ominous decree, in which he affirmed that, as for the procreation of a presumed heir to the Beringheld family, nothing more was to be expected, short of divine intervention. Hearing this sacerdotal pronouncement, the Count bowed his head in an embarrassed manner, and his wife threw him a glance that was very difficult to interpret, given the multitude of ideas it suggested. The Count smiled at his wife in a way more meaningful than usual, and all of this, considering the nature of the two spouses, indicated something extraordinary.

In fact, the prospect of seeking in the secular realm a means of remedying the Countess's infertility had been on the mind of husband and wife for a whole month: they considered for a long time, before presenting it to their confessor, whether this matter held no hint of heresy, and whether or not they were able to pursue it; the Countess had even dared to mention the powers of Lagradna, but this woman had too much of the taint of magic and witchcraft about her for the Count to dare call upon her. The Countess, emboldened by the hope of having children, contented herself with cherishing this thought within her own mind.

It was during this silence, as the couple reflected upon the lack of success of their proposal that the caretaker arrived and announced that a stranger desired to speak with the lord of the house.

"Bid him enter," said the Count.

At once the officer appeared and greeted the Count, all the while examining him attentively, after which he addressed him in the following terms:

"Monsieur le Comte, several months ago I returned from the United States, where I loyally served the revolutionary cause. In doing so I received a gunshot wound that I was unable to pay back, which means that I still owe one to Cornwallis's soldiers. After having paid the surgeons over there in vain, who were unable to cure me, I returned to France in order to halt the course of my sickness, the consequences of which were serious enough that they would have become fatal. After having consulted—and *paid*—the most famous doctors without the least result, I resolved to return to my place of birth and spend the remainder of my days there: I am from Angers. Fate had it that I found lodging there in the house where the executioner was living. I found out about it only too late," the officer added, noticing the movement that escaped from the Count, his wife, and Father de Lunada, "but all in all this hangman seemed a rich man, and one who owed nothing to anyone.

"His wife was on the verge of death, and I heard everyone say that it was becoming strange that she didn't die, all the more so as no doctor was attending her. Soon, however, she began to get better.

"I ask you to excuse me, but all of this is linked with my presence here, and from Angers to here, I spent much money, and money is hard to come by!

"Sensing some mystery, and seeing the husband anxious, I kept a close watch on what was going on. Sleeping little because of my pain, I finally realized that every night an old man, remarkable for several unusual traits, and especially for his extreme decrepitude, visited the house. Astonished by this mystery, I questioned the executioner; he told me that the man had promised to cure his wife; what he asked for his services, that was none of my business! The next evening, I waited for this old man as he entered the house, asking him to heal me, if he had the power to do so. He looked at me, Monsieur le Comte . . . ah! I can say that the man's face will remain in my mind forever! A black flame . . ."

At this instant, the officer, happening to glance accidentally at the portraits that covered the walls of the room, let out a scream; and, tottering on his legs, fell into a chair, pointing at one of the paintings. Everyone turned to look: it was the portrait of *Beringheld-Sculdans*, called the *Centenarian*.

A visible consternation clouded the face of everyone.

"Do you see him? . . ." the officer cried, terrified. "His eyes are still moving! I just saw them move . . . It is *he!*"

What doubled the stupefaction of the stranger was the fact that on the frame beneath the portrait was written the following inscription: "*Beringheld anno 1500.*"

"I swear to you" the officer repeated, "that the eyes in that portrait cast upon me the same blazing fire that I saw in the eyes of the old man, and that they moved!"

Terribly frightened, Father de Lunada glanced back and forth between the Count, himself pale as death, and the portrait, whose black eyes showed no sign of that devilish fire the officer had described.

"Look," the latter continued, "something is moving the canvas!"

No one dared to look in order to verify this fact, and the Count rang for his valet: "Saint-Jean, remove that picture . . ." And the Count, trembling, pointed at the portrait of Beringheld the Centenarian.

Saint-Jean tried in vain to take the frame down: it seemed to be imbedded in the wall. The spectators looked at each other in amazement, and Father de Lunada, maintaining in spite of the emotions that moved him the ecclesiastic sang froid proper to his order, asked:

"Finally, Monsieur, might we learn what brings you here?"

"You will know that soon enough! . . . But, where was I?" the stranger asked, troubled, and unable to take his eye off the portrait.

"You were mentioning the old man . . ." the Count answered trembling.

"That supernatural being smiled at my request, and pronounced the following words, whose unique nature made me remember: 'Child of a day, you want to live out your day? . . . I'll grant it. I will cure you, but swear to me you will do what I ask of you . . . and you will be cured!' Nothing seemed more reasonable, I gave my oath, and the heavens are witness that I had every intention of keeping it.

"'I want of you,' the old man continued in a broken voice on the verge of fading away, 'but a very small service! It is to take a letter that I will give you and deliver it in person to Count Beringheld at his castle!'

"He explained to me exactly the way to this village, and even described the entrance to the castle, the turning house and the mountains.

"Monsieur le Comte, my cure was swift, I found the letter on my table the day after my recovery, and I hastened to carry out my promise. *Whatever you have gotten from another must be given back,* whether it be silver, gold, words, or services."

Saying this, the officer drew from his bosom a letter that he handed over to Count Beringheld, adding: "Now, I owe nothing to anyone."

The latter took the letter with trembling hands, opened it, and seemed to fear the letters scrawled on the paper. He read the following:

"*Count Beringheld must know that his race is not destined to die out. On the first of March, in the year 1780, a man will arrive at his castle to remove all obstacles. Care must be taken that no person unknown to the family, be found in the main suites of Beringheld Castle on the day in question. The doctor will arrive during the night and should find the Countess in the formal bedroom of the castle.*" B.S.

Such was the content of this strange message. The Count grew pale as he read these words. His face showed signs of anxiety; he dared not think, and strove to keep himself in a state of imaginative torpor, a sleep of the soul, so as to banish the thought that terrified him. He handed the letter to his wife and fixed his gaze on the visage of the Countess. When she had finished, she looked at her husband, and both of them, moved by fear, turned toward Father de Lunada.

The habitual perspicacity of this latter let him easily ascertain that there was something mysterious in this letter; not lacking in monastic craftiness, a quality of those whose self-interest obliges them to study the human heart, he lowered his gaze, and appeared to have no interest in learning the contents of the letter, knowing that sooner or later the two spouses would tell him about it. This adroit way of never overstepping his bounds was what gave Father de Lunada his strongest hold on his noble patrons.

Nonetheless, for the Reverend Father, the pallid visage of the Count revealed that he was unable to prevent a multitude of bizarre thoughts from swarming around in his imagination, overwhelming it with the dull forebodings of a painful dream; in contrast, the Countess's face expressed real joy, the joy of a woman who conceives the hope of soon becoming a mother; but this joy was visibly weakened by the fear that Father de Lunada might find perils to the conscience in something that seemed so supernatural.

Nothing could be said of this matter in the stranger's presence. After exchanging a few commonplaces with him, the Count ordered him to be shown to the apartment destined for friends who occasionally visited the castle, and when the officer was gone, the Countess exclaimed:

"Whatever mystery lies at the heart of this affair, I can't help rejoicing, if it brings the happy outcome that is announced to us."

"It is natural," said the Count.

"Isn't the first of March the day after tomorrow?" the Countess asked.

"I don't know," answered Beringheld.

"Tomorrow is the first of March," said the Jesuit.

"True," said the Count.

"Tomorrow! . . ." his wife repeated the word with a movement of surprise, and fear. "I didn't think that . . ." and she fell into a deep reverie.

"Good night, my son, peace be with you!" said the priest as he took his light and went slowly toward the door.

No matter what the Countess might say, she could get no more than monosyllables from her husband: yes and no; she got not even the glance, the smile, or the friendly words that the Count usually had on his lips when he spoke to his wife. At the moment when she was getting up to retire, the noise of several confused voices was heard, the door suddenly opened, and Lagradna burst in crying: "I must enter! . . ."

"My Lord," she said, taking advantage of the fright her extreme old age produced, "I cannot hide from you that the spirit of Beringheld the Centenarian is loose in the region, and that he is in the castle! I saw him enter! . . ."

At these words, the most extreme fright gripped the Count, his wife, and the two servants who had wanted to keep Lagradna from entering. The Count motioned with his hand for the midwife to be quiet, and then he added, after a moment of silence: "We must go and fetch Father de Lunada."

Only the Count's valet and the Countess's serving maid had not gone to bed; they followed their masters, as did the midwife, and all went in the direction of Father de Lunada's apartments. Saint-Jean was carrying the two torches, and silent with terror, this group passed through the long galleries of the castle.

The Count was trembling the most, but in order not to let it be noticed, he walked along with assurance. All at once a piercing scream echoed through the galleries, and one easily imagines the fear this scream must have caused in the souls of people weak in inner resolve, alone and wandering in a huge castle, far from all succor, in the middle of a gloomy night, accompanied by all the noise and clatter caused by the winds of the winter equinox. Saint-Jean dropped the two torches; one of them continued to burn, casting a pale glow that lost itself in this immense gallery. They stopped to listen, and despite the wind that howled through the place, despite the cries of night birds, the sound of woods and waters, rapid steps were heard approaching . . . a man appeared at the other end of the gallery, he stopped, raised his lantern so as to identify the people who were before him, and the Countess, who did not have the same reasons as her husband for trembling at what had just occurred, recognized their guest, who was coming toward them, with all the signs of fright on his face.

"Monsieur le Comte," he said in an altered voice, "I am a brave man, and do not fear measuring myself against the first man to confront me, provided that it is a man of flesh and blood like myself! . . . you offered me hospitality in a gracious manner, I owe you my thanks, will you please accept them? . . . but not if you gave me an empire would I remain in your castle; I just saw my doctor again, my guide, and your ancestor! . . ."

At these words, each became dizzy with fear, remained motionless, holding his breath.

"Oh! I clearly recognized the model who sat for that portrait hanging in your drawing room! I owe that person my life, I know it! But I acquitted my debt in doing what he asked of me. I have nothing of his, nor he of mine, and now, I have no further interest, after all that has happened, in finding myself in his presence. I would rather be out this very night on horseback, on the *Vallinara*, even lost, rather than here in your castle with this devil of a man who doesn't even seem to be a *man*! For, if I read the caption on that portrait correctly, this model was either born, or sat for the portrait, in 1500! . . . I am neither religious nor superstitious, and I even admit that there are strange things in nature, there can be more distant resemblances yet, the whole thing can be a trick! . . . Nonetheless, I am an honest gentleman from Anjou who believes in God and wants simply to live in peace. I let the great lords of the Earth find their amusement where they will . . . By this token, I won't even try to explain what I have just seen with my own eyes, because it is inexplicable, and besides is none of my business; simply, I am prudent, I like neither secular justice nor ecclesiastical justice . . . These are all worthy institutions in their own right . . . Consequently, as everything that has happened here has become much too strange for me, I take my leave, Monseigneur! I owe you nothing, you owe me nothing; I've fulfilled my oath, I'm square now, it matters little to me what comes of it, it's your affair! I have the honor to salute you."

With that the stranger, brushing the chalk from the wall off of his sleeve, made a low bow to Count Beringheld, and hurried off down the staircase. He was heard heading for the stables; he led his horse into the courtyard, set his light down on the front steps of the castle, and rode off at a full gallop.

Chapter nine

AN APPARITION — LUNADA REDUCED TO SILENCE —
THE COUNTESS IS CONFINED TO HER BED

It doesn't take much imagination to understand the degree of terror that took hold of this group, when they saw a brave soldier preferring to flee into the cold, stormy night, rather than remain in a castle inhabited by a being about whom there had always existed at Beringheld the most contradictory of legends, legends however that, in all versions, were of the strangest sort.

The Count ordered Saint-Jean to go to his quarters and to await him there. He asked his wife to retire to her room; then he went, alone, to Father de Lunada's apartments.

Beringheld found the Reverend Father reading his breviary. Seeing the Count enter, he set his book down on the table, and, closing his eyes, placing the first two fingers of his right hand against his cheek while moving the rest of this hand to his lips, he appeared ready to listen to the Count.

"Father," said Beringheld, "do you recall the avowal I made to you at confession, at the time of the death of Commander *Sculdans*?"

"I have forgotten it, my son," said the crafty Jesuit; "it can only be recollected during confession."

"Never mind, Father; at the time you had seen it as an instigation of the devil, but today, the existence of that being Uncle

Beringheld spoke of on his deathbed can no longer be placed in doubt; he's here in the castle . . ."

"*Here in the castle!*" exclaimed the priest; leaping up with all the marks of fright.

"Lagradna and the officer have seen him," the Count went on.

"It can only be the devil, or, if not, then your ancestor has made a pact with man's eternal enemy."

"Think, Father," Beringheld continued, "think: if the Commander died of fright, what will happen to us!"

"My son, God is just; he never allows the Tempter to triumph."

"But what shall we do?" the Count exclaimed, for *he* commands that all strangers to the family must leave the castle tomorrow evening for the whole night; and *he* will set aside all obstacles that prevent us from having an heir."

"What did you say?" cried Father de Lunada, "let me see that letter."

The Count gave it to the priest, who read it. Father de Lunada was not lacking in a certain resolve, and his first thoughts proved to him that the devil did not write at all, that it was physically impossible to resist him; he thought also, deep inside, that the presence of beings of this sort had never been an article of faith, that for a long time such an idea had been banished to the realm of dreams.

Nonetheless, in this case, a great number of circumstances presented themselves in a supernatural light; then he recalled that several prisoners of the Inquisition, when facing certain death, confessed that they possessed a power that was unknown to them and which they could not explain; finally, the executions of several sorcerers came to mind. He fell into a reverie that his penitent dared not interrupt, and the result was this: that one must be on one's guard, everyone must be armed, and that he would spend the night of the first of March at the door of the great hall, with holy water, the scriptures, and the sacraments at hand; that everyone should engage in prayer, and that one should take all necessary precautions to resist, either this demon, or men; finally, that the Countess must not be exposed to this mysterious adventure.

The Count, reassured by the words of the good priest, was preparing to leave when he heard a slight noise.

"I think," he said, "that someone is walking in the corridor."

"Quiet," exclaimed Father de Lunada.

They halted, and held their breath.

The door seemed to move, the priest and the Count felt themselves freeze with horror when the movement in fact became a reality; and when, the door opening, an old man of enormous size, his eyes darting a sardonic fire, advanced slowly and in a *disembodied* manner! . . . This mass *enchanted* them, *charmed* them, as if through some sort of *incantation*. The darkest of horrors seized the two onlookers. The old man stopped; he looked fixedly at them; they were gripped as if by some higher force, a thing inexorable, outside of nature.

Beringheld recognized his ancestor, the original of the portrait, but he was ravaged by signs of most terrible old age, by a decrepitude so great that one imagined hearing the cracking of the dry bones of a skeleton. The count's mind was seized by the deepest terror, by that cold, insidious terror that possesses a man body and soul. Indeed, ever since this apparition, he fell subject to mental lapses; and his reason, without failing him entirely, suffered intermittent blanks. At these moments, he sank into a deep reverie.

This huge magical shade, and the appearance of life that animated it, made Father de Lunada's hair stand on end; vainly he called on the powers of reason to help him dispel the icy feeling that had penetrated his soul, but try as he would, he was unable to doubt the presence of this *vapor of a man*, nor the ironic gleam of his two eyes which, by themselves alone, revealed that life was present here.

The old man raised his arm, and with his finger he pointed at Count Beringheld, who believed he saw the infernal depths open wide before him.

"Count Beringheld, leave us alone! . . . And fear not, my presence is, for your family, never anything but a source of prosperity! . . ."

The sound of this deep voice, that seemed to issue from a crypt, possessed a sort of kindness, a tone of friendliness that nonetheless was far from reassuring. An inner power, superior to physical force, radiated from a single movement of the arm of this man who seemed to have risen from the tomb, possessed of all the supernatural powers. This moral force came from ideas alone, and subjugated the Count. He left the room, his eyes haggard and his mind in a state of confusion difficult to describe.

While this was going on in the confessor's apartments, the Countess, whom we left in the gallery with the midwife, turned toward this strange woman, who seemed not at all startled by this extraordinary happening, to ask her what she thought of it all.

"Madame," Lagradna told her, "nothing could be truer . . ."

"Come into my quarters," the Countess interrupted, "and you can tell me everything."

Madame de Beringheld sat down beside the hearth, and was astonished to hear Lagradna tell her:

"Madame, believe me, you will have children! I was saying the same thing just two hours ago, and I repeat it now: the spirit that watches over the Beringheld family reveals itself only on the most important occasions. This huge old man eats no earthly fare! My grandfather saw him as old then as I saw him just now! . . . My great-grandfather met him in 1577 at the foot of the Andes in Chile, and I have only a partial memory of the tale of a young Peruvian girl, who perished in a large earthenware jug and whom my great-grandfather buried. At that time, there were those who hunted *the Centenarian* to give him over to the Inquisition, but he escaped, it seems, from all these attempts. Whatever the case, my great-grandfather told my grandfather that the rumors that circulated about the *Centenarian* soon died out, for the deaths of those who had seen him, or claimed they had, gave the investigators nothing to go on. Reports made to ministers got lost, and men in high places no longer believed such tales because interest in *magic* and the *occult sciences* gradually waned, because the more things went on the less they were believed; finally, interest lagged because the old man was rarely seen twice in the same place.

"The Beringheld family owes its splendor to him! *He frequents kings!* One has met him in various disguises, sometimes on foot like a beggar, other times in a splendid coach under the name of a prince.

"If he comes, Madame la Comtesse, be assured that you will have an heir." Lagradna's incoherent tale put the Countess in an extraordinary state of mind; she was astounded as she heard this series of sentences uttered that were apparently dictated by madness, and yet an invincible curiosity moved her, because the midwife's statements matched the instructions given in the letter she had read.

"But," said the Countess, "surely they will prevent me from being alone tomorrow night in the huge formal suite of Beringheld Castle, and it's there only that . . ."

"But, Madame, why are you supposed to be there?"

"It's the order given in the letter."

"A letter written by the *Centenarian!*" exclaimed the midwife. "You must go there, Madame; do everything in your power to do so."

"But how can I do so?"

"You must," Lagradna added, "feign the most violent illness, retire early, take yourself there and remain; I will hide there if you wish."

The hope of becoming a mother gives birth to the most violent acts, and one has seen women willing to do much more than what was asked of the Countess; and so the latter had already decided, by herself, to obey the orders given by the author of the mysterious letter.

The midwife had just gone out, leaving the Countess plunged in reverie, when the Count entered his wife's quarters; she was terrified by the expression he wore on his face, and Beringheld, sitting down on a chair, spent the whole night without saying a single word.

Father de Lunada never opened his mouth about the scene that must have taken place between himself and the strange creature Lagradna called a *spirit*. Even on his deathbed the good priest never uttered a word about it; and, whenever anyone would speak to him about this encounter, the Reverend Father made it emphatically clear that questions on this subject displeased him greatly.

Whatever the case, the next morning he came down, as was usual, to say mass. When he saw Count Beringheld, he calmed the fears of his penitent with soothing words, he sought to prove to him that there was nothing extraordinary about the apparition they had both witnessed, and he added:

"My son, you must never neglect anything which concerns the fame and prosperity of your illustrious family; you yourself will be to blame if you don't seek to profit from advice offered by a stranger; no harm to Madame la Comtesse can result from it, because no one has any reason to do her harm; and, my son, the Lord sometimes acts in devious ways. Thus, I am going to obey by leaving the castle for this night, and should we have the joy of seeing an heir befall you, I will gladly take his education in charge."

"But, Father," exclaimed the Count, "what makes you think that . . ."

The priest had already departed, and was walking as fast as he could go toward the village across the wide meadow that stretched between the castle and the turning house.

The Count, not knowing which way to turn, spent the entire day in the throes of the most violent doubt.

"Monsieur le Comte," said the Countess, "what do you think of this letter, and what should we do about it?"

"Do exactly as you wish, Madame."

"Do you think there is any danger?"

"In this matter, I think exactly the way you do."

"Would I do well then to go to the great room tonight?" the Countess asked.

"You would," said Beringheld.

"But what if I don't go, Monsieur le Comte?"

"You are responsible to yourself alone," he replied.

"Lagradna prepared the room this morning," Madame de Beringheld continued.

"Ah? . . ." exclaimed the Count; then he fell into a reverie from which it was impossible to withdraw him.

The evening arrived; the Countess finished her toilette and, leaving her husband alone in the living quarters, went down to the great room that was located at the center of the castle's façade, facing the park. There she found the old midwife, who had prepared everything. Eleven o'clock sounded, and Lagradna, at the behest of the Countess, withdrew after lighting a lamp that she placed on the mantle. This lamp cast a faint glow, insufficient to light the vast room where Madame de Beringheld now went to bed.

When she found herself alone in the great bed that, as far as memory reached, had served the counts of Beringheld on their wedding nights, a strange dream befell her . . .

Chapter ten

NIGHT — THE COUNTESS IS PREGNANT — WHAT WAS
SAID OF THE EVENT — AN AMAZING BIRTH — TULLIUS
ENTERS THE WORLD

It is two o'clock in the morning, the night is calm, the voice of the storm subsides, the moon bathes the vast room with a pure light that effaces the lamp's reddish glow; outside, the snow that covers the mountains and trees reflects a light that is bright but harsh. Countess Beringheld sleeps a deep sleep, as does the entire castle, the village, all of nature, everything, except for *him who never sleeps*!

In the midst of her sleep, and after having thought she heard the slight sound one imagines ghosts to make, the Countess felt ice-cold hands touching her, a deathly shiver ran through her body, a voice was heard, a glow lit up her nuptial bed. She thought she was still dreaming, so much did this glow seem to issue from a supernatural source, so much did this vague and inexpressible voice resemble something one hears only with much difficulty in dreams; but an infernal heat soon followed, she remained passive, and . . .*

The Countess had never been gayer and livelier than the morning after her night spent in the bridal suite of the Countesses Beringheld. What is more, insofar as she maintained till the day she died the deepest silence as to the events that transpired after her awakening, we have replaced the gap caused by this discretion with a blank, and have ended our narrative with the final circumstances which she rendered in detail.

"We will be able to have children," she said to her husband the next morning at breakfast.

"Do you think so?" he responded.

"I'm positive of it," she added.

"The Lord be praised for it! . . ." And with that exclamation their conversation ended.

Father de Lunada returned to the castle. Three months later there was rejoicing in the village, the castle and the environs, when it was officially announced that the Countess was with child.

Yet one could not prevent the most absurd rumors, all far from the truth, from circulating; nor could one prevent reports of the circumstances that surrounded this pregnancy being accompanied by commentary and observations that bristled with maliciousness.

In spite of its remoteness and small size, the village of Bering-

*[Editor's Note: Wherever there are such blanks in the text, they will indicate that we have excised things of little interest that were written down in the General's memoirs.]

held had a notary; this little notary was a wit, a fact to be noted; he had a nasty character, which made him a formidable enemy; his back was slightly hunched, his weasel face told of his falseness, yet none of that stopped him from being a notary, or being a wit; nonetheless, as his wit gave him neither an occupation nor deeds to execute, he talked more than he wrote: thus he took the liberty of saying, when he learned all the details of this affair, that Madame la Comtesse, being more clever than she looked, and hiding her designs behind a feigned silliness, had put one over on her husband, her confessor, and the whole household; that, in collusion with Lagradna, the ghost of Beringheld the Centenarian and the officer were one and the same person; that, according to what he had heard, he tended to believe that this person was identical with the physique of a charming young musketeer who, two weeks before the event, had been in the next village, and who came to the mountains every summer to hunt, hunting in fact more than one kind of animal; that, finally, in the eighteenth century it was a disgrace to believe in ghosts and witchcraft.

About all this, and in answer to the little notary, Lagradna, mounting her stool of prophesy, observed that the *spirit* had not yet left the region, and that sooner or later woe would come to this little notary if he persisted in his slander.

If there were a thousand people on Lagradna's side, the notary also saw many people side with him, thus there were two factions at Beringheld, but both were soon reduced to silence.

Shortly after having spread all these calumnies, which had a slight hint of truth to them, the little hunchbacked notary was returning from making a lucrative inventory of goods; he was crossing over the fearful Vallinara on his mule, in the midst of darkest night. A farmer who came after him along the same road found the scribe fallen in a swoon; he carried him back to the village of Beringheld, and the poor hunchbacked notary died that night, the consequence of being frightened out of his wits.

In spite of the best possible care, his face never showed any expression but that of the most awful fear; his eyes rolled in convulsions and strayed wildly around the room, as if he dreaded finding there some object of horror! . . . And whatever questions were asked him, he passed away without saying anything other than: "*Yes, I saw him! . . . I saw him!*"

Lagradna, who did not refrain from making windy speeches in the room, exclaimed that this was probably *Count Beringheld the Centenarian*! Hearing these words, the little notary struggled to make an affirmative nod with his head, but he gave up his last breath without even being able to complete this movement: his members retracted and shriveled from the effect of the violent convulsion that ended his life.

This death left a mark of deepest fear in the village, in the castle and surrounding region; no one dared to go afoot at night, and the Vallinara was seen as a place of great danger.

Madame de Beringheld's pregnancy was pleasant and uneventful, for she felt none of the discomforts that usually beset pregnant women.

It was observed that she often contemplated the portrait of Beringheld-Sculdans, called the Centenarian. As for the Count, he suffered a strange decline both in mental and in physical powers. One was astonished to see the Countess engaged in frequent conversations with the old midwife, who told her all she knew about the *spirit* of Beringheld: Madame la Comtesse took a strange pleasure in listening to the tale of his magical adventures, which Lagradna amplified considerably. The midwife, by means of these mysterious tales, opened the door of the castle for herself and attracted the attention and good graces of the Countess.

The month of November finally came: the old midwife asserted with certainty that *Beringheld the Centenarian* had not yet left the region nor the mountains; she added that she had seen him atop Mount Peritoun, his favorite summit, and Lagradna, taking a clue from this apparition, predicted a host of ills.

The Count, seeing that all these utterances had a dangerous effect on his wife's mind, and moreover not caring for this subject of conversation, which always caused him attacks of melancholy, forbade that such legends, traditions, and anything concerning his ancestor be discussed in the castle; Father Lunada, as well, seconded the Count in this matter.

Nonetheless, it was impossible to prevent the Countess from learning things from the midwife: (1) that Commander Sculdans had revealed to Count Beringheld the existence of the head of the junior branch of the Beringheld line; (2) that Sculdans the Centenarian caused the Commander's death by appearing to him; and that the *spirit* of the *Centenarian* had appeared on 28th February, 1780, that very year, near the castle, in the castle itself, and so on. Finally, Lagradna did not forget the tale of Butmel, condemned to be drawn and quartered at Lyon, nor the story of the Peruvian girl, nor that of Count Vervil, and on and on.

Thus it was that 2d November arrived. The Countess herself was surprised that she had not yet gone into labor; and, as she felt no particular discomfort, no one had taken the precaution to ensure the presence of a doctor, as up till now Lagradna had been sufficient to guide Madame de Beringheld, who had a singular confidence in the knowledge of the midwife.

This particular year, the month of November was marked by an absence of its usual fog and chill; the trees still retained a few leaves of a deep yellow that fell with the least stirrings of the air.

The Countess, seated at her window, was admiring the rich hues of the sunset, which in the Alps never fails to produce most picturesque effects: now the vivid red sun tinted the sky and the battlements of the castle with a whole spectrum of hues that were most apt to induce meditation; and thus the Count, plunged into a deep state of reverie caused by several words his wife had just uttered that had to do with the Centenarian, stood silently by.

At this instant, extraordinarily violent pains struck Madame de Beringheld; she complained, withdrew from the window and sat down: the pains were felt anew, with increased violence! At this, the Count ordered a servant to mount up and go to the adjacent village, to fetch a doctor at once, for, to judge from the enormous size of the Countess's belly, it looked as if she might give birth to twins.

The pains came more frequently; Father de Lunada himself

was obliged to fetch Lagradna. She came, her white hair disheveled and her face filled with extreme horror: she whispered in the Count's ear as she entered that she had just spied the *Centenarian* standing on top of the battlements which overlooked the Countess's chambers, and that despite the strong wind blowing, not a piece of his great brown coat moved.

The screams of the Countess became terrible to hear, and her voice, piercing the walls, resounded outside: soon Lagradna declared, in a low voice, that Madame was in the greatest danger, and that if she were to be saved, more than human help would be needed.

Desolation reigned throughout the castle; Count Beringheld, terrified, and with a character unable to sustain such emotions, was weeping all the tears of his body, seeing his wife on the verge of death, and hearing her as she uttered heartrending screams.

Lagradna, seated next to the Countess, was unable to gather the wits needed to begin an operation as difficult as it was urgent; so, letting nature take its course, she contented herself with merely announcing the danger.

It was amidst this scene and the turmoil caused by such a happening, at the moment when the Countess had reached the ultimate degree of human suffering, had apparently yielded and ceased to struggle, that Lagradna, glancing at the Count, who himself remained mute and motionless, warned him that his wife was going to die because she would not be able to bring her child into the world, and that she would need a dangerous operation, which she feared to undertake on the Countess.

At last however, at that terrible moment of silence that precedes death, footsteps of an astounding heaviness are heard in the gallery: the floorboard trembles under a mighty weight, the door swings open with a clatter, and the huge old man, the living image of the Count's ancestor, steps forward! The Count faints at the sight, Lagradna attempts to look upon this terrible witness of so many centuries, but remains motionless at the sight of this mass, its withered hands, and especially that eye at which none could look without harm.

The Count is suspended between life and death, waking and sleeping; he knows not what to believe, and experiences all the effects produced by African serpents on their prey. Frozen to the piece of floor where he is standing, he resembles a man that lightning has struck without being felled.

The Countess, feeling a pair of icy hands run over her body, awakens from her state of deep prostration! She cries out, and attempting to raise her leaden eyelids, she tries to see the being who, with skilled movements,[18] and by means of potions that he drew from assorted phials, is alleviating the terrible workings of nature . . . Her gaze, as she faints, perceives the petrified skull of this *shadow of a man* . . . She recognizes the subject of Lagradna's tales . . . and a terrible cry of fright issues from her parched throat. The terror that fills her soul is such that it overcomes all her physical suffering.

During the time she fell prey to the pains of this moral and physical agony, the huge old man, drawing a blade of shining steel, that made Lagradna shiver, succeeded in saving both the mother and the child.

The midwife, during all these procedures, that demonstrated the most profound scientific knowledge, and were carried out with the most touching sense of devotion, stood *dumbfounded*, and contemplated these happenings as if in a dream. She thought, indeed, she must be dreaming, for several times its seemed impossible that the Countess could still be alive after such a dangerous operation; and every movement he made, every aid, every remedy, to the degree these assisted or rather mastered nature, seemed to Lagradna to far surpass the common order of things.

The Countess, in a state of swoon, was placed comfortably in her bed by the Centenarian. The old man poured a liquor between her teeth, a liquor whose powerful effects brought back the colors of life to the cheeks of this mother in pain: she fell into a peaceful sleep . . . then the stranger performed a most unusual exercise: it consisted of a series of movements, executed with *incredible* slowness, by which he seemed to take command both of her pains and of nature. Lagradna noticed that, although he studiously avoided touching the ailing Countess, whom he seemed fearful of approaching, the efforts of this astonishing old man nevertheless drew from her what remained of her sufferings, and the face of the sick woman became increasingly radiant the more this magic doctor tired himself in performing such a bizarre operation. She soon noticed (a thing incredible to see!) beads of sweat pour from the huge gray skull of the supernatural being she was observing. All the celestial power he deployed had, as it poured forth from his vast machine, invaded the room, now become too narrow for this conqueror of death: Lagradna saw nothing more except through a cloud of bluish smoke . . . Finally the cloud thickened, and the old midwife fell into a swoon! The same happened to the Count, whose impressions were if anything less precise and vaguer than those of Lagradna, for, as he witnessed this strange scene, he seemed more like the dust of some tomb than a being endowed with the organs of life . . .

Lagradna awoke at last. The room was purified, the air redolent with an odor rendered beneficent by its delicate subtlety. In the light of several candles the astonished midwife perceived the fearful colossus smiling down at a baby boy three times bigger than a newborn child ought to be; he rocked the baby gently, and the vast and strange face of this old man took on an expression impossible to describe: his eyes seemed a thousand times brighter, and the flame that escaped from them expressed nothing but gentleness. The smile that played upon his face resembled one of those half-storms that furrows the vast ocean, but only at a single location. A while later, he set the child down on its mother's bed, gave Lagradna a commanding gesture, showing her the night table, and an elixir that the Countess must take; then, casting a last look at mother and child, he made preparations to leave: Lagradna already believed she saw him fly out the window, vanish in a puff of smoke, melt away by degrees like a ray of dying sunlight, when, overcoming her fear, under the influence of his silence and *enchantment*, she fell to her knees, and cried out: "And what about Butmel? As you are master of life and death, Butmel, give me back my Butmel!"

Lagradna believed she saw a horrible smile play upon the lips of this man, and she regretted her outburst: suddenly, the *Centenarian* raised his huge arm and with a gesture at one and the same time full of power and majesty, he pointed to the east and said in a solemn voice: *"You will see him again!"*

At the sound of this voice, at this sound that seemed to issue from beneath an aqueduct, and that imparted to the soul an idea of what the voice of God on Mount Horeb or in the Sinai must have been like, Lagradna, trembling, not daring to interpret this sinister pronouncement, remained on her knees, her hands stretched out toward this strange being who, turning toward the sleeping mother, placed his hand on her forehead, directing to that spot all the vital fire of those eyes that burned like two pyres. Then the huge mass, whose head nearly touched the ceiling, withdrew with slow steps, without making the least noise: this *human monument* seemed to move by means of some power or force outside of nature. He passed by the Count, stopped, held out his hand to him, shook it, and vanished from the room, the gallery, the castle, and the entire region with such ease, such rapidity, and such mystery, that no one, since his appearance, ever saw him again. The Count's hand remained extended; the hand of the stranger was icy, and transferred to the Count's hand all the cold of the North Pole.

Lagradna uttered a piercing cry, when she noticed that the large infant looked exactly like the old man, but with this difference, that where the *Centenarian* had upon him signs of the decay of the grave and the coldness of death, the child bore a character of youth and freshness. Hearing her scream, the Count came running and was stricken with astonishment; his organs were deranged forever, such a sight was too powerful for his soul devoid of energy, and for his puerile imagination: he himself, from this moment on, lapsed into childhood; the tomb remained his best hope, indeed the only thing one could wish for him, given his sad existence.

The night was well under way; Lagradna and the Count spent what remained of it at the bedside of the Countess, whose face, calm and rested, smiled as she slept. The dawn soon covered the turrets of the castle with its morning colors; and daybreak caused the light of the candles to pale;, the Countess awoke: and what an awakening it was! . . .

"Are you in pain, Madame?" asked Lagradna.

"Me, not at all," she answered.

"You suffered quite a bit," the Count interjected.

"When?" she asked, caressing her child, whose eyes were already open.

The midwife was greatly astonished at these words; or rather there are no words able to describe her state; she remained dumbstruck, looking back and forth from the Count to the Countess.

The joy of a mother who sees her firstborn is quite excusable; but what proved that the Countess had but the faintest memory of that night's happenings was the fact that, even though she knew she was a mother, she nevertheless got up as usual and went to the window to take a breath of air.

"Madame, aren't you risking your life?" exclaimed the midwife.

"*He told me* I could do it, (imagine the surprise!) *he told me* I had nothing to fear."

And the Countess, as if remembering instructions that *Beringheld the Centenarian* might have given her, turned toward the night table, and drank down the potion found there in a single gulp.

"No one spoke to you last night!" the Count said.

"No one?" she exclaimed with a slight hint of irony "*He* spoke to me all night long."

"Who?"

"*I don't know* . . . I have an unclear recollection of it, as I do of my pains and my sleep. *His* is not an ordinary constitution; *his* bones are ten times bigger than ours, *his* nerves are taut, *his* muscles like rods of steel."

"'Whose?" asked the Count.

"*His*," she answered with childlike innocence.

"But . . ." the Count was terrified.

"I don't know anything more," she went on, "and . . . *he forbade me to tell the rest!*"

With these words she looked at her child, whom she was rocking in her arms, but without being struck by the resemblance he bore to the portrait of *Beringheld-Sculdans*, called the *Centenarian*; and she offered him her breast, having the joy of hearing him utter a cry—her first joy! She thought the child had spoken to her.

"He was born on the day of the *dead*," said Lagradna.

"He is perhaps *destined to live a long life*," answered the Countess.

The whole castle experienced an inexplicable surprise, on learning all these happenings, which were made all the more incredible by means of the commentary that was added to them. It was taken for granted, throughout the entire region, that the *devil* had delivered the Countess of her baby, and that the Count's son was a fearful prodigy. In the midst of this tumult and gossip, Madame de Beringheld remained calm, and busied herself solely with her child, whom she adored.

Chapter eleven

BUTMEL AND LAGRADNA — THE TALE OF BUTMEL —
TULLIUS'S CHILDHOOD

Count Beringheld had his son baptized by the ever-obliging Father de Lunada, with the name Tullius, that of the first head of this ancient line.[19]

Marguerite Lagradna returned home, the day after the baptism; the Countess had given her a large sum of money and had told her:

"Here, Lagradna, it is by *his* order that I give you this small fortune; *he* told me to repeat to you the words that *he* spoke to you, following the prayer you uttered that you might see Butmel again."

Lagradna, remembering that Madame Beringheld was at that

moment immersed in the deepest possible sleep, and that *the man* had contented himself with placing his hand on the countess's head, no longer doubted that it was the spirit of Beringheld who had risen from the grave, by a decree of heaven, to work such marvels.

"'*I don't want,*' he told me, '*that Lagradna should suffer any longer, her term has expired, if I had known it earlier, had I passed by this place earlier, I would have lightened love's misery with good fortune! . . . so that she might be happy, completely happy, at least for a little while.*'"

The Countess, repeating these words exactly as spoken, seemed to have had them engraved in her soul by a force at once superior and immutable in its effects . . .

Lagradna was walking toward her cottage, at that moment when the setting sun was gilding the mountains with its magnificent colors: stormy clouds were forming slowly in the east and seemed like the shrouds of the day, soon ready to vanish; a gentle warmth made itself felt, and this beautiful autumn evening, which seemed more like spring, produced in the soul an effect of *rebirth*; one would have said that nature here was unwilling to die without regret, summoning its forces for a final effort, in order to see itself decked out in a springlike appearance one last time, before shrouding itself in the funereal garb of winter.

The village, located in a picturesque setting, shone with all the splendors of nature: its vista of tree groves, gentle, sublime, and full of a throng of harmonies, brought about, at this moment especially, a delightful sensation; and yet this sensation gave the midwife a pleasure filled with pain; and only heightened her delirious melancholy. Indeed, this was an evening exactly like the one when she and Butmel had exchanged tokens of their love and pledged their hearts to one another.

The poor woman recalled that moment; gentle tears rolled down her wrinkles.

Not believing for a moment in the Centenarian's prophesy, she walked on, surrounded by the charming glory of nature, feeling her heart become young again; and already, her gait no longer had that heaviness of old age.

"Well," she told herself, "if Butmel were to return, it could only be only at such a moment as this . . ."

She approaches her dwelling, and on the bench by her door shaded by a rosebush planted by Butmel's own hand, she sees an old man with white hair, sitting faithfully in that spot Butmel used to occupy long ago, a spot that ever since had never been occupied by another. The old woman hurries forward! . . . she recognizes Butmel who holds out his arms to her! His dusty feet, his forehead covered with sweat, tell that he returns from a long voyage.

"Butmel! . . . my dear Butmel!"

"Marguerite, my dear Marguerite! . . ."

The two aged ones mingle the silver of their locks; the midwife, in rapture, reveals, with a wild gesture, the necklace of glass beads that has never left her neck; and Butmel shows her the modest cup that she had given him.*

The Tale of Butmel

Once the rapturous tears of joy had ceased to flow, when Lagradna and her dear Butmel found themselves alone in front of a fire of pine boughs, the old lover, now nearly a centenarian, asked

*[Editor's note: The loves of Butmel and Marguerite Lagradna comprise, in the General's manuscript, a story that he has told with such a simplicity and a naturalness that we did not see the need to reproduce it here, indeed to extract it from the whole of this relationship, of whose telling it is a central part. Here an account of this adventure, from which we have removed many details, would obviously be detrimental to the topic of our narrative. We have therefore retained only those circumstances indispensable for the reader, in order that he have knowledge of the life of the midwife, insofar as Lagradna plays a role in the memoirs of the General; we repeat, however, that we have transferred the entire story of the midwife to another work. One will find a note that refers to this adventure, at the end of the fourth volume. There, those who take pleasure in feeling their souls moved by gentle and natural emotions will be able to satisfy their needs.]

by what stroke of fate they had found each other again after more than a half-century. Here in a few words was Butmel's reply:*

"I was taken to Lyon, where I was arraigned by decree of the attorney general. My trial was over quickly: two or three witnesses, whom I did not know, and whose names told me that they were not from around here, testified against me. My conviction seemed to me sealed even before any of these three men had spoken. They said much more than was necessary to make me seem a horrible criminal . . . I don't even remember their names! My fate was sealed, and had I been sure of living I would never have held it against them. There was one of them however who seemed to me a thorough scoundrel! I pitied him from the depth of my soul. All I had in my favor was my innocence and my simple, artless way of speaking, I was found guilty. I was taken back to my prison, I began to think of you, of your pain! . . . I thought just how much more unhappy you would be than I, because you would survive me!"

Lagradna moved closer to Butmel, took his withered hand, and pressed it in her hands no less withered; and then, taking that sacred hand up against her heart, she combined all the fires of love in the tender look that she gave to this old white-haired man.

"Look at these wrinkles," she exclaimed, "see my marks of suffering! . . . You are the only man who has ever entered this cottage since you left!"

There was a moment of silence; soon old Butmel resumed his tale:

"The night before my execution came all too soon (Lagradna trembled), I was in the deepest sleep, and I was dreaming of you, when I heard in my dream the noise of a heavy fall; it was fol-

*[Editor's Note: This adventure, containing information about the Centenarian, we have left in the text: it is clearly related to the story of the General, and to all the events that we have just recounted, in a word, it forms a single body with all the documents that the General has assembled concerning his ancestor.]

lowed by the sounds of a sepulchral voice that called me by my name, 'Butmel! . . . Butmel!" This voice had in my dream such a sense of reality that I awoke . . . Imagine my terror when, in the midst of my underground dungeon, surrounded by thick walls, I perceived a man of such a stature that he was obliged to bend his enormous head earthward. I still shudder with horror when I think of his locks, of his forehead, and the great size of his limbs. He held a lamp and was looking at me with a kindness that made me tremble. The iron door that sealed my prison was closed tight: the idea of some supernatural power seized upon my faculties at the sight of this being, for whom I could find no place in all creation."

"It is the spirit of Beringheld the Centenarian!"

"That was exactly the idea I had! He spoke to me in a dull voice, which no longer had any of the characteristics of the human voice, for the sounds it made were hoarse, almost indefinable: 'Butmel, you are innocent. I know it! The true culprit was destined to set himself above such punishment as these children of men meet out to their kind, for there are simply some things that must be. The reasons for such, beyond the merely human, cannot be explained to those who live but a day. Learn that Count Beringheld was innocent as well; but human justice could not do without a victim, and to your misfortune I chose you!'

"These words cast turmoil in my soul, and I was incapable of thinking.

"'It is my duty therefore,' he went on, 'to set you free, and not to allow you to die. Follow me, and observe how the knowledge of all those places where man brings his fellow man to despair, gives me the power to cheat the executioner, on those occasions when one is guilty . . . and to save the innocent as well.'

"With these words, he raised his hand to the vault; and an enormous stone, that he held up without effort, came loose: he took me by the feet and lifted me up into the opening formed by the absence of that stone; then, handing me the lamp, he commanded me to move to the left, and placing his hands on the edge of the broken vault, he lifted himself to my level by the sole force of his wrists. In a flash he was at my side; a rope tied around the stone that lay below allowed him to return it to its proper place in the dank ceiling of my cell; and, uniting our forces, we drew it up until the old man, examining a black line traced on our side, judged that it had reached the level of the other stones. Some mortar was there, all prepared; he faced the stone, in such a manner that in twenty-four hours it would be impossible to tell the place from which we had fled.

"We crawled through a narrow conduit that led us into one of the city sewers and from there to the Rhone where a boat was waiting for us."

"Every order this magical creature gave to me carried such force, there exuded from his entire being such great awareness of his superhuman power that he seemed to know in advance that no one could resist him.

"His influence over me prevented me from making a single remark, I did not have the courage to think; and, when I wanted to speak to him, it was as if my tongue were frozen in my mouth. By fleeing like this, I admitted I was a criminal! . . ."

"Such was the idea that I had, when we arrived in Marseille. The old man took me on board a ship and we sailed for Greece: I saw that land of antique souvenirs, then we arrived in Asia, all the while my guide had not spoken a single word to me: he knew all languages and cast terror in every soul. He took me as far as India, to a country whose name I do not know.

"We passed through a horde of lands and nations,[20] and everywhere my miraculous guide sought out, in obscure quarters of cities, old men and women whose language he spoke and whom, by his aspect alone, he plunged into the deepest astonishment. To judge by the homages proffered him, it was easy to imagine that people took him for a *god*. Some gave him plants, the fruit of long research; others animal products or rarities that were found but once in a century, such as the seed of the *Soan-Leynal*, or the tumor that forms in the brain of the tiger, which the Tartars call *likai*.

"Finally, we came to a fantastically high mountain, near a

river of astonishing width. The huge old man made me climb this mighty mountain: about halfway up, we came upon a deep cave, at whose entrance was a venerable old man. As soon as he saw my guide, he threw himself at his feet and kissed them: the Centenarian did not seem to pay much attention to such tokens of respect, to which he seemed accustomed.

"'Butmel,' he said to me in French (these were the first words I heard him speak since Lyon), 'Butmel, it was impossible to leave you in France where you would have been discovered; and, for a number of reasons, you can no longer go back there: foremost among these reasons is that I do not want you to go.

"'You will have everything you need in this place; you will be pampered. You will be made to live a long time; you will have all you desire, except for freedom; for I forbid you to set foot off this mountain. When all these countries we have just visited will have put on a new face, when a generation will have gone by, if you are still alive, then you will be allowed to see your homeland again! Though I may be at the other end of the universe, I will give the order to release you, and these ancient ones, sacred vessels of an unknown science, will hear my voice, will see my signal, and then the day of your deliverance will be made known to you.'

"Having spoken, he turned to the old man, conversed with him in some barbarous tongue; then, the next day he disappeared, accompanied by a crowd of oddly dressed old men, all of whom looked upon him with respect, and followed him for a long time with their eyes.

"They assigned me, as dwelling place, a cave lined with shells and decorated with a variety of things. All the delights of the Orient were lavished on me, but every time I wanted to leave the mountain, I encountered an armed man, who rushed to prevent me.

"On that mountain I became acquainted with men and women from diverse nations: they taught me their languages; and all these beings, spirited away from their homeland by the arm of my guide, told me the most surprising things: their adventures seemed to vie with one another as to which could present the most supernatural events, events in which the Centenarian always played the principal role."

"On many occasions I will tell you some of these, and you will tremble more than once.*

"I made the following reflection to myself: all of these individuals punctually obeyed their guardians, and seemed to love them. At certain times, a guardian would arrive, taking the hand of the person who was placed in their charge, and immediately, the man or woman would lower their head, and follow the person they called *the Brahmin*. I questioned them several times about this oddity; no one was able to give me an answer; only once, on one single instance, did someone offer a remark: *I am going to bed!*"

"Finally, about *nine months ago, toward the first of March, 1780*, my Brahmin told me that the Centenarian had just given him the order to let me leave, at last. He told me that you were waiting for me, and he called you by your name, Marguerite Lagradna. I was dumbfounded; I left at once . . . and here I am."

The marks of the most profound horror appeared on the face of Lagradna.

"Butmel," she said, "the Centenarian was here two days ago; he was here nine months ago; and nine months ago, when I opened the gate for him, I cried out to him: 'Butmel! Butmel!' He broke out then in a frightful laugh and answered *that you were not dead at all!*"

Butmel remained petrified; these two old people, looking furtively at each other, dared not turn around: the sound of the wind terrified them; they let their many thoughts wander through their weakened imaginations without seeking to convey them to each other: only Butmel, after a long silence, exclaimed: "I was told things even more astonishing! But, on learning of such happenings, the mind remains ever terrified . . . Marguerite, let us fear God! And let us not seek to fathom such mysteries . . ."

*[Editor's Note: These adventures have been collected, and will be published under the title of: Memoirs of the College of the Brahmins of Mount Coranel.]

Such were all the circumstances that accompanied the birth of General Tullius Beringheld: we have set them forth with the greatest fidelity, because the General, in his manuscript, seems to attach a good deal of importance to this.

Therefore, it is only at this moment that the General's life begins. We will see, subsequently, how this life is attached to all the events in the past, the present, and the future of this narrative.

Chapter twelve

THE DEATH OF THE COUNT — TULLIUS'S CHILDHOOD — HIS
NATURAL TALENTS — HOW THE BERINGHELDS WERE SPARED
BY THE REVOLUTION — VERYNO PLAYS A ROLE

Madame de Beringheld nursed her child herself; she lavished on him all the powers of maternal love in its highest degree: it was as if this soul, weak and lacking in all else, had been compensated by nature in receiving a dose of tenderness, in which all the spirit and feeling that can animate the soul of a woman found refuge. Her son was everything to her, she adored him, she was content with a gesture, a glance, and a gentle correspondence seemed to take shape between the mother's eyes and those of her son.

She tasted, in continuous pleasure sweet and delightful, all the joys of motherhood. She watched over the development of this tiny being as if watching a play, and relished all the difficulties of the task. She was witness to each smile of her son, his first word, his first step; happy and a thousand times happier than the soul that soars up from limbo bound on its celestial journey.

Father de Lunada also came to have much affection for little Tullius, and he saw, in the heir to this house of Beringheld, signs that indicated that he would be the one to restore it.

As for Count Beringheld, he died a year later in a state of imbecility that made his death seem a blessing. Indeed, for a long time now, the Count was already considered as if dead and mourned in the soul of Madame de Beringheld. His death only produced the effect of a happening that one announces to a person who has already known it for a long time.

The Count had designated Father de Lunada as his son's tutor, jointly with his mother; but the good Father found his powers restricted solely to things which lay beyond the Countess's sphere of duties; he accepted this naturally, of his own volition, for ever since the Countess had had a son, her character had taken on a sort of consistency; indeed, her soul seemed *retempered* by this event, which bestows on the female machine so much vigor, disposing it to all forms of courage and effort: this is the source of all their admirable traits, and of all their weaknesses!

Tullius's childhood was marked by a number of peculiarities, remarkable in that they augured what he would later become. From the age of eight, he deployed an extraordinary tenacity and passion in all that he undertook. Everything he touched had meaning for him, and even in the mud castle that his childish fingers shaped with joy, one discerned a refinement, a good taste that revealed a soul in love with the harmonies and diverse traits of nature, which the painter, the poet, and the musician have all called *unity, ideal beauty*. He possessed a unique talent for discovery, for seeking and finding; but once he had achieved his goal, once he had reached a result, everything was over, and he would fly on to another conquest. For example, a new game would captivate him body and soul! Once mastered, he dropped it, becoming suddenly bored with the game.[21] And it was the same with everything he did. Tullius used all of his powers to conquer, desiring nothing but the combat. For him, the state of rest was a disaster.

Father de Lunada was amazed at the progress Tullius made in the basic sciences the Jesuit taught him, and was even more struck by the distaste the young man displayed for the treasures of monastic learning and the logic-chopping of theology.

Tullius's ideas grew as he grew in an astonishing manner; his mother, reveling in his perfections, idolized him, and young Beringheld became accustomed to seeing all obstacles bend before his will. Such obedience on the part of those bigger and stronger than himself, far from making him despotic or capricious, taught him, once and for all, that he must never ask for anything that was not just and honest. Acting in this manner differently from all other children, he revealed himself, in this anomaly of mind, a being already extraordinary, one whom reason had infused at an early age with its divine light.

Mathematics was especially pleasing to him; he learned all that the good Father de Lunada knew about them, and soon knew more that his teacher.

Amidst all these qualities, there was one that shone forth in the ultimate degree: it was a certain tendency to exaltation, blended with an equal dose of chivalrous grandeur, which caused him to consider *faith in the oath* as a sacred thing; this brought him to admire Regulus, who returned to Carthage seeking Aristide and certain death, to admire the Spartans, and Themistocles, choosing to die rather than fight against his country, and so on. His fiery soul seemed to have been fashioned out of the rarest substances with a meticulous care by the man who brought him into this world. As soon as one spoke to this young child, one forgot the spiritual ugliness of his strange countenance, and admired the liveliness of his responses, and saw a soul shaped on a grandiose scale, out of all that is noblest and most sublime in human nature.

Nevertheless one noticed further (we owe these observations to Father de Lunada, for he remarked all these characteristics), one noticed, as I said, that his passion for making discoveries led him to a deep loathing for things human, put him in a state of extreme melancholy; the sole conclusion to be drawn from this was that our young genius would surely perish unless he found an object of study that he would never be able to exhaust.

Once he had lost faith in whatever it was, his enthusiasm waned, everything came to a halt, and he had to have something new to feed his curiosity and passion. To look at him, one would have said that fire flowed in his veins, that it roiled there in torrents, and that such mighty activity, such vital energy, in no way lessened his natural goodness and tender compassion.

One can thus imagine with what ability and enthusiasm he ranged over the vast field of the sciences. The Beringheld library gave him all the books and instruments he needed. He devoured it all.

His love for his mother was excessive; if indeed excess is possible in the case of an emotion that, however intense it may become, will never wear the name of *passion*, because in it there is nothing of that which mars the passions. It contains only that which is pure and grand. It is perhaps the only perfect human sentiment that exists.

So Madame de Beringheld, now happy, lived life through her son, and trembled to think with what fury the passions would rage through this great and powerful soul, incapable of the half-measures that reveal a petty mind and its narrow ideas. For him, it would be either great acts of virtue, or great crimes, according to the situation; such are the colors, such is the standard borne by those natures destined to soar like eagles, or to perish woefully in the mire.

"Reverend Father," he would ask as a little boy, "why is the universe round?"

"Because God made it that way."

"But man has not explored the whole universe, how does he know it is round?"

Father de Lunada rubbed the sleeve of his cassock; lowering his eyes, he was at wit's end:

"One imagines it is so," he answered.

"Ah, I see," said the child with a crafty smile, "people say that in order to get rid of the problem; because if it weren't round, how would they ever find the end; they would go on forever."

"But that's exactly it, my child," Lunada continued." It is infinite."

"What does 'infinite' mean, Reverend Father?"

"It means God," the Jesuit said, to cut things short.

"I don't understand," the child exclaimed, and he would ponder all day long, casting a sly glance at Lunada.

When he was ten, he listened eagerly to the tales that old Lagradna and Butmel told him, one after the other, of the mysteries of his birth, the legends that circulated concerning his ancestor Beringheld-Sculdans the Centenarian, who was still alive, even though born in 1450, and who had roamed the world for three and a half centuries now, mastering all the sciences and acquiring all the powers.

One imagines, obviously, that all these miraculous happenings of which Lagradna and Butmel spoke, claiming to be witnesses, must have had a strong effect on the young child's imagination, disposed as it was to all things romantic and extraordinary.

As for the facts that the old midwife had learned from her father, and her grandfather, concerning Beringheld the Centenarian, they fit together so perfectly that it was impossible not to believe them, and Tullius found happiness only in the company of these two centenarians, still in love, who told him these tales in their broken voices, inside their cottage, sitting beside the hearth fire that they kept burning thanks, as they put it, to the generosity of the Centenarian.

In addition, all the stories of the inhabitants of Mount Coranel were a rich mine, which old Butmel rendered inexhaustible through his slow and ponderous manner of narration.

All these prodigies, these miracles, the myriad descriptions of the Centenarian, and the bizarre forms in which he appeared in all the countries of the world, were etched in Tullius's young brain: he admired the happiness of this privileged being who must have known all the sciences, all the languages, and all the stories, and who carried within his skull the entirety of human knowledge.

And so, from earliest childhood on, Tullius was struck by the truth of these tales, and when he would return to the castle, watching out over the *Peritoun* in hopes of seeing the huge old man, he would ask his mother whether these stories told by the centenarian couple were true, and Madame de Beringheld, assuming an air of seriousness, would answer him:

"Tullius, I've seen the Centenarian, I owe my life to him: when

I gave birth to you, we would have perished, you and I, without his science. You will see him one day, Tullius, for *he* loves you."

"But, mother dear," asked the child, "is he really 300 years old?"

"I don't know, Tullius, all I can say is that I saw the man that old Marguerite has told you about."

"And I look like him! . . ."

Hearing this, but avoiding answering, the Countess took her child, showered him with kisses: then his aroused curiosity made him return to Lagradna's place, in order to hear once more everything Butmel and his wife knew.

At the age of twelve, Tullius dreamt only of the Greeks and Romans; he wandered the mountains, giving them the names of all the famous places in ancient history; and here he became excited, seeing the Peritoun, which he baptized the Capitol; he admired Thermopylae, Cape *Sunium*: and the Vallinara became, successively, Orchomenus, the plain of Chersonesus, the Field of Mars, and the Forum.[22]

At fifteen, he grasped the mysteries of life in society, he saw that men were ruled like horses, with a bit and bridle, that is, by becoming master of their appetites, flattering their vanity, and catering to their passions. He saw the world divided into two distinct classes, the strong and the weak, and realized that every man had first, if he were to ensure his own happiness and bring about that of others, to place himself among the class of the powerful.

At sixteen, he could no longer think of anything except battles and glory; and of all things resplendent in life: power, lofty deeds, triumphs seduced him, and the brilliant trumpet of fame which aroused Themistocles now deafened his ear.[23]

It is here, at this age, that we take up his story, consigning to silence his hunting expeditions in the mountains, his excursions and pranks, which nevertheless all bore the singular mark of originality, as well as his ideas, ideas most children are not allowed to have, and that condemn them to being considered *geniuses*.

The year was 1797. The effects of the Revolution[24] had not been felt at all in the village and castle of Beringheld, whose location made them inaccessible to the murderous consequences of the system at that time. Young Beringheld was a minor; he could not be the object of any envy or hatred.

On the other hand, the People's Representative from Beringheld, and the head of the district which included the village of Beringheld, happened to be former monks, friends of Father de Lunada, with whom this latter had maintained clandestine relationships concerning the Society of Jesus (relationships which were criminal in nature, which may explain why the spirit of the Centenarian had been able to impose silence on the Reverend Father during that famous evening encounter); in this manner Father de Lunada, tutor in the house of Beringheld, was able to keep his pupil and mother safe from all harm.

Now is the moment to return to the head forester of the crown and his charming young wife. This man, whose name was Veryno, was charged by Father de Lunada with the management of all the Beringheld properties. Upon the death of the Count, the extent of these holdings made the task of governing them too great for Father de Lunada and Madame Beringheld; Veryno, in managing this vast fortune, was in his element; he was by nature both an honest man and an able administrator.

At a period when each citizen was able to claim his part of the general domain, Veryno encouraged this first impulse of our Revolution; he took part in it as an honest man, committing no barbarous act, and backing up his opinion with gentle means, means that any man could admit to, with honor even.

He was able to discover the large sums of money the Beringheld family had in Parisian banks, and foreseeing the difficulties to come, he had the presence of mind to send this gold to Beringheld, where it now slept peacefully locked away in vaults. The Beringhelds possessed as well several large castles in various districts; everywhere, one saw this Veryno going about his business, a man made invulnerable through the power of a series of high-placed individuals, who succeeded each other in the Republican machine. Ultimately the honest Veryno convinced Madame Beringheld that these useless castles should be torn down, because their demolition, at the order of her son, Citizen Beringheld, would bring her money without diminishing her revenues, and, more precious yet, would provide a safeguard through having given consent of sorts to the system then in power. What is more, Veryno spread the rumor that young Beringheld intended to enlist in the army as a common soldier.

Veryno's skillful maneuvers succeeded in warding off all possible blows, and the house of Beringheld did not suffer at all from the storms of revolution. One day only, when Veryno was absent, an order came for the arrest of Madame Beringheld and her son as being *aristocrats*; an invisible hand however sent the signer of this order to the scaffold.

Veryno received very fruitful advice from a man he never met. It was thus that this wise administrator increased the holdings both of the Beringhelds and of his own family, through operations spelled out to him in certain anonymous letters, operations that never failed him.

All these preliminary explanations being given, we shall now take up the details of the General's life.

Chapter thirteen

TULLIUS'S DESIRES — ESCAPE IS PLANNED — IT FAILS —
A MARQUISE DROPS IN UNEXPECTEDLY

The year was 1797.[25] Young Tullius, now age seventeen, frightened his tender mother each day with his talk about the French armies, of their victories, their defeats, and of his excessive desire to go and win his share of the laurels that were adorning so many foreheads.

"Am I made for spending my life in a Gothic castle, amidst

these mountains, and living as a gentleman farmer, without any-one being able to say after I'm gone: 'He was a Tullius worthy of his ancestors?'"

"My son," said Madame Beringheld, "glories there are that do not cause mothers to tremble for the lives of their children."

"The sciences," said old Father de Lunada, "offer a vast field where one can reap such laurels that partial misfortunes can never tarnish. Come, Tullius my boy! Discover a planet, write a poem, be a Newton, or an orator, or musician, and your name, my child, will resound from age to age!"

On hearing these words, the young man's eyes lit up; he saw a tear on his mother's cheek and rushed to wipe and kiss it away.

Then Madame Beringheld redirected the passion of her son to another subject by speaking of his going to seek out Bering-held the Centenarian. In this way, she obtained a few days of re-spite, for the young man fell into deep dreams whenever he pon-dered the mysteries at the heart of the existence of Beringheld-Sculdans.

A hundred times over he read and reread the mysterious letter that seemed to have been written by the person who had aided his mother in her painful labor, the initials that served as sig-nature seemed to him obviously those of the names Beringheld-Sculdans. An event came along that countered his uncertainties as to the likelihood of such a fact, a fact his reason made him call into question. Veryno, the administrator, came to the castle; and, making a report of all his operations, spoke of anonymous let-ters: Tullius asked immediately to see them in order to compare them with the letter of February 28, 1780.

Veryno, drawing the first one that came to his hand from his wallet, presented it as follows:

"Leave Paris today, as an arrest warrant has been issued against you by the party in power.

"Return the day after tomorrow, as the danger will be over then."

"Sell your promissory notes as soon as you can, as they are about to lose their value." B.S.

Young Beringheld shuddered and paled when he recognized the large, heavy, loose, and trembling handwriting of the mysterious letter. Soon however, as he recovered his energetic character, the result of this event was that his level of curiosity was heightened to an even stronger level, and that he could no longer doubt the existence of a mysterious being that protected his family.

Finally, the news from the army became such that it counterbalanced everything else in the mind of young Tullius, and without saying anything, on March 10, 1797, he was making plans to leave Beringheld with Jacques Butmel, the nephew of Lagradna's fiancé, when something occurred that prevented him from doing so.

One of the tasks of Father de Lunada, indeed his main task, had been to preserve the young man from *the sin of the flesh*, to use one of the old Jesuit's expressions; he had been able to do so by keeping Tullius in a state of perpetual mental activity, by means of overloading him with studies and projects. On the other hand, he never depicted the fair sex to him except in the most dismal colors; he demonstrated to him that in giving in to women, one prepared for oneself sorrows caused by their petty passions and their whims that subjugated us by some singular law of nature; that great men were able to conserve their genius and their active nature only by not wasting their energy in this material and unappealing commerce. Finally, the good Father, always retaining a weak spot for his Order, explained that what made his Society so powerful was that all of its members made vows of chastity, which turned their minds toward *elevated things*, and great discoveries.

At such times, Madame de Beringheld would bemoan seeing her son deprived of one of the most intense pleasures, the source of so much sweetness, but she found no overcoming arguments when Father Lunada would tell her that her son would save himself from hell by means of chastity, and also that his passion for women, in any case, would arrive soon enough.

Madame de Beringheld would think that if such privation

might procure for her son the happiness of angels, then it was truly necessary that she take the Jesuit's side, because eternal happiness was worth much more than a few instants of fleeting pleasure.

Then Father de Lunada would make the observation that this was no privation for Tullius, because one cannot desire what one ignores.

The Countess, silent all the while, and despite her great devotion to Lunada and confidence in his advice, could not prevent herself from wishing, deep in her soul, to see her son be the happiest possible: and, as a woman, in such matters, knows what the story is, she found that her son was unhappy. She would not dare to touch this most sensitive chord; but she would gladly have sacrificed something so that a woman of high quality, between thirty-five and forty years old, might have lived in a chateau a mile away from hers; that this woman might be beautiful, witty, and that—wise inheritor of the maxims of a ruined court—she would have loved young men rather than men of a certain age.

Tullius, as ignorant in this area as he was learned in others, nonetheless felt what Saint Augustine called the *advisings of nature*. Each time in the mountains that he would meet a young girl, pretty, and slender of waist, he would feel himself on fire, would look at her, yet would dare neither to speak to her nor shake her hand; to kiss her seemed an impossibility. One sees that *lycées* did not exist in this part of France; for had the young Beringheld spent but twenty-four hours in one, I guarantee that he would, once class was over, have kissed young girls, without blushing, or with blushing.

Nevertheless, Veryno the administrator had a daughter in 1781 to whom he gave the sweet, almost Italian name of *Marianine;* she was now going on sixteen; often she would meet young Beringheld in the mountains, but as the one was as timid as the other, their discourse would never go beyond a half of the third of the alphabet of love, and their walks would barely go as far as picking flowers, catching birds, or hunting, Tullius with his rifle and Marianine with a bow and arrow. Marianine and Tullius, having a tender inclination for each other, remained at the stage of shaking hands; nevertheless, the young girl, comparatively the older, was also more advanced in the alphabet; and Beringheld, as ugly as he saw himself in his young and timid imagination, seemed to her nonetheless the prettiest boy in the world, having the most beautiful and candid soul that could be found anywhere.

The tender Marianine never expressed anything without a smile, and this smile became indefinable, by force of charm, when she spoke to Tullius. For her, Beringheld deployed all his powers, his eloquence, his knowledge. These two charming beings loved each other without the young man even suspecting it; as for Marianine . . . the question remains open.

Thus, on 10th March, Tullius was making ready to leave his beloved mountains, the good Lunada, Marianine, and his mother: he was to depart during the night, and he only returned to the castle after agreeing on a signal with Jacques and making preparations.

The dinner was eaten in silence; Madame de Beringheld noticed with anxiety the unusual expression on her son's face; his face was a faithful mirror of the thoughts that jostled in his soul; one could read it like a book. Thus, one does not leave a beloved mother, one does not leave her in sorrow, without serious thoughts, and Madame de Beringheld, too poor a physiognomist to divine them, was still too good a mother not to see that her son was troubled and that some project or other was churning around in his young and turbulent brain.

The young man rose abruptly after the lunch, and went from the dining room out onto the porch of the castle; his mother quietly followed him there.

"What is troubling you, my son? You are frowning, and your face resembles that of your ancestor *The Centenarian*! . . ." and she began to smile, but this smile concealed a mortal fear.

Tullius had turned away; his mother, following the visage of her son, spied tears, which caused tears of her own to flow: Tullius in turn looked at his mother, and, taking her in his arms, he hugged her with force while kissing her several times.

"You feel sorrow, Tullius, tell me, is it so? It is perhaps nothing, and if it is something, then we will be two to weep."

These moving words shook the soul of the young traveler.

At this moment, they spied, in the avenue that passed in front of the servant's stable, a strangely dressed horseman who was pushing his mount for all it was worth, so much so that the steed seemed to have taken the bit between its teeth.

Tullius knew no one in the region who was skillful enough to handle a horse with so much dexterity, and what disturbed the conjectures shaping in his mind even more, was the fact that this horseman, dressed in white, wore a feathered hat that he was unable to recognize because of the distance.

Soon, the horse passed by the servants' stables; now Beringheld saw a dress, a woman's hat, a large shawl, and the androgynous legs of the rider fell on either side of the horse and were shod with women's rider's boots.

In a flash the meadow is crossed, the horse all bloodied falls dead on the porch, Tullius arrives just in time, and is agile enough to catch in his arms a woman who otherwise would surely have been killed: he places her on the ground, she begins to laugh, bounds blithely up the stairs, all the while making the porch ring under the iron of her boots, which were covered by a dress of white cloth, then she touches Tullius's nose with her gloves, saying to him: "We thank you, my handsome page!"

With that she turns to Madame de Beringheld, and tells her: "Am I or not a good rider, Countess?"

"Ah! . . . what adventure brings you to arrive here in such an outfit?" Madame de Beringheld exclaimed.

"Oh! You'll find out in due time!" And the young woman flings her boots gracefully to the left and to the right, moving her legs as if she had wanted to give two kicks; out of each enormous boot she removes two of the prettiest legs and two of the daintiest little slippers of white satin which one could ever see; then, taking the Countess by the hand, she entered singing into the dining room, sat down, and asked for something to eat while taking off her hat; then, she revealed her beautiful black hair, and a neck that seemed to have been sculpted by Myron and set upon her shoulders by the hand of Phidias.[26]

The wit, the kindness, the effervescence—the whole graceful ensemble of all the movements of this sylph, had turned the young Tullius to stone: he could not have imagined such a woman, because Madame de Beringheld and the other women of the village, with the exception of Marianine and her mother, gave him no exalted idea of the sex. Marianine, the lovely Marianine, had a type of beauty exactly the opposite of that of the stranger, whose vivacity and piquant gracefulness had plunged Tullius into the deepest astonishment.

The strange phrase by which she had thanked him for having saved her life, the little importance she seemed to accord it, the tap of her glove on his face, the pretty movement by which she removed her big boots, her delicate foot, the beautiful shape of her leg, the studied nature of all her manners, were so many traits that altered the ideas of poor Tullius.

One can imagine his haste in following the mysterious lady,[27] and in keeping close to his mother, while keeping his eyes fixed on the stranger.

The young woman, when she noticed him clinging to Madame de Beringheld's dress, began to laugh, and exclaimed:

"He looks like a little chick who won't come out from under mother's wing. Why did I call him my handsome page? In all truth, I regret having done so! . . ." These words, and the subtle smile that accompanied them, cut Beringheld to the quick; he blushed and swore to himself that he would show that he was more than just a chick.

"But tell me, my dear . . ." the Countess continued.

"Yes, yes," said the pretty woman, who was eating with a hearty appetite, "I think, my dear friend, that you have heard all about what is going on in the country right now. Well, our marquisates are no longer in fashion, and for seven years now the nation has been looking for another style of dress: now we wear our hair in the manner of Titus, our dresses à la grecque, and our hats à la victim; and there are some women who look divine . . ."

And all the while the stranger went on eating and smiling in the most charming way. Every movement was grace itself, every gesture a seduction, every word a pearl she cast forth.

"For a long time we were considered a polite people," she continued, "and in former times one would have never permitted the imprisoning of a Marquise de Ravendsi; everything has changed now: one fine day, without waiting till I had finished my toilette, they locked me up without even so much as asking, *Are you a dog, are you a wolf?* . . . And, my dear, that's not all; they wanted to kill me, can you imagine it! . . . A young officer in the gray musketeers helped me escape from town to town, from forest to forest, and I came to this region; once in G——someone recognized me, how I don't know."

"By your beauty," said Madame Beringheld.

"It's possible," the Marquise laughed, displaying the prettiest little teeth between two lips of coral." In short, I found there an honest 'citizen,' for we call each other *citizen now*—you and I are *citizens!* . . . this citizen's name then was Veryno . . ."

"He's our administrator."

"Ah, you still have administrators!" . . . exclaimed the Marquise de Ravendsi. "Ours dropped their masks! They're as rich as we are now: indeed, everything changes! However that may be, this morning I put on the leather pants of a gendarme, took his horse, his boots, and here I am. I came in a hurry, because they sent some people after me, but more for the form. An old Jesuit, a friend of a certain Father de Lunada who is supposed to be here with you, this same old Jesuit or Capucin, is now an unworthy representative of the French people, he took it on himself to close his eyes, and Citizen Veryno told me that I would not be bothered here at all. As for my possessions, my mansion, my diamonds and my wardrobe, who's going to look after all that? . . . No one. But as our servants used to say before they became people, the sun shines for everyone, so it must shine for marquises as well."

Such glibness, the wit that the Marquise put into her least words, her gestures, her smiles, her least little attitude, caused young Beringheld to feel the effects of an *incantation*. He could not move a muscle, and his eye followed all the lively, mischievous, and graceful movements of this young woman. Madame de Ravendsi was supremely flattered by this silent homage, this credulous admiration, which is more telling proof of a woman's beauty than the most exalted words of praise, than the most sincere compliments.

"For a while then, my dear Countess, you will be my sunshine and my providence, though I wish you will never have to come and have the favor returned at Ravendsi."

"You are most welcome here," the Countess spoke with a composure and solemnity that never left her except when it was question of Tullius. This remark thus spoken possessed a quality of truthfulness, of frankness, that put the listener at ease." I would never have believed," the Countess continued, "that you would ever come here as someone banished, after having seen you so brilliant during the last ball at court in 1787!"

"You haven't been back to Paris since then?" the Marquise interjected.

The Countess indicated, with a gesture, that her son had occupied all her time since then. Young Beringheld kissed his mother.

For Tullius that day was but a moment: when night fell and Jacques gave the signal agreed upon, Beringheld went down and informed his friend that their departure would not take place for several days.

I don't believe that one can depict, or render in words, the millions of ideas that ran through the young man's head during that night when he realized during that day, obscurely and for the first time, that a woman held in her hands all his happiness, and that all men depend on such. Tullius dreamt only of Madame de Ravendsi: he mulled over in his mind everything that he might say to her; he formulated his sentences in advance, his imagination returned again and again to the mischievous and graceful expressions that animated that pretty face, so full of vivacity and spirit, and he no longer knew what to think of this new feeling that was creeping into his soul.

He compared her to Marianine, and was surprised to discover that Marianine only inspired in him feelings of unimaginable candor, of divine sweetness, while the memory of a single gesture of Sophie de Ravendsi dazzled him, arousing in him a flood of desires: one woman spoke to the heart, the other to the senses and the head.

Chapter fourteen

A DECLARATION OF LOVE — MARIANINE'S SORROW —
TULLIUS'S HAPPINESS

A young butterfly that flits from flower to flower; a swan playing on the waters of a lake; a thoroughbred horse deploying its forces, giving itself up to spurts of innocent cheerfulness, in the field that witnessed its birth; a crystal whose facets shine with a myriad of colors, changing at each moment; the caprices of a child, and the caprices of a wave that molds itself graciously into the sinuosities of a sea rock; these are but imperfect images of Madame de Ravendsi: having exhausted the three kingdoms in order to give an idea of her, nothing more is left to me but to leave the field open, to something that has never been placed in any category. I speak of the brilliant imagination—a gift divine!—that allows one to figure in one's mind the image of this petulant marquise with a turned-up nose, eyes of a limpidity full of malice; a being as volatile as gunpowder, graceful as a woman is, possessing wit to the end of her fingernails; pretty like a grace, but a malignant grace! original, like nature itself. And I am willing to give up my *Mémoires de Bramines de Coranel*, if that which you imagine is not the truth!

Next to this portrait, place that of Tullius Beringheld, having no idea of the tone and manners that make up the code of the fop, saying what he means out loud, having an awkward air in those attitudes that one is obliged to assume, awkward in the compliments that he attempts, enthusiastic, forgetting all he knows in hopes of deciphering the *book of love* and seeming to understand nothing in it; seeking advice from Father de Lunada who was not very learned himself in such things, not daring to look at Madame de Ravendsi, who was making fun of him; finally, look at him, cherishing even the very mockery that pierced him through and through; with this, you will have some idea of what was about to take place at Castle Beringheld.

One month after the arrival of this vivacious Marquise, young Tullius was no longer recognizable and his mother took secret pleasure in the changes that the barbed remarks of Madame de Ravendsi were causing in her son's manners—Finally, one night, Tullius was sitting beneath a poplar tree beside the Marquise, who could not help admiring the sublime nature of this evening in the lovely month of May, that harbors all the promises of nature, witness to its first leaves and first buds.

"I would have never imagined that the countryside could be more beautiful than a set at the Opera," said Madame de Ravendsi.

"The Opera must be most beautiful then," exclaimed Tullius, "if men have been able to give any idea of such a spectacle as this: behold, Madame, these distant mountains, whose pyramidlike peaks stand forth with pride against the azure of the sky! These vast and airy valleys seem as if they sought to restrain the streams of purple and light, the source of which expends itself in coloring these snow-covered heights with hues of such richness that no brush will ever be able to render them! Behold this vale, whose every blade of grass contains an emerald and a diamond, created by the strange effect of rays of sunlight that wend their way through the mountains!. . . and this spectacle is now complete, because two beings such as we are present to admire and understand it. Standing here before nature, next to its masterpiece, at the sight of such magical vistas, how could the soul not yield to extreme emotions? . . ."

Giving in to his enthusiasm, Tullius spoke with an eloquence whose inspiration was drawn from the eyes of the Marquise and who, totally astonished, observed this torrent pour forth from the young man's lips; she felt her superficiality disappear, her soul participate in the ardent imagination of Beringheld, and she held her eyes fixed on his face where all the features of ugliness were transformed into traits of genius and enthusiasm.

"I love you!" Tullius finally pronounced in a voice that, however sonorous and majestic at first, modulated toward a tone of timidity and prayer.

These words brought the Marquise back to herself; she broke out laughing and exclaimed: "Why I've known it for a month! . . . But," she added in a tone that transported Beringheld with joy and happiness, "it has only been an hour, a minute, since the thought in my head passed into my heart."

Beringheld, not knowing that for cases such as this there were a stock series of responses such as *Charming lady! Adorable creature! etc.*, contented himself to hold the Marquise in his arms, to sit beside her, gazing at her with an expression whose description I will leave to those same geniuses who have depicted Corinne and Endymion.

Madame de Ravendsi easily perceived the young man's ignorance from these movements dictated by nature alone, and she began laughing; this made Tullius ashamed and set him to trembling: he thought the Marquise was mocking him, and he told her so with such violent words that they announced a soul in the throes of suffering.

"Poor child! . . ." cried Marquise de Ravendsi. "Come, let's go home," she added with that accent of tender compassion and gentle irony which women know how to employ so skillfully. She took him at once by the arm, and pressed against it in such a way as to bring Tullius's embarrassment and incertitude to a peak; he could say nothing more until they were back at the castle.

Madame de Ravendsi let Beringheld sink deeper and deeper into that sea of delight that overwhelms the soul of a man, once he has uttered the words "I love you," and has seen that the person to whom he addressed these words responds fully to their meaning; the Marquise, however lively and witty, became far more involved with this naive soul than she would have ever imagined she would need to, and she drew Tullius into that vast realm of genuine emotion.

Nevertheless, she did not remain at the first letters of the alphabet and, without going all the way to Z, one can safely say that, according to the admission of the General, Madame la Marquise made her young friend spell out more than two-thirds of it, which would have him stop at the seventeenth or eighteenth letter.

One can imagine with what ardor a youthful imagination and a man of Beringheld's character threw himself down the path that this first sensation opened to him: although his heart felt nothing for the Marquise (which he didn't perceive at the time), because this woman appealed to the senses and to the head in such an astonishing manner, what resulted was an image of a moral sort that led the young man to believe that such a passion was indeed his first love.

The Marquise had subjugated his soul to the point that, as she was now living at the castle, the memory of Marianine was blotted out of Tullius's mind, to such a degree that it was as if he had never known her, and yet, one could strongly affirm that she alone had etched herself in his soul and in his heart in an indelible manner; and, had he been in the mountains, had he seen Marianine, the brilliant prism of his love for the Marquise would have shattered like a soap bubble that struck against a boulder. But Beringheld, held fast under her too powerful domination, did not even leave the castle and knew but one place—that occupied by Madame de Ravendsi.

If the Marquise had put no tender feeling at all into the *education* of young Tullius, she would have played the role, in the eyes of certain persons, of a woman of vile character: nonetheless, this latter way of acting would have saved the young Beringheld from a precipice toward which he was rushing as fast as he could.

The fact was that the Marquise, in turn subjugated by contact with this sublime soul and thus elevated toward all that was noble and generous, herself followed the slope that Beringheld traced for their feelings each for the other: and Madame de Ravendsi, forgetting her past life, the time, the place, and the circumstances, abandoned herself to the inexpressible charm of creating happiness for a man worthy of her, the first she had met—alas, too late. She had too much finesse and wit not to perceive that Beringheld did not love her for love's sake, and, in order to prevent him from realizing this himself, she kept him constantly off guard, and blended with her ravishing caresses an authority such that, while yielding to each and every desire, she maintained a dignity and willfulness that contrasted strangely with her bent of mind, the piquant charms, shafts of wit, and manners that did not seem to entail such domination: in the end, she was a mistress who remained always the *mistress*.

Beringheld Castle seemed to Tullius, as well as to his charming friend, to be the only place that existed in the universe: their days passed in the midst of sensual delights that seemed all the more lasting, in that the spirit, the taste, and the soul participated in these pleasures, and varied them through enchanting conversations. The young Marquise seemed to know all the sciences, and she listened to her friend with an intensity that charmed him. Madame de Beringheld was radiant in the sole expression of her joy. This mother, this tender mother had never spent moments so agreeable, especially when she came to reflect on the fact that the Marquise thus was keeping her son away from the dangers of the army that he had desired to join.

Finally, young Tullius, believing in *faith in the oath*, saw this liaison in a strange light, but one that resulted from the inflexions of his character. He joined his entire soul to that of his mistress, she was everything to him, he focused on her all his affections. His happiness rested entirely on this brilliant gossamer of joy, of hope, of feelings, and of pleasures, that Madame de Ravendsi wove before him. She had extended this fragile net with her agile fingers over this young hothead, who, at each instant, made her swear to love him forever.

Thus she would say laughingly to the Countess: "Your son is charming; he is naive enough to ask me whether I will love him all my life! . . ." and she would burst out laughing until tears came.

That deep enthusiasm, which imparts to truly sensitive souls pleasures so violently pure and grandiose, pleasures that so differ from those of the vulgar that they mark the difference that exists between the pyramids of Egypt and the mediocre buildings of *modernity*; such enthusiasm, let us say, is also the source of pains, of falls that are every bit as great. Such hearts that beat for things immense and for powerful concepts, experience nothing but the infinite: as a result of this impulsion, that elevates them to the heavens, they find themselves either in the clouds or plunged into a hell of suffering, because they are unable to recognize the fine line that separates these extremes.

The soul of Beringheld, as we have already said, had a penchant toward disgust and melancholy whenever he reached any *summit* whatever and approached the end of a given career. Madame de Beringheld, not possessing enough knowledge of the human heart, could imagine nothing fearful for her son, but Father de Lunada saw obscurely a cloud gathering on the horizon.

The state of young Beringheld's soul could not have remained a secret to anyone: in the entire village, everyone was talking about Madame de Ravendsi and young Tullius . . .

This gossip reached the ears of Marianine; it caused her rosy cheeks to pale. She loved the companion of her excursions; she loved him with a true love.

For if Madame de Ravendsi was light, bright, and sparkling, Marianine brought together the opposite qualities in a same degree of perfection.

Marianine, pale with a pallor that did not exclude the timid glow of innocence—Marianine, touching and contemplative, given to meditation by her character and by the beautiful scenes that were constantly before her eyes amidst the mountains, was meant only to conceive, and did conceive, feelings of a purity and loftiness equaled only by the mountain peaks of the Alps. The thousand curls that graced her black hair seemed fashioned by the hand of nature, and when she shook her head in order to chase them from that seat of innocence, her forehead of ivory, one saw her two eyes shine like two stars that pierce through the black veil of a night cloud. All who saw her seated on a rock, holding her bow and arrows in one hand, and in the other the gentle turtledove she regrets having felled, would have surmised that the first torch that love lit for her, would remain alight to mark her final steps in life; that she would be beautiful forever with all the beauties of the soul as of the body. Her father and her mother thus idolized her, she was all their love, their pride, their joy, their life.

At one time, they feared that her svelte figure, her lovely waist full of sensuality, grace, and elegance, risked becoming deformed; a learned surgeon ordered her to do much exercise with her right arm; and so Marianine became a young huntress who roamed the solitary mountains that bordered on Beringheld Castle. Insofar as no danger menaced her, for the forest wardens constantly escorted her on foot, she yielded to the urgings that drew her toward the woods and the boulders; finally, she went everywhere where nature, lavishing its magnificence, impresses on the soul an inclination toward purity, exaltation, and such idle reverie where one wanders about in gentle madness.

Beringheld and Marianine had together contemplated torrents, banks of moss, glaciers, sunrises and sunsets; thus Marianine loved Tullius: she loved him as one was supposed to love, forever.[28]

When news reached the administrator's house that Tullius was in love with Madame de Ravendsi, Marianine's color faded, and from that moment melancholy took hold in her soul. She resembled the lily smitten by a spring frost.

What could she hope for? "Did he not say to me, 'I love you!'" she thought. "Ah! Why did I remain silent? Why didn't I take his hand and vow to him that my eyes could never forget him even though he would no longer be before my eyes?"

She roamed the mountains, she gazed at the torrents that, long ago, they had so often crossed together; she spied on what was happening in the park, she set the print of her agile foot in those paths Beringheld loved to wander. She sat on the same stone where he had been when, one day at sunset, the young mathematician revealed to her, in a most eloquent speech, the secrets of the heavens: by what means and what laws the earth turned on that immortal axis traced by the human imagination around the middle of this globe, the object of so much scientific inquiry! . . . She believed she heard him speaking still. These places so full of poetry had for her all the charms of things remembered, but such charm also had a sharp edge. Melancholy caused Marianine's lovely face to grow pale, and, in all her actions, a keen eye would have detected the sadness of a love scorned.

She understood Beringheld so well that she would exclaim to herself: "Oh, if he only knew!" . . . But Marianine's pride took the upper hand, and she dared not bring herself to go to the castle.

The lovely Marianine had imagined that Tullius's ugliness would keep him faithful to her by putting him out of reach of the schemes of other women: "His soul must have shone through! . . ." she told herself.

There was no dear friend to brush away her tears, for she cried in secret, and the forests, the streams, the cliffs were her only witnesses. Her light and pure voice no longer sounded for those shepherds and goatherds who, long ago, would pause to listen to the least strain of her voice.

Her mother began to worry; her father often took her by the hand, asking her if she were sick, and she would reply: "No, father." But these sad words, void of expression, were even more troubling to him. Even so, a tender smile played upon her lips . . . and yet that smile resembled a flower that grew on a newly constructed tomb.

Beringheld knew nothing of the condition of the sweet and lovely companion of his games and rambles. How could he have known of it? For, always at the side of Madame de Ravendsi, he doted on each shaft of wit that flew from that charming mouth, the coral of whose lips he imagined would be his forever.

Two months went by, and these two months were for Tullius an ocean of happiness: he imagined that his whole life would be thus; his ideas of glory fled on the wings of reveries and dreams, and love with all its charms seemed to Beringheld the only thing for which one should live.

Father de Lunada would have wished that his pupil had not put all of his soul into this passion, and he regretted being too old, which prevented him from being a guide to Tullius.

Often the old man, stopping Tullius in the gallery, spoke to him with an earnest air, made all the more impressive by his snow-white hair and long black cassock: "My child, woe to him who invests his entire fortune in a ship, before seeing whether or not it will make the trip to India!"

Yet Sophie had such a seductive look, her body was so beautiful, her smile so delicate!

His mother, frightened by what the good father sensed, would say to him on occasion: "My son, women are not everything in this world; there are balances that must be maintained; there are necessary blows that one must bear, and when one has not seen them and they arrive, one falls prey to despair. Take care, my son!"

A single gesture of Sophie however carried the day . . . Sophie was so pretty!

If Sophie had said in a moment of cheerfulness, "Beringheld Castle bores me, let's burn it down . . . we will rebuild it," all Beringheld and its antique towers would have been ashes.

Had Tullius learned that Marianine, the young girl who moved him so much, was dying . . . a glance and a gesture from Sophie would have stopped him from rushing to her side.

If Sophie had said, "Die for me," Beringheld would have laid his head on the block.

Finally, Tullius forgot everything, even his ancestor, of whom he spoke no more, even though a person of his age should have lived only to seek the truth behind such a phenomenon.

Chapter fifteen

DISASTERS IN LOVE — MADAME DE RAVENDSI LEAVES
THE CASTLE — TULLIUS'S GRIEF — HIS FIRST MEETING
WITH MARIANINE

If Beringheld was so violently in love with Madame de Ravendsi, it was because he truly believed that his mistress shared
this love in all its amplitude, and that nothing in the world, other
than himself, could occupy her or move her. Tullius's soul was
made of such strong stuff that, once satisfied, his love—no longer
prey to fear nor hope, happy with all the blessedness of paradise—
endured and never seemed to have to end, even though his love
for Madame de Ravendsi was feeble compared to the love he might
have imagined for Marianine, had Marianine presented herself
to his gaze at that moment when he first conceived of love and all
its charming mysteries.

The month of September arrived: Tullius, for the first time in
a long while, had gone for a morning walk in the mountains, having left the Marquise alone in her apartments.

Beringheld returns to the castle thinking to find his friend
prey to all the delights of a voluptuous awakening: he imagines
beforehand seeing her hand move languidly over a soft pillow
which sleep had not yet abandoned; her eyes, fearing the light of
day, close and open in turn; he savors in advance the pleasures
of those innocent frolics that follow an awakening, and that the
sallies, the half-content, half-pouting air of the Marquise, make
so charming. He walks along, buoyant, contented and full of love,
thinking of what he is about to do: he arrives in the long gallery, and, as soon as he enters, he hears bursts of laughter and
the voice of the Marquise. Beringheld imagines it is his mother
who has preceded him; he approaches, and the masculine sounds
of a man's voice echo in the room and reach his ears. Then he
slows his pace, walks on tiptoe, and he overhears a long speech
made by a stranger, whose manner of speaking and tone indicate

a person of elevated rank; from time to time the Marquise laughs and seems playful. Beringheld thinks he hears the slight rustling of the sweetest kisses. Finally, on approaching, not ashamed of spying on his mistress thus, because jealousy, a base passion, never calculates in advance, his ears are struck by the following words:

"Really, Marquis, this air of *banishment* becomes you marvelously!"

"You think so?"

"Yes indeed! You've never been so seductive before . . . I don't know whether it's because it's been such a long time since I saw you last, and that you have, for me, all the charm of something new; but who in the devil would recognize you in those peasant's clothes . . . Ha! . . . ha! . . . ha! . . . ha! . . ."

With this, the Marquise teases, the Marquis answers, and there ensues a shower of kisses punctuated with bursts of laughter, provoked by Sophie's bursts of wit.

Beringheld is dumbstruck; he remains in the gallery; standing motionless as a statue, as if in the end he didn't exist at all.

This scene reveals to him an intimacy that had all the hallmarks of the one that had grown up between himself and Madame de Ravendsi. His entire brain is thrown in turmoil; his ideas become confused and jostle so violently that, as in a whirlwind, his thoughts scatter.

"What! Will I go with you? Certainly. In fact," she says, "I'm beginning to be bored in this castle: there are neither balls nor amusements, and, when one is in exile, one changes location every day, one has fears, and hopes, and one sees people; here, it's as if they had buried me . . ."

At these words, Beringheld advances in a furious manner, and at the sound of his steps, the Marquise cries out: "Hide, hide! . . ."

"How, Madame . . ." Tullius says, his face pale and his eyes wild, "How could you do this . . ." He stops, his voice fails him at the sight of the tranquil manner with which the Marquise approaches him, she takes him in her arms, puts her pretty finger on his mouth, drawing him outside as she closes her door, telling him: "Shh, Tullius! . . ."

Beringheld, dumbstruck and frozen, lets himself be led outside, and the Marquise is with him in the park, beneath a poplar tree, before he has the time to recognize where he is and gather his wits.

"Will you explain to me, Sophie," he says, crossing his arms, staring at her with concentrated rage and refusing to sit down at the place she indicated to him, "will you explain to me this strange scene that has just occurred?"

She bursts out laughing with a playful grace and tosses her head in a gesture full of a malicious compassion that doubles Tullius's anger.

"Laughter is no longer in season, Sophie. When one has totally blighted the existence of a man, one should, it seems . . ."

"But, my dear Tullius, how charming you are, ah! . . . your face is too sublime in its vexation, for me to wish to soothe it, let me revel in this spectacle . . . really! . . ."

"It's not by joking that you intend to answer me, I hope?"

"And if I don't have any desire to answer you, believe whatever you wish . . . really, your stubbornness is so amusing! . . ."

"What! That man in there seems to have the same rights over you as I do, you seem to love him . . ."

"And why not?" she said with a subtle smile.

"You say you love me! . . . And you dare to profane the name, the sacred name of love! Enough, adieu, Madame, farewell, for your forehead does not blush, and the anger of him who should be dear to you provokes in you nothing more than an outburst of gaiety, and my sorrow, a sorrow which shall cast bitterness over my entire existence, means nothing in the least to you, adieu!"

The Marquise was laughing all the while, and exclaimed: "What a sermon! . . . But you *are* full of pathos; you would be wonderful in the pulpit, indeed you would be marvelous preaching to the *infidels.*"

"Who is that man?" Beringheld asked in a tone of absoluteness and with a look that fascinated the Marquise.

"Why, he's my *husband*! . . ."

The phrase, this word, confounded Tullius to such a degree that had lightning struck at that instant two paces from him, he would not have heard it. The Marquise spoke for a long time without his understanding a single word she was saying. Finally, emerging from his torpor, he exclaimed:

"What? This man has loved you, he married you; you must have loved each other then? . . ."

At this remark, the Marquise could not restrain a long burst of laughter: "Love each other," she continued, "but that's not necessary in order to get married. Oh, my poor Tullius! Have you no idea then at all of the things that go on in this base world of ours?"

"How base indeed!" Tullius said with a sardonic expression. "What! You were able to betray a man who loved you, who married you, oh! . . . had I only known that beforehand! . . ."

"Why didn't you ask me then?" she replied curtly.

"So, you are not mine at all! . . . All those words by which you chained me to you, were not spoken for the first time to me alone! . . . We are not going not walk the same path together our entire life through! . . . *I am alone!* . . ."

At this word, which he spoke with an accent of such profound sorrow, a tear rolled down his flaming cheek, and he sank into a reverie that overwhelmed him.

The Marquise made him sit down beside her and lavished tender caresses on him; she spoke to him for a long time, hoping to explain to him, in a way that was plausible and in speech full of wit and original considerations, those maxims that govern the life of a woman in high society; she revealed to him the perversity of their morals with such honesty, justifying her conduct with so many examples, that Beringheld no longer knew what to think. The scene that she unveiled before his eyes was new to him: virtue depicted as a chimera, love as a *perpetual round of beddings*, changing partners a duty, constancy a thing ridiculous, lover's playthings, and pleasure the sole guide to follow. Nothing was left out, the Marquise's speech was an accurate portrait of this century of corruption, its code of vice; it offered a veritable *Cat-ilinian conspiracy* against virtue.[29]

Beringheld recognized in Sophie's words a tone of conviction that pierced his heart; he realized now that she had loved him in good faith, but only as much as she was able to love, and as much as a woman of Madame de Ravendsi's character was expected to love.

Tullius, examining his inner being, admitted to himself that he bore the punishment for having been born too late; he imagined that Madame de Ravendsi had made an exception for him, that the tender heart of this woman cherished him alone; if he sank into a state of deep chagrin, at least one consolation came to soften his anguish: he believed he was the only one she loved.

Five or six days later, he witnessed, in the park, a scene of the same sort between Madame de Ravendsi and another stranger, a friend of Monsieur de Ravendsi. Sadly, he asked for an explanation; it was short:

"He's the first lover that I had," Sophie said.

Tullius's only answer was a convulsive movement, akin to that of a criminal who is undergoing torture, and who, having endured the first pains, can no longer prevent his body from betraying the emotion that the latest blow causes him.

From this moment on, young Beringheld fell prey to the deepest melancholy: he tumbled from that peak of happiness and voluptuousness on which he had been dwelling. This experience determined his way of thinking for his entire life to come. He judged woman to be a creature too feeble to endure an infinity of feeling; in a word, he was cured of an illusion that he had created for himself . . . and it was toward one of the great moments in life, and one of the principal sentiments of mankind, that he directed this his first sense of disgust.

Indeed, he had traveled an immense distance, he found himself at the end, and his empty soul experienced the malaise that an ambitious man would feel after having conquered the earth. The cup that he thought brimful and inexhaustible lay now at his feet, containing nothing more than dregs of absinthe.

He began to curse life, nothing more moved him, he began each day repeating the same things with an insurmountable disgust, and he resembled a machine driven by some ingenious mechanism. His mother was unable to console him, and Father de Lunada was dying at this time.

Beringheld, always at the bedside of his old teacher, and witness to his final struggle with death, found him happy, and judging from the aspect of the Jesuit's funereal bedside that mortal existence was of little value, he pondered life, like a man suffering an attack of spleen.

The Chevalier A——y, the Marquis de Ravendsi, and his wife left the castle and took the road to Switzerland, in order to rejoin their parents and friends in exile. This departure only added to Tullius's melancholy, because of the indifference visible in the feigned tenderness of the Marquise.

"Farewell, my young friend," she said, "I hope I will always have a place in your heart."

Thereupon, she began to laugh as she mounted her horse, and said to Tullius:

"We are on the same porch where earlier you saw me for the first time; in truth, I wish a painter could paint your face of today, and compare it with that of that former moment! . . ."

Such flippancy hurt young Tullius; nonetheless he followed Madame de Ravendsi with his gaze until he could no longer see her, and stood long afterward contemplating the trace that her lovely foot had left in the sand.

The character which had been Beringheld's since his earliest childhood destined him to an unhappy life, and, passing from one deception to another, he had come to the midpoint in his career, surfeited in all things, after having gone through everything, tried everything, and assessed everything.

One easily understands how completely he must have been struck down by this first defeat, which hit him before he was able to see it coming and at a time when his heart shone with all the glow of youth, when all his faculties were being deployed for the first time with a growing energy.

These events planted in Marianine's soul a faint seed of joy and sorrow. The genuine love she had for Beringheld allowed her to share his sorrows, and yet Marianine no longer wept: her sorrow was sweet to her, and her joy celestial. She thought that Beringheld would go back to the mountains; she returned there full of hope, her heart full of consolations ready to offer her young friend.

The echoes that had forgotten the sound of her voice resounded again with several songs of love; the waters that had no longer seen her face now reflected its features when she looked several times to see if roses had returned to infuse their hues into her formerly faded cheeks. Her gaze was more often directed toward the castle, and she would have wished that her thoughts, leaping over the distances, might resonate in the withered heart of Beringheld so as to spread there a sweetness of friendship, a freshness of love that might revive her dear friend, who was the constant object of her thoughts.

Do you see, on an isolated rock, covered with those dead leaves that autumn sheds from her pale crown, do you see a young man seated toward evening on an ancient stone? He is contemplating in sadness the sight of this evening whose events are in harmony with the state of his soul. Nature seems to be dying, she accepts the farewell of the sun that is setting: the mountains are reddish, the sky is dull, and no longer retains that *Italianate* purity with which it sparkles in summer.

"And although nature dons a winter shroud, it is reborn in spring," he said to himself. "But in my case, my soul is buried forever, and for me love no longer exists. That chariot, resplendent and heaped with roses, in which I saw myself spirited away, now lies shattered forever. Woman is unworthy of me; or is it rather I who am not flexible enough for woman? . . . Life is a disappointment, a mere instant, and to live or not to live is a thing of indifference . . ." With these words, he bows his head to his chest, and listens to the mournful tolling of the village bells, for at that moment Father de Lunada is being buried.

All at once a young girl rushes toward him, she runs with a naive and innocent joy, revealed in her bounding strides, that resemble those of a fawn hastening to rejoin its mother; yet, when she perceives Beringheld's eye, that deep look of calm despair and that majestic severity that results from recent meditation, she halts, a look of amiable timidity comes across her countenance, and Marianine seems to ask pardon as though she had offended. Even as she solicits the permission to approach, her attitude reveals that she is going to withdraw, her face and her entire person however desire the contrary.

Nonetheless, at the sight of her friend's sorrow, she leans upon her bow, and her soul ultimately becomes one with that of Tullius. Marianine awaits but a smile and a word before she runs to sit down on the moss of the great rock where Beringheld sits; a tear escapes from her beautiful black eyes and rolls down her cheek when she realizes that the companion of her games speaks not a word to her. Then putting aside all feminine pride, she advances, sits down next to Beringheld, uttering in a low voice: "Love is the science of self-abasement." She takes Tullius's hand, and says to him: "Tullius, you have sorrow! I would rather cry with you than laugh with the entire world."

The young man looks at Marianine with astonishment, yet he shakes his head, and falls back into his melancholy pose.

"Ah! Tullius, I prefer insults to your silence! Tell me, does Marianine mean nothing to you?"

"Nothing," Beringheld answered in a dull voice and with a mechanical tone that made it seem like an echo.

Marianine burst into tears with the artlessness of a child of nature; she looked at Tullius with an expression that said: "Look at my complexion and my bloodless lips; you are the cause of this pallor . . ."

At this moment a shepherd on the plain sounded the feeble strains of a rustic melody; the sounds of this pastoral flute seemed prophetic, they repeated the refrain of a song of love. Marianine was filled with hope.

"Tullius, do you think you have loved?"

The wretched man turned to the young girl and made a movement of his head that expressed all his suffering.

"Oh, Tullius, love lives only through sacrifices . . . Were any made for you? . . ."

Marianine stopped, she feared to make too much of what she was doing at this moment, and no longer able to bear the sight of this sad smile of one who was not listening to her, she seized his hand, got up, and crying many bitter tears, she moved away with slow steps, looking back at him, her face full of beauty . . .

Beringheld returned alone to the castle; his somber lethargy terrified his mother. .

[End of Volume Two]

Chapter sixteen

BERINGHELD *Loves* MARIANINE — A LOVE SCENE —
HE WISHES TO LEAVE — HE GETS A COMMISSION —
HIS MOTHER'S ADVICE — FAREWELLS

Marianine's words, the sound of her voice, her artless ways, the contemplative beauty of her spiritual face, awakened in the depths of Beringheld's soul a welter of powerful memories, and he shuddered to realize that, in the space of a few days, Marianine had taken possession of all his faculties; now he could compare the difference between a true love and that artificial love that Madame de Ravendsi had inspired in him; nonetheless, he resolved never again to expose himself to such a stormy sea without having absolute proof of a love that is eternal.

Several days after this meeting, he returned to that mossy rock where Marianine had come to find him: on climbing the mountain, he saw her sitting on that piece of rock; he saw that the place where he had sat was religiously respected.

"Marianine," he said with a vague sense of fear, "I come here, pursued by the charm of your words; I have examined my heart, I found your image there and it is you that I love with a real love!" These were the first words he spoke, they came tumbling out one after the other; then he remained speechless, holding the hand of Marianine.

In order to understand the ecstasy that seized the young girl, on hearing these words one needs depict the magic scene that opened out before her gaze: a tranquil valley at the foot of the Alps, a village elegantly situated, an admirable view, and a plain colored by the dawning light of day. At this moment, nature resembled a young fiancée who blushes at the first kiss of her betrothed, as he comes to meet her.

Marianine cried for joy, she wanted to respond, yet was only able to make a delightful smile, that shone through her tears, like a morning in spring.

"But," Beringheld continued, "do you know what love really is?"

"Even if I did know it, I would wish to forget, so as to hear you describe it again for me and to know whether I do love."

In uttering this last sentence, Marianine let it be seen that she was convinced of the very thing that she put into question: nature teaches women the delightful art of depicting everything that they feel in words that appear to say exactly the opposite.

"Marianine, *to love* is not to be *yourself*; it is to make all human affections: fear, hope, sorrow, joy, pleasure, depend on a single object; it is to take the leap *into the infinite*; to see no limits to feeling; to give oneself to another person, in such a way that one lives and thinks for that person's happiness alone; to find grandeur in submission, sweetness in tears, pleasure in pain, and pain in pleasure; to unite all contradictions, all contrasting things, except hate and love; finally, it is to absorb yourself in *the other* and to breathe with its breath alone."[30]

"I do love," Marianine said softly.

"Love is," Beringheld continued in rapture, "to dwell in an ideal world, a world magnificent and splendid with all the splendors, for there one must find the sky more pure and nature more beautiful; one must have but two ways of being and two divisions of time: *absence* and *presence*; and no other seasons but spring when you rejoice in *presence,* and in the winter that *absence* brings; for no matter whether the flowers were born smiling, or the sky were of the purest azure, all withers then; the world contains only one single person, and that person forms the entire universe for the lover . . .

"Ah, I do love," Marianine exclaimed.

"To love," cried Beringheld, his visage aflame, and unleashing the full force of his soul, "is to watch for a glance the same way the Bedouin spies a drop of dew in order to slake his burning palate; it is to have ten million ideas, when one is apart, and to utter none of them when one is together with the other; it is to give as much as one receives, but to force each other mutually to give more, to emulate each other in making sacrifices."

"Ah! I am certain now I love!" Marianine replied, whose enraptured pose and the fixity of her gaze would have made one believe that she was listening with her eyes alone.

"Are you in love, Marianine?" Beringheld asked.

"Yes," she replied, adding a look that appeared to *blush* with naive modesty.

"In that case you have devoted yourself to pain and sorrow, all for a glance, for a dubious word."

At these words Marianine lowered her head thinking of the suffering she had felt with Beringheld's terrible silence, when she had come to bring him her consolation.

"You have so thoroughly mingled with another," Tullius continued, "that no trace of individuality remains; you live with another life than your own, and yet you feel yourself exist through the happiness of another; at that moment, you would renounce your faith, you would abandon your own father."

"Yes, my father!"

"Your mother."

"My mother!"

"Your country."

"My country!"

"And at a single one of his glances, at his first command; from that moment on, religion, parents, country, honor, everything that is sacred is to you nothing more than a grain of incense that you will burn in his honor. You will renounce everything for his smile . . ."

"Yes," she said, lowering her voice and blushing for love.

"But," Beringheld continued, "such love is thus the exaltation of all our qualities of feeling; it is the constant inspiration of a Pythian Apollo on its sacred tripod; it means carrying *poetry* in the heart, in life itself, and hurling oneself at the heavens in scorn of the earth; it is thus one worthy of the noblest efforts, the greatest deeds; and, if one has sacrificed everything on the altar of the heart, one is then capable of adorning it with the garlands and wreaths of glory, of genius, and the divine laurels of those who have loved the most. In a word, love thrives only in the most extreme circumstances, and however childlike it may be, it raises its head to the clouds while its feet remain in the mud of this miserable globe."

Marianine was caught up in the most blissful rapture that could ever seize upon a woman's heart. Beringheld, having in his exaltation made vibrate all the strings of her soul, fell into a deep reverie, he mingled his gaze with that of the tender and contemplative Marianine, and an august silence served to veil this moment full of charm, this delightful sensation whereby two beings pledge themselves to each other tacitly and forever. The two held their hands joined; in turn they gazed at stars being born in the sky, at the mountains, at each other. Here and now Beringheld realized the delights of first love, feeling as if, inside himself, his entire soul participated in this charm that is fleeting like youth, like clouds in the sky, or like figures in a fading dream.

But he understood as well that he was no longer worthy of this young girl: the thought of this tormented his heart, which was chaste and full of a nobility unknown to those born amidst the whirl of society.

Poor Marianine, in the wake of this grand love scene rendered beautiful by all the fires of a pure heart, believed she had entered the temple of bliss, when all at once Beringheld stared at her in confusion.

"Marianine, you are as pure as the heavenly snow that nothing has soiled, your soul is the dewdrop that graces a young flower, beloved of nature—I am no longer worthy of you."

The young girl remained silent, yet her eyes spoke, improvising the tenderest consolations of love; she understood none of this, but her instinctive tenderness allowed her to realize that Beringheld was grieving.

This last glance, filled with all the melodies of love, and contemplated amidst the most beautiful harmonies of nature, made Tullius realize just how great was the tenderness he had for the lovely Marianine; he was terrified of it, thinking that this brilliant prism, this union of all delights all at once could dissolve, and, judging his future sorrows by the one that Madame de Ravendsi had caused him, he rose, in a moment of sudden inspiration, and, seizing the hand of Marianine, drew the slender young girl to his bosom, held her tightly, placed a kiss on her lips, and said to her: "*Farewell!*" He showered a torrent of tears on her cheeks decked out in the crimson of hope, then broke away suddenly, leaving her prey to the keenest anxiety. She watched her friend run off amongst the boulders; he turned his head often, but each time resumed his flight. Then a sharp pain caused the girl to feel the cruelest torments, for this sudden denouement, exceeding all that seemed possible, terrified her.

Marianine returned home with weary steps, and this scene of love remained in her memory forever . . .

Beringheld lapsed into his deep melancholy; all of his thoughts shaped by the somber philosophy that was his mark, proved to him that eternal love, where women are concerned, was a chimera, and that he was heading toward a future of misfortune. Nonetheless, Marianine's gracious image, her penchant for exaltation, struggled mightily with the fears and arguments of Tullius: whatever the case, he resolved to end this struggle by renouncing his loves forever, until he found a woman who might give him unquestionable proof of that fidelity he demanded.

A short time later he went to see Veryno, who had relations with one of the members of the Directory, and he succeeded in getting Marianine's father to take the necessary steps to procure for him a commission in the army, as well as a letter of introduction to the commanding general of the Italian campaign. He requested that Veryno keep this secret, and set about making preparations for his departure, trying to conceal these from the probing eye of his mother. Jacques Butmel received a second time the order to stand ready to accompany Tullius, who awaited nothing more than the arrival of the papers he so ardently sought.

Marianine could not doubt Tullius's love for her, but, when she learned of his plans, she cried bitter tears, which she swallowed in silence.

Madame de Beringheld was not long in perceiving, as Father Lunada had predicted, that her child—who at six years would fly from game to game, who at eight could find nothing to satisfy his zeal, who at twelve devoured all the sciences, who at eighteen had tired of love—thirsting for glory, would end by craving power, and would die of grief at thirty if something immense did not come along to absorb all his energy, his passion for the unknown and great things. For this reason, the good father had directed Beringheld's mind toward the natural sciences, which, because they offer discoveries without end, could keep him in suspense.

For the moment, Tullius had come to desire glory, and his mother understood that nothing in the world could stop him from abandoning this peaceful life; that would never be in harmony with his character. His disconsolate mother cried tears of blood.

One evening, she summoned her son, who, ever plunged in a deep reverie, could not dislodge Marianine from the place she occupied in his heart. Beringheld found his mother seated next to the huge fireplace in her bedroom; she did not get up, and, pointing to a chair on the opposite side, forced Tullius to sit down with an imperious gesture, full of a solemnity that Tullius had never before known in his mother.

"My son, you want to abandon your mother, your mother who loves you so! . . . I know it," she said, perceiving a gesture made by her son, "I cannot prevent it, but I must acquit myself of a duty that I swore I would execute.

"The day I brought you into this world, the being who spoke to me in a voice that I could not hear with any of my physical senses, imparted to me these words, enjoining me to repeat them to you whenever you expressed the desire to give yourself over to unavoidable dangers: hear them, my son! I am going to repeat in my own voice those memorable words that only today it has been given to me to remember, through the medium of that *invisible and real* power that once dominated my entire being; hear them."

At this moment, Madame de Beringheld stood, pondered, and then spoke with a visible emotion:

"I can prevent you from dying, but I cannot stop you from being killed; I can watch over you and give you immortality *only if you remain in the same place, unless chance brings us to encounter each other somewhere else."*

Madame de Beringheld sat down and said nothing more. Tullius, on hearing these strange words, was plunged into an astonishment caused, in part, by the sight of that deep conviction visible in the attitude of his mother, and by the enthusiasm that her look expressed. He wanted to question her; she indicated with a wave of her hand that, because of her emotion, she was unable to respond.

The pain that Madame de Beringheld exhibited would no doubt have stopped her son from leaving, much more than the strange warning that seemed to emanate from *Beringheld the Centenarian,* or from the being who bore this name; but, soon after this scene, Tullius received from Paris a commission as captain, along with a very flattering letter of recommendation that he was to give to Bonaparte; his departure was therefore irrevocably settled, and he steeled himself to resist the shock that the farewells to his mother and to Marianine would cause to his heart . . .

It is five o'clock in the evening: Madame de Beringheld is standing on the porch of the castle, she looks back and forth at the place where her son has just been, and the path she has just walked with him: the castle, the countryside, nature itself seemed empty; she is no longer where her son is, but she follows him with her soul and accompanies him; tears furrow the cheeks of this forlorn mother. "I have seen him for the last time," she tells herself, "I will die before I see him again!" And she returns home, despair in her heart.

At dinner, when she will see her son's place empty, she will for several days ask that someone go fetch him: she will go into his room as if to look for him; henceforth the bell on the gate will never again be rung; no one will ever fire a single rifle shot in the mountains without her trembling, without her thinking of her son; the newspapers will be avidly read, and even more often her chapel will find her praying that a fatal bullet may spare the love of her life; she will have but one thought in her mind, and that thought will be a sad one; nor, finally, will she live much longer, because sorrow will devour her.

At this moment she cries! She did not cry when she had embraced her son; Tullius had bathed his mother's face with heartfelt tears, and his mother's dry eyes had frightened him; he had wavered, but the sound of Jacques's rifle brought him to his senses. Then his mother had escorted him up to the mountains: she was not tired when following him, it was only when she returned that her legs gave way under the burden of suffering; the words "Adieu, my mother!" still echoed in her ear, as did his sad accent and the sound of her son's final steps. Poor mother! He who would not pity her is unworthy of the name of man! Each night and each dawning will witness her tears, and her shade invokes a sigh from all those mothers whose sons have fallen, their heads crowned with laurels.

Another scene almost as terrible (who would dare to choose between these two griefs) was waiting for Tullius where he did not expect it. Timid Marianine, that model for lovers, wept in solitude; she had not gone to bother her young friend with her tears, for she understood how her lover must love glory; thus she had wept, without wishing, however, to deter him from his projects.

But could she renounce seeing him again before his departure? No, no, she wished to revel in the sorrow of his departing glance: and, jealous of the mother's love, Marianine, making use of the natural ruses of lovers, informed herself through Jacques of the mountain route Beringheld, her dear Beringheld, was to take. The road passed not far from the rock that had witnessed their kiss: thus, Marianine slipped away from her paternal household and, long before Beringheld had left the castle, she was sitting on the stone bench; here she awaited the arrival of her beloved, her ear attuned to the slightest noise.

It was at that time the cold season of winter, the first days of the month of January 1797; a residue of whitish light, produced by the last rays of the sun sinking over the snow, revealed a nature in mourning: Marianine shivered from the cold and burned for love; the ice-bound torrent had long ceased its murmur; the shepherds no longer sang their joyous songs; all around her was in harmony with the state of her soul: nature seemed to participate in her sorrow with its mantle of snow, as it had earlier reflected her joy with the pure and delicate tints of dawn.

While Marianine awaited his arrival, her feet buried in snow, Beringheld trudged toward the mountains, surprised all the while that he had not seen his Marianine, who had given him proof of so much tenderness; her desertion only confirmed him in his terrible resolutions to forget her: and, mulling this affront over in silence, he let Jacques talk, who was calculating the days and distances so as to determine at what period they would arrive in Verona, the theater of the war, and whether or not they would be able to participate in the planned battle.

Beringheld climbed up the mountain; now, his steps were easily recognizable, and a gentle voice cried out: "*It is he!*"

Having thought that Marianine had abandoned him, and having drunk an entire cup of gall, just at the moment when Beringheld was finishing the dregs, to hear her voice, at this very spot, was a sensation almost painful.

At this moment the moon appeared on the horizon; it covered, as if by enchantment, the vast rocks with a broad mantle of silvery light, which the reflections of the glaciers and snows rendered almost mottled. Emeralds, sapphires, diamonds, and pearls adorned the dawning of this beautiful sun of the nighttime that appeared as if to cast its light on this scene of love's farewell.

The beautiful white and naked arms of Marianine offered up a stunning spectacle to Beringheld, and her eyes, full of love, followed the course of this beautiful luminous planet.

"Tullius, nature has always displayed its riches for us; it approves of our love."

"And you were there?" exclaimed Beringheld! . . .

"Yes, I was there," she replied, "awaiting the final glance that you would cast on your homeland, so as mingle with this sacred love the memory of Marianine, of Marianine who will love you always! . . . who loves you, a little for herself," she said, smiling the smile of angels, "but more still for you yourself! . . . She sees you rush with pleasure towards glory, she has tried, Tullius, to hide from you the spectacle of her tears."

"Marianine," cried Tullius, shaken, but steeling himself so as not to seem so, "I respond to so much love on your part, that I must forget you, that I will at least attempt to do so! As for you, Marianine, I order you to do so! . . ."

At these cruel words, the beautiful child burst into tears, staring at her friend in fright.

"Beringheld," she said, "I love you!"

"Marianine, you think you do, you do so at this moment in good faith, but in ten years, in twenty years, you will not love me anymore, and . . . I want an immortal love! . . . But such is not in the nature of man, who receives at each instant a new existence; therefore, seek not to be faithful to me . . . I dispense you from it. Adieu."

This girl of the mountains felt, at this moment, a savage and terrible form of energy surge in her young breast, as she heard these dreadful words; and seizing Beringheld's hand, she exclaimed in a voice that could pass for the sublime outcry of truth and of feeling scorned:

"Beringheld, by this pure light that clouds must soon obscure, by these immutable stones, by this place sacred to me, by all of nature, by whatever else I can invoke, I swear never to love but you! It is upon this altar, lit by the stars of night, that I wed myself to you forever . . . Go, run away, be absent five, ten, twenty, a hundred years . . . You will find Marianine waiting for you, just as she is in this moment . . . As for her soul . . . though I am beautiful now, I will no longer be so then, and sorrows will consume me. Adieu! . . ."

Saying this, the young girl compressed her entire soul into one final glance, hurled it into the astonished eyes of Beringheld, and ran off with the nimbleness of a gazelle; yet one could hear her sobbing in the distance, and the echoes repeated her sighs.

Beringheld remained deeply moved by such an uncommon outburst of energy, by this sublime protest against his odious thoughts, a protest that the young girl uttered with burning energy, amid the majestic scene that these magnificent mountains presented.

Jacques saw tears streaming down the cheeks of the young soldier; thus he hoisted his rifle and shouted: "General, on to glory!" And marching enthusiastically at the pace of an assault, he swept Beringheld along with him.

Chapter seventeen

TULLIUS IN THE ARMY — THE BATTLE OF RIVOLI —

BERINGHELD IN EGYPT — THE BATTLE OF THE PYRAMIDS

— THE CENTENARIAN AT THE PYRAMIDS

On the morning of January 13, 1797, Jacques and Captain Beringheld arrived at Verona,[31] and Tullius introduced himself immediately to the Commander in Chief.

Bonaparte was on the eve of launching the battle of Rivoli; he was studying the map when young Beringheld entered his quarters and presented the letter from the member of the Directory. The General raised his head and was struck by the unique physiognomy of the audacious young man. He read the letter, committed the name and face to memory, and, abandoning his meditation on war for a moment, he began to question Beringheld.

It suffices to say that the republican General formed a high opinion of this young man: he stationed him in the 14th Half-brigade, gave him a note to take to his post, which was at Rovina, and dismissed him with these words:

"I am convinced that we shall meet again! The future of France is full of great men, so . . . till tomorrow."

By a thing of the most astonishing nature, Beringheld justified the very next day the horoscope Bonaparte had just cast.

The captain found himself part of that army corps which, during the Battle of Rivoli, attacked, under Joubert, the left flank of the Austrians.

The French army was positioned on three hills. On the right, a French brigade defended the bluffs of San Marco, which the enemy sought to regain; two other brigades occupied the high areas on the left, called *Trombalaro* and *Zoro*; finally, the 14th Brigade, Beringheld's, was assigned the center, at Rovina. The battle began.

The Austrian vanguard, having already been pushed back toward San Giovanni, engaged the major part of the French forces. A battalion, where Beringheld was, spurred on by the zeal of this newcomer and by Jacques, who never ceased his cry: *À la gloire!* advanced to take San Giovanni; at this moment the Austrian army under Liptay attacked the French from the left with superior forces; and, taking advantage of a ravine that concealed their movement, the Austrians hit a brigade in enfilade so hard that, in order not to be cut in two, it was obliged to retreat; then, the 14th Brigade was overrun on its left, and, in order to fall back on its right, which was holding, found itself in the necessity of abandoning the company that Beringheld commanded.

The young captain, separated from his forces with a handful of brave men, entered San Giovanni with a superhuman effort, and defended themselves at this spot with such bravery, such fiery courage, that the Austrian army was halted.

Bonaparte saw the terrible damage that this rout on his left flank might bring; he abandoned his position on the right and rushed to repair the damage, for nothing less was at stake than preventing an enemy column from reaching the plateau of Rivoli. Seeing the enemy letting itself be outflanked, he could not imagine what could make an obstacle to stop Liptay from triumphing; and, while dispatching the tireless Massena with his 32d Brigade, Bonaparte, moving away from the right and center fronts where the army was winning, went to see what was keeping the enemy occupied around San Giovanni. It was Beringheld, who was defending the village, and Berthier, who, at the head of the 14th Brigade, was holding his position, while dispatching other battalions to help Beringheld. Massena came to relieve them, and the advantage was regained, thanks to a brilliant resistance.

Berthier, Massena, and Joubert[32] all presented the young officer to Bonaparte when the latter arrived at this location in order to change positions, following the enemy retreat. The Commander in Chief began to smile when he recognized the young man from the day before.*

This valor silenced all those who felt tempted to grumble about the Parisian commission that placed young Beringheld at such a high rank. It was at the Battle of San Giovanni that the entire battalion gave Jacques Butmel the nickname "Lagloire," which remained with him always.

This campaign ended with the peace treaty of Campo-Formio. Young Beringheld returned to Paris with the general in chief and witnessed the honors that were bestowed on this army of heroes.

Beringheld occupied the splendid town house of his family: he entertained the Commander in Chief there, who, at that time, was planning his expedition to Egypt. The latter had passed judgment on Beringheld and did not hide from him his plans, telling him that he counted on him to be a battalion commander. Tullius was dazzled by the idea of visiting the ancient land of the priests of Isis, and he joyfully accepted the General's offer . . .

Beringheld is now beneath the burning sun, under the leaden sky of Egypt.[33] The battle of the Pyramids has just taken place. It is nine o'clock in the evening; the terrible cannon has ceased its roar; cries of victory are heard, and retreat is being sounded.

*[Editor's Note: One can imagine that from here on out we will no longer offer detailed accounts of Beringheld's feats of arms; we only narrated the conditions of the Battle of Rivoli because this was his beginning. We will pass rapidly over the events that happened over the space of fifteen years, during which our armies swept across Europe: we will extract from them only those facts that have bearing on our story, while inviting the reader to transport himself, in his imagination, to the various locations where they took place.]

The colonel who commanded Tullius's regiment has perished in battle; Bonaparte, witness to the valorous actions of his aide-de-camp, pins on his shoulder the insignia of the fallen colonel; then he orders Beringheld to pursue the fleeing enemy, and after that to return and bivouac at Gizeh.

The Mamelukes fight on the run, but the terrain, especially in front of the famous pyramids, is littered with their bodies. Tullius passes without saluting the ancient monument that defies the genius of ruins; totally absorbed by his duty, he runs, he flies, and decimates the remainder of the enemy, who is retreating in the distance.

Once Beringheld has settled his regiment and the whole army is bivouacked, he goes back to the Commander in Chief, makes his report, and attends the dinner, receiving praise from the various generals, and, much more important, the warm handshake of the chief, who confirms his promotion to colonel, remarking that Beringheld has not yet reached his majority.

But as soon as Beringheld has fulfilled his obligations, he slips away, leaves his army sleeping, and returns to the pyramids, drawn by his genius and his taste for things grand and sublime. The night shines with all the brilliance of oriental nights, and nothing disturbs the august silence of nature, except for the dying gasps of the Mameluke soldiers, stripped of their armaments. The more Tullius advances, the more expansive his thoughts become, these huge monuments, which he has seen since the beginning of day, grow greater to his gaze and in his imagination; so much so that he barely heeds the cries of the wounded who have not yet been fetched or who have been forgotten. He sits down on what remained of a caisson and sinks into a deep reverie, contemplating these arrogant summits that proclaim to all eternity that, here, was found the people of Egypt.

This spectacle that flatters human ingenuity proved to be nothing in comparison to the one that now presents itself to Tullius's gaze. He is deep in contemplation, looking up toward the bold summit that stood out clearly against the sky, when a faint sound brushes against the base of the pyramid and makes it resonate; it seems to him as if someone is speaking; he lowers his gaze, and dares not believe his eyes! . . .

This indefinable being that Marguerite Lagradna, that Butmel, that his mother had so accurately described to him, appears at the base of this immense construction, and the eye of the old man seems to say with its vital and piercing fire: "I will last as long as these!" He stares at the pyramids, as two equals would face each other; Beringheld remains frozen with astonishment watching him disappear beneath the monument, dragging in each hand the body of a Mameluke. Without heeding in the least their anguished cries, the pitiless old man drags them through the sand, at which their hands clutch in vain, and he moves with a slow, immutable step, like that of *Destiny* itself.

The moon lit up this scene with a glow that the shadows and the presence of the pyramid transformed to the point of giving it a greenish hue, which contributed much to the effect of this tableau.

The old man was completing his fourth trip, and already there were eight Mamelukes in the vaults beneath the pyramid; at this moment the young Beringheld creeps closer in order to get a good look at his ancestor, if by chance he might come back a last time: all at once, he hears horrible muffled screams issuing from the opening of the vast monument, and soon the cries ceased.[34]

An indefinable horror seized Tullius, the idea of death on the battlefield surrounded by the dead and dying had not terrified him, and although these Mamelukes would have eventually died of their wounds, their cries of despair were too woeful, too accusatory, not to move him. Their screams, followed by an immutable silence, stirred him to the depths of his being, and he felt his hair stand on end. The stories told by Lagradna now flooded back into his memory. The idea that this man could live for four centuries took on meaning, and this legend no longer seemed to him a chimera.

After an hour or more lost in meditation, he perceived an enormous shadow that was projected outward; he turned around and found himself face to face with a man who bore a perfect resemblance to the portrait of Beringheld-Sculdans, called the Centenarian. Tullius's initial reaction, at the appearance of this motionless mass, was to retreat a step or two. He stood spellbound.

"You have not followed my advice! . . ."

These words issuing from the huge mouth of this strange personage struck the ears of Tullius, who stood transfixed as if by the effect of a spell; he looked around for the huge old man; he had disappeared. Beringheld rubbed his eyes as if awakening from a dream, or as if the strange light from the Centenarian's eyes has clouded his gaze.

He returned to his quarters, believing still that he saw before him this magnificent *human pyramid*, bending beneath the weight of three centuries. The dry blazing fire of his infernal gaze, the few movements he saw this being make, were such *incorporeal* things, and had so dulled his imagination that he felt a nervous fatigue overcome his entire body. He returned deeply stressed, and, in his sleep, he did not cease to see his ancestor.

Beringheld had too clearly recognized the unique and almost savage traits traced in the portrait of Sculdans the Centenarian to refuse to believe that this was not *the being* itself.

Surmising that the impossibility was too great that two beings could resemble each other to such a degree of *physiognomical* perfection, and seeing that this being had the same white hair and the same great age as Lagradna had seen when she was young, Beringheld fell prey to the most violent curiosity and could doubt no longer what his eyes had seen.

This singular adventure absorbed all his attention, even though this was only the dawning of his desires for glory, ambition, and power.

Chapter eighteen

BERINGHELD IN SYRIA — THE PLAGUE OF JAFFA —
THE CENTENARIAN CURES THE SOLDIERS AND SAVES
TULLIUS — TULLIUS IN FRANCE — HE ACHIEVES A
HIGH DEGREE OF POWER

And yet Beringheld, swept along by the rapid momentum of the war, and by the torrent of visions of grandeur that assailed him, was torn from his meditations by increasing dangers, by the necessity of being on the battlefields, and the misfortunes of our armies; though not forgetting the Centenarian, he no longer thought of him so often.

The Commander in Chief had taken the war to Syria, and the army was stricken with a horrible plague.[35] An ancient convent of Greek monks, situated on a hill near Jaffa, served as the main hospital, and its keeping was assigned to Colonel Beringheld. He revealed, in this dangerous mission, where the danger brings no visible glory, a truly heroic courage.

The vast monastery was in ruins, only the church remained standing. It was there that they took the sick who were considered beyond cure.

The nave offered a spectacle where all the woes and feelings of human nature came together to erect a Temple to Suffering. On the broken tile floor, each sufferer had staked out a tiny place. There, wrapped in overcoats, lying on pestilence-ridden straw, these Frenchmen, far from their homeland, abandoned themselves to the darkest despair.

The livid faces of these warriors, who quailed before so terrible a death, comprised the most terrible spectacle that the human imagination could conceive. Their cries were but feebly heard beneath the vault where once sounded the futile prayers of the Caloyers. Today, as then, such prayers are in vain, and the vault retains its same impenetrability.

Daylight passes barely through the vaulted windows; it casts on this vast tomb a faint light, a deathly glow, and the cries of the birds that had taken refuge in the high vaults of this three-hundred-year-old building, mingled with the moanings of the sons of France.

One, in a corner, puts his parched tongue against the damp walls, hoping to find something cool to calm his suffering. Another, sitting upright, keeps the same position: he is silent, his arms are folded, his eye stares at the ground, and his sublime resignation makes one shudder with horror at this imposing portrait of a suffering that is wholly Roman, or rather wholly French; he is old: he knows how to suffer.

Farther along, a young man bows his weakened head, he is about to give up the ghost, his hand is on his saber; he attempts to smile, and this smile rends the soul every bit as much as the other man's resignation astonishes.

Another seeks out the hand of his comrade in arms in order to bid him adieu; he takes his hand, he touches it: it is cold, his friend is dead, he is about to follow him.

An old soldier cries out in pain: "I will never again see France!"

A young drummer answers him: "I will never again see my mother!"

"Water, water!" cries a group of parched men that rises up in a body and demands with savage fury some slight relief for their suffering.

Not far from this group in rage, who appear as if they were lifting the marble slab of a common grave, one hears soldiers hurling gibes and insults at each other, in order that the genius of the nation be heard even in the grave.

A symphony of groans blends with these diverse tableaux; it seems as if each stone were speaking, each pillar responding, and this multitude of heads, contorted in pain and expiring, offers something like a vision of hell, a vast panorama of the Palaces of Satan.

Some die while shaking hands, others in the arms of a friend. Two enemies make peace and care for each other in a way touching to see. They expire crying out: "Long live France!" Others cry out: "Long live the Republic!" and these cries of victory contrast with the silence of death that reigns in other parts of the building. To make this tableau of human emotions complete, one sees soldiers counting their money and making the coins ring. One watches in sadness as two dying men fight over some water or a bit of straw; others hasten to claim for themselves goods left behind by their neighbor; they die as they retrieve a cup of lemon water, and this precious inheritance passes from row to row, until the one who is least sick has time to drink it before he himself passes away.

The air one breathes is akin to fire, one hears only sighs and sees only death, that pale and horrid specter which advances with slow steps. It is the Palace of Pain: the dying are heaped on the dead.

Beringheld passes through this place spreading the balm of consolation; he is blessed by those who see him; he appears a god when he brings appeasement, as much as when he bestows gentleness. In the midst of this tableau, one witnesses a woman full of compassion, devoted to the cult of suffering, and who lavishes her gentle ministrations. She appears as a divinity; she garners an abundant harvest of praise, of those touching words that make us shed tears, words that reach the ears of angels.

The sun casts a few of its dying rays on this scene of horror; soon the Eastern night arrives to bring a coolness greeted by a concert of outcries. At such a moment, individual man has disappeared; the enclosure has become but a single mass of beings, and this suffering mass gives thanks to nature!

Beringheld goes outside, he looks up at the sky; his soul, crushed by the sight of such human sufferings, seeks a moment of respite; he sits down on a broken column, resting his gaze on the pile of cadavers that are being brought out of the convent to be burned.

At this instant, a cry from the guard post at the entrance to the convent causes him to turn his head suddenly, and he spots the Centenarian slipping into this house of suffering, looking like a shade that has escaped from the tomb.

Beringheld goes back into the monument to witness the general astonishment caused by the sight of this bizarre being, who succeeds in quelling all human emotions and uniting them into a single feeling that never abandons mankind—curiosity.

The Centenarian is in the middle of this temple of death; he places on the debris of an altar a large vase, the contents of which he ignites, the flame bursts forth and the air is purged of the pestilential vapors that thickened it; a bluish light reflects in the face of the *man*. The terrified colonel notices the cadaverous flesh and the century-old wrinkles of the silent and immobile old man, who is stirring his flaming potion; it alters the atmosphere, and the movements and attitude of the stranger give him the air of a god.

Once the air has become pure, the old man passes from row to row, distributing small draughts of a liquor contained in a great antique amphora, which he holds without effort and stirs with such ease that it gives a striking idea of his strength.

Beringheld does not dare interrupt him in his operations, and he shudders on seeing the man advance toward him. His ancestor has, in fact, visited each soldier, he is now ten paces away from Tullius; he approaches, and, throwing him a glacial smile, says to him: "*Imprudent one!*" Then, taking off the blue overcoat that he wore over his shoulders, he wraps his descendent in it, adding: "With this, you need fear nothing more."

"Who are you?" the colonel asked dumbfounded.

With the question, the old man transfixed Beringheld in such a way as to fascinate him and render him motionless; he held out his hand, took his, and answered: "*The Immortal One!*"

His thunderous voice resounded in such a bizarre manner, that the vault seemed to tremble. One need not be astonished by the stupefaction of all those who were witnessing this strange creature, for even the boldest of men would find himself invaded by the overpowering feeling appearing to emanate from the body of this magical being, distilling terror in the form of some invisible and penetrating fluid.

Nevertheless, Beringheld revealed his willingness to follow

the old man, who prepared himself to visit each of the patients a second time. The stranger, however, halting the colonel with a movement of his hand, said to him, in his sepulchral voice: "Stay there! Only I can enter that place now."

Indeed, he now commanded the woman, the soldiers, all those who were not sick, and whom he designated with an imperative wave of his finger, to leave immediately. He remained alone with the sick, and he closed the door.

The group of those he had just sent away, gathered around the colonel who, plunged in a deep reverie, did not notice the unusual odor, unrecognizable and penetrating, that issued from his overcoat; everyone was watching Tullius with silent curiosity; and the impression made by the appearance of this old man lasted for part of the night, until a soldier finally exclaimed: "What an eye!"

"It hurt me to look at it," said the young woman.

"*He* looks like you, colonel," exclaimed a warrant officer. Beringheld shuddered.

'He must be at least a hundred years old," said one of the men who had carried the bodies.

"Who is he?" another person asked. Beringheld remained silent.

At that moment the door opens, the huge old man appears; he is worn with fatigue, his eye is dull, his features distorted, he utters a sigh, and without paying attention to those who are watching him, he walks through the group of people that parts respectfully: he says in an extinguished voice:

"*They are cured*, at least!" then he walks with a slow gait, toward the road to the mountain, and disappears like a will o' the wisp. Fearful for the life of the patients, everyone rushes to enter the nave of the church: a frightening silence reigns there, and in the light of the dawning day, one sees each soldier stretched out on the floor; one approaches, and one perceives the light breathing of peaceful sleep; a color of health, the absence of all suffering, shines on faces that are now less pale, and all have on their right arm an incision in the form of a cross stuffed with some black substance, which one recognizes to be burnt paper.

The air is pure, a faint odor of sulfur reigns in the building, and the terrible spectacle that, but a few hours earlier, over-whelmed the mind, has now completely ended.

A soldier awakes, gets up, takes his clothes, gets dressed, and when one runs up to him, asks him questions, he does not answer anything, is amazed at the questions, does not understand how someone has given him an incision, and knows only one thing, that he is cured. It was the same for all, and the eight hundred soldiers take up battle positions, and all kiss the hand of their colonel.

The greatest astonishment came over those who could not deny they had seen the old man; they returned to headquarters, where stories that were more or less fantastical were spreading concerning this apparition and this mysterious night. All the soldiers who had been in the least way touched by the sickness went to the church, and the power of the air that filled the place, of the beneficent fluids with which the old man had impregnated the walls, made all symptoms of the plague disappear.

It was during this time that the sickness went away.

The Commander in Chief was alone in his quarters when the colonel came to make his report concerning this unique happen-ing, concealing from him, however, those facts he had known since his childhood, and which concerned his family.

"Colonel," the General said as he drew Beringheld apart in a corner, "I saw this old man; it is to him that I owe my *invulner-ability*, and . . . *many other things*!" the General added with that piercing gaze that set him apart from the rest of men; "But," he continued, "You bear resemblance to him, colonel! . . ."

"That is true!"

"What a man!. . . And what an eye," Bonaparte replied. "It will be the first time in my life that I will have trembled! . . ."

This adventure was hushed up by events known to all, and of those who were witness to it, only Beringheld returned to France; the rest of them perished on the plains of Syria and Egypt.

We will not enter into details about the happenings that took place in France and in Europe from the return of Bonaparte up till the war in Spain; we will merely recount in a succinct manner the things that pertain to our hero.

It is well known that Bonaparte was very fond of those who followed him to Egypt. Beringheld was appointed, in rapid succession, brigadier general and then major general. When the Consul became Emperor, Beringheld often served as ambassador to various European courts.

It was then that our hero, now at the apogee of fame and power, was able to judge for himself how the great of this world lived. Arriving at *this new acme of human accomplishment*, he fell into that state of loathing that usually took hold of him whenever he arrived at any *acme*, and he saw that, even sitting on Earth's greatest throne, with all the power and glory anyone could desire, one remained the same person one was before; that nothing altered the basic pattern of life; that, to use the common expressions, the drinking, eating, sleeping of a sovereign were identical to those a poor wretch, with the sole difference that while the former drinks his poisoned wine from a crystal cup, the latter drinks with tranquility from his own cupped hand; that while the one eats exquisite foods in silver plates, the other eats his rude fare from a clay dish, without a care in the world; that while the sovereign's feather bed is at times exceeding hard, while he has nothing more to wish for, the poor man revels in the treasures of his own desires, which his imagination, constantly yearning for that which it lacks, ever conjures before his eyes.

Beringheld, deprived since his departure of the ineffable pleasure of seeing his mother and Marianine, abandoned himself in advance to the supreme joy he would have on delighting in their surprise, when he would find himself among them both, in the castle, adorned with all his badges of power and insignia of his honors. He burned up the pavement with the wheels of his coach, so as not to lose a single instant: wasn't he going to see his mother again, the dearest of all mothers? He had just arrived at G—— when a messenger, sent by Veryno the Prefect, informed him that Madame de Beringheld had just passed away, with the name of Tullius on her lips, complaining gently not to have seen him again and saying that her death was *indeed a bitter thing*! Marianine had constantly been at the bedside of her beloved's mother, lavishing on Madame de Beringheld care worthy of a tender and sweetly loving daughter: what is more, the proud beauty wrote not a line about this to the General.

At the moment that Beringheld was in the throes of the deepest sorrow and was blaming himself for not having written to his mother to tell her that his diplomatic missions, his important functions, permitted him rarely but short stays in Paris, and as he was giving the order to go to Beringheld, another courier dispatched by the Sovereign brought him a message that recalled him immediately to Paris, where the Sovereign wished his arrival in order to brief him, and to place him in command of an army in Spain.

This message surprised Beringheld, because Bonaparte had the praiseworthy habit of distancing from himself those great and strong men capable of opposing him, and who, by their frank and stern advice, might thwart his ambitious projects; for this same reason, the General had fallen, for a long time now, into a sort of disgrace. Despite this, Tullius obeyed.

Beringheld, deeply sorrowed by the news of his mother's death and disgusted with everything, went to Spain with the idea that he would perish there in combat, and end in glory an existence that weighed heavily on him.

It is here the place to make the remark that such a moral malady as this always takes hold of souls like Beringheld's, whenever they reach the height of their aspirations. He found himself one of the richest landowners in France, he himself did not know the extent of his fortune, which doubled because of the prosperity of France and its agriculture; he knew of no pleasure that was not within his grasp; he was surfeited with power; from love he took only the pleasure, and his illustrious reputation in this area made him labor so hard, that his disgust reached its peak. The human sciences offered him nothing more; we must, however, make an exception of the science of chemistry, which he had not had time to cultivate. In similar circumstances, and for a soul like that of

Beringheld's, life was nothing more than a mechanism without prestige, an opera set of which he saw only the pulleys and levers; thus, when all curiosity is sated, when one has run out of desires, happiness dies, life becomes joyless, and the tomb a refuge.

The death of his mother cast a further pall over all these meditations, and he set forth, in 18—— for Spain,[36] with the firm resolve to leave his mortal remains behind, in that proud land.

Chapter nineteen

THE BATTLE OF L. — THE GENERAL'S SICKNESS — THE
TALE OF THE YOUNG SPANISH GIRL — THE GENERAL AT
DEATH'S DOOR — THE END OF HIS MEMOIRS

Beringheld's bold courage, and the touching goodness that emanates from all those whose soul is assailed by the singular malady that beset him, won him the love of his men. Death did not want him, and this harshest of goddesses, like all women, refused an offering he made so often and with such steady stubbornness.

Bonaparte was in Spain, and personally directed all operations. At one action, the last one at which he was present, Beringheld succeeded in giving himself a loathing for war and for power.

The Spaniards, having taken refuge on a hill that was accessible from only one slope, kept it under constant fire from two well-positioned batteries. Thus defended, this position blocked the aspirations of Bonaparte, who wanted to achieve the total defeat of the enemy, by the most incredible means.

His heart boiled with rage as he looked upon this resistance. Four times his ferocious grenadiers mounted an attack, but four times the decimated survivors returned; they then denounced this dangerous undertaking as the ultimate folly. At the moment when Beringheld at the head of a corps of Polish cavalry arrived to announce the rout of an opposing force, Bonaparte, driven to the final degree of that rage that seized him at times, ordered the elite of his officers to follow him, and he marched toward that mountain of death as if he were marching to a festival: his visage shone with a terrible fire.

"Don't tell me what is impossible; nothing must be impossible for my grenadiers!" he uttered in a stern voice, to the officer who had just excused his soldiers.

"Sir," the officer replied, "if you command it, shall we go back and die?"

"You are no longer worthy to do so! . . . It will be my Poles: I reserve for them the honor of taking that battery. It's yours, Beringheld!" . . . An ill-thinking person would have thought that Bonaparte wanted to rid himself of a general whose transcendent genius worried him.

At his leader's command, Beringheld gave the sign to his troop and climbed the hill at full gallop; he reached the plateau with twenty soldiers, where he massacred the Spaniards and seized their artillery. The rest of his unit littered the hillside.

This charge sent a shudder through the monarch and his general staff, but when Beringheld returned to Bonaparte with what remained of his detachment, he carried with him the germ of a mortal illness, enflamed by the extraordinary emotion this harvest of brave men caused him, all sacrificed in vain; for one could have surrounded the mountain and cut off the Spaniards, who would have died of hunger or been forced to surrender, but such slow methods were not to the taste of *the rash and hasty man* who ruled.

Beringheld and a large part of his division were left behind in this spot: the General was in the throes of a sickness that the army doctors declared to be fatal. His distraught soldiers were plunged into sorrow at this verdict, which circulated in the town; each wept for a father, and the officers, for a friend.

Before the General fell sick however, he had become singularly interested in a young Spanish girl, and during his sickness he often inquired about her. She lived in the house next to the General's quarters.

Inez had loved a young French officer with all of the passion of the girls of this sunburnt land. Inez's brother however, rendered fanatical by the presence of an enemy on the soil of his homeland, swore an oath to kill any Frenchman he met, armed or not, young or old, friend or foe. Don Gregorio murdered his sister's lover just as this latter was leaving their house. Inez heard the Frenchman's last cry, and witnessed his final breath.

This young girl, a veritable portrait of Hebe, went mad; her madness was of the most touching sort.[37] Constantly seated on a bench at the spot where her dear Frederic had expired, she would gaze at the spot his blood had made on the tiles of white marble and which she refused to allow to be washed away; she spoke not a single word. Only at eleven o'clock in the evening would she utter a muffled cry and say: "Gregorio, don't kill him, have mercy!" . . . After having pronounced this solitary sentence, she would weep and lapse into silence. People placed food for her on the windowsill of her deserted house, and she never ate it unless she could no longer endure the hunger.

She made no movement, kept the same position, let her beautiful hair loose, suffered no one to remove her bloodstained dress; and, keeping the same set of clothes, she remained like the statue of despair, petrified, smiling at those who would question her or who would stop; but the smile she gave was exactly the same for everyone, and bore that mark of madness that rends the soul even of the most insensitive beings.

At all hours of the day and night one would see her; if by chance she left her spot, it would be to go to the door by which she admitted Frederic; and there, seeming to listen, she would crane her pretty neck with all her might; her eager ear would listen for a noise no one else could hear, but which remained etched in her memory, and with her eyes wandering over the garden, she would attempt to see the desired object; after a few minutes, she would cry out: "The door is closing, there he is!" . . . She would run to greet a being that her deceiving imagination conjured in a manner so strong and enduring that the poor young girl would believe she held Frederic in her arms: she would kiss him, would take him with a charming care, full of all the rapture of a lover, toward her room; then, she would utter a dreadful cry, and coming out of her illusion, her eyes horribly dry, her face contorted, she would return to her spot.

During the day, one would see her occasionally, bur rarely, looking to her side as if she had perceived her friend; she would contemplate him attentively, her dull gaze would seem to come alive, to take on expression; there was nothing so astonishing as these rapid movements of her eyes between life and death. Darting from the vague and indefinite, her gaze, passing through unnoticeable shadings, would rise to all that memories of love possess of the most graceful and most exalted;, it shone with all imaginable splendor; then, gradually, it would imperceptibly return to the blankness of mental death.

One evening, the General, on the verge of succumbing to the increasing ravages of his illness, inquired about this young martyr for love. An officer answered that something extraordinary had occurred the night before in Inez's house, and that since the morning she repeated over and over: "What an eye! . . . It is an infernal and blinding light! . . . It is the devil! No matter, I will become his servant, because he will let me see my Frederic again!"

She had then donned a beautiful dress, she fixed her hair, and the officer added that he had just seen her in the most sumptuous attire, looking constantly at the street with a delirious expression and saying over and over:

"Why is he not coming! . . . Why is he not coming!"

Black clouds cast their pall over the splendid Spanish night, the plain on which *Alcani* is situated took on a somber hue, a stifling heat afflicted the earth with a heavy mantle, and the windows of the General's bedroom had been opened. The officer had just finished giving his short account of Inez's newest folly, and departed after shaking the General's feverish hand.

Indeed, this colonel, having noticed the profound changes that took place in the features of Beringheld, who during his account seemed locked in a struggle with death, felt that this spectacle was too painful for him and, not having the courage to face it, he left this death room, where only two surgeons remained, who glanced at each other with anxiety and with despair.

This fatal news that the superior officer announced in his quarters caused icy consternation in each person. The courtyard filled with a crowd of soldiers and civilians. People sighed in silence, questioning with looks and gestures one of the surgeons who was at the window.

The General was still partly conscious, and his soul was still functioning; flickers of thought and memory wandered through his suffering brain.

In the midst of this scene, a tall man, of colossal stature, arrives at the door of the hotel, he advances at a slow pace, concealing his enormous head beneath a brown-colored greatcoat; he passes through the crowd, climbs the staircase, and enters the General's bedroom, whose eyes were just closing.

The two surgeons freeze in terror at the sight of the slow and uncertain movements of the stranger, but especially at that of the inscrutable rigidity of his features and the infernal splendor of his eyes. The old man goes up to the bed, feels the sick man's pulse, and immediately casts off his coat and sprinkles throughout the room drops of a liquor contained in a phial: all at once a penetrating cold creeps into the air, and the General, who was dying of suffocation from the heat, opens his eyes . . . The first thing that he sees is the stern brow of his ancestor; he shudders and cries out: "Let me die, I wish it! . . ."

"Child," answers the booming voice, muffled and hollow, of the stranger, with an accent of pity, "*I want you to live!* You were told that *I can prevent you from dying but not from being killed!*"

At these words, the General raised himself in a sitting position and looked at his ancestor, asking him: "Are you Beringheld the scientist, born in 1450? . . . If that is true, I consent to live in order to know you!" . . .

Without responding, the old man stirred his white locks, making a slow movement with his head; Beringheld thought he saw flickering across these lips, burned at their center, the weak smile that a man whom one is flattering cannot conceal.

"In two hours I will return to save you!" said the specter, placing his hands on the General's skull and directing toward that place the entire beam of light from his flaming eyes. An irresistible calm took hold of Beringheld, and the old man, as he left, ordered the two surgeons to do nothing and to prevent anyone else from entering the room.

The surgeons looked for traces of the liquor that had just been sprinkled about. It was in vain.

The old man wrapped himself in his coat, and hiding his horrible hoary head, beneath a sort of hood, left the hotel.

He went toward the window where the young and beautiful Inez, a smile of hope on her pale lips, was waiting with impatience. He placed himself in front of the mad girl, adjusted his hood, and fixed her with one of those looks of absoluteness that attract and subjugate.

The young girl became as pale as death, looked for a last time at the trace of Frederic's blood, and her look lasted for a long while; the old man tired of waiting, called out to her in his slow, sepulchral voice: "What difference does it make to you! . . . Aren't you insane? . . . Come, what are you doing in this life? . . ."

Inez lowered her head, opened the door, made it turn on its hinges, which had not sounded for six months, and she followed the old man . . .

Two inhabitants were witness to this singular scene . . .

At two o'clock, after the thunderstorm has raged in the fields of the sky, and the night has regained its solemnity, the huge old man enters the courtyard of the General's lodgings: the courtyard is empty, he climbs the stairway, he encounters the two surgeons, who, in tears, stop him and make a sign for him to listen. Oh, how dreadful! . . . The ghastly death rattle echoes in the stairwell . . . the General is dying!

With a leap as rapid as thought, the old man is at Beringheld's bedside. .

The surgeons had remained on the stairs; they were witness to the departure of the Centenarian, who held in his hands a phial that appeared to be empty. The old man was never seen again. The surgeons and doctor found the General asleep. Soon he awoke. Beringheld had no memory of what had happened; he knew only that the center of his lips seemed as if burned; he often carried his hands to this spot.

Three days later he stood parade with his entire division.

A banquet was given in his honor, by which the army under his command wished to celebrate the miraculous recovery of its general. It was then that Beringheld was informed of the strange circumstances surrounding his cure.

Some soldiers had seen the old man during the storm leading Inez toward a cave, he came out without his young companion; she was never seen again. The General's soul was filled with the most horrible imaginings

He was not to see his ancestor again for four years.

Here Beringheld's memoirs end: the following is what he added before entrusting them to the Prefect.

"The being we were concerned with yesterday is absolutely the same the person whom I encountered at the pyramids, in Jaffa, and who saved my life in Spain.

"It would have done better to have let me perish, for life has become a burden to me, and if I live, it is only in hopes of some-day solving this astonishing mystery. Weary of glory, of power, of everything, I intend to give my resignation to the emperor and devote myself with passion to seeking out this strange being for whom life itself has become the problem.

"If I do not succeed in resolving this matter, I will return to Beringheld, and if Marianine has remained faithful to that passionate oath she took before me there upon the mountain, I will bring to her a soul cleansed and reward her for her love."

As they finished reading this manuscript, the magistrates found themselves seized with an uncanny feeling of horror; they thought they perceived the old man, and each looked at the other with an expression of fear. When they retired, the Prefect demanded that they keep the most absolute silence concerning what they had read.

A copy of the manuscript was made and was sent to General Beringheld, along with an account of the events that had taken place in Tours, in order that he transmit these documents to the Minister of Police.

Let us now follow the General on the journey he was taking to go to Paris.

Chapter twenty

THE ANCIENT ONE AGAIN — THE GENERAL CATCHES UP WITH

HIM — THE RUINED CASTLE AND ITS OWNER — THE STORY

OF A PRETTY WOMAN, TOLD BY A STAGE DRIVER — THE

GENERAL NEARS PARIS

Having read this brief account of the character and the principal events in the life of General Tullius Beringheld, one understands the nature of his meditations, at that moment when he was sitting high atop Grammont Hill.

If there was anything that kept him alive, it was the hope of finding Marianine, for this soul, deprived of its hopes in all other domains, liked to find solace in the consoling idea of a true love.

But now that he had seen the old man again; now that those scenes of which the city of Tours was the theater had revealed the being he called his ancestor in a positive light; now that he was convinced that this being was a man, an extraordinary man, in truth, but in the end, purely and simply a man, the General's thoughts took another direction, and Marianine became for Count Beringheld little more than a secondary thought; Tullius's main concern was now the search for his singular power, and especially for the secret behind the longevity of this bizarre being.

Thus, as the General's coach rolled toward Paris, his thoughts took on a less somber and lugubrious tone, and he began to see a vista of immense sweep, one that would ultimately engulf and consume the ardor of his soul.

This vast field was that of the natural sciences, whose infinite horizons always leave the human mind in the hope of some new discovery, even after one has lifted up a corner or two of the veil that enshrouds nature. Indeed, the General was unable to conceive of the possibility of the old man's existence, except by means of the secrets of a science for which the word "impossible" no longer has meaning.

But the last event of which he had been witness made him shudder, and he dared penetrate no further into the abyss of the horrible thoughts that came to him along with this memory. He called to mind the words of his mother; he compared between them the various effects that the old man produced, and he came to think again that his ancestor combined the power of life extension with powers more extraordinary yet.

One understands just how deep a man's reflections become at the sight of immortality in the flesh, and in the hope of new powers that promise him an absolute mastery over the things of this earth. In a weak brain, such ideas lead to madness, and thus had Beringheld's father succumbed. It is a fact, however, that our soul receives a grave blow from such *knowledge*, and there is not a single man who would not be greatly excited at the hope of making a discovery in this realm, even one of little importance.

In the grips of this new train of thought, which just now had kindled in him a *passion* that, this time, was to absorb his entire life, Beringheld arrived at Maintenon, plunged in a deep reverie.

The General climbed out of his coach while the horses were being changed, and at that moment he overheard in the stables a conversation between two coachmen, and this conversation was of the sort that interested him greatly.

It took place between an old coachman who had just returned and a younger coachman who was preparing, for a comrade, the horses destined for the General.

"I tell you that it is *he*!"

"Phooey, it's impossible."

"I recognized him, he hadn't changed a bit, and not one of his hairs, white like the stem of a brand-new pipe, has changed; only, his eyes seemed to me more sunken than the last time, and I bet you my whip breaks next time I use it to get out of a rut, if they were not brilliant like the button of a new coat that shines in the sun. That giant there knows a lot."

"Well, the old man . . ."

"Old," the older coachmen interrupted, "I don't think our man knows what old age is, because, when I drove him in 1760, he was already over a hundred, unless he was born the way he is, with those eyebrows of old moss and his forehead of granite; as for his skin, it's as tough as the leather on my saddle."

"I'd gladly give a crown to drive him," the younger driver continued, "and six francs to see him."

"I believe it!" said the old coachman, "and you'd be ahead of the game too . . . here, Lancinot, my friend, open your eyes, and feast them on this brand new napoleon! It's my tip; and I drove him lickety-split, for he said to me, just like that: 'Lad, get me to the next station by noon, there's a louis in it for you.'"

"Lancinot," said the coachman taking the arm of his young comrade, "we made it by eleven-thirty! . . . I even had to walk the horses back. That man there, you see, is some German prince."

The young coachman returned with the General's horses, and Beringheld continued his journey. Arriving at the next station, he asked for news about the person who had preceded him, and he described the old man. The driver who had brought him was in the tavern and drunk as a monk, all the General could get from him was this sentence: "Ah, what a man! What a man!"

Beringheld lost the trail of Beringheld-Sculdans, for at the next station the coachman admitted to the General having driven the old man's magnificent carriage to a former royal residence, which was located several leagues inland.

Tullius, leaving Lagloire to mind his coach, mounted his horse and had the stage driver lead him toward this chateau. After an hour's ride, Beringheld found himself in an immense and gloomy avenue, for the trees were at least two hundred years old, and he perceived a huge building whose surroundings all in ruin testified to a reprehensible negligence on the part of the owner.

The General dismounted, asked the driver to wait and to conceal the horses behind the trees of the avenue; then Beringheld proceeded on foot toward the entrance of this sumptuous domain. Grass was growing on the dilapidated walls, and the handsome caretaker's cottage was surrounded by greenish stagnant water, weeds, rubbish, and noxious creatures. One could no longer see the paving stones of a circular courtyard that was immense in size, and the grass that had invaded it still held the marks of the four wheels of a carriage, which the General noted led in the direction of the stables. The windows of the chateau, the doors, the front steps, the fences that surrounded the walls, all were in ruin, and birds of prey had long since taken possession of the crest of this splendid building. The General could not help lamenting the state of this chateau, all the while looking for the bell cord. It was not without a certain difficulty that he found it, and the sounds that echoed through this ruined shell made a noise as if the building were complaining. Silence returned, yet no one came. The General rang a second and a third time, but still no living being appeared.

Beringheld was already climbing over the gate, when he perceived a little old man come out of the stable door, which he closed after him slowly; the man walked with a slow gait toward the main gate, where the General was now hastening to abandon his efforts.

The little old man came up to the gate, and his aspect caused the General a moment of surprise. In effect, the dwarf, who was at least eighty years of age, had features that bore a vague resemblance to the General and to the huge old man; but his compressed features were of proportions as hideously small as those of the old man were large and austere; seeing this dwarf, one doubted it was a man.

The little old man raised an eye that had no spark, a dead eye, and inquired in a dying voice:

"What do you want?"

"Didn't someone arrive here a while ago, at this chateau?"

"Perhaps," the tiny caretaker answered, looking at the General's boots, while maintaining a hunched-up and awkward position.

"An old man, perhaps?" Beringheld asked.

"That could be," the stranger answered dryly.

"Who is the owner of this chateau?" the General asked.

"I am."

"But," Tullius continued, "I didn't hear you spoken of, but of another man, very much bigger."

"Believe what you like."

The General, getting impatient, continued: "Will Monsieur allow me to visit this magnificent chateau?"

"For what reason?" the little man said, adjusting his wig, which was the color of Spanish tobacco.

"In order to see it," Beringheld answered ill-humoredly.

"But you are seeing it, and if this façade is not enough, take the first path on the left; you can admire the façade of the gardens."

"But the interior, the rooms . . ."

"Ah, I understand, you are curious, a lover of fine things."

"Yes," said the General.

"Well, Monsieur amateur, I am not in the habit of showing them, for I would be swamped with visits, and I don't like them."

"Monsieur, do you know that I am General Beringheld."

"That's very nice indeed."

"If I wish, I can get an order to enter from S.M. . . ."

"As you wish."

"To enter here by force . . ."

"As you wish."

"Extraordinary things are taking place here."

"Perhaps."

"Criminal things . . ."

"I won't say no to that, for it is most extraordinary to see a stranger come and insult an honest man, who pays his taxes regularly, who abides by the law, and has no quarrel with anyone. But . . . as you wish."

On that note, the little man folded his hands behind his back, and walked away with slow steps, without looking back once.

From the tone and manners of this singular bit of a man, the General foresaw that, even if he were to make a forced entry, he would find nothing in the chateau, and that the old man had given his caretaker the means of discouraging curious visitors; he thus decided to return to the coach station, and as he rode along, he asked the driver for information about the castle and its owners.

"General," the guide answered, "this chateau, *from what my mother said*, belonged before the Revolution to the R—x family: when the Revolution began, the Duke emigrated and his chateau was sold; it was bought in 1791 by a little man in his fifties, the man you must have seen, though he rarely shows himself to anybody. He cultivates by himself an apple orchard and a garden full of strange plants and shrubs that provide his food; but there are those who say he is a sorcerer—*You get what I mean, General?*" the driver added, with a shrewd smile that signified that the guide did not believe in sorcerers.

"Monsieur Lerdangin is usually seen only once a year, at the tax collector's, to which he brings the taxes he pays on his land and his castle. Most people think he is crazy: I heard someone tell my mother a strange story about his father and mother, for he is from the region; I don't even know if I remember it all"

"Of course you can, tell it to me," the General said.

"It was," the driver continued, "about a giant with whom the mother of this owner was in love, and this stranger came every night to visit Madame Lerdangin, without her being able to learn from where he came, by what means, or why. *It seems in any case, from what my mother said*, that Madame Lerdangin was madly in love with this giant, whom she never saw except at night. *Do you understand me, General?*

"The first time he came, it was—*my mother said*—a winter night when Madame Lerdangin was all alone; her husband was traveling at that time on business. She was going to bed, and was even in bed—*my mother said*—when her door opened and . . . at that point, General, *my mother said nothing more*, because Madame Lerdangin was silent as well.

"But Madame Lerdangin was extremely young and pretty, and her husband jealous, ugly, and brutal. Jealous, because it seems—*my mother said*—that the poor dear man would have rather let the world end than lose her; and brutal, because he feared that his wife . . . *You get my message, General?*

"Madame Lerdangin loved clothes and jewelry, and the stranger always left her gold a-plenty; it seems, *as my mother would say,* that this giant stranger was a man, but what a man! *You get me, General?*"

The General began to smile on seeing the gaiety of this driver, whose grinning face and carefree air revealed him to be the country village orator, and who, without doubt, used his mother's authority to lend credence to all of his tales.

"Madame Lerdangin admitted to my mother that, in a single night, the stranger . . . . as true as the way I'm telling it to you, General, but I wasn't there!

"How could it not happen, General, that pretty little Madame Lerdangin would not get pregnant? And when she was, she had cravings, and the biggest of these was to know the father of her child. She believed, *from what my mother said,* that it was a farmer-general who lived some six leagues from there; but my mother explained to her that a farmer-general never did novenas . . . *You get my meaning, General?*

"Monsieur Lerdangin returned and resolved to get rid of his wife; he took her away on the pretext of going to a fair, and Madame Lerdangin returned from there completely frightened. As for her husband, it appears, *from what my mother said,* that the stranger had annihilated him, at the very moment he was about to kill his wife; for Monsieur Lerdangin was never seen again.

"That pretty little woman, one night, saw the giant issue from a coach, and come toward the door to the garden of her house; then, she hid a lamp and when the giant was in bed she got up and ran up with the light . . . it seems, *from what my mother said,* that she would have seen a monster, for she fell in a swoon, and no one ever heard any more talk about the giant, *you get me, General? . . .* This whole story is easy to see through, women know how to play more than one trick on us, and . . . just don't get married, *mon Général!*

"Madame Lerdangin died giving birth to this little *extract of a man,* who became the owner of that beautiful castle. Don't you think, General, that the giant's gold helped him buy it? . . . But it seems, *from what my mother said*, that the giant had revisited his son, in order to teach him the secrets of black and white magic: the fact is that he lives in a very strange manner, and that this coach that comes to the chateau every ten or twenty years, or something like that, gives a person a lot to think about."

The General had arrived at the station; he climbed into his carriage, deep in thought, exclaiming:

"Damn, that man will haunt me forever."

All at once, the General saw a hat held out before him, and heard a voice that said to him: "Do you get my meaning, General?"

Beringheld realized that his preoccupation had prevented him from compensating his guide; he tossed him one ecu to buy drink, and another for his skill in storytelling.

The rest of the General's trip was uneventful; and, moving on toward Paris without any other adventures, he easily caught up with his troops before they entered the city.

Chapter twenty-one

MARIANINE IS FAITHFUL — WHAT BECAME OF MARIANINE
DURING TULLIUS'S ABSENCE — HER STEADFASTNESS —
SHE SEES BERINGHELD AGAIN

Ever since the papers had announced that General Beringheld was returning to Paris, on orders of the emperor, with the division he commanded in Spain, those persons who were working at their windows, and who, consequently, would notice everything that was taking place, would see a water-green carriage heading, at the same time each day, toward the tollgate of the Bons-Hommes, and returning every evening.

An extremely beautiful woman, bearing in all her manners the mark of an exalted soul and a sweet melancholy, was in this carriage, with her personal servant. Certainly the bourgeois of the Gros-Caillou district, and the young girls who, under the watchful eye of their mothers, arranged a little corner in the windows by pulling back a bit the muslin curtain, did not fail to make conjectures about this matter.[38]

At the sight of the pallid complexion and the languid manners of the beautiful stranger, the old men who came down to digest their dinner on the concourse, leaning their chins on their canes and watching the passersby, were all in agreement in thinking that the young lady was dying of consumption.

The young girls, having noticed the beauty of the panels on the carriage, and the rich livery following it, were of the opinion that the lovely woman awaited the return of a colonel who was not, was, or was about to become her husband.

The mothers, not seeing in this present matter the possibility of spouses for their daughters, paid no attention at all to it; nonetheless, as the key player always has to play her role, and as the tongue of a mother is always worth that of a daughter, the mothers ended up remarking that this young woman was animated and almost rosy with hope when she went to the tollgate, and pale, almost moribund, when she returned.

The servant of a household, where mother and daughter were vying with each other to see which would be the most curious, took it upon himself to go, on the advice of a chambermaid, to the tollgate, and he discovered that, for two consecutive days now, the landau had ventured out to the Versailles road.

And finally, a young man, former aristocrat of the ancien régime, from the Gros-Caillou district, thinking that the young woman was simply taking in some fresh air because she had nothing else to take (for doctors never tell you to breathe the air until their science is exhausted), this quondam young aristocrat, already speculating on this conquest, sent his footman to drink with her driver whenever the landau would stop, thereby even running the risk of seeing his drunken servant burn down his house.

The young man learned in this way from his lackey, who did not get drunk and burned nothing down, that the beautiful stranger was the daughter of Monsieur Veryno, Prefect and former member of the Council of the Five Hundred.[39]

The faithful Marianine came indeed each day to watch for the return of Count Beringheld, and these thirteen years of absence had in no way altered the purity, the ardor, and the sublimity of her love: in a word, she loved even without hope, and her pride was always the equal of her love.

When Beringheld had left with the army, Marinanine sealed up her passion in the depths of her heart. From that moment on, she sought to make herself worthy to be the bride of that being whose first steps on the path to glory were giant steps.

Her father, having proved his loyalty to the Republic, was launched on an administrative career, and step by step rose to such high posts in government that Marianine felt a secret joy when she saw that her lover would not be disgraced by their alliance. She took lessons from the best teachers. The study of painting, music, literature, and the rudiments of science seemed a pleasure for her, when she thought that it was for the sake of Beringheld that she embellished her mind. Every dispatch from the army caused her poor heart to contract with fear; and when the paper had been read completely, and Beringheld was deemed to be alive, a joy, or rather rapture, took hold of her senses.

Her room was always full of maps of the lands that the army corps to which Beringheld was attached had crossed; and each morning, each evening the pretty finger of Marianine traced the progress of our armies: pins stuck in cities indicated that Tullius had stayed there.

Thus this charming girl badgered people with questions about the customs of these cities: whether the climate was pleasant, whether the French were liked there, the girls beautiful, the city attractive, the food expensive, the inhabitants friendly, and so on.

If a bulletin announced a battle for that day, Marianine, pale, her eyes always in a meditative state, neither painted nor sang nor touched her harp until an end was put to her mortal fears by the battle being fought and won, with Beringheld still alive.

Each day she would look at the spot on the map where he was

to be, and speak sweet words to him as if she were seeing him in person.

There were only two paintings in her room: one represented the scene in the Alps where Beringheld had come to find her seated on the mossy rock; the other depicted their farewell. The portrait of the General looked exactly like him.

Bad luck would have it that every time the French forces returned to Paris, Veryno had been obliged to remain in an outlying district, and Marianine in love had never been able to see her beloved Beringheld in the midst of the court, brilliant in his glory, his opulence, his fame, *and perhaps still faithful!* . . .

The town house that was situated in Paris right across from Beringheld's splendid mansion came up for sale: Marianine urged her father to buy it, bringing to bear a flurry of arguments that had nothing to do with her love, but in which her love shone through. She did not understand how her father could do without a town house in Paris, when surely any day now he might be called upon to head up some administrative office; what is more, didn't they need a house during their stays in the capital? Wasn't her father's fortune great enough now to permit this? Wouldn't it be necessary to take up residence near the General to whom her father would soon have to give an accounting of ten years of property management? Would it not be better to live near a person whom you knew?

The town house was bought.

During this long period of time, a thousand occasions arose for Marianine to marry; several men of high distinction loved her with a real love; Marianine refused everything: honors, fortune, love.

Her life, in the absence of her dear friend, was that of a saint prostrate before her altar, it became confused with pleasure in the hopes that she entertained of later enjoying a heavenly happiness, something that she often glimpsed by means of an angelic ecstasy.

The young and pretty huntress of the Alps lost nothing of her beauty: whenever, decked out in the refinements of an elegant toilette, she would sit before a large gathering, she would ring from her harp all the riches of harmony and of skill, and in a passionate performance she would express all her love and the deep exaltation that sustained her life.

If at this moment the curls of her hair were held prisoner to art, if her eyes had less vivacity than they formerly did in the mountains, if her hand no longer held a bow and arrows, if her words and manners were now measured, nonetheless an astute observer would discern that her young bosom still harbored an eternal passion.

Did someone in the drawing room of the Prefecture proclaim the success of our armies? Did Beringheld's name strike her ear? ... If so she would, in turn, blush, become pale, be beside herself with pleasure. Indeed! At such a moment a young applicant, or an old supplicant, or a man in danger of losing his position, all were sure of obtaining her favor; she would, I believe, have smiled at an enemy, if she had had one! The very name of Beringheld, any praise of the General, all would have a magical effect on her.

Everything the poor received was given in the name of her love for Tullius; she even loved Cicero, because the name of the Roman orator was that of the General.

O passion of beautiful souls, O love, divine love, O Marianine, Marianine! . . . I do not know whether Cicero would have used such an oratorical flourish to thank her, I use it only because it pours forth from myself, and when one writes, it is the least one can do to write down what one believes. There are so many people who cannot arrive at this moment! . . . Fearing that such a thing might happen to me, I seize this opportunity to set down so clear a sentence, one which depicts my thoughts so faithfully.

The death of Marianine's mother followed that of Madame Beringheld, and these two mothers were sorely missed by their daughter, in a touching manner. Marianine thus became responsible for managing her father's household, and she revealed just how much good sense, order, wisdom, and greatness she had in her ideas.

When rumors began to spread concerning the return of General Beringheld's army, Marianine made it clear to her father that she should go to Paris, in order to petition the Emperor to make good promises he had made them. Nothing less was at stake here than to relocate Monsieur Veryno in Paris, by making him head of an administrative office there.

Sure enough, it was part of Bonaparte's plan to mingle old guard Republicans with the old ranks of feudal nobility at court, and there was no stauncher Republican to be found than Veryno.

This was easy to determine, for his name bore none of those titles of count that Bonaparte had spread about so lavishly.[40] Veryno had steadfastly refused any aristocratic distinction, and he was one of the sharpest critics of the First Counsul's ascension to the throne of emperor; in a word, he had the misfortune to be numbered among those few honest men whose are always constant in their beliefs, whatever they may be.

Veryno, knowing the severity of his daughter's principles, and her pride, saw no inconvenience in letting her go alone to Paris: her age, her experience, set aside all danger, and besides, this good father, knowing without revealing it his daughter's love for Beringheld, and full of admiration for her constancy, could not bear the cruelty of forbidding her the innocent pleasure of the sight of her idol.

Thus, Marianine came to Paris with her father's steward; each evening she would go out in hopes of meeting Beringheld, and each morning she would go up in the attic of her town house, to see whether they were not preparing the General's house. For eight days, she went to the tollgate of the Bons-Hommes, and quite in vain; thus she was sad: her servants always saw her steeped in deep reverie, which imparted charm to her, and which no one dared interrupt. The harp remained untouched, the brushes remained packed away; she was preoccupied only with Beringheld; and, when she was not on the road to Versailles, one would see her sitting in a wing chair, her face in her pretty hand, and her eyes fixed on Beringheld's portrait.

Finally, one morning, the little woman was eating her lunch, when the old steward came up with the newspaper; she interrupts her lunch, opens the seal, reads, and cries out:

"He's coming! . . . he's coming! . . . tonight! . . ."

Hurriedly, she rings, rings again, she breaks the cords, walks about, becomes impatient; the chambermaid enters:

"I'm going to get dressed; have them harness the horses; what dress shall I wear? How shall I fix my hair? Which belt to wear? . . ."

A flood of questions pours forth, and the chambermaid is dumbfounded at the sight of such exuberance in the sweet Marianine.

"Julie, the Emperor has returned, he has given the order to return by forced march. Oh! . . . the poor soldiers! . . . But that's not important . . . Ah, he did well to drive them! . . . tonight! . . ."

Julie no longer understands her.

"But, what are you doing here, Julie? Get everything in order!"

Then taking up the paper, she reads again out loud:

"General Beringheld arrived yesterday at Versailles, where an order from His Majesty informed the General that he wished to see him lead his division in a parade today in the Tuileries . . ."[41]

"Julie, go and get everything ready for my toilette. Hippolyte will do my hair. You send for him, have him come at once . . . Oh what happiness!"

She ran at once to the attic of the house and trembled with joy upon seeing a servant in the General's courtyard cleaning a coach that had arrived the day before; the shutters were open and a certain activity was everywhere to be seen.

At once she went down, and went back to considering what clothes she should wear when she appeared again to the General's eyes. After many hesitations, she went and got the painting that depicted the scene of her farewell to Beringheld and decided to dress exactly as she had at that time, when her heart had been so cruelly upset.

A simple white dress was arranged on the spot, similar to the one of the young huntress; hair tumbling over her shoulders in thousands of ringlets, forehead almost covered by a lovely net, such was her adornment, one that memories of love made yet more delightful and full of charm.

Long before the troops arrived, the inhabitants of Gros-Caillou saw the elegant carriage pass, in which Marianine, bright and beautiful with all possible beauties, looked ahead excitedly. A bit of remaining pride, of modesty, caused her to carry a veil, with the option to set it aside . . .

She waits one, two, three hours; she begins to fear. At four o'clock, she shivers, hearing the faraway sound of drums: it is impossible to render the burning and stinging sensation that caused her all her blood to rush to a single place, to her heart, which is not able to contain it, and sends it back.

This drum roll tells her now that, finally, she is going to see once more, after fifteen years of absence—and what an absence it was—the person whom she, in the mountains, in the midst of the gentlest nature, had chosen to be her idol, the one who ever since has been the constant object of her thoughts, the one whose glance holds sway over her soul and her life, who holds all her happiness in his hands! . . .

The drumbeat is getting closer; soon clouds of dust arise, yet their disagreeable presence is not perceived by Marianine. Finally she hears the marching step of this mass of soldiers; she sees their sunburnt faces and their eyes that brighten up as they catch sight of the capital of their fatherland. "Do you see him, Julie?" Marianine exclaims, trembling with excitement, "Do you see him?"

The drums cease their clashing noise, and a martial music fills the air with the sound of magnificent harmonies, the general staff is arriving! . . .

What a look! . . . How much did it express! Yes, Marianine at last looks upon General Beringheld, who is holding in check the wild spirits of a Spanish mount.

Alas! Tullius's calm attitude, his decorations, his brilliant uniform, the pomp, the cries of "Long live the Emperor!" and "Long Live France!" . . . shouted by the soldiers, all this was too much for Marianine in love: she faints, and her happiness has lasted but an instant.

Frightened, Julie orders the driver to return to the town house . . . O happy maid! Marianine comes to, and sees that her coach is following the general staff; thus, an ardent look thanks Julie for her idea.

At last Marianine, at the height of happiness, can now become intoxicated to her heart's desire; at times her coach moves in front of the group of officers, at times she follows them . . . But although she has devoured the charming sight of Tullius, surrounded by officers covered with decorations and wounds, the General once again has not yet noticed his gentle and faithful Marianine.

Several times the officers and Beringheld glanced at the carriage, and they were joking to each other, trying to discover on the face of the beloved cavalier the blush of pleasure that would betray him.

No one could attribute the presence of Marianine to any of those who were in the General's suite, and on seeing the veil of the beautiful Marianine each denied it was he. Finally, she abandoned all pride, and seizing the moment when the landau was almost beside Tullius, she threw off her veil, and the General, who was looking at her with a sly curiosity, was struck dumb.

He approaches, Marianine thrills, and she hears Tullius say in a low voice:

"Is that you, Marianine?"

"Yes," she answered, "it is Marianine! She has not changed!"

"I can see that, for here is her same mountain attire . . ."

Hearing those words, Marianine trembled with joy, with a movement full of love.

"Here is," Beringheld continued, "all her youth embellished by the spark of the summer of her life, and her heart . . ."

"Tullius?"

This simple word uttered by Marianine, comprised the most powerful of questions: thus, the General heard it, and ceased to doubt the love of Marianine; yet the touching girl regretted the severity of her glance, and of this word.

"Yes, my friend, I love you, and have never doubted your love; therefore, I have set aside all virginal pride, and I say this because it was not a sacrifice for me, I felt too much sweetness coming here each day."

Beringheld had, as he listened to these tender words, a pensive air that frightened Marianine, and, seizing the hand of Tullius, she exclaimed:

"Oh, Tullius! tell me you love me, tell me, am I not always dear to you? But you do still cherish me, don't you? . . ."

The General, at the height of happiness, and troubled, glanced in the direction of the Tuileries; he saw that his general staff was soon about to arrive there.

This movement, whose reason Marianine ignored, broke her heart.

"Tullius, if you leave me, I will die! . . . Oh, yes, but once I shall be dead, you will say, on seeing the village at the foot of the Alps: 'All in nature changes, but here there was a heart that did not change, and that beat for me alone!' Such remorse is my only vengeance." Tears ran down the beautiful face of that sweet lover.

The General took the hand of his friend; he showered it with tears, and a most passionate kiss. Then he rode off at a gallop to rejoin his staff without looking at Marianine, to whom life was returning.

She hurried to the Tuileries to watch the General again, as he marshaled his many troops in battle formation.

"Look, Julie, how graceful he is! . . . He has much changed since the day he left the mountains, but I'm not really sure in which garb I like him better."

The Monarch passed his army in review and entered his palace with the General.

Then, Marianine, intoxicated and burning with all the fire with which a love can burn, when fifteen years of absence, of thoughts, and desires, had kindled its flame, returned home. She continued to contemplate the General's mansion, listening whether his carriage was going to fetch him at the Tuileries, or was returning from doing so.

Chapter twenty-two

BERINGHELD ACKNOWLEDGES MARIANINE'S CONSTANCY
— MARRIAGE IS PLANNED — AND SUSPENDED — THE WOES
OF VERYNO — HE CONSPIRES WITHOUT CONSPIRING — HE
IS BANISHED AND MARIANINE GOES INTO EXILE

At eleven o'clock in the evening a coach comes galloping up to the gate of Marianine's town house: an intuition causes her to rush to the vestibule, and she hears the steps of Beringheld as he climbed the stairs: they fall into each other's arms! . . .

"Tullius," she cried, in the midst of tears of joy, "I recognize the Tullius I have always dreamed of!"

"Marianine! O tender and constant Marianine! . . ."

The General had just heard at the Tuileries, in the Emperor's circle, a senator tell about the behavior of Mademoiselle Veryno, who refused all suitors, and who insisted she would be married, he said looking intently toward Bonaparte, only upon the order of His Majesty.

Beringheld, at the height of happiness, had rushed away to cast himself at Marianine's feet.

She herself was too happy to scold him about his silence, or about the fact that he had not written a single line that might have consoled her poor heart; no, she held his hand in hers and contemplated him in sweet ecstasy: it seems that the moment when they parted was so close to the present moment that the interval between was abolished, and that there had never been an absence. Their hearts are young in feelings, they have lost nothing despite the distance of place and time, and they now open up each to the other.

"Marianine," the General says at last, "your father is about to receive the order to come to Paris, to take a high administrative post. But, my dear friend, I will be leaving soon; the Emperor has refused to accept my resignation and has ordered me to the Russian front,[42] to put a stop to the recent problems there. Upon my return, Marianine, and I hope it will be soon, I will marry you."

A glance was Beringheld's reward, but what a glance!

"I swear," he continued, "to never have another wife but you . . . I swear it simply, without infusing it with the same charming enthusiasm by which a certain young girl, formerly, enflamed her delirious promises, those she proclaimed to the summits of the Alps."

Remembering this, Marianine saw that she had at times occupied a place in his memory, and carried the warrior hand of her friend to her grateful lips, placing on it a grateful kiss. What a delightful proof of love!

"Tullius," she said, "why must we postpone our happiness? I don't know, but to delay seems to be courting misfortune: one always fears not to get there when one has desired to do so for so long."

The naïveté of those words, the sweet exaltation of Marianine, the simplicity of her soul, aroused in the General an emotion unlike that any woman had ever given him.

"You are," he says, "the woman of my heart, of my thoughts, the only thing that can make me want to live! And so, Marianine, I make you the mistress of my being . . . command me!"

"It's for to me to obey," she said, with the docility of a child, and the pliant submission of a woman. "I fear I have asked too much." But her glance was gaining a hold over him.

"No, no," Tullius exclaimed, "I will return to the castle, and I will incur disgrace in the eyes of the Emperor, rather than cause you the least pain."

"Beringheld, if you can serve your country, I will wait! Three thousand Frenchmen should not suffer for one woman's love. Nevertheless," she spoke with a charming smile, "if we could reconcile the two . . . Ah! I would be very happy . . . I would follow with the army . . . What would I not do for you!"

Beringheld kissed Marianine, said farewell, and returned home. Marianine watched him as he crossed his courtyard; she followed his light up the staircase, she was not able to sleep all night. Her happiness overwhelmed her.

The next day the General went to the Tuileries. He returned

to dine with Marianine, and as soon as he entered, his troubled brow told the little woman that his efforts had been in vain. The color left her face.

"Marianine, His Majesty is taking me in his carriage; he has promised to make me a Field Marshall . . . I don't know if I will be eight days more in Paris."

The eyes of the General's tender friend filled with tears.

"Tullius, how wretched I am . . . I foresee only danger and suffering." Marianine became sad, but her sadness was offset by her happiness in seeing Beringheld.

"What shall we do?" Tullius asked her.

"Let us get married as soon as possible!" . . . she responded, with one of those smiles that would intoxicate a Stoic.

"Ah, my dear friend, who more than I would wish that?"

"I do! . . ." she added, "for I love you with all the love possible; something inside me torments and casts a pall over my heart: yes, I believe that these fleeting moments shall be the last of my life . . . When I came into this world, Lagradna predicted that I would die unhappy, and that an old man would torment me . . . I don't know, but at this moment, when you announce to me these new delays, something I cannot define brings about a slight shiver in my soul: it is the trembling of nature at the approach of a storm. This cruel war, your courage, all this frightens me . . . If at least I could be at your side! . . . if only I could follow you . . . I would have to be your wife . . . Do you hear me, Tullius, Tullius?"

"Your words make me shudder! But," he said with a slight movement of his head, "I forget that you are a *woman*, and that I am a man; these little superstitions are part of your charms . . . However, Marianine, you have frightened me, because it was *you* who spoke."

"I won't talk anymore," she answered, "because all I really want is to bring pleasure to your heart. I hope at least we will profit from this week to see this famous city of Paris, the rival of Athens of yore, and of Rome today!"

"Yes, my love, yes! . . . there is more, I'm going to obtain a dispensation from the Chief Justice for our union; and if the Emperor joins in agreement, perhaps he will marry us in the Tuileries, in its chapel, before I leave."

Marianine was in a veritable ecstasy! . . .

Nonetheless, we must not forget to take account of one of the main circumstances of the General's interview with Bonaparte. Tullius gave him all the documents that pertained to the huge old man. Once Napoleon had considered all that is discussed in these papers, once he had gone through the descriptions we readers have already read at the beginning of this work, he gave Beringheld an indefinable smile. Like all great men, Bonaparte was superstitious, and his smile encompassed a number of thoughts . . . Did he have knowledge of the powers of Beringheld-the *Centenarian's* mind? Did he desire to possess them himself? . . . We have no answers to any of these questions, and the General, to whom we owe these thoughts, never again heard Bonaparte mention this extraordinary man.

Whatever the case, the Emperor gave the order at once to seek out the *Centenarian* with the greatest thoroughness, and whatever suspicions might surround him, to do him no harm, to treat him with distinction. In everything that he set to paper, one easily saw that he attached great importance to the arrest of this singular person; but, he testified to none of this in writing.

Some time later, the Prefect in Bordeaux informed him, in a telegraphed message, that before the order of His Majesty had arrived, the huge old man in question, displaying an order from the Emperor, which forbade anyone from hindering his movements in any way, and so on and so forth, had embarked on a launch which carried him to an English vessel. The Prefect, not knowing whether His Majesty might be sending this extraordinary being on some secret mission, let him depart, not daring to retain him . . .

Bonaparte seemed quite concerned at this news, and instructions were sent to the headquarters of the Imperial Police. The safe conduct carried by the *Centenarian* was henceforth to be considered null and void, and a secret injunction sent to all authorities to apprehend this new *Proteus*, and send him to the Emperor, no matter where he might be.

The week of General Beringheld's stay in Paris was spent with Marianine: his time was divided between her and the Château des Tuileries, where important decisions were being made. From these discussions that took place, the Emperor gained a high opinion of Beringheld, and such tacit recognition of Tullius's merits only served to confirm the promise to give him the first commission of field marshal that might become available.

Marianine's father soon arrived, he made his reports to the General, and this worthy father was overjoyed, when he saw that absence had not altered Tullius's feelings for Marianine, and that the honors, glory, riches, had not altered the brilliant personality of his friend. This old man, who looked like one of those Romans, one of those old republicans born from the strokes of Corneille and of David,[43] smiled at the future happiness that such tender passion presaged.

This week was, in Marianine's life, the first moment of real happiness she had ever enjoyed. The young woman savored the delights of a pure existence, of a full life, and this pleasure bore no resemblance to any other human pleasure, pleasures that are always tainted by a touch of bitterness, for Beringheld now entertained the hope of marrying Marianine. Bonaparte joyfully consented to this union, which married the blood of a patriot to the blood of the ancient line of Beringheld, that antique pillar of the feudal system. The order was given to the Chief Justice to dispense with the necessity of posting bans.

Marianine was introduced everywhere as the fiancée of the illustrious General; celebrated by all the Court, admired, praised by the Emperor himself, Marianine swam in a sea of bliss.

French society saw her in the company of her friend. Where before they had more than once felt their hearts beat in unison before the magnificent spectacle of nature in the Alps, now together they admired the splendid interiors of the Parisian theater, and in their praise, their enthusiasm, they were in perfect harmony with each other. She visited the monuments of our capital, leaning on the arm of her lover, as he had so long wished.

Sitting side by side, in the same carriage, swift horses carried them through this city so full of sights, and the dizzying motion that caught them up still could not prevent their two hearts from feeling alone. Amid the sublime thoughts of three centuries, contemplating the museum itself, this great monument erected by artists of all the ages of modernity, Marianine held tightly to Tullius's arm, looked at him with an expression that said everything, as she stood before either Poussin's *I Too Was in Arcadia*, or the paintings of Raphael. A head of Correggio's, of Guido Reni's, of Francesco Albani's, sufficed to offer the two a quiet feast of love.[44] Nothing else expresses the beauty of a true union of souls as does such mutual admiration, such *spontaneity* of thought, in the presence of the great works of man.

Finally, what crowned Marianine's joy, was that a difficulty, suddenly raised by a German court, halted the Emperor's departure, and now she truly conceived the hope of marrying Beringheld; the latter shared her hope, for he believed that the departure of Bonaparte might be even more delayed than his Majesty had foreseen; he imagined that only a letter to the Court of B——, written in his all-powerful hand, could suffice to remove all obstacles. One can thus picture the celestial joy felt by tender Marianine. She slept no more; and, every day her heart fell prey to a cruel excitement, as she saw that day diminish the lapse of time required by the law. In her desires she bore exact resemblance to Tantalus, who at each moment lunges in vain to drink the water that could quench his thirst.

At last the day was near.

All gathered, one morning, in the sumptuous dining room of the General's town house; they were in the midst of eating, and had abandoned themselves to the charms of this impending bliss. The goddess of joy herself was pouring the wine, she gave inspiration to the conversation, the words of love, the glances . . . All of a sudden, one of Bonaparte's aides-de-camp entered, saluted, and hand on cap, spoke:

"General," he said, "His Excellency sends me to tell you that all opposition from the Court at B—— has been resolved thanks to the skill of our ambassador."

"What is it?" Marianine asked, pale and trembling.

"The Emperor, General, leaves at four o'clock, and has reserved a seat in his carriage for you, in order to communicate his instructions to you en route as to what you will need to do . . . It is your army corps that will begin operations . . ." The aide-de-camp withdrew, and his horse was heard in the courtyard rushing away at full gallop.

What a sudden fall from the heights of joy to the depths of despair!

Marianine did not have even the strength left to curse the skill of that meddling diplomat. She no longer had the luxury to wish for new complications, for her lovely head, as if frozen, sank upon the breast of Beringheld, and she remained there, pale, downcast, like the sweet leaf of a white rose that the wind had cast upon the foliage of an oak. At first, she did not sigh, she wept not a tear, dared not even look at Tullius.

This latter looked mournfully at Veryno, and the old man fell silent. The graceful goddess of pleasure, that had intoxicated them, had abandoned this place for another, and the pain that follows reigns in her stead! . . .

When at last Tullius made a movement, Marianine, raising up her noble head, uttered a cry of dread.

"Can I not follow you, my friend?" she exclaimed; and her eye was dry with desperation.

"That cannot be! Marianine, the Emperor wouldn't allow it."

"Here is what I call a master!" exclaimed Veryno.

"But," the General continued, "once our armies have regained their illustrious position, I will return at once."

"Shall we ever see each other again? . . ." she said sadly: "I've been so happy that I fear that fortune toys with us! . . ."

How can one describe the looks by which she blasted each of his preparations for departure?

When the General, dressed in traveling clothes, came to take her in his arms, when he came to place his farewell kiss on her bloodless lips, Marianine wept, and wrapped herself around his arms, as if not wishing to be torn away from Tullius.

The gentle superstitions of fearful Marianine cast upon this farewell a veil of suffering, and made it painful to bear.

"Remember, Tullius!" she cried. "Remember my premonition!"

"Marianine, take heart!" answered Beringheld; and he took her on his knee, caressed her lovely hair, holding forth with a long speech, filled of love and consolation.

She believed him, for he believed everything the General said to her; when, however, he climbed into his coach to go to the Tuileries, she leapt into her own carriage, saying:

"I want to be with you right up to the last minute! . . . Alas, it may be truly the last minute for us!"

The two coaches entered the courtyard of the Tuileries; and the warrior's lover, casting an reproachful look at the Emperor, who smiled at her sweetly, gave Beringheld a final intense look, and the imperial coach whisked him away.

For a long time, the young lady remained standing at that spot where the carriage had been; finally, she returned home, pale, downtrodden, without strength, and near sickness; all had become unbearable to her. The first week she spent in a state of morbid melancholy, viewing over and over in her mind the parting gesture of the hand that the General had addressed to her, as the carriage of Bonaparte swept him away with the speed of thunder; her soul had foreseen this misfortune, as in nature the coming of a storm.

The poor child, her eye fixed on a map of Russia, would wander in those forests so fatal to the French army. Beringheld's name was constantly on her lips. Finally she fell seriously ill, when, at the end of six months, she realized that the General was not coming back, and that perilous actions and bloody combats were taking place each and every day.

At this moment, misfortune seemed to have cast all its darts, one after the other; and, in an increase of fury, now the blows follow each other in ever crueler manner.

Half of Veryno's fortune had been invested in the undertakings of a famous banker. This latter absconded, leaving his business in the most acute disarray: he was declared bankrupt.

For a long while Veryno, who had purchased property that had been formerly owned by the state, was now in litigation with the Crown over the right of ownership to his main acquisition: he lost his trial at the Imperial Court, at the moment when he believed the Emperor's protection would have put an end to the litigation. He hurriedly appealed, and wrote to Beringheld to have him intervene on his behalf with the Emperor.

The General, in one of the bloodiest battles of the campaign, had been seriously wounded and taken prisoner. This news carried Marianine's dismay to its heights: she no longer got out of bed, and a violent fever took hold of her ravaged body.

It was during these unfortunate circumstances that the final blow of fate struck her father and reduced him to despair.

He had been the intimate friend of certain generals, who at that moment were attempting to mount a conspiracy against Bonaparte; the goal of this conspiracy was to reinstate a Republican government. Without being totally involved in this conspiracy, Veryno was in the confidence of these generals, and saw with a secret joy an enterprise whose object was the freedom of France. Veryno, ever faithful to his principles, had never hidden his leanings, even at assemblies and at Court. This steadfastness of opinion had won for him the esteem of all honest men, and his commoner's name, his buttonhole free of decorations, the services that he declared having rendered to the motherland alone, all were proof of his enthusiastic adherence to the Republican ideal.

The conspiracy was soon unmasked, and its conclusion fatal to all conspirators, as all Paris learned, at once almost, of their undertaking, their conviction, and their death. Bonaparte gave the order to try Veryno, whom he stripped of office, unless he would accept to go into voluntary exile.

The Minister of Police informed Veryno, through a mutual friend, to leave the country at once and wait until the Emperor's anger had passed, promising that he would do all he could to appease him and ensure Veryno's return, taking upon himself the justification of his actions. As one would certainly expect, following all this, Bonaparte rejected Veryno's request for an appeal in the matter concerning the lawsuit over the contested property of B——, and the Court of Appeals upheld the earlier verdict.

Marianine was near to dying and could not accompany her father: she stayed behind in Paris, sold their town house, gathered together what remained of her father's fortune, liquidated his brilliant livery, dismissed the servants, who all said goodbye with tears in their eyes, and retaining only her Julie, she modestly took the public coach and went to join her father as soon as her health would permit it. Amidst these sorrows, the most poignant of all was to have no news at all from Beringheld, whom her unbridled imagination depicted in exile somewhere in Siberia, suffering, dying of cold, of fatigue, of sickness, or from his wounds.

Veryno had taken refuge in Switzerland; the presence there of his cherished daughter acted like a soothing balm on the wounds of this respectable old man. He had chosen a modest sanctuary, a small house in the mountains; he tended his own garden, Julie did her best to keep the house in order; and Marianine, in this cruel situation, mustered a rare courage, the sort of courage common to a contemplative personality. She sought to overcome her pain, in order not to add to the misery of her father by exposing him to the pangs of love; this latter however, detecting the rouge his daughter used to enhance her colors, was only grieved all the more!

Marianine was like a young flower that a worm eats away at its root: she was elegant, and still retained some of her colors, but she was unable to prevent the onset of paleness: she withered despite the sunshine, and finally succumbed. Marianine wept in solitude; her attentions for her father bore a stamp of melancholy that nothing could erase. Despite her desire to sing happy songs, she could only come forth, in an involuntary manner, with a few sad sounds; and when all three gathered in the evening beneath the poplars that were before the door, they awaited the end of the day as they listened to the strains of Marianine's harp.

Newspapers were beyond their means now: Marianine's father went on foot every three days and read them in the neighboring town. And so, the young girl, full of anxiety, pale, would go out on the road to meet her father, she would sit on a rock that resembled the rock in the Alps, and whenever she spied the white locks of the old man in the distance, she would spontaneously rush to him; but when she saw the sadness in that paternal face, she would weep, would dare not ask a question, and, when later, back home, she would finally gather the courage to ask:

"Well, father?"

Veryno would answer her in his sad voice:

"There's nothing, my daughter."

Marianine would play no music that night; Julie and Veryno would not speak a word; and the moon would surprise this silent group beneath the poplars, that alone were murmuring their airy complaints.

Six months went by like this: the old man, resigned to his fate, suffering to see his daughter cruelly wasting away; and Marianine, for her part, seeing with joy the marble of the tomb open wide to receive her. Nonetheless, this house of misfortune retained its dignity: the strictest cleanliness replaced luxury; Marianine, clad like a peasant girl, spent time making lace; Veryno cultivated his garden with feeble hands; and all, sharing equally the burden of misery, would have found that burden light, had Marianine's heart not been surfeited with suffering. Now and then she would smile, as if seeking, through this semblance of joy, to lessen the melancholy of a soul near death. But what a smile it was!. . . Her father would turn away his eyes, and Julie would burst out crying! . . . Marianine did not complain, and yet heartrending cries would have been more bearable than her somber and courageous behavior. A great effort was made never to pronounce the name of Tullius or of Beringheld.

However, at night, her harp had barely sounded beneath the beautiful poplar trees, when his memory and his image would preside over this small assembly. Often, Marianine, thinking she was alone, would cry out, fixing at a point in empty space the form of a cherished object, conjured with the power of her imagination.

"You hear me, do you not? . . . You are thinking of me!" . . .

The old man and Julie looked at each other, and in their look of compassion this thought was expressed:

"The poor wretch! . . . She's delirious! . . ."

At other times, imagining that Beringheld was dead, Marianine, casting a dull glance at the silvery disk of the moon, would play an air of somber harmonies, to which her rendition lent new force, and she would cry out:

"Your soul is floating up on those airy clouds! it soars through the air! Its loving influence surrounds me! . . . You are calling to me! . . . I hear you! . . . Soon enough I will come to join you! . . ."

Then the old man would take hold of his daughter's arm, and say:

"Marianine, that's enough. Let's go inside, it's getting late! . . ."

The harp lay still, all went to bed in silence, and Julie would hear Marianine crying the whole night through!

The events, however, which were to hurl Bonaparte from the throne were close at hand;[45] and yet Veryno saw in the papers no news of Beringheld . . . At last, one day, the old man, who never tired of going to the neighboring town, went for the thousandth time, and saw a paper that announced that General Beringheld was alive and had just been transferred.

Marianine awaited her father, sitting on the rock; it was almost nightfall. All at once she heard steps so rapid that at first she did not recognize they were her father's. . . She arose, the old man, half dead with fatigue, came rushing up in a sweat and cried out:

"Beringheld's alive! He's in charge of the reconnaissance corps! . . ."

The tender lover fell into the arms of her father, and her joy burst forth in a torrent of tears; she did not speak, a funereal happiness was suffocating her.

Marianine, half-conscious, was brought back by her father to their little hermitage. A spark of hope had been rekindled in the poor girl's soul . . .

"He's alive," she told herself, "he's alive . . . I can no longer marry him! But he's alive! . . ."

A modest celebration was held in honor of this news. Marianine placed the General's portrait at the table; she herself picked strawberries from her father's garden; they drank wine from their beloved France; they toasted the success of our armies a thousand times, armies that defended their beloved soil, and Marianine yielded herself to the sweetest of hopes. The grandeur and generosity of Tullius's soul was too well known to her that she might doubt that he had forgotten her in her misfortune, but, in this new situation, her resurging pride commanded her not to take a step in Beringheld's direction; yet, what if he were to come and fetch her in Switzerland? . . . In that case, she would have waited for him in the humble hall of the hermitage.

Chapter twenty-three

MARIANINE RETURNS TO FRANCE — VERYNO IN DISTRESS
— MARIANINE IN DESPAIR — SHE RUSHES TOWARD DEATH

Let yourself imagine a young woman, wearing a plain dress of blue calico, walking with an old, white-haired man along the main path of the Luxembourg Gardens . . . See with what infinite care she places him on a stone bench, though next to the bench there are chairs! . . . See how tenderly she looks after his every need! It is Antigone leading her father.

The sad and dreamy old man thanks his daughter with the frigid smile of old age.

This woman is wan, wasted, exhausted; she is young, beautiful, her body is softly curved, her black eyes shine with a savage fire, beneath a white and cold forehead, like that of the statue that is near to her. She is a plant that is young, beautiful, elegant, that needs only a little water to be reborn: a single ray of life-giving sun would restore her radiant color and her beauty; but, at the moment, these are faded. The young woman seems to drag herself along, and to be saying to the old man: "It is I who will go to the grave before you!"

This woman is Marianine . . . But did I say Marianine . . . Her name is now Euphrasia, and the old man is Masters, her father.

A trustworthy friend had sent word to Veryno that he and his daughter could safely return to France, provided they used an assumed name, and lived in an out-of-the-way district of Paris; their situation would change in time, *perhaps.*

On the faith of this word, *perhaps,* on the hope that Marianine had, *perhaps,* of seeing Beringheld again, who was still defending the soil of his homeland, Veryno had sold his sanctuary; he had once again eaten away the slim the resources left to him, had made this expensive voyage, and now father and daughter have found lodgings in the Faubourg St. Jacques, in a second-story flat, but still too expensive for their meager means.

Veryno, a man of honor in every sense of the word, had not wanted to compromise the faithful friend who had helped him with his advice.

Therefore, no one then knew his assumed name except this friend, who, alone, knew the address of the exiles and made only rare visits: he still worked for the administrative bureau Veryno had formerly directed, and would have lost his position had there been the least suspicion.

For two months now Marianine and her father had been living in the Faubourg Saint-Jacques,[46] where they endured all the privations their difficulties imposed on them: but most painful to Marianine was the fact that she alone, having charge of expenses for the household, saw to what degree and with what frightening rapidity their funds were diminishing. She concealed from her father this gnawing distress, for she could not bring herself to deprive a single pleasure to this being who was so near to the tomb.

When she had sold their town house, and before their exile, Marianine had not wanted to invest what was a sizeable sum of money for fear of losing it all in another bankruptcy. She did what she thought best, in leaving that sum in the hands of the buyer; but, drawing small sums on this principal from time to time, she ultimately exhausted it. Finally, in order to make the trip home from Switzerland, she had withdrawn the last remnant of this money, and the sum was dwindling away each day.

One morning, Marianine took Julie aside and said to her:

"Poor Julie, you have given us constant proof of your devotion, you can be sure we are most grateful for it! . . . But," she added, in tears, "our slender resources will not allow us to keep you on any longer. Julie," she continued, taking her hand, "I want to spare my father the grief of learning the true state of our affairs, listen . . ."

Julie was crying openly, and in the midst of her sobbing pronounced the name *Mademoiselle*, not knowing what else to say.

"Listen, Julie, I've got to have some pretext for dismissing you . . . Can you find something? . . . Otherwise my father will guess that, if I don't keep you on, it's because we can't afford it . . . and this will kill him outright!"

"Mademoiselle . . . I cannot leave you...I'll . . . work for nothing . . . I'll share your misfortunes as I did your good fortune. . . Ah! . . . Mademoiselle, please, don't refuse my wish!"

And Julie, wiping her eyes on her apron, threw herself on her knees in front of Marianine; reproaching her for ingratitude toward a loyal servant.

"Mademoiselle, you will marry the General, you know it . . . I predict it! . . . Grant me the favor to stay in your service without wages."

At this memory, and this word, Marianine held out her hand to Julie and kissed her.

The old man, hearing their sobs, shuffled toward them: he had overheard everything. He entered the room, sat down beside Marianine, and exclaimed:

"Oh, my daughter! . . . Oh, Julie!" Imagine how heavy the silence that ensued!

Henceforth Veryno deprived himself of a host of small pleasures, yet his daughter's heart filled with pain. The most severe frugality held sway in the little household, and this brilliant beauty, once the ornament of the most distinguished circles, was obliged to do needlework in order to make ends meet.

The efforts of Marianine were in vain; she saw the frightful moment of indigence at hand; and, at the height of her misery, she noticed that Julie was deceiving her, making her pay much less for things than they actually cost; she was spending her nights doing laundry, handwashing, and ironing in order to avoid spending the family's money, and to maintain Marianine in some semblance of that luxury which is cleanliness.

The suffering of Veryno's daughter reached its ultimate degree. Her father no longer left the house, but spent his days sitting in an old yellow Utrecht velvet wing chair, and eating the least possible, using as his pretext that he was not hungry. Soon, in order to have the same amount of food, they were obliged to buy the coarsest fare. Julie cried at night, and, knowing the character of her mistress, did not dare confide in anyone.

Marianine wished she could die: but how could she die without seeing Beringheld again! How could she die without speaking to him once more! Or die leaving her father dying of hunger! . . . In these moments of reflection, a fearful force awoke in Marianine and gave her strength.

At last the moment arrived when she was obliged to pay the rent; Marianine realized with a movement of horror that there was not enough money left to do so! She was stupefied . . .

The poor old wretch was sitting in his wing chair by the window, with the unfortunate Marianine at his side. It was almost night; she was thinking about their horrible state of destitution. Her haggard eyes were unable to cry, her solitary heart was swollen to the bursting point.

"What is the matter, my daughter? . . ." the old man said. "Are you suffering?"

"No, my father . . ."

"Did you sigh then? . . ."

"No, my father, let me be, I beg of you . . ."

Marianine's voice was not the same; there had been a change, a tilt toward anger in it.

"What, my daughter, don't you have confidence any longer in your old father? . . ."

"But, my father, don't you have everything you need? Are you not *pampered, waited on, content*? My God! You only have one *torment* to deal with! . . . Those who suffer on all fronts, wish on occasion to have time to meditate! . . ." These last words were spoken with a slight tone of reproach.

The old man looked at his daughter with an expression of docility, or remorse, of paternal suffering, of surprise, which brought Marianine to her knees: "O my father! Forgive me! . . . It's the first time in my life, I think, that I have ever been disrespectful to you! Forgive me!"

The voice of a parricide begging for mercy could not have been more heartrending.

"No matter," the old man said, "you will always be Marianine!" . . . and he took his daughter in his arms. "Poor child, this is the most beautiful moment of my life! . . . You have made me shudder in my very heart and soul. I was wrong, my daughter! . . . There are sorrows before which silence is a duty."

The old father, the dying daughter, accusing each other, could only be depicted by the brush of Poussin.

Marianine had not a penny, and the next day she had to pay the rent; she was thinking about what she ought to do, when her father, who had no idea of such distress, questioned her. On top of these painful thoughts were added the pains of love as well . . . She had just learned that General Beringheld had been wounded at Montereau![47] What a night Marianine had!

The next day she obtained a few days of respite from the landlord. She was returning from that visit, at which her courage and pride had been rudely shaken, where she had debased herself in supplication before a man far from able to understand how to come to the aid of the unfortunate. All at once her eyes fell upon her two Alpine landscapes, the only decoration in a room now almost bare.

At the sight of these, an idea came to her; this idea however caused her to pour forth a torrent of tears. She did not dare to make this sacrifice herself; it was Julie who took the paintings, placed the fatal *For Sale* sign on them, and went off into the populous quarter of the capital.

For three days, she came back, but no buyers were found; no one even looked at the two paintings. Despair seized upon the souls of the two women. Julie considered pawning her clothes and the few jewels she owned.

Finally, on the fourth day, a merchant came along who offered two hundred francs for the two precious paintings.

When he saw how attached Marianine was to these landscapes, he concluded they must be by some master; and in order to tempt the young woman he made the pieces of gold ring, and spread them out before her on the table . . . Marianine wavered for a long time between the sum of money and her two memories, her tear-filled eyes went back and forth from the paintings to the metal . . . Finally, she succumbed to the infernal necessity: She made a painful gesture, the merchant understood her, and the poor child saw her Alps no more.

After she had paid the rent, the money that remained would surely not take the poor household very far . . .

Allow me to spare you the heartrending details of this terrible misery . . .

All resources were exhausted! It was no longer possible for Marianine to bear the sight of pallid face of her old, resigned father, whose gloomy silence appeared to have been foretold by the immortal author of *Le Retour de Sextus*. Marianine preferred death.

Julie left the house; she had gone to see friends in order to borrow some money, without telling her proud mistress.

After casting a final glance at the barrenness of the place to which she was abandoning her father, Marianine gave him a final kiss and took her leave with respect, abandoning this future tomb to the night. She retired, and closed the door softly.

"She leaves me now, just when I am so hungry! . . ." the old man cried out with the voice of madness.

"My Father, I'm not leaving you," Marianine said, coming back into the room.

Veryno had gotten up; he stared wildly at his daughter; and, taking her hand, he squeezed it:

"Stay, my daughter, my dear daughter! . . ." he cried out with a heartrending voice.

"No!" Marianine cried out to him.

The old man, fixing her with a terrible energy, and gaining back for an instant the awesome authority of his paternal dignity, pointed despotically at the door.

Marianine rushed out screaming: "Oh, Marianine, this last blow was all that I needed! . . . Ah, Marianine! All that remains for you is to die! . . ."

She wandered aimlessly, in the throes of the most dreadful thoughts, and so great was her preoccupation that she went toward the gate to the Luxembourg Gardens, not thinking that it would be closed.

"Before he made that horrible gesture, and gave me that vengeful look, did he not smile at me? . . ." she was saying to herself, "Did he not call me, in his failing voice, 'his dear daughter'? Yes! . . . But how to feed him? Oh, my poor father! My tender father! What will you say when they come to tell you: Marianine is dead! . . ."

She found herself in the Place de l'Observatoire. She walked on gazing with a dry eye at the moon that shone with a bright and pure light, despite the large black clouds that encircled it: the moon with its sweet light seemed locked in combat with these airborne giants, and the contours of the clouds took on tints of its silvery glow.

"Why am I not able to open this gate?" said the distraught Marianine.

"Who goes there?" . . . cried the sentry, hearing someone speak and rattle the gate with force.

"Does everything in nature reject me? All doors are closed to me," she continued, moaning.

"Who goes there?" the sentry cried out a second time and backed away.

"Cursed gate! Now I'll have to take the long way around to get to the river."

"Who goes there?"

The soldier raised the butt of his rifle to his shoulder and aimed it into the dark; and his finger, seeking out the trigger, was about to satisfy the wishes of the imprudent Marianine, when all at once a booming voice, which seemed to come from beneath the Observatory, cried out:

"Citizen!"

With that single word, the soldier froze with horror!

At the same time, a man of gigantic stature took hold of Marianine and carried her off with a movement of extreme rapidity, down the street to the west. Marianine no longer belonged to this world . . . She let herself be carried away, and the huge old man hurried to lay her out on a stone slab that was as cold as she was: it was exactly like the eagle or the condor, who, having seized a prey on the plain, takes it to the summit of its desolate crag, where from its cruel talons it releases a pure white lamb, already dead from fright.

[End of the third volume]

Chapter twenty-four

MARIANINE IS SEDUCED — SHE SAVES HER FATHER —
SHE RETURNS TO SEE THE OLD MAN — THE POWER OF
THE CENTENARIAN

We abandoned Marianine just at the moment when an old man of massive proportions had set her down on a stone.

"Young girl," he cried to her in his sepulchral yet dominating voice, "you seemed willing to let yourself be killed!"

Bewildered, Marianine, looked around wildly; carefully she gathered up her beautiful hair, now all undone from the brusque movements of her savior; slowly she responded:

"But to what danger did I expose myself? . . ."

"The sentry was preparing to shoot you . . . He was speaking loud enough for you to hear."

"I didn't hear him!" the girl replied.

The experienced old man, learned in the *great sufferings of* mankind, recognized in this answer the tone and manners of a person close to madness.

"Child," he said, "no one on this earth knows suffering as I do; all pains are my vassals! The condemned man who goes to his death, the young girl maddened by love, the parricide, the son who can no longer bear to see his father suffer, the man who cannot survive his dishonor, the mother who loses her child, the man on the verge of committing a crime, the soldiers who, on the battlefield, call upon death when their wounds are incurable, indeed all those who suffer and who wish to find death find it in me! . . . I am the judge and the executioner! Without rest I haunt the receptacles of human misery: prisons, those repulsive madhouses, the dens of opulence and satiety, the deathbeds of crime, and no man can fool me! Young girl . . . shade of a day barely at its dawning, you are suffering . . ."

As she listened to these somber words, Marianine felt herself petrified with horror: she attempted, in the silvery light of the moon, to look upon the extraordinary being who was speaking to her, but his appearance only augmented her terror. The man was colossal in size, and his massive frame, shrouded in a brown overcoat, seemed to overburden the earth. The glow in the stranger's eyes astonished her, the naive Marianine let escape a gesture of horror; she made a movement to flee, but felt herself restrained by the cold, dry hand of the man.

"You look at me up and down" he said, "and my appearance frightens you? Yet, such as you see me, I have all the world's powers at my command; and anything you may desire, I have in my power. Young child, one takes from me without shame, for I have assumed the role both of *destiny* and of *chance*!"

As Marianine listened to the stranger, his unusual voice appeared to change and became almost melodious: with suavity its sound insinuated itself into her ear; that same serpent who long ago seduced the first woman must have had a voice like this extraordinary being, who focused the full beam of his eye on the white forehead, pure and virginal, of Marianine, all the while holding her hand in his.

"Listen, child of a day," he continued, "seek to know me, you will find that I have the attributes of a divinity . . . and to prove my power, I am going to tell you in a few words the story of your life."

Marianine shuddered; some magical force held her at the side of the huge old man, who was able to modify the disturbing power of his gaze, adapting it to Marianine's weakness. All the while he held the young girl's hand, studied her face with the thoroughness of a doctor, and examined all her features. And, on seeing her body, and the physical signs that characterized Marianine, the austere and immutable countenance of the old man expressed astonishment, and a look of satisfaction introduced itself into his odd smile.

It seemed as if he had found a thing he had long sought in vain. He gave his voice a paternal expression, and said to the one he wanted to seduce:

"Poor child, I feel sorry for you . . . You are in love, and what you are feeling is your first passion and your last! . . . You are unhappy! . . . And if you have a father, a family, hunger and misery are presently exercising their implacable rigors among them: you are proud, you have received a brilliant education, you are suffering and you rush to destroy yourself!. . .You are mad! . . . You do not know what death is, for you have yet not seen, as I have, many men drawing their last breath . . . They all regret life . . . because life is *everything*! . . ." With this word, the old man seemed to grow ten feet, his tone assumed a force of conviction that caused Marianine to tremble; she began to come to her senses, and was surprised at the truth of the old man's remarks.

"Ah," he continued, "it is only when life leaves us that we understand this cruel truth, and that all our vain systems come crashing down. Young girl, if you were right now at the bottom of the Seine, choking on your last mouthful of water, thinking your last thought, you would regret that some strong arm did not come to rescue you . . . Child . . . look at my white locks, they have seen more than one winter, and this mind knows much about life."

Marianine, *charmed*, felt her morbid thoughts dissolve away inside her like a block of ice melted by the rays of the sun. She said to the old man:

"But what can I do?"

"Live!" he responded in a sonorous voice that issued forth, full of all the male tones of a superhuman energy.

"But how?" the young girl exclaimed.

"Listen to me," the old man said. "Didn't you want to die? Look at me as if *you were dead!* . . . (Marianine shuddered) You now no longer exist: I will take possession of your body, and I swear to you I will never allow it to do anything that would dishonor you . . . *You belong to me then!* Will you come to me occasionally at night? . . . I will lavish on you everything that nature, power, and wealth offer that is most splendid. You will be a queen, you will be able to marry your lover, to crown him . . . and . . . in exchange for all that royal opulence, the only price I ask is to have you request of me on occasion the permission to live . . . You are in no danger with me, for, poor child, if you were in any danger! . . . (This word was spoken with a diabolical expression.) We are far from any help, the sentry will not leave his post, and before I allow your cries to reach human ears, I will have accomplished all my plans: as for my strength, look! . . ."

All at once, before Marianine could utter a sound, he took hold of her, and lifting her by the waist like a doll, a fragile toy, he set her pretty feet on the palm his left hand, then, raising her high in the air, he stretched out his arm, and, after having lifted her beautiful head fifteen feet off the ground for ten minutes, he set the young girl down, without the least fatigue, on the spot from which he had taken her.

Terrified, Marianine felt her heart swell.

In his movements and words the colossus had demonstrated an irony and a power that struck Marianine dumb; in a sense, she was transported by the force of thought into a supernatural world.

"Consider," the old man resumed, "that my glance can kill a man, that the strength that resides in my arm, in its deadly swiftness, is equal to that of the keenest weapon; and yet, see here my hoary head (and he showed her that enormous head, which he lowered with a movement of horrible slowness), do you see this aged skull? Do you think that a centenarian could have such desires? . . . That he could be feared by a young beauty? Come, young girl, pour all your sorrows into the depths of my heart, it is fertile in consolations, and in my person you see all the qualities of a good father: kindness, humanity, tenderness. My hands are full, I ask nothing more than to cast forth those riches placed in my charge. I go back and forth on the earth and help to soften the blows of fate, as implacable in punishing crime as merciful in aiding misfortune, putting an end to incurable miseries and healing all wounds, redeeming the *effects of a cruel fatality* through a multitude of good actions!"

This voice, which had become honeyed, sweet, harmonious, had to it an unctuousness, a saintly nature, that conjured in Marianine's soul the strangest ideas. She felt an inexpressible pleasure in remaining at the side of this man, and she admired this human mass, unable all the while believe in his reality. She was imagining, dreaming . . . "Think, young girl," the august old man went on. He seemed in the eyes of Marianine a sort of *genius.* Indeed, nothing more resembled Ossian singing of tempests, summoning the dead, than this hoary old man, seated on this rock, his chest covered with a long silver beard, and raising his hands toward the heavenly vault in the midst of night, alternately somber and radiant.

"Think," he said, "that the gods of this earth punish parricide, and your father is dying perhaps! He accuses you! He calls to you! . . . How joyous to return home laden with gold! To see him in the midst of abundance, savoring, in his declining years, all the blessings of a happy life! He will press your hand, kiss you, and will say to you: 'O my daughter!'"

Marianine felt tears flow down her cheeks on hearing this vision, to which the gestures of the old man imparted a form of life.

"And in exchange for all this I only ask of you that you come back and see the poor Centenarian from time to time . . . My child! You wanted to die, would it not be better to die in order to save your father?. . ."

This horrible proposition did not frighten Marianine at all . . .

"So!" exclaimed the old man, "I'm going to bring you your wages!" . . .

Marianine recoiled in horror at this word, but the old man, directing the fire of his eyes and all the energy of his will upon the face of the young girl, caused this amiable being, who resembled a turtledove fascinated by the eye of some devouring serpent, to come back to him.

"Young girl, I understand you, for no human thought shapes itself in the lobes of my brain, without my being able to *see it;* yet I have given you proof enough of decrepitude and of youth, of strength and of debility, of power and of weakness, to change your ideas toward me. The union of all human contradictions, of all there is that is uncanny, is that not enough for you? Is it in my presence that such human sentiments are to be deployed? What does your shame signify, in the presence of one who takes what he pleases from the life of a man without making him die? Who masters all illnesses, who can transport a *substance*, a woman, a man, one hundred, one thousand, ten thousand miles away, without it leaving its place, without it seeming to move?—Everything in nature obeys me, not in its entirety, but in its parts: I am the master of all that, I depend neither on death nor on time, I have *conquered them*! . . . Gaze upon this aged skull! It has been warmed by a sun four hundred years older than the one that shone upon you this morning. You may think me an angel or a demon, it makes no difference to me—but listen well to this: you would accept gold from the hand of a prince, why then do you refuse it from *the Eternal One*?. .

At this word Marianine, rooted to the spot by some invisible force, felt her memory, her faculties slip away like shadows; she fell into a state difficult to define: although not asleep, she had the appearance, the immobility of sleep; her shining eyes were fixed on the celestial vault; and, when the huge old man with his locks of silver came to the end of his fiery speech, she thought she heard the strains of divine harps. She saw (and yet her expiring will no longer left her the force to make a single movement), she saw the old man disappear at such a languishing pace, that one can give an idea of it only by comparing it to smoke that is gradually clearing: Marianine's eyes followed this shade, which vanished in the direction of the Observatory, and soon she saw nothing more . . .

Marianine hears the clock strike one; she wants to flee, but a magic force holds her there, for she vaguely remembers that the old man said to her: "Wait for me! . . ." Marianine thinks, but her thoughts follow a path directed by some impulse she cannot define: her mind succumbs to rapture, and the ecstasy lasts for an indefinite moment! Finally, in the midst of a profound blackness, she perceives a large, luminous mass approaching so slowly that its approach makes her suffer, gradually she makes out the head of the old man, and a voice calls out to her: "Your father is dying . . . hurry! . . ." And the colossus vanishes with the words: "Till tomorrow!"

An extraordinary sound strikes the ear of Veryno's daughter. Marianine, immobile, dumbstruck by a scene that seems to issue from the realm of dream, rubs her beautiful, tired black eyes with a mechanical movement, and, by the glow of the moon, she perceives the color of gold shining through the rude cloth of a sack.*

"My father is dying," she said, "why shouldn't I sell myself to save him?"

Even so the old man's words came back to her mind, and an involuntary dread made her shiver. She picked up the sack, and had incredible difficulty lifting it up on the stone, so heavy was it.

Marianine contemplated this treasure, while giving herself up to a thousand contradictory thoughts, but the idea of placing her father again in the midst of abundance, of surrounding his final days with all the splendors of wealth, carried the day.

"And what," she said, "if he were the enemy of mankind, an assassin? . . . Provided that he doesn't ask me to do anything dishonorable, that he attacks only *me*! Must I not help my father . . . ?"

With this thought, she lifted up the too-heavy sack, attempting to put it over her delicate shoulder . . . Steps were heard, and fear gripped the trembling Marianine: she deposited this gold behind the big stone and hid . . . Someone was approaching . . . coming toward the spot where Marianine was; it was a woman, who sat down and began to cry:

"I have no friends left," the woman said, "I don't dare go home! . . ."

By her voice, Marianine recognized Julie; she stood up, Julie, frightened, let forth a scream, but she saw her mistress who was pale and haggard, and who, with a delirious gesture, showed her, by the white light of the moon, the too-heavy treasure.

*[Editor's Note: General Beringheld, when Marianine told him of the magical happenings of that strange evening, wrote down a note that proved that, at the time he wrote it down, he had already acquired all the powers the old man deployed, and he has affirmed in writing that these belong to a science that has long been known, and was not even unknown to the ancients.]

The most gruesome thoughts entered Julie's soul . . . She looked at her mistress with an eye dry with despair; she didn't know whether she should admire her, or retreat in terror. However, in this moment stamped with the dismal seal of misery, of hunger and of horror, Marianine cried out in her sweet voice:

"Julie, my father will have bread!"

These words brought the servant back to herself; she cast upon her mistress an observant look, and the sight of her face, pale, yet sublime in its innocence and suffering, caused all Julie's thoughts to vanish; she blushed at them as if they were a crime. Then they silently took up this mass of gold, and carried it with plodding steps, heading toward the lodgings of Veryno . . .

The old man had accepted in a passive manner the final look of his daughter: prey to an involuntary horror, he followed her with his eyes when she had disappeared, and this look, dumbly mournful, spoke of a deep agony. Veryno, feeling an excruciating hunger, had not dared speak of it to his daughter: he awaited death joyfully . . . His eyes were already fading; he could barely make a movement.

"She's not coming back," he murmured, and he listened carefully to the hour that tolled.

At eleven o'clock, the old man got up, and rummaged through his rooms, looking everywhere to see if there was not some scrap left over to appease his hunger.

"They have left me nothing!" . . . he said, "and, I am alone! . . . It is late . . . If I die, who will close my eyes?"

He spied a crust of dry bread, and tried to chew it. At last, the old man succumbed to weakness; he fell to the floor and could not raise himself . . .

"My daughter!" he cried out now and then. "My daughter! You've abandoned me . . . Perhaps you as well are dead! . . . Your thinness and your pangs of love, your sorrows are more than enough to . . . Marianine! . . . My dear Marianine!"

At just the moment when the old man had fallen silent, and when a somber desperation had taken hold of him, Julie and Marianine entered.

This latter cried out in despair at the sight of her father's white locks, shining as they spread out over the tile floor; the lamp was going out, there remained a mere glimmer of light that in its feebleness resembled the pittance of life that remained to the old man; nothing was lacking to this scene of horror!

Marianine threw up her arms to the heavens, and dropping the burden, as did the exhausted Julie, the gold spilled out over the floor, which made it ring.

At this sound, the old man awoke, he cried out:

"My daughter, I'm hungry, I'm . . . dying!"

Julie grabbed a handful of gold pieces and rushed out with the speed of lightning, while the daughter, tears in her eyes, held up her old father, and took him toward his wingback chair. There, his first word was: "Marianine? . . ."

This simple questioning word, spoken after Veryno had contemplated these cascades of gold, bore an admirable character of sublimity: honor, which overcame both hunger and pain, was the first thought of this generous old man, who was almost in his grave.

The proud Marianine met her father's glance, and could only reply with the sweetest smile that ever this goddess of innocence had allowed to pass across her naive lips. At this *answer*, the old man drew his daughter upon his feeble knees, and placed on her forehead a kiss that was almost cold.

Julie returned with all kinds of things to eat, and there was a splendid feast. The old man and the servant devoured everything in sight, but Marianine, preoccupied by the magical scene to which she owed this liberating gold, dined in sadness. Her face expressed terror, and the image of the colossal old man was ever present in her memory.

"They are eating my life," she said to herself. "I no longer belong to myself!" Then, no longer able to believe in such a bizarre happening, such a singular adventure, she attempted to find an explanation for this vision.

"My daughter, you are sad, sadder than yesterday, and yet we have plenty! I imagine that our banker must have reimbursed us . . ."

At this word, a thrill of joy went through Marianine: an idea came to illuminate her with a shaft of light—her idea was to take to the old man, as reimbursement for the sum he had given her, the credit notes they were to get back with the liquidation of their banker's assets.

Now, Marianine could share her father's joy; and there was but one thought that poisoned her: "If only I could see *him* once again!" she said to herself, thinking of Tullius.

When the dinner was over, they counted the money Marianine had just brought, and found it to be 35,000 francs.

The next day the first thing Julie did was to go and buy back the two paintings.

When evening came, Marianine went toward the Luxembourg Gardens. On the main promenade, she found the old man who was strolling with ponderous steps; everyone stopped to look at this giant; he was simply dressed, and no longer wore his great-coat; a hat in the contemporary style covered his forehead of brass and his hair of silver; spectacles prevented one from seeing the thin thread of light that darted from his sunken eyes; he held his withered hand over his lips; and, as he assumed such a meditative pose, there remained only his gigantic size, and his huge bony frame, that set him apart from the rest of men.

"My girl," he said, in a voice that was soft but hollow, "I was waiting for you . . ." and he went and sat down on a bench along with the trembling Marianine.

She felt a movement of respect and passive obedience invade her as soon as she was at the side of this miraculous old man; in vain, she sought to ward off a new sense of being that took hold of her soul, she felt an invisible *je ne sais quoi*, indistinct, indefinite, gradually taking possession of her, like the infusion of some fluid imperceptible to the senses, but whose invasion was felt in the soul itself.

This singular humor became an invincible force once the old

man had held Marianine's hand in his own for five minutes: the stranger's hand conveyed a sensation of icy cold. Marianine, not daring to withdraw her hand, placed her other one on top of the old man's hand, and found it intolerably hot. It seemed that between this burning hand and that of Marianine, all the cold of the North Pole had introduced itself by means of some layer thin as a geometrical line.

"Young girl," the old man said, "what is your name? For there is among all women one *lover* whom I must never come near."

"My name is Euphrasia Masters," answered Marianine, not realizing that such misinformation was fatal to her. Hearing this name, the old man made a movement with his hand, taking the hand away from his lips and chin. As it was still daylight, Marianine was dumbstruck when she noticed that the old man bore a resemblance to Beringheld . . .

Then, all that she had heard about the spirit of Sculdans the Centenarian came back into her memory, and a certain horror overcame the feelings that held her in thrall. This inner struggle caused her to remain silent and motionless.

At this moment, the hour arrived when the gates were to close, and mechanically Marianine followed the old man, who led her toward the stone where the night before he had spoken of things so strange and incoherent seeming.

"Monsieur," Marianine said, "you have put me in your debt with a graciousness and goodness, for which I would not know how to thank you; but, as you seem so generous, I come to propose an arrangement to which you will surely be unable to refuse your assent.

"My father is creditor of a sum of 300,000 francs, owed by a well-known banking house, which, in this moment, has just put their affairs in order: I offer to let you have these notes for a sum equal to that which you have had the generosity to lend us, and you will, by this, relieve both my father's heart and mine; we are too proud to have anything given to us, even by a prince: my father has for a long time, indeed always, placed kings at the same level as other men."

The old man began to smile and said:

"That's fine, my child, I ask nothing better . . ."

At these words, Marianine, delighted at the possibility of escaping from this magical being, drew forth the papers; but the old man, casting at Marianine a profound look that stirred her heart, took her by the hand and said:

"My dear, the day is fled, how do you want me to see these papers? . . . Even though the Centenarian never picks up what has once fallen from his hand, he consents that the river may flow back to its source; that his money may return to his treasury . . . but will you come into my palace? And there, by the light of an immortal flame, we will read these characters traced by the hand of those who live but a moment. Would you not like, you young girl, you who despair of marrying the one you love, would you not like to see your lover? Once there, in my palace, a supernatural light, the fruit of my all powerful craft, can show him to you, no matter where he might be.—You will enter into the pure and vacant atmosphere of thought, you will traverse the ideal world, that vast reservoir from which issue *Nightmares,* those *Shades* that lift the curtains on deathbeds, all the arsenal of *Incubi* and *Magicians*; you will experience the shadow that is cast by no *light,* the *shadow* that has no sun! You will see anew, by means of a way of seeing that lies *outside the way one perceives in the living world!* You will move without moving; and, as the universe becomes nothing more to you but merely a simple place stripped of all its forms, all its circumstances of time, of color, of substance, then you will contemplate your lover! Such vision depends neither on time, nor on any inherent circumstance. The bolts of a prison, the thick walls of a fortress, the distance of oceans, you will overleap them all, you alone will see him!"

"Can this be true?" . . . Marianine exclaimed involuntarily; forgetting all else at the charming idea of seeing Beringheld again.

The old man began to smile in a disdainful manner, and this smile had such a force of conviction, that the young woman felt gripped by the most violent desire that had ever assailed a woman's heart; at this moment, however, all the tales she had been

217

told as a child came back to her mind, and she asked the old man with the most childlike naïveté:

"I was told that those who approached you risk danger, that your voice is like that of a Siren for those whom you charm, and that it terrifies the rest of men: finally, are you not Beringheld-Sculdans, called the Centenarian? . . . Are you body or spirit? And, what do you want with me?"

"Young child," the old man interrupted, "be quiet! . . . *The Man,* as he said that, fell into a deep silence: he took the hand of young Marianine, and holding it in his own for ten minutes, he directed toward that hand all the fire of his eyes: then, he moved away slowly, after having said to Marianine: "Will you come tomorrow? You will see the one you love!" . . .

Marianine walked back toward the rue du Faubourg Saint-Jacques, feeling in herself a violent desire to elucidate this mystery.

"What do I risk?" she said to herself! . . .

Chapter twenty-five

MARIANINE'S VISION — HER STRANGE STATE —
BERINGHELD IN PARIS — A SCENE AT THE CAFÉ
DE FOY — ALWAYS THE CENTENARIAN

The next day Marianine spent the whole day thinking about the pleasure she would have if the stranger were to show her the General. The strangest ideas struggled to take hold in her soul.

"In any case," she said to herself, "am I not obliged to go and give him back the sum that we owe him? . . ." This motive, along with hope, made up her mind.

As soon as it was evening, Marianine went out and ran to the place the old man had taken her to. She didn't find him there, and her desire grew strangely as she waited; she experienced all the torments brought about by such torture of the soul.

At last she heard the heavy and slow steps of the old man; indistinctly she perceived the bright light of his eyes. At that moment, a vague hint of danger made her tremble, and from this moment on, she was gripped by all the fevers of a delirious fear.*

Marianine feels the icy hands of the old man seize the tips of two of her fingers; and, through the pores of this vulnerable part of her body, a mist insinuates itself that takes hold of her entire being, more or less the way night, little by little, invades nature. The young girl attempts to defend herself, but some invincible power irresistibly causes her eyelids to become so heavy that they droop, and she resembles Daphne whom a magic bark came to enshroud.[48] A pleasant sensation, vast in its extent and suave in its particulars, inundates Marianine, once she lets herself go, tired of a futile combat, with the current . . . she is passing way . . .

Her brain, calm and rendered unable to register the stimulus of sensations or to receive ideas, no longer makes its moral influence felt. Night holds sway over Marianine's existence, and all that possesses life seems to abandon her . . .

To describe this condition, she made use of a comparison that is almost trivial, but which we will use because of its accuracy. She found herself, inside of her being, in that situation one is in when one awaits, in deep night, the pale lights and the magic effects of a phantasmagoria. One is in a bedroom, in front of a spread-out cloth; in vain the eyes strain, they see nothing; soon, however, a feeble light illuminates the cloth upon which appear lucid and bizarre phantoms, who will wax, wane, and vanish all at the will of the clever magician.

But this bedroom in this case is the brain of Marianine, *she is looking inside herself*, and finds there an absence of colors . . . After an indeterminate time an undefined gleam begins to appear: this

[Editor's Note: We have attempted to depict in a manner more thorough and lucid yet those strange ideas, incoherent events, and this unique relationship that General Beringheld had put down on paper, based on what Marianine had remembered. We are in no way responsible for the vagueness of terms, for missing ideas, nor for the extraordinary nature of this narrative.]

light has the vagueness of that of dreams . . . At last, it finally becomes increasingly real and brilliant; and Marianine, without moving from the spot, feels herself carried away with unequaled speed, and in the midst of these sensations of light and of travel, she perceives the old man who is always by her side: at one moment he disappears, the next he is back in her sight, which resembles that sight given to *the shade of a dead man*, yet at all times *she feels him* at her side.

Marianine was never able to tell the time precisely, for no human circumstance acted on her any longer, yet there arrived a moment when she lost sight of the old man, and when she had nothing else before her but the following spectacle.

Through a thin, diaphanous cloud, luminous, comparable to a veil of gauze, she *saw* an inn; this inn faced toward a street. She *read* above the door: "*Vanard, innkeeper, lodgings for travelers on foot, on horseback*"; she *saw* the sign, *The Golden Sun*; she *climbed* a rude staircase, and opened herself the door of a bedroom, on the second floor, without anyone speaking a single word to her, *because no one could see her, she passed* through the bodies of people, without their making the least movement. On opening the door, she *cast* a glance through a window into a courtyard, and *saw* the carriage of General Beringheld: she *saw* his coat of arms on the panel, and entering the bedroom, she uttered a cry! . . . She *saw* Tullius but he made not the slightest move. Then Marianine, forgetting she was invisible, began to cry.

Beringheld was sitting in a chair, in front of a rude table, he was finishing a letter to his quartermaster. Marianine came closer, *read* the letter. Tullius was ordering his quartermaster to make all efforts to locate Marianine; he supplied him with letters of introduction to Ministers of Police, of the Interior, and of War, asking them to help him in his search. Marianine heard the noise of a cannon.

Tullius heard it as well, he set down his letter, got up, and, pacing back and forth with great strides, he exclaimed: "What is going to become of France! . . . O my country! . . . In any case, I have greatly paid my debt to you, for I have abandoned Marianine and her father . . ."

"Tullius!" Marianine cried out, "Tullius! . . ." She held him in her arms, yet Tullius walked on as if nothing were touching him. Marianine bathed his face with her tears! He walked on!. . . The young girl suffered the pains of a martyr.

At that moment, Lagloire entered, and said: "General, we must leave, the enemy is advancing! . . ."

Marianine, as if the lamp of the phantasmagoria were going out, sank into the deepest darkness, and *saw* nothing more. She returned to that same state of limbo that had previously taken hold of her. She was passive like the toy that a child torments.

She remained in this state for a long period of time, during which the most bizarre and most extraordinary things took place: all of these were outside the realm of things possible, yet she did not retain the memory of any of them. She had the memory only of the sight of Beringheld, and of a promise that she made to the old man to return in four days, at eleven in the evening, to the vicinity of the Observatory, to the entrance of a house that was located in the middle of a large garden strewn with ruins and buildings.

She saw vaguely both the path and the entrance to this building, to which she promised, *in an unflinching manner,* to go.

There remained in her mind the vague memory of a very hard struggle she had yielded before making the promise, but the huge old man had smothered her under a mass of vapor, and he triumphed.

Marianine had gone to the rue de l'Ouest, at ten o'clock in the evening, the old man had come to her at eleven, and at eleven-thirty she began no longer to exist! . . .

Marianine awakes beset by indefinable feelings. She thinks she is in the rue de l'Ouest at eleven-thirty at night, but it is *ten o'clock in the morning*! . . . and she is in her bed, in her bedroom, in her father's house . . .

She opens her eyes with great difficulty; she sees Julie and Veryno seated by her bedside. The period of time between eleven o'clock, the night before, and ten o'clock the next morning, is simply taken out of her existence, and she remembers only two things: she has seen Beringheld, and she has promised the old man to meet him in his palace four days from now. What is more, she feels a solemn obligation to say nothing of these happenings. At each moment of the day, she wants to inform her father, but an invincible power holds her tongue captive.

"Have you suffered greatly, my daughter?" were the first words of her father.

"How do you feel this morning, Mademoiselle," continued Julie.

"What do you mean?" Marianine answered in an astonished voice.

"The doctor thought you would never come out of it," said her old father. "Here, look, Marianine."

The little woman, totally surprised, contemplated her father, and saw his eyes swollen and still red from all the tears he had shed. She broke out laughing; and this laugh, open and full of youth, of force and of health, far from reassuring the old man, terrified him. He made a gesture to Julie, and Julie, for her part, shuddered; they believed that Marianine had gone mad.

They finally informed her that around one o'clock in the morning she had come home, her eyes staring straight ahead, her tongue so cold that she was unable to utter a word; that she made no response to all the questions that were asked to her; that she went to bed in a mechanical manner, as if she were all alone, though she was in the presence of her father, whom she did not see; that, alarmed by such a condition, they went to find a doctor, who had just now left, after having pronounced that no human aid could bring her out of a condition for which no precedent existed in the annals of medicine; that every time the doctor, Julie or her father had touched her, she had uttered in a dull voice a plaintive cry . . .

Marianine understood nothing of such a story, and to the great astonishment of her father and of Julie, she got up, and seemed in no way ill disposed . . .

Beringheld and Lagloire were, in fact, in a village in the vicinity of Paris. The General, learning of the events of Fontainebleau and the abdication of Bonaparte, mounted in his coach, and went to Paris.

We are going to leave General Beringheld in his town house, distressed at not having any trace of Marianine and her father, although he has sent an enquiry to Switzerland to learn the route they had taken to return to France, and so on. As well, let us take leave of the tender Marianine, who ceaselessly thinks of her lover, who learns from the papers that he has just arrived in Paris, and who swears not to take one single step to go to meet him. Marianine's pride has grown during her tribulations: nonetheless, tears flow down her cheeks, whenever she thinks of that day of joy and happiness, that day, when she saw Beringheld once more as he was returning from Spain.

"At that time," she said "I could have gone to meet him! . . . I had a magnificent carriage then, I was daughter of a Prefect, rich! . . . Now, I am poor, the daughter of a pariah; it is his duty to come to me now! . . .

One evening, in the Palais-Royal,[49] and in a corner of the Café de Foy, seven or eight persons were gathered around two marble-top tables, which were littered with empty demitasses and saucers on which a few lumps of sugar remained.*

"It is unusual," said a small man as he put the remaining pieces of his sugar in his pocket, "it is even astonishing that the government has never looked into such strange things: happenings like this deserve its attention . . ."

"Monsieur," a man with a pale face answered, "this science has been known for a long time, and everything you find so extraordinary results from this same science, which demands minds capable of devoting themselves entirely to the knowledge of na-

*[Editor's Note: We will see how this fragment, that finds its natural place at this location in the narrative, was able to come to the attention of the General, in those manuscripts from which we have taken this information.]

ture; indeed, a long time ago, in one of my treatises, I made notice of the very thing that astonishes you so, and I myself have witnessed most unusual experiments."

The five other persons shook their heads to show disapproval of this discourse, and the victory went to the little skeptic, who exclaimed:

"Chimeras, my dear Sir; I know all about Mesmer and his bucket:[50] but one must put all that in the same boat with the magicians of the fifteenth century, with the makers of gold out of water, with the alchemists, with judiciary astrology, and god knows what other so-called science, that rogues abuse in order to dupe honest property holders . . ." and, the little man, getting hotter under the collar, went on: "It is like the Rosicrucians, who were looking for the secret of human life. . ."[51]

At these words, a huge old man who had not spoken a single word since the beginning of the evening, seemed to stir. He was seated right in the corner; as he was sitting on an extremely low stool, he concealed his great height and seemed to be at the same level as all the others; his hat was pulled down over his eyes. When he had come in to sit down, he was not noticed among the crowd that filled the café; but, when he sat down, each of the regular customers in the group looked him over, seeking in vain to find some explanation for the extraordinary size of his clothes. The old men glanced at each other, as if to ask each other's opinion, but the stranger, his nose buried in his frock coat, appeared to have dozed off after having drunk a bowl of punch; soon no one paid any more attention to him.

One began by speaking of the recent political events, but, as this conversation soon waned, they switched to talking about progress in the sciences, and among other things, about chemistry which was developing in a frightening manner, and so on.

"Is there," said the little pensioner dressed in black, "is there a single Rosicrucian, a single transmuter of gold, a single astrologer or alchemist, who ever added a stone to the magnificent edifice of the human sciences? And yet, how many honest property owners and pensioners have they cheated!"

The old man, halting the arm of the pale-faced individual with a movement that was almost despotic, turned to face the little pensioner; and these actions, coming from this silent stranger, drew the attention of the circle, that now became silent and attentive.

"Monsieur, your round visage reveals a property owner, and the lack of relief in your facial features, indicates that the sciences have never been your exclusive occupation![52] Admit that the cares and the intellectual activity of certain property owners, bourgeois of this city, who have never traveled farther than Montargis, never go beyond the instigation of a lawsuit over the common wall of their house in the Marais—for that is where you live, is it not? And before ten o'clock you'll be safely back home . . . So, my good Sir, admit that it is at the very least thoughtless of such people as you to want to speak about the sciences. You merely paddle around in that vast ocean and find yourself there like a freshwater sailor in the Sea of Spitzbergen, or rather you resemble the rat in the fable who mistook a molehill for the Alps."

With these words, at the magic sounds of the broken voice of this old man, several savants came to join this group of old regulars; several leaned on their elbows, and they listened to the stranger without paying attention to the gestures of discontentment of the little property owner.

"Monsieur, you dared to speak of the Rosicrucians, and about a science that one despises in our day, and you have spoken of it with the disdain of those who have never ventured deeply into anything. As for the Rosicrucians . . . is it no small thing to venture into a science whose goal is to make the life of man longer, almost eternal? To seek what is called the *vital fluid*? . . .

"What glory it is for mankind to discover such a thing and by means of certain precautions to acquire a life as long lasting as the earth! You would see such a scientist hoard the treasures of science, lose nothing of individual discoveries, constantly pursuing, unceasingly, and forever, his investigations of nature; making all powers his; roaming the entire earth, knowing it in its smallest details; becoming, himself alone, the archives of nature and humanity. He would avoid all inquiry into his activities; taking refuge in all lands: free as air, avoiding pursuit through an exact knowledge of places, the caves and catacombs upon which cities are built. One day donning the rags of misery, the next taking the title of some defunct line of aristocrats and traveling in a magnificent carriage; saving the lives of good men, and letting the wicked perish: such a man replaces *destiny*, he is almost *God*! . . . He has in his hand all the secrets of the art of ruling, and the secrets of each state. He learns at last the truth about religions, about man and his institutions . . . He looks down on the vain contentions of this earth as if from the height of a cloud, he wanders among mortal beings like a sun; in sum, he passes through the centuries without dying."

With this thought, the old man raised himself a bit, his hat was removed, and the listeners began to falter in their inner resolve; the desiccated hand of the old man made meaningful movements, movements they feared to interpret.

"Don't you imagine," said the colossal old man as he sat up straight, "how great the sacrifices must be to have such an existence, and if one must make cruel sacrifices, who among you would dare to make them?"

At this question, the listeners felt themselves prey to some indefinable horror.

"And if a man discovered this vital fluid, do you think he would be stupid enough to tell about it? . . . He will profit from it in silence; he will seek to avoid the gaze of men who live but a day; he will watch *the river of their lives flow, without seeking to make a lake of it.* Fontenelle[53] *told me* that if he had his hand full of truths, he would keep that hand closed. He was correct! . . . Listen to me, Monsieur," he addressed the little property owner, "the next-to-the-last true Rosicrucian was alive in 1350; he was *Alquefalher the Arab*, the last grand master of the order: he found the secret of human life in the caves of Aquila, but he died for not having known how to keep the flame burning in his retort. Since then, what great steps science has made, walking side by side with the science that you scorn, and with the *true* medicine! . . ."

With these words, the old man stopped; and, looking at the astonished assembly, he made the gesture of a man who realizes the mistake he has made, but that his adversary has not yet seen. The old man thus got up, and his gigantic height, the thickness of his bones, were revealed; all present believed that they saw his head and his bronze forehead threaten to touch the ceiling. He cast on those present a glance that plunged them all into a state of involuntary terror, doing so by means of the inexorable force of that thread of light that issued from his hollow eyes. It seemed to all present that they had each been struck in their inner being by a bolt of heavenly thunder.

The stranger walked away slowly, and those who were able to observe his manner of walking, had the idea that here was some bizarre alliance between life and death, shaping a hideous human construction that belonged equally to both. He vanished like some phantasmagorical shadow, and astonishment reigned in the café . . .

Chapter twenty-six

THE GENERAL IN PURSUIT OF HIS ANCESTOR — HE DOES
HIS OWN INVESTIGATION AT THE CAFÉ — MARIANINE'S
PRIDE — THE FATAL DAY ARRIVES

In the midst of the important events of which at that time Paris was the scene, this incident at the Café de Foy* received little publicity, and thus did not cause a great sensation. Those who told of it were scoffed at by those who listened to them, and soon the former feared they must have let themselves be deceived by their eyes and ears.

Nevertheless, news of this incident reached General Beringheld. He was at that very moment actively engaged in his search to find Marianine, and this occupation absorbed him entirely, and

*[Editor's Note: We have changed the name of the café, just as we have changed the name of the towns and all the characters in this singular story.]

the memory of the old man had yielded to that of his tender lover. We know that, for Beringheld, there could be no half-feelings; and since, after fourteen years of absence, Marianine had come to meet him, and he had found her faithful, all of his thoughts went to this charming girl.

Although the dangers for France, the turmoil of battle, the woes of a long captivity, and the bloody struggle in which France had just been defeated, had prevented him from seeing Marianine, and from helping her father in his disgrace, he had never forgotten them; and, when after two years of forced absence, he saw his town house again, his first thought was for Marianine. He ran to all the Ministries, he questioned the buyer of their town house, he sent Lagloire to Switzerland: all was futile; all his investigations in vain, and the General's despair knew no boundaries.

For two days now, Tullius had returned to Paris for good, having resigned his commission and forever abandoned the vicinity of thrones. The day after his arrival he heard mention made of the scene in the Café de Foy. All at once, he thought no more about Marianine, but left the salon where he had been, and immediately went to the Palais-Royal, thinking to find one of the eyewitnesses, and perhaps once again see the man who had preoccupied him from the day he was born, and who flitted like a shadow through his life.

At the moment when the General came up to a group, a man, who was being listened to with attention, raised his head and was dumbstruck; he stopped and cried out:

"Here he is! . . ."

The General stood motionless and waited until the commotion of the group had subsided; a constant murmuring continued still, and several persons said: "Why not arrest him? . . ."

"Messieurs," said the General, sitting down, "I can see, from your astonishment, that you are speaking precisely about the man whom I have come here to find out about, because it is said that he made an appearance here. This man, or rather this being, looks like me."

The man who had been speaking nodded in agreement.

"But, Messieurs, he cannot be me, for I am General Bering-held! . . ."

Everyone bowed.

"Don't let my presence bother you; continue, please."

"General," the speaker said, "the person who looks like you came here yesterday, for a second time; sometime later I will tell you what happened the first time, but now I want to continue my other story, and finish it for these people."

"Yesterday, we were sitting here talking about the Bourbons, and among other things, about Henri IV and his reign . . . a man decorated with a *cordon bleu* was over there (and he pointed to the corner where the stranger had taken a seat). His clothes were those of a courtier in the ancient style; he wore green spectacles, and was wrapped in a huge frock coat. A lawyer (who knows a lot about financial matters) spoke of Sully,[54] and comparing that great man with our ministers of today, he found him much more agreeable in manner, and of much greater talent . . . The old man, however, interrupting his discourse, said to him: 'Sully, agreeable! . . . Young man, if you have ever known a prison door, you will have some idea of how gracious Sully was: he was haughty like time itself, and there wasn't a single important figure at court who wasn't plotting against him. I *saw* him very near to being disgraced . . .'

"As he said this, you can imagine our surprise; we thought the man must be out of his head, or that it was a *lapsus linguae*: yet the strength of his convictions caused us to persist in our first opinion. The young lawyer then went on with his conversation, inciting the old man to tell us tales of the most distant times; the man spoke occasionally in the first person, and made himself an actor in the scene. He said he had treated François I and Charles IX. As he went on, the oddest things, narrated with a unique kind of wit, issued from his large mouth. Soon however, one of the regulars, whose name I don't know, who came to sit with our group, seemed struck with astonishment, and told us that this strange personage was the same man people were talking about. Hearing the stroke of ten, the old man arose and amazed us all with his skull of bronze, of steel, of stone, for one does not know what name to give to the matter that formed its indestructible base! . . . But what surprised us even more was, when he removed his green spectacles, the infernal look he cast on us. With that, he walked off with a gait so slow that no idea exists capable of rendering the effect produced by such *incorporeality*, if one may use such a word."

"I know him," said Beringheld, "and I know what you want to say."

At these words, each person looked at the General with astonishment, but the intrepid speaker went on:

"The young lawyer went to follow this walking cadaver: I saw the young man again this morning; he said that the old man had climbed into a hired cab, and the lawyer followed him in a carriage. The old man stopped in the rue de l'Ouest, across from the Luxembourg Gardens; the young man let himself off a bit farther on, in order to spy on where this strange personage was going. He saw him head towards the Observatory, at the extreme end of the street: at the most deserted spot, he saw a young woman of about thirty who was waiting."

"Oh, the wretched woman!" exclaimed the General, "how I pity her!" The look of horror that appeared on Beringheld's face struck everyone.

"All at once," the speaker went on, "the old man turned around, and looking around him, saw the young man who was ten paces away from him . . . In a twinkling of an eye he was beside the lawyer . . . This young man, however much I entreated him to do so, has never wanted to tell me more about what then happened: it seems that the old man forced him then to return the way he came; by what means? . . . I don't know . . . How? I don't know; all I can say is that the more I pushed the lawyer to tell me, the more a vague terror came over his face, and he told me as he left: 'My friend, what I can advise you, for your peace of mind, is not to talk about this old man, and whenever you meet him, if he is on the left, you go right; and if you are facing him, take care not to bump into him! . . . For sure, the police and the government should keep an eye on a man who seems so extraordinary, and who possibly is dangerous."

"The police," interjected a dry little man with a tone of smugness that betrayed him, "the police know more about this business than you think."

"Yes," added the General, "for if Monsieur is working for that branch of government, he must remember that the order for this same stranger's arrest was issued more than two years ago."

The dry little man looked at Beringheld with amazement, and as with an ordinary freemason who stands before an officer of the *Grand-Orient*, the General only responded with a withering look of contempt.

"I imagine," he said, "that you were listening to this with pleasure . . . You would love to get hold of this old man; learn, however, that, by the strength of his arm alone, he would kill three such *insect-men*, for there are many people who deserve this name and no other."

The dry little man, when he learned that the one speaking was the General Count de Beringheld, left without saying a word, as he belonged precisely to that class of men who, when one spits in their face, or wipes their *feet* on them, answer thank you.

"Drive away," the General exclaimed, "always drive away, Messieurs, such wretches! . . . Insolent in the face of misfortune, wallowing in the mud before grandeur, a spot in the stream—they are created and put on earth to show us just how far human nature can debase itself; their back is made of flexible rubber; their soul is slime, their heart in their belly; the vermin of power, the bilge of society, they are, within the State, its most horrible sewer, and they must be disgusting even to a man who lives in the company of snakes." Beringheld, continuing his philippic, added that he had no idea how any human being could communicate with them:

"Apparently," he said, "there are degrees of baseness: at the top of this scale one finds an *honnête homme*, below there is the ordinary man, and above him there is the person who traffics with the chief of police."

The General withdrew in a pensive mood, and returned to his town house. He sent for Lagloire at once.

The old soldier immediately appeared before his General, holding his hand respectfully against the rim of his police hat: "Present, General! . . ."

"Lagloire," said Beringheld, "you must remember that huge old man we saw four years ago, on the road from Bordeaux?"

"Do I remember him, General! To my dying day I'll never forget that eye, and that skull, shining like a gun casing."

"Well, Butmel, he's here in Paris at this moment, in the Luxembourg quarter, near the Observatory: his stalking ground is in that district, and you must locate him for me."

"If this is the order, General, it will be carried out; the enemy will be pursued, beaten, taken prisoner, and destroyed!"

"But Lagloire, no violence—use craft, and as you will have need of money, take some! . . ."

The General showed the old soldier his open writing desk.

"You will also need," the General said smiling, "to refurbish your headquarters."

"If that's the order," answered Lagloire, laughing as well, "it will be carried out! . . ."

"Don't come back," Beringheld added, "until you have located his house, the name of a young girl he is seeking to seduce at this moment; and, if you succeed, tomorrow morning we will look for seven or eight of my old grenadiers . . ."

"If there are any left," Lagloire said sadly. "The General forgets that in our last conversation with the Russians, there were many who talked too much! . . . Where are they? . . . God only knows! . . ." And the Sergeant raised his eyes to the ceiling with a movement full of such sudden melancholy that it moved the General. The Sergeant straightened his moustache, went away slowly, and left the General prey to a flood of reflections . . .

The political events that had just taken place allowed Veryno to take back his real name and to think of requesting, from his many friends, the means of getting out of his state of exile. The first person the old man thought of was General Beringheld.

On hearing this name, Marianine stopped her father:

"Think of it, my father, how can we go and solicit help from Tullius, when before leaving he promised to marry me! It would be too humiliating a move, both for you, and for me! . . . The General must come and seek us out in our exile, and I am certain that he has not forgotten us!"

"My daughter, your observation would be true if you were to accompany me, I admit it; but nothing could be more natural than my going to see him by myself! . . . How do you expect him to find our dwelling, when I have changed my name and when I am living in an out-of-the-way district? No matter how much good will he has, how can he guess where our lodging is in a city like Paris?"

"Ah well, my father, I prefer to stay in this house the rest of my life, rather than see you go, with your white hair, to the house of a person who was supposed to bear the name of your son-in-law. O Father! I beg you, will you wait? . . . Perhaps tomorrow, soon, you will be in a position to satisfy yourself; don't make Marianine suffer! . . . Your own daughter! . . ."

The old man yielded. He promised not to go back and see Beringheld, and Marianine, after this lively discussion, fell back into the dark melancholy that had gripped her for three days. Tomorrow she was to go to the old man's place, and a vague idea of mortal danger held sway in her soul, although that thought was unable to triumph over her repugnance, and stop her from keeping her rendezvous; an invincible force constrained her to do so; she found a thousand reasons to go: curiosity, the desire to give back to the old man the sum she owed him, the hope of seeing Beringheld again through the power of this magic being, and thus to read into the soul of Tullius, and assure herself that he still was thinking of marrying her, which would have decided her to accompany her father to the General's town house.

Nonetheless, the sadness that had taken possession of Marianine, since the night when she had brought back that sum of money, had not gone unnoticed by Julie, any more than the nocturnal errands of her mistress.

Julie, among a thousand good qualities, had one defect: she

was curious, and the next day, after the evening when Marianine had promised the old man to go to his palace, Julie asked questions all over the neighborhood, and learned that Marianine had gone to the Luxembourg Gardens, and there had followed an old man, so easy to recognize that people were able to give Julie an exact description.

Julie thought that Marianine would return there each evening; she was much deceived when she saw her mistress stay home for three days. Nevertheless, the melancholy and taciturn air of Marianine worried Julie immensely.

Finally the day arrived when Marianine was to go to the old man's house. That morning, Veryno's daughter, as she did her toilette, looked at herself in the mirror with sadness and sighed, seeing how much her beautiful face was altered. Even so, one still noticed the expression that shone through the marks of her suffering: even now the great and meditative soul of the girl who used to hunt in the Alps cast its glow on her withered face; her eyes still sparkled with all the fire of a violent love.

"Can I hope that he might see me! . . ." she exclaimed, and she shed a few tears. Julie dressed her mistress in silence.

"Mademoiselle, will you be needing me after dinner?"

"Oh, Julie, soon I won't be needing anyone anymore! You can go out if that pleases you! I will be going out as well . . ."

Already Julie was hatching the plan to go and find General Beringheld, and to tell him of the condition of the proud and gentle Marianine.

Chapter twenty-seven

MARIANINE SAYS FAREWELL — JULIE GOES TO THE
GENERAL'S HOUSE — MARIANINE'S PREMONITION —
SHE REACHES THE CENTENARIAN'S HOUSE

The day that came bore the mark of the most profound sadness. Marianine sat embroidering beside her old father, and at each moment she looked at the clock with visible fright: it seemed to her that her life was reaching its term, and the speed of the clock hand made her shudder.

Veryno contemplated his daughter with pleasure but a certain uneasiness on his face was clearly noticeable, and he made known his desire to be alone.

In fact, Veryno had indeed promised not to go to the General's house, but he had not sworn not to write to him or not to let him know where he lived, and the presence of his daughter was uncomfortable to him, for she would certainly have disapproved of his Jesuitical little ruse.

Evening arrived in the midst of a perpetual combat of questions and pretexts that the old man would come up with, and which the pale and dreamy Marianine would skillfully deflect. As the hour became later, the uneasiness of the young woman became more disquieting.

She called Julie, and went with her into her chambers:

"Julie," she said, "if I don't return tonight, I give you permission to go to Count Beringheld. My dear," she added breaking into tears, "to prove to him how much I loved him, you need only tell him how I lived: for two years there has not been a minute during which his memory has not been part of all my activities . . . and, if I don't return, you will give him this letter . . ." Marianine added—she seemed to have death in her heart—"Farewell, Julie!"

The faithful servant, in tears, kissed her mistress, but to herself she clearly resolved not to wait until her mistress had gone out, in order to rush to the General's house, through this act hoping to save Marianine, whom she suspected of wanting to die. Julie was hurrying to leave, when she felt herself stopped on the stairway by Veryno, who was waiting for the servant to pass.

"Here, Julie," he said, "take this money, hire a cab, and hurry to General Beringheld's; you will give him this letter, and I have no doubt that he will come here at once. My daughter is wasting away, and I cannot bear the heartrending spectacle of her passion any longer . . . Go, dear Julie, you are the messenger of destiny! You carry with you the fate of my tender child, may the heavens be favorable to us. Do everything you can to reach the General: but if perchance he really is not home, leave the letter with his old soldier, and beg him, for Veryno's sake, to take it himself to the General."

Julie ran off with the rapidity of a hunted deer . . .

Veryno went in, and his daughter, after a moment of silence, came to sit by his side; she led up to her farewell with a thousand little attentions, the motive for which he was unable to fathom, but which astonished him by the mixture of regret, of pleasure, and of soft pain that characterized them.

The incertitude these caused in Veryno's mind, the fear that Marianine felt, cast over this moment something indefinable.

"Farewell, my father! . . ." Veryno shuddered unwittingly; he looked at his daughter, and detected this accent of deep emotion, that caused the remaining strings of his heart to tremble.

"And why are you going out, Marianine? . . . You are going to leave me alone . . ."

"Perhaps I am leaving him alone for good! . . ." the trembling Marianine said to herself, and this thought caused her to remain silent.

"Why don't you answer me? . . ."

She did not even hear her old father's request, so astonished she was by the fixity of his eyes . . . "My daughter? . . . What is wrong with you? . . ." he repeated.

"There is nothing wrong, my father," she said with a delirious gesture, never moving her eyes that were fixed on some imaginary object; "but don't you see? He will never marry me, and the grave beckons . . . Yes, *I must do it!* . . . Besides, my father, I have promised! . . ."

Amazed, the old man listened to his daughter in silence. This weight of feelings that dominated the soul of poor Marianine was something strange and even frightening to see. She had a foreboding that she was going to her death, and this foreboding was spreading through her soul a black vapor of thoughts, similar to sea haze as it invades a clear sky. Despite her suspicions, she felt herself dominated by a supernatural force that made her appearance before the old man a *necessity of nature*.

She said to herself: "I am going to die, I am going to abandon Beringheld whom I love, and whom I believe faithful; *but it is necessary that I* go to this subterranean place that I had a glimpse of . . .

"My father cannot live without me; my death will kill him . . . but *I must go to this subterranean place.*

"I see before me a life of pleasure, of happiness, adorned with everything that luxury, opulence, riches, honors, and the art of creating happiness, can offer that is most brilliant and enchanting . . . Then I see a tomb, black, deep and silent . . . *I must go!* . . ."

Finally, in order to depict this situation in a manner that is both vital and true to fact, let us imagine Marianine on the crest of a rock: she has lost her balance, she is leaning over an immense precipice . . . The push is given, she falls, she is at this moment in the middle of her fall, she seeks in vain to hold herself back, *she must* undergo her fate; she looks up to the top of the mountain and the flowers that adorn it, but *she must* say farewell to the sky, to greenery, to life; a moral weight draws her toward the old man, at the same time as her physical weight drags her toward the bottom of this precipice.

"But, my daughter, what do these words mean? . . ."

"Farewell, my father, farewell . . ."

"Marianine, come back soon: don't leave me alone for long; promise me! . . ."

"Yes, my father, farewell!" And she kissed him with a frenzy of filial love that should have enlightened Veryno as to what was happening.

He followed her with his gaze, accompanied her down to the street, and did not come back up until he could no longer see her . . .

Once she had disappeared, a horrible terror took hold of this desperate father . . .

Marianine walks, or rather wanders, along, she struggles against a will that is not her own; but her detours, and her hesitations, only result in causing her to resume the path that she perceived in a visionary manner, and toward which a vague memory is leading her. She looks at the sky, which the night invades, she says farewell to all that she sees, her heart is already as if dead, and her ideas possess only the strength to show her where her final steps lead.

"No," she said, "I want to resist and stop myself from going on! . . ."

She sat down on a stone, for she was more tired than if she had taken the longest possible route.

After a deep meditation, she got up, saying: *I promised!* And she set out again, muttering as only Marianine could mutter, that is, gently, against this invincible arm that dragged her along.

Formerly there used to exist, behind the Observatory, a rather large field; it had been a garden; since then, buildings had been constructed on that spot.

The trees and plants in this garden grew wild, without fearing the hand of a gardener, and nature spread itself forth in wild profusion. This garden was cluttered with a multitude of ruins and debris from demolitions: enormous building blocks lay about, and bore witness, by their sooty hue and the moss that covered them, to the fact that the vast constructions they were supposed to shape did not yet exist except in some architect's plan. The large buildings that surrounded this receptacle of ruins cast huge shadows over them, and the trees, growing unchecked, without being pruned, added an even more somber cast to this night.

This place imprinted in the soul the kind of horror that results from a series of natural circumstances, the confluence of which plunges mankind, despite itself, into a vortex of dark thoughts. One cannot explain this phenomenon; and yet, if the soul is moved when one passes through a vast, silent forest at night, when one wanders in the midst of a ruined abbey whose vaults echo one's steps, how can a person not experience a sort of fear at the sight of this wooded area that resembled the remnant of a forest beaten down by the armies of Caesar? . . . The deep solitude of this garden, filled with ruins nuanced by a thousand accidental splinters of light that traced the forms of bizarre phantoms, would have terrified even the boldest man.

Nothing revealed any human interest here: the gate, another ruin, stood open, and gave free rein to curiosity, and to the covetousness of thieves.

At the end of the garden stood a dilapidated porch formed by arches of brick; finally, two or three windows closed by broken shutters seemed to indicate that someone was living in this singular dwelling.

Now and then, neighbors had seen, at different periods, an old man come from this ruined building, and spied his white head wandering among these ruins; but this was only hearsay, and since 1791, he had not been seen again. One never glanced into this garden except by accident, and an old serving woman who claimed she had seen the old man recently in the garden was dismissed as crazy. This serving woman was given support by the testimony of a coachman from a nearby house who vouched for the truth of the woman's assertion. The wits replied that they must not always have seen clearly, and that the imaginations of these two were the main subject of this story.

It was toward this very place that Marianine was heading; soon she arrived, and halted when she found herself in the midst of this imposing ensemble. She sat down on a stone, and, if someone had been able to see her, in the night, her head bowed, gazing straight ahead, her face pale like the light of the moon, he would have thought he had seen the figure of *Innocence* weeping for all the ills of the earth, before taking her ultimate step; . . . Marianine has few regrets for her earthly stay, yet casts upon it one final glance . . .

Chapter twenty-eight

While Marianine was hastening to her death, the General waited impatiently for the return of his old soldier. He trembled each time the heavy knocker at the gate of his town house announced a visitor; and when the General, rushing to the window, did not recognize Lagloire, he would go back to sit down again, with a movement of vexation.

It was nine o'clock in the evening when the General heard the plodding steps of his old soldier. He ran to open the door and hasten in the grenadier who was tapping out his pipe in the chimney of the drawing room.

"Come on, Lagloire, . . . come on! . . ."

"But, General, respect demands that I put out my pipe before . . ."

"Hang it! Smoke all you like, but if you've learned anything, tell it to me, immediately! . . ."

Lagloire muttered under his breath: "But what's wrong with the General tonight, wanting me to smoke in his presence like that! And what about respect then? . . ."

He set his pipe aside, and giving his moustache a twist he followed Beringheld.

"Come on, Lagloire, sit down!"

"No, General, that is not done any more than the pipe! . . ." and the obstinate Lagloire remained standing.

"Come on, come on, hurry up, sit down! . . . (Lagloire made a movement) or don't sit down, do what you wish, but no more stalling, tell me everything."

"General, following your order, I went to the Luxembourg Gardens: I asked in all the taverns in the neighborhood if anyone had seen go by a certain old man, whom I described as best I could, and no one was able to give me a satisfactory answer . . . *So*, I did an about face, and changed my tactics, I placed myself in the role of sentinel, and I mounted a watch at the Observatory."

"Yesterday in the evening, I saw the old man come out of his billet, and I followed him to the Luxembourg Gardens; *so*, when I spied some bourgeois who were pointing him out to each other and whispering, I mixed with their group as discreetly as I could, showing them my campaign ribbon, so that no one would take me for an informer. *So*, General, I found one of those old fuzzywigs who give me some information about our *bird*. It seems that he appeared in the neighborhood no more than fifteen days or so ago: and the day before last a young lady had come to meet him on the main promenade of the Gardens, where my *old civilian* had seen her. I asked him the name of the young girl, but—nothing!"

"He told me she is pale, tall, scrawny, and sad, that she has eyes that shine like polished platinum; a large white forehead; hair black like a spit-shined cartridge pouch, and what is more, she walks her old father now and then. This young girl, my thorny old fuzzywig told me, is unhappy, and it is easy to see that she suffers in her heart . . ."

At these words, the General thought of Marianine, and stopped listening to Lagloire, who, noticing the reverie of his General, stopped speaking as if he had heard the word: "Halt!"

"You said, Lagloire, that the girl is in love! . . . Continue!"

"Then, General, I invited this old geezer to go drink a shot, but he refused me on the spot; *so*, I did a left face, and I went back to my post."

"What post?

"A little public house from which one can see what goes on in the street, on which the entrance to the garden of old *Eternity* is located. I reconnoitered the terrain: all I saw was an old shack that wouldn't stand up against a rifle shot, and a pile of stones, that looked as if someone had demolished a fortification.

"*So then*, I returned to my headquarters, and when it was night, and the old man had gone into his fortress, I followed him like a skirmisher, maneuvering among the rocks, the brambles, and the trees. The fellow went into his shell, I followed him . . . Here, General, the magic begins, for the nest was empty, and I went through the little house in vain, all I found were apartments in ruins, doors open, and no old man. And yet, General, on my honor as a sergeant in the grenadiers, I saw him go in there!"

"Come, Lagloire, my horses, let's hasten to that house . . ."

"Just a moment, General . . . I have one more bit of information. . . . I was returning, this morning, through the Faubourg Saint-Jacques, when I ran into an old comrade.

"*So then*, we renewed our acquaintance over a little bit of *eau de vie*, when the wine merchant exclaimed: 'Look, there's that young girl!'

"At once the mother and the daughter leapt to the doorway, and came back inside saying to themselves: 'And she is going alone . . .'

"*So*, I said: 'What, pray tell, is going on here, good woman?'"

"'Oh!' she said, "it's a young woman—that is to say, she is at least thirty years old, and there is a story to be told about her doings, because she returned, in the night, to her house, and didn't know where she was . . . and Monsieur Flairault, the police commissioner's clerk, told my daughter that that girl was seeing an old man who looked like the walking dead and whom they were going to nab; this caused a stir in the neighborhood, because, ever since she's been living here, she's seemed so decent, and as you see . . .'

"*So*, General, I got the address of the commissioner's clerk, and, armed with the recommendation from Mademoiselle Pamela Balichet, the daughter of the fat wine merchant, I waited for the clerk until this evening, when he returned home. After a few preliminary words, and an added syllable *of a monetary nature*," Lagloire said, rubbing his fingers as if counting his money, "the man declared, in a low voice, that the girl lived at 309, rue Saint-Jacques, and that her father had been previously banished, because of some conspiracy during the reign of *little bald pate* . . ."

"Lagloire, my God . . . it's her! . . . It's he!"

"Who, General?"

"Marianine, Veryno!. . ." And, terrified, General Beringheld leaped up.

"No, General, the man's name is Masters, and the girl's name, Euphrasia; it's not they. *So*, I came back." The General fell into a reverie, and only returned to himself in crying out:

"No matter, Lagloire, let's hurry; we must save this victim."

"What victim, General?"

"Come on, Lagloire, on the double! Tell the servants to harness the black horses, and grab your saber, hurry . . ."

Hardly had Lagloire left, when the concierge knocked three times discreetly at the door of the bedroom where the General was pacing back and forth with large strides; he went to answer:

"Monsieur le Comte, a young girl absolutely wants to speak with you, only with you."

Thinking that it was Marianine, Beringheld bowled over the concierge and rushed out . . . He flew through the rooms and down the stairs, and came to the door. He saw Julie and did not recognize her . . . A mortal pallor came over his face when he realized his error, and he turned around without saying a word. Julie ran after him.

"Monsieur, I came to find you without my mistress's knowledge, but Mademoiselle won't be long for this world if you do not see her again. Monsieur Veryno . . ."

Hardly was this name pronounced than Beringheld turned to look at the chambermaid, and exclaimed: "It's you, Julie! . . ." It seemed as if he could already see Marianine! . . . The accent that accompanied his simple phrase was one of happiness.

"Alas, Monsieur le Comte, she is in dire straits, she has given me a letter for you, in case she does not return tonight, but I have not waited . . . It's my idea that . . .

"Give it!" . . . and the General took possession of the letter of Veryno. He opened it and recognized at once his old friend's handwriting; he held out his hand to Julie, to take from her the letter of Marianine that she still sought to hold back.

Marianine's Letter to Beringheld

"Farewell, Tullius! I have cherished you right up to my dying breath; my final words and my last breath were for you! I can tell you all this now . . . Happy, if only I had been able to see you and to bask in your gaze, perish in your arms, and to prove to you that my oaths were not in vain. I write these words attaching to them all my soul and all my love: when you read these lines, imagine Marianine seeking out your eyes, in order to place there her final look. I flatter myself to think that this testament of love will often be read by you, that you will never forget her who wrote it, that she will live forever in your memory. I take this idea with me joyfully, it consoles me . . . I am going to die, Tullius, a secret foreboding tells me so. Farewell."

Your Marianine of the Alps.

"Alas! this letter calls to mind a flood of sweet moments, the most beautiful of my life, had I not had eight days of happiness before this fatal campaign, the source of all of France's woes as well as ours. Farewell, forever! . . . Forever! . . . What a terrible word it is! . . ." The General, moved, weeping, held her letter in his hand.

"Poor Marianine, where is she? . . ."

"Oh, Monsieur, I don't know! By now," said Julie, "she must have gone out, and no one knows where she has gone! . . ."

A horrible suspicion beset the soul of the General: his face became distorted, he looked at Julie, and with a weak voice he asked her:

"Where are you living?"

"In the Faubourg Saint-Jacques . . ."

"O my God! It's her! . . . The old man! . . ."

"Oh, Monsieur, then you know the stranger with whom she has been having dealings? Ah! how sad she has been ever since she laid eyes on him . . ."

Beringheld, having fainted, heard nothing more. Coming to his senses, he cried out: "My horses! . . ." and he ran to the stable, to the sheds, to rouse the servants.

"Laurent, a hundred louis for you, if you can get to 309, rue du Faubourg Saint-Jacques in a quarter of an hour!"

At once, the General takes Lagloire, Julie, and Laurent into his coach: they traverse Paris at full gallop, crying out: "Out of the way!" . . . They burn up the pavement, the General's horses devour the distance, never has anyone seen such speed as this . . .

"Sir," said Julie, " we came back from Switzerland nine months ago, but Monsieur has been obliged to change his name in order to stay in Paris. We have been in the most dire straits, and never once did Mademoiselle want to let you know about her situation."

"How fatal! How wrong she was to be ashamed! . . . What misplaced pride! Me, her friend! . . . Her husband! . . . Oh! . . ."

"At last, five days ago, one evening, Mademoiselle came back from the rue de l'Ouest with a large sum of money . . ."

The General's fear was at its peak, he tore the braids from his uniform in rage, and, leaning out the door, he cried:

"Laurent, full gallop! . . . Faster! . . ." and Laurent rushed down the rue Saint-Jacques, yelling back: "We're losing the horses! . . ."

"Will we make it in time?" the General said.

"We must hope so," answered Lagloire, who, putting his head out the window, shouted a warning to those who found themselves either in front of or behind this coach that seemed carried along by a furious wind.

At last they came to Veryno's house. The General rushed up the wooden stairs with a rapidity never seen; he burst into the room of his old friend.

Veryno was alone; his lamp gave off a feeble light. The old man, his head in his hands, was deep in thought; and the fact that his eye was fixed on the chair that Marianine usually occupied all day long, revealed that all his thoughts turned upon his dear daughter. When he heard the noise at the door, the old man stirred his hoary head; he lifted up his eyes swollen with tears, and he saw the General in a condition that was difficult to describe. His horrified face, his terrifying attitude, moved Veryno so deeply that he acknowledged Beringheld without daring to speak to him.

"Marianine! . . ." was the first word the General uttered.

"She's gone out!" was Veryno's answer.

Beringheld wrung his hands, and raised his eyes heavenward with an expression of pain, of fear, and of fright, which was noticed by all. He went slowly toward his old friend, took him in his arms without saying a word; let his tears flow over this aged face, and, turning to Lagloire, he gave him a sign they must leave.

The General left the old man plunged in the deepest astonishment; a vague fear, a glacial terror gripped his heart, and he looked searchingly at Julie. Julie made no answer to this tacit question, and silence reigned; the astonished old man walked back and forth with feeble steps in this room void of life.

Meanwhile, the General and Lagloire rushed toward the place where Beringheld the Centenarian had made his temporary dwelling. They arrived, spurred on by the hope of arriving in time to save Marianine. They entered a place that seemed to be the palace of the spirit of destruction, and the temple of terror.

The General's curious eye swept over this vast panorama; his gaze rested on the nearly ruined house, and there, the moon, breaking out from behind the thick shadows of a large cloud, lit up with a swath of light the porch of this savage haunt. This magical scene *stunned* the General: for suddenly the huge old man appeared in the opening of the house, he carried on his shoulders Marianine, who had fainted; her lovely head rested against that of the Centenarian, and the jet-black of her long locks mingled with the silver tresses of the old man; the arms of his faithful lover hung down without strength, and in their weakness revealed that she had let herself go: this pose, this *laissez aller*, took hold of her entire bearing. The old man carried her with indifference, as if she were some lifeless object. Her lovely face full of sweetness, her eyes, lifeless and closed, Marianine's pallor, rendered whiter yet by this sudden ray of moonlight, all were in stark contrast with the fire that darted from the eyes of this *baleful* old man: it was death carrying off the dying. Add to this his slow and immutable gait, the rigid expression of his face, and his *monumental* stature, and one will have an idea of the most terrible picture that the imagination can envision. This spectacle was more than terrifying for the General, for he knew that Marianine was going to her death. Thus, hardly had he spotted the old man and his prey, when he rushed, with the speed of a bullet, toward the ruined house. He went inside, and found nothing there; he went through all the rooms, and saw no way out whatsoever; he examined the floor of flagstones where the old man seemingly vanished, and he found no issue. Lagloire was dumbstruck, but he rushed to get light, weapons, and tools: during this errand the old soldier exulted, he swore he would tear down everything, rather that not find Marianine.

"Rally round me, friends of the 3d Regiment! The enemy is here!" he cried.

Three or four persons heard Lagloire's cry, they followed him toward the tavern where he had already set up his headquarters, during the campaign he had raised in hopes of finding the Centenarian's dwelling, and as chance had it they were former soldiers from Lagloire's old regiment.

Chapter twenty-nine
MARIANINE IN THE CATACOMBS — PREPARATIONS
ARE MADE FOR HER DEATH — HER FINAL VISION

As soon as the old man had entered the underground tunnel with his victim, he hurried to take advantage of Marianine's being in a swoon, in order to transport her to the place he called his palace. The dankness of these deep vaults,[55] which began beneath the Observatory and to which the Centenarian had secret access, gripped Marianine, and she awoke from the deep sleep to which she had fallen prey.

A mortal fear took hold of her soul when the feeble glow of the lamp that the old man was carrying revealed to her the horrible place they were passing through. The young girl, never having heard spoken of the catacombs, was terrified by their appearance. These mountains of bones, piled in rows with unique regularity, seemed the archives of death. This eternal silence, barely troubled by the steps of the being who carried her, and, more than this even, the presence of this extraordinary being who in so many ways shared his existence with the inhabitants of these tombs, all these things concurred to place her under the invincible *spell* of fear; this condition drained her of the energy and the means of escaping from her fate; she could only follow this magic being, who as soon as he saw that she had regained consciousness, placed her on her feet.

They had been walking in silence for quite a long time, and were about to find themselves at the end of the catacombs, when the poor Marianine, gathering up all her strength, stopped and said: "Where are you taking me?"

"To the Louvre . . . Here, child, look! . . ." And the old man showed her the vault.

"But, what is the purpose of going to the Louvre?"

"You will see a palace where all the sciences converge; you will discover a place where all powers have been united: if you wish to see your lover, you may contemplate him to your heart's content; if you are unhappy now, you will cease to be so . . ."

The old man had a sardonic tone that made Marianine tremble. At last, she arose and followed the Centenarian who was walking with a silence terrifying like that which follows the executioner as he drags his victim to the scaffold.

Soon they came upon a huge slab of stone that started as part of the ground and rose up until it surpassed the vault. This announced that they had reached the end of their subterranean journey. The bizarre position of this mass of stone indicated that the past generation that had exploited this quarry had stopped here, either because the quality of the stone had not been the same, or because the mine had ceased to yield any stone at all. Marianine sat down on a block of stone; her eyes, straining and empty of any vital expression, wandered over the sinuosities of this underground rock, over the holes that still bore the marks of man's tools. She dared neither to look at the Centenarian, nor to turn her head: finally, if the human mind is in some way capable of understanding that state of being where one has nothing left of life but its animal breath, where one is deprived of sensations, of feeling, and too feeble to set in movement the springs of the soul, then one will have an imperfect idea of Marianine's situation.

In the midst of this deathly silence, one heard nothing but the noise of dripping water, that filtered drop by drop, and whose monotonous succession alone was capable of plunging the soul into a state of melancholy.

The Centenarian, searching in the vault for an object that seemed familiar to him, found it after a few moments. Although Marianine, because she had reached an unheard of degree of passive suffering, remained incapable of astonishment at the new wonder before her eyes, she looked on mechanically, as if watching some ordinary occurrence, as this great mass of stone rose up in the air, and the Centenarian fastened an iron chain, that dropped down from the vault, to a large ring set in the wall of this rock. Then the young girl perceived another tunnel, whose eternal darkness was lit by a glow so feeble that only served to make the darkness more terrible. This sad light, which came through the cracks in a door located at the end of that gallery, imparted a rather strong color to the two sides of this dark sub-terranean corridor; this glow however soon faded and died, in imperceptible shadings, in such a manner that the spot where Marianine stood was plunged into total blackness. This effect of nature caused in the soul such emotion, that Veryno's daughter was to a degree drawn from her torpor, and she uttered a loud scream.

"There you see the portals of my palace!" cried the old man, taking hold of Marianine and forcing her to enter this strange place.

She was agreeably surprised, when she felt that she was walk-ing on a hardwood floor, covered with a carpet that must have been precious, to judge by the softness of its feel under her feet. The vault and the walls of this gallery were hung with black vel-vet, draped with elegance and fastened by clasps of silver. Mari-anine, in the midst of the royal luxury of this gallery, regained a bit of her courage, and she began to pass her pretty hand over the velvet and the ornaments, like a person who, though dying, still picks flowers, make plans, and by some secret law of the nature of the human mind, conceals from himself the horror of his future death by playing such ephemeral games.

Marianine followed far behind the old man; suddenly, her foot stumbled against a sonorous object, the noise of which frightened her; she looked down at her feet and, in the light that became stronger as she advanced, she thought she recognized a skeleton, the bony hand of which was still holding a piece of tapestry. Marianine shuddered at the horrible idea that rushed to her mind of the many people her guide must have sacrificed in order to ensure that the location of his subterranean dwelling remain an inviolable secret. At once, all this splendor faded, she thought only of the deaths of the workmen the old man had employed, and her reflections led her to think that she would never leave this tomb . . . She turned as if to flee, but as soon as she raised her eyes, she encountered the Centenarian who was blocking her passage. She trembled at the sight of the horrific looks he cast upon her.

"What is all this mystery?" she demanded, pointing to the bones of the skeleton with an accusatory finger.

The Centenarian began to smile scornfully; and in the midst of all this silence the sound of his sardonic laugh terrified the girl . . .

"Do you think that I caused him to die?" . . . Marianine shuddered as she saw the sagacity with which the old man discovered her thoughts. "Euphrasia," he continued, "fifty men, during the several past centuries, have worked on this *gnome's* palace; there is not a single one of them *who knew they had built* my palace . . . If ever I do sacrifice a living *being*, it is always the rarest of occasions, and I do so with weeping, because at that moment I am following the laws of necessity . . . onward! . . ."

At last they reached the end of the gallery, and there, before entering, Marianine noticed a number of precious objects arranged with taste. Among these curiosities she remarked several pieces of burnt wood placed respectfully on a piece of velvet as if they were a precious object.

"What is this?" she asked, looking at the huge old man.

"Those," he answered, "are pieces of *Joan of Arc*'s stake; next to them, we have one of the last stones from the Bastille; farther on, the skull is that of Ravaillac;[56] this book is Cromwell's bible; that blunderbuss belonged to Charles IX. Take a good look at this map of the world: it is that of the great Christopher Columbus; here is Queen Elizabeth's veil! There you have her sister Mary's necklace, Louis XIV's riding crop; the sword was Jimenez's, and the pen belonged to Cardinal Richelieu; the latter is not the pen that signed poor Montmorency's order of execution, but the one that wrote *Miramé*. Look, here is a ring that belonged to Pope Sixtus V: all the things you see are, in short, souvenirs that bring to mind my many friends and bygone centuries."

When he had finished speaking, the Centenarian pushed open the door, and the astonished Marianine was struck by another spectacle. She saw a vast circular room whose walls were hung with rich tapestries. On a huge table, covered with green cloth, stood a bronze lamp that looked as if it was intended to light this place of horror through all eternity.

Indeed, several human skulls were on the table: skeletons thrust forth their hideous heads; they seemed to chortle aloud and to call to Marianine. When she cast a glance in the another direction, she shuddered as she saw a number of steel instruments that shone in the light and seemed to be harbingers of death; spheres, bones, maps, strange substances, the forms and colors of which she could not distinguish, all terrified her eyes. She saw no books at all, only dry parchment scrolls, half unrolled and covered with cabalistic signs, which comprised the entire library of the Centenarian. Not daring to think, Marianine let her gaze wander about this room that here, at the center of the earth, appeared to contain all the secrets of nature. She came to her wits all of a sudden, and her first impulse was to attempt to flee; she turned around, she saw no way out, and, as if by magic, a chair covered with a black sheet rose up out of the floor behind her—she thought, at least, that the object this fatal sheet concealed was a chair . . . She looked around to find the old man and ask him what it was, and was petrified with horror! . . . The Centenarian had sat down in his chair, he had stripped himself of all the trappings and clothing that concealed his form, and the pallid light of the lamp, shining down on top of his skull, gave it such a yellowish hue that one was unable to distinguish the old man's head from those other heads, deprived of life, that lay before him.

But much more astonishing to Marianine was the change that had come over the face of the singular being facing her. The Centenarian's attitude, the stiffness of his behavior, was such that it would have humbled the most intrepid of beings. A brusque severity dominated his face, giving it all the marks of cruelty. He did not dare look at his victim, who, pale, with disheveled hair, and beautiful in her candor and innocence, seemed to plead with him with her eyes alone, lacking the words that she could not pronounce. The barely visible light of the lamp, along with an unrelenting silence, lent to this subterranean scene an unimaginable eloquence. One would have thought one was witnessing, at that moment, Mary Stuart alone with her executioner, awaiting the mortal blow in that room Schiller[57] depicts decked out in regal opulence.

Marianine soon noticed frightening signs in the old man, manifestations of some impending dissolution: the somber fire of his eyes softened imperceptibly and seemed to fade. This was either an effect of the uneven nature of the lamplight or of some *anomaly* of his supernatural existence, for she thought she saw the artificial complexion of this being pale to a degree such that the bones of long dead generations could not be whiter. At the moment when this poor child was contemplating him with the maximum of attention, he looked at her, and even the furtive glance that Ugolino cast on the limbs of his children dead from hunger, however horrible it is in Dante's rendering, was less ferocious and intense than was his look at this moment.

After using this look to bring about in the soul of Marianine a stupor that he apparently wanted to exploit, the old man got up; but feeling his existence weaken, he was forced to drag himself along, leaning on the furniture as he went, in order to go and fetch a number of items.

He took up a glass tube that ended in a blowtorch, the extremity of which was coated with platinum, he set it down, with all the precautions of old age, on his table, he attached to it some phials whose contents Marianine could not ascertain, for some substance made of an alloy of several metals fastened each beaker together, the upper part of which alone remained uncovered. Once he had placed on the table everything he seemed to need, he took a mortar made of gold and placed it near Marianine, who watched all these preparations with a childlike curiosity. The poor girl, I believe, would have played with the same ax that would be later used to cut off her head.

"But why," she said softly to the old man, "why all this?"

The cry of the hyena that finds its long sought-after prey was not more savage that the laugh of the Centenarian.

"What a terrible voice," exclaimed Marianine. "Oh, let me go, for I no longer exist! . . .

"Your life is mine," the old man said, "you gave it to me, it no longer belongs to you! . . ."

"What do you want with it?" she asked with innocence.

"*When you learn that, you won't know anything more about anything!*" the Centenarian responded laconically.

"My God!" exclaimed Marianine, wringing her hands and raising her eyes to the vault; she had reason to tremble at that instant, seeing above her head an immense bell made of some transparent substance,[58] that seemed to be hanging but by a thread. She uttered a cry of horror, and fell to the ground but, fortunately for her, to one side of that fatal instrument concealed beneath the black sheet.

The Centenarian continued his preparations with stoic impassiveness, and did not even lift up Marianine, who was attempting with all her might to crawl toward the door that had now become invisible; the old man, however, from time to time cast a glance at the movements of his prey.

At this moment, a rather extraordinary noise echoed through the tunnels they had just entered; the old man, astonished, listened for a long moment; but, as the noise suddenly stopped, he paid no further attention to it. A faint ray of hope shone in the soul of Marianine, she was on her knees and sought to discover what was hidden under the lugubrious black sheet, placing her hand near it. She felt an unbearable heat, and did not dare to determine whether the hidden fire whose force was so violent was burning beneath the grotto, or whether it was contained in the bronze itself. She looked over the top of the black sheet, and saw a vapor whose presence was suggested by the movement of the objects that were this side of the sheet.—"Come," the old man exclaimed, advancing toward the young girl, "Will you get up?"

Marianine got up, and ran to take refuge on the other side of the room, seeming to fear the approach of the old man. The latter began to smile at the fright of his victim and said to her:

"Euphrasia, you are in my power, and nothing can save you from it . . . What ear could hear your cries, what arm could come to your aid? We are two hundred feet beneath that same ground upon which the men of a day walk . . ."

"And what about God?" said Marianine.

A terrifying smile passed over the cauterized lips of the Centenarian; seeing this sardonic laugh worthy of Satan, the young girl cried out: "I am dead . . . I see it now."

A second smile was the only response, and the old man, contemplating the sublime beauty of the being that he was about to destroy, let several tears flow down his pale cheek . . .

Marianine, falling at the feet of her executioner, raised her hands in supplication and said in a tone of voice that would have softened a tiger's heart:—"At least, will you let me pray to God . . . for a few minutes? . . ."

"If that makes your death less cruel, I consent to it . . ."

With that, the old man returned to his chair and, examining one by one the substances contained in the phials, he began to compose a mixture of them, while Marianine, kneeling on a square of velvet where other victims like her had perhaps prayed before, lifted up her innocent supplications to the heavens.

"Alas," she said out loud, "perhaps I should thank the Almighty for taking away my existence: it will spare me much future pain. Indeed, Almighty God, up to now, the sum of my misfortune has outweighed that of my happiness, and for those few fleeting moments of joy, how many pains I have suffered! . . . If such were the case during the most beautiful part of my life, sadly it does not augur well for the rest of that life! . . ."

As this idea invaded her soul, she arose with calm, and offering herself up to the old man, she spoke to him in a sweet accent of innocence: "I'm ready now . . ."

The Centenarian, not expecting such submission, looked at her with astonishment.

"Could you tell me," she continued with a voice that in no way complained, "could you tell me what I did to you to make you want to kill me? . . ."

"Why did you cross my path? Did you not admit to me that you were going to your death, that you desired it? . . ."

"Yes," she exclaimed, "I desired death . . . Oh! I didn't know what death was! . . ."

"Because you wanted to die, is it not better that your life's breath, rather than dissipating and losing itself in the mass of existing things that comprise our earthly globe, comes to me to prolong my life? . . . Young girl, now my breath is dependent on yours, I pity you if you have deceived me! . . . Even if you love life, you must leave it . . . If only you had warned me . . . I would have sought out other victims! They are not lacking in Paris . . . Indeed the dives of the *Palais de Richelieu* furnish me with more than I can use . . . There is no time left now . . . In a little while I will expire . . . I feel already that my ideas are barely able to shape themselves and that the vital fluid is lacking . . . Your death is now a *necessity,* and as you have a beautiful soul, I will speak to you bluntly . . . Poor child! I will regret you perhaps more than all those you are leaving behind on this earth . . . and there are memories that are most painful to me!"

Finishing these last words, the Centenarian seemed oppressed, and a residue of human feeling triumphed over the cold and mournful truths that his *omniscience* had brought him to conquer.

"Then," said Marianine, "will you use your divine art and plunge me into the sleep of the soul, and let me see the one I love? . . . While I will be absorbed in this sweet vision, detached from the world, you can take from me the breath that I will no longer need . . . for *if he did not come to marry me, it is because he no longer loves me.*"

The old man seemed enchanted by this proposition that would save Marianine the pains of death and spare him the terrible spectacle of a victim who struggles against death. A flash of joy returned to animate his face, which had already taken on the appearance of that of a skeleton, and he took hold of Marianine's hands . . .

Marianine's Final Vision*

As soon as the Centenarian had taken Marianine's pretty hands in his own, she plunged into the void, and a night deeper than the night of the heavens invaded her with a swiftness equal to that of the arrow that pierces the dove. The young girl entered thus into that vast kingdom whose domain begins where our universe ends, a domain where no one enters without being at one and the same time both *dead* and *alive*, where man summons all of nature to appear outside of itself, as if a mirror were revealing its least secrets, shaping them into material substance; it is a domain ruled by a power that cleaves the entire earth in two, as with a sharp razor, uncovering within its most hidden treasures; a domain where in involuntary manner one is able to name the

*[Note of Monsieur de Saint Aubin: I do not need, I think, to reiterate, in relation to this passage, the observation I recorded in the note that the reader must have read earlier, when I recounted the first dream of Marianine. The present passage was also left intact by the Editor, who did not wish to cut a single word of it.]

names of all the plants and animals, where one understands the ideas of all peoples, where one soars across the universe with the ease of a fly that flits from one room to another. It is a splendid kingdom, in which one forgets everything, retaining only that agreeable sensation one compares to the charm of a dream of happiness. It is, in sum, a place where a person looking at himself sees nothing but the precious elaboration of things that comprises the faculty of thought.

Marianine is no longer in the catacombs, where in fact she physically lies.* Her lovely body remains there, it is true, but her soul soars at the command of a being whose dominating yoke she is unable to shake: it seems as if he possesses the magic wand with which peoples of the East arm their fantastic divinities, and that he manipulates nature as if in play. The young girl remains plunged in this funereal night, and her inertia becomes so great that, according to what she would later say, *death lying in the tomb* could not be more inanimate and motionless than she was at this moment.

And yet, in spite of this palpable night, she feels an immanent danger, and she has a vague sense that someone is about to cause her pain.

At the end of an indefinite length of time,† (because Marianine could not have any sense of duration) she begins to *see daylight inside herself*, and this time, *the dawn that came up in her soul* has a whitish hue, similar to the glow cast by a night light set in a vase

---

*[Editor's Note: I put this narrative in the present tense, as if the Editor himself were telling the events or were witness to them, in order to avoid confusion].

†(My dear A——, it is the multiplicity of sensations and the human faculty of thought that have rendered tangible the succession of instants, and have made Time a thing that is almost palpable; thus, from the moment when one withdraws the faculty that modifies space, reduces it to seconds, minutes, hours, the duration of a day becomes a unit that, even though much vaster, still offers no more space than a minute. This metaphysical problem requires more argument in order

of alabaster. She then begins to *walk* in the same subterranean passage she had just taken with the old man; yet her steps make no sound, her breathing no longer echoes in the vault, and she strikes the piles of bones in vain, they make no sound.[59]

A sudden illumination *made her move forward* at an incredible speed, she *heard* the noise of a number of confused voices, and then she moved in the direction of those people she *sensed* were approaching.

In order to arrive there sooner, she leaned (as if to draw more force from it) into the *shadow* of the Centenarian, whom she *felt* at her side, without however seeing or hearing him, and yet she *knew* he was there. Having thus attained a stronger dose of *incorporeality* and an energy that resembled that of *animal vitality*, she suddenly *saw* a scene that caused her to utter cries of joy; yet, although Marianine mustered all her bodily powers in order to cry out, no sound issued from her *body*, no word came, and her tongue remained stuck to her palate, *even though she made it move.*

Indeed, General Beringheld, Lagloire, three soldiers, Veryno, Julie, Tullius's coachman, all formed the group that Marianine *perceived;* some held torches, and others armed with picks were digging at the floor of the Centenarian's house.

"Courage, lads!" cried Butmel, "Grab those picks *by the rifle butt!* The General gives a *hundred louis* if it's finished in an hour!"

"Two hundred," said Beringheld, "and thirty thousand francs if we save Marianine!"

When he heard these words Veryno, who had just arrived, understood the danger his daughter was in, and fainted dead away into Julie's arms. The General, too busy with his digging, paid no attention to the old man's fainting; he grabbed a pick and set to

---

to be proven; *I simply mention it in passing in order to make my letter more intelligible; for in the end this explanation was useless even for you: you understand my drift.) [Note of General Beringheld] [Editor's Note: I have respected this note, which as you can see I have written down verbatim.]*

work: seeing this, Lagloire gave his moustache a twirl, swore out loud, while exclaiming:

"And what about respect then, my General?"

"Marianine! Marianine!" Tullius replied, striking such mighty blows on the stone floor that the walls seemed to shake from them. "All we will find is her body!" he exclaimed.

"My father is dying!" Marianine uttered in her soft voice; "Tullius, you are digging too much the left; it's on the right, there is only one big stone to lift up . . . it's here! . . ."

The *extraordinary thing* about this magic vision was that Veryno's daughter found herself only halfway along the path through the catacombs, that she was separated by a vault of sixty feet of earth from the spot where the scene was taking place; and yet *she saw it*, not by the visual power of the *external eye*, but by an *internal vision*; and in such a manner that the problem to be resolved here is the following: to know whether the place itself came to her and appeared *inside her*, or whether it was she who was transported to the place?

Finally she *was there*, and when she came up against the vault, she passed through it as if no barrier existed between herself and the group of workers. She uttered a cry of joy that was no more heard than any of her other cries. She placed on the forehead of her father a loving kiss, but it did not seem to affect him.

She said in vain: "Hello, Julie! . . . In vain she threw herself in the arms of Beringheld and held him in the embrace of a *soul* filled with love, but the General did not in the least stop delivering mighty blows to the slabs of marble—Although Marianine had earlier experienced an example of this same intangibility (*but she had not retained any memory of it*), this was like the first time for her, and she poured forth a torrent of tears, which she wiped away with her lovely black hair.

"Hurrah!" cried Lagloire, "I know the way now! General, here's a stone that comes loose."

Marianine, weeping and grieving, did not share in the joy of the group, she sat down beside her dear Tullius, and took pleasure in the admiration in which she was plunged as she contemplated the ardor with which he pursued this excavation. The General paled with happiness and hope, when Lagloire showed him the immense stone of which each sought to guess the secret of its opening.

"At last, General," exclaimed Jacques Butmel, "we are going to enter the headquarters of our old bandit of a Cossack!"

"There must be a counterweight somewhere," murmured Veryno, "in order to raise this mass; I don't believe that there can be any other way."

"Here! It's here! . . ." cried Marianine, taking hold of the hidden spring that operated the counterweight; but her efforts to move it were in vain, the stone never moved an inch from its place.

"To hell with the counterweight!" cried Lagloire; And, going through the ammunition pouches of his soldiers, he took out some cartridges, tied them together, and forcing them into the cracks at each of the four corners of the stone, he drew out his flint, his pipe, his tinder box (objects he carried wherever he went); and, looking at the three soldiers, he told them:

"You, my old troopers, you are going to stay with me!—General, Papa Veryno, and you, my pretty little pistol," he said, addressing in turn the General (to whom he bowed respectfully), Veryno, and Julie, to whom he gave a chuck under the chin, "you are going to go back to the street; once the charge goes off, and we are again masters of the terrain, you can return! . . . Let's go . . . General, we must evacuate the caserne; I'm giving the orders today!"

Everyone withdrew, and Lagloire remained with the three comrades that he had recently found; he made a trail of powder, and once he had gotten a reasonable distance away, he ignited it.—The stone was blasted away, *Marianine was sitting on top of it, she felt no jolt whatsoever*, and even when there was only a hole remaining, Marianine did not change her place.

They all returned to examine the spot where Marianine still sat, crying when she noticed that they could not see her at all. A salvo of cries of joy filled the air as they found the steps of a stairway, and Lagloire, forgetting that the government had changed, rushed into the tunnel with his three men crying: "To glory! On-ward, charge, and *long live the Emperor!* . . . of Morocco!" he added prudently, as he entered the subterranean place.

Marianine still wandered feebly, following them with her eyes, but everything vanished and the scene faded gradually, as when the mind loses the trace of a memory, if it is possible to compare material objects with the effects of thought . . .

Finally, like Eurydice, when she vanished in smoke from the arms of her husband, her soul, no longer illuminated, seemed to return to inhabit the lovely body that lay rigid in the horrible amphitheater of the Centenarian. And yet Marianine felt, at the moment when she *saw* nothing more, that the Centenarian had abandoned her, and that his icy hands had ceased to wander over her body . . .

The End

Is Marianine dead? Does the Centenarian still exist? Has he been seen again? . . . Is all of this merely some fiction, the ravings of a sick imagination? To all these questions the editor's only answer is the phrase that Socrates found the most difficult for mankind to utter: *"I don't know . . ."*

Paris, 18th April, 1820

First Editor's Note

Paris, 20th August, 1822

Here, effectively, is the last of all the information concerning the Centenarian that I was able to procure.

What kept me so long from publishing all these documents, in reducing them to a coherent narrative, is that I felt that this ending, this denouement which in fact unties nothing, would never satisfy the curiosity of those who seek in a book an action in accordance with the rules of dramatic art, and who absolutely must have a fifth act and a marriage, instead of being thankful to the author for all the feelings they experienced before they get to the last page, and who consider all such emotions of no importance if one does not leave them something to play with in the end.

One would have especially blamed me for the vagueness that reigns in this final chapter, and the soul, I feel, is grievously affected at the thought that Marianine had to perish. Finally, a sort of impatience must erupt when one finds himself in the dark as to the fate of the Centenarian.

At least, these were the feelings that disturbed me as I assembled my manuscripts. I am going to give an account of how chance placed in my hands the letters that provide the conclusion to my story.

I have a brother, whose fate is unknown to me, for he sailed five years ago on a trip around the world. This brother, before he embarked, placed in my hands part of the information that serves as basis of this tale, and as he has a great interest in the *natural sciences*, and as he is very absent-minded, he gave me this bundle of papers, but in a most incomplete state: without the help of some influential friends, these papers would have been quite useless to me.

Six months ago, my brother was rumored to be dead, and as we are several brothers (they will soon be known), his room was sealed off: about two months ago, in breaking the seals, I recognized some letters that were in the handwriting of General Beringheld.

Having already made proof of my skill in extracting documents, during my adventure in the Père Lachaise (see the preface of my novel *Le Vicaire des Ardennes*), one can imagine the subtlety I used to get hold of these precious letters, which will now comprise the conclusion to this story: indeed, I did so right under the nose of my brothers.

My brother (the one presumed dead) was a true scientist, having most extraordinary opinions on the *nature of things*. His was a mathematical mind, that advanced from proof to proof, and which never worked but with *Analysis* (he claimed that one does nothing without it); and since a long time ago I went in the opposite direction, and gave everything over to imagination, I have often made fun of the so-called discoveries of my brother, of his ideas and of his systems. It finally got to the point where he considered me unworthy of his confidence; and this explanation should reveal the motive he had for concealing from me the adventure that gave him the occasion to meet General Beringheld.

Insofar as it is but recently that I came across these important pieces, I have not had the time to alter their form, and so I publish them exactly as they are, without taking anything out or adding anything; I beg the reader to make up for anything that may be lacking.

Horace de Saint-Aubin

CONCLUSION

Letter from Monsieur de Saint-Aubin senior to
James Gordon, Paris . . .

My friend, there are more adepts in the world than we admit and I have a terrible fear that the powers we have conquered may soon be the property of everybody. Listen to what happened to me.

Yesterday, after I left you, I went to the meeting at Jeannes's house, who, as you know, lives at the other end of the earth. Everything that we had to do there took much more time than we would have thought, and soon it was midnight. I was returning at about two in the morning, and I was, I believe, some six hundred feet from the *Hospice des Enfants-Trouvés*, when I heard piercing screams: I headed toward the place they seemed to be coming from, and saw a man come out of that fenced-off area I have often pointed out to you: a man carrying a woman in his arms.[60] . . I thought it was an abduction, for as the light of the moon was not sufficient to distinguish things clearly, I did not have a complete view of the woman's face, whose disheveled hair and countenance gave me reason to think that the screams I had heard were made by her. Immediately, I rushed forward, and violently seizing the abductor, I wrenched his victim from him and went toward the house of a baker, whose light I saw still burning.

As soon as I had the woman in my arms, she began to moan in the most unusual manner. I was forced to give her up, for the stranger who was holding her, blocked my way, and asked me to give her back in a tone and manner that proved to me that he was not at all a scoundrel. And so I helped him carry this young woman, who had fainted, back to a house in front of which a carriage was standing.

There we entered the lodgings of a concierge, who appeared to be extremely upset, as if an extraordinary event had happened in the neighborhood. The body of the young woman was placed on a bed, and once she was there, the young man, examining her pallor, believed she was dead. Then he gave himself over to the most awful despair to which a human being could fall prey, but I calmed him suddenly, for after having taken the pulse of the one he called his *dear Marianine*, I told him she was still alive: he looked at me with an air of astonishment, and for a long time fixed his eyes on me, and on the young woman.

"This," I said, "is most extraordinary . . ." All at once, I took up the lamp and, heating up a brass wire, I laid it red hot in the hand of Marianine. The stranger shuddered, but he was astounded to see the immobility of Marianine, who uttered no cry, even though her skin was burned by the brass wire.

Then, taking the hand of the stranger, I said to him: "Monsieur, I answer for this young girl's well-being, and thank the stroke of luck that permitted us to meet each other, as she would die of hunger, were I not able to bring her out of the lethargy in which you now see her immersed."

I *awoke* her immediately: she cast an astonished look at me, but when she saw the stranger, her eye was no longer dulled by the haze of *sleep*: it burned with an almost supernatural light, and she cried out in most charming voice: "Tullius!"

At this word, the stranger, becoming fanatical, took her in his arms, and left hurriedly; he placed her in the carriage, crying out to his driver: "Laurent, a hundred louis if you carry us like the wind to the relay station. You will not encounter any cabs, so full speed ahead."

I stopped him, and asked him, by way of recompense, to send me the account of whatever strange adventure led to this young girl having been *put to sleep*: I gave him my address, or rather I threw it at him, for his carriage was off like a shot; and at the moment he left, I saw the two embrace each other and the young girl rest her head on the shoulder of her lover.

I tell you, she was as beautiful as an antique statue; I have never seen such soft forms, and despite her extreme pallor and thinness, she was still perfect.

Insofar as I was extremely tired, I went home, saying to the old concierge that I would return the next day in order to find out from him all the incidents that he had wanted to tell me about.

You see, my dear Salvator,[61] that we are not the only ones interested in that science, whose wonders surpass the miracles of yore.

I returned the next day: I learned that the stranger was General Beringheld, and that three hours after I had left, horrible screams had been heard coming from a house located in that enclosed space I mentioned earlier; that the girl's father, her serving lady, and an old soldier came out of it, leaving behind, they said, three soldiers struggling with the demon.

This is what I learned that was most understandable from all the ramblings of the old gatekeeper; when I will have received news from the General, I will fill you in on the rest of this adventure, and awaiting this, I remain sincerely yours . . .

Letter from General Count de Beringheld to
Monsieur Victor de Saint-Aubin Senior, Physician.

Monsieur, you made me promise to explain by what strange adventure the young girl that I so rapidly carried off found herself in the condition from which you rescued her.

If I left you so abruptly after having received from you a service that ten million francs could not requite, I beg you to allow me to begin this letter then by expressing my infinite gratitude, and I offer you with pleasure my reputation, my heart, and my purse.

Whatever your knowledge of the human heart, in the moral sense, you must imagine that when you brought my dear Marianine back to life, when her eyes turned toward me, and she called out to me: "Tullius! . . ." putting into that word all the love that has animated it since the beginning of time, the first impulse of a man who *loves* (and Monsieur, there are not many who *love*) is to take hold of such an adorable and adored woman, and to take her away from all possible malign influences, from heaven knows what demons that have dogged us ever since the war in Russia.

The few words that we did exchange convinced me that you were very well versed in the sciences; and the *inconceivable service* that you rendered me, made me see that you possess one of the secrets of that extraordinary being whose fate I still ignore.

Take yourself back, Monsieur, to that night of terror and suffering, and picture me followed by four old soldiers, throwing myself into the immense abyss of the catacombs, seeking there a woman who, a long while earlier, had been dragged there by an old man, about whom I will later give you enough information to allow you to know all the horror of the position in which I found myself. Let it suffice for the moment that I tell you that this old man had taken her there *in order to kill her.*

We wandered a long time in those tunnels, but the zeal that drove us on, and whatever spirit that flies between lovers, led me to follow in obstinate manner the right route.

Ah, Monsieur, what a sight! . . . In the depths of the catacombs, after having passed through mountains of human bones, we came upon a cave, whose door we broke down, and there I found my dear Marianine in the state in which you saw her, ready to be cast, by this old man, into some device about to be covered by a bell of bronze . . . I rushed forward, and overcoming an invincible terror as I approached the old man, I snatched his prey from his hands, while my three soldiers held him at bay at gunpoint.

At that instant a horrible fear appeared on the face of this extraordinary *being*, and he cried out after me while I was fleeing: '*My son!* . . . *My son!*' . . . I heard no more, and I succeeded in escaping. I can boast of having, like Orpheus, and more fortunate than he, gone and brought back my bride from the underworld.

As I have not seen Monsieur Veryno or my aide again at all, I cannot give you any more details. As for informing you of the adventure that led to Marianine being put in the power of the Centenarian, I will soon send you some documents whose contents will give you food for thought.

Let it he known that for three days I have been reunited with my dear Marianine, and that I have sent a courier with a message

to her father, so that he may come and bear witness to our happiness.   Sincerely............Beringheld.
P.S. Whenever you might wish to do us the honor of coming to Beringheld, you will be most welcome, and I admit that I would be curious to discuss with you the immense career that now opens up before me.

Excerpt from Monsieur de Saint-Aubin senior's Reply to General Beringheld

General, I took myself back to the place where the Centenarian had his abode, and after the most thorough search, I found nothing except a huge overcoat, brown in color.

Editor's Note

What remains to be published about the Centenarian, about General Beringheld, and Marianine, will comprise, I think, another work that will have for title *The Last Beringheld*. I do not know when I will be able to produce it, given the fact that it still requires a lot of work and research, and what is more, I do not know whether the work that I propose will have any success with the reading public.

I promised the adventures of *Lagradna and of Butmel*, a story whose naïve simplicity makes it worthy of being known; but this is perhaps only another reason that more work needs to be done, in order to elevate this story to the level of *nature captured in the act*.

In concluding here, I request great indulgence of those who will have read this work, that they do not judge ill things whose *degree of plausibility they ignore.** Thus, one will cry out against the alliance of certain words that jar, against incoherent sentences, and inexact expressions; but happily I have taken my precautions, and I declare moreover that I know what I have risked: the greater or lesser success of this work will decide whether I shall henceforth remain silent, or continue.

*[*One can see that I begin to regret not having believed my brother.*]

I have no illusions that certain readers will find this ending less than satisfactory; they would have wanted to see Beringheld and Marianine reunited and the scene of their marriage: this radical omission is not of my doing. If I had merely written a piece of fiction, I would have neglected nothing, and I would have pleased everybody, if that is possible, but, as a historian, I have faithfully told everything that I have learned.

THE END

The Centenarian in the *Comédie humaine*

The author, in an "Avant-propos" to his *Comédie humaine*, written toward the end of its creation (1843), repudiated *The Centenarian* along with all the early genre work not signed with the name "Balzac." It is clear as well by the end of *The Centenarian* that Balzac's mythic scientist must not, in the form of a flesh-and-blood character, enter the contemporary world of Restoration France. And yet avatars of the Centenarian are everywhere in the *Comédie*. He has been "domesticated" in any number of self-centered and maniacal figures—Balthasar Claës, Gambara, the Père Goriot, Vautrin, Gobseck. Readers are often at a loss to reconcile Balzac's "scènes de la vie" with his "études philosophiques." Their dialectic, in fact, is a continuation of the dialectic between the two Beringhelds in the early novel. Even more central to the deep structure of Balzac's mature work, in fact, is the dialectic that occurs between the mind and body of the Centenarian himself. Once what is literal in the Centenarian's overreaching aspirations and cannibalistic methods is removed, the same struggle can be restated on a more general, and figurative, level—that of the *peau de chagrin* (the "wild ass's skin" of Balzac's novel of that name). As with the title of Balzac's early story, "Melmoth réconcilié," his social comedy hopes to "reconcile" the Centenarian. In doing so, it transposes his character's raw, personal struggle with the human condition to the level of social, and ultimately material, law. If the Centenarian's presence is no longer felt in individual dramas, it informs the abstract principle that regulates these dramas. This figure lies at the source of Balzac's famous social code based on "scientific," positivist principles. It is but a step from the Centenarian's elixir of life and its expense to the concept of *volonté*, or natural will, that will govern all further relations between individuals in Balzac's social world. Let us describe briefly how the Centenarian is domesticated in the *Comédie humaine*, the vast social comedy that is the written corpus of his work, and how this is perhaps essential to a fuller understanding of the nature of Balzac's work.

The Two Endings of The Centenarian

Balzac's novel has two endings, and in each of them the Centenarian appears to perish physically, thus neutralizing any possibility of his playing a significant role in any future dramas. If the testimony of Balzac's mother is correct, the novel originally ended with Tullius rushing to find the entrance to the Centenarian's lair, while Marianine begs for her life, pleading to be hypnotized so that she can "see" her lover one last time.[1] And it is precisely at this moment that the reader senses a possible change in the character of Marianine. Where before she was cardboard cliché—the submissive "faithful" lover, the dutiful daughter, the innocent victim—we now find a strong, possibly calculating woman.

The narrator compares Marianine, as she faces the old man's terrifying laboratory equipment, to Schiller's Mary Stuart before her executioner. By virtue of this comparison, the simple mountain girl suddenly becomes noble, and more significantly, crafty as well. She watches his preparations with "a horror mingled with curiosity." This allows her to detect on his face "signs of impending decomposition." From this she deduces his secret, his urgent need of physical energy, which she can withhold from him by means of ruse. All at once, she is more perceptive than the weakened Centenarian. An "extraordinary noise" is now heard in the tunnel, which he does not heed, and "a ray of hope" shines in her soul. She at once realizes that Tullius is coming to her rescue and that she needs to stall, causing the old man to waste his vital force. She asks to be teleported, in discorporate form, to see her lover one last time. She begs for the favor in such moving terms that the old man grants her request. The Centenarian is thus forced to draw upon his own vital fluid in order to "accompany" her, a presence she exploits consciously: "In order to arrive there sooner, she leaned (as if to draw more force from it) into the *shadow* of the Centenarian, whom she *felt* at her side, without however seeing or hearing him, and yet she *knew* he was there. Having thus attained a stronger dose of *incorporeality* and an energy that resembled that of *animal vitality*, she suddenly *saw* a scene that caused her to utter cries of joy."

Though she cannot break through to Tullius's plane of reality, she seems to have succeeded, in vampiric manner, in expending the life of the old man. In the final paragraph of this first ending, it is no longer Orpheus who vanquishes the powers of the underworld, but this new Eurydice, capable of manipulating the science of magnetism: "Finally, like Eurydice, when she vanished in smoke from the arms of her husband, her soul, no longer illuminated, seemed to return to inhabit the lovely body that lay rigid in the horrible amphitheater of the Centenarian. And yet Marianine felt, at the moment when she *saw* nothing more, that the Centenarian had abandoned her, and that his icy hands had ceased to wander over her body." In terms of transfer and conservation of vital fluid, Marianine appears to defeat her antagonist on his own ground.

Balzac however added a supplemental ending, one that (more than just serving as padding or to add to the word count) significantly redirects the primal struggle of the first ending toward the world of the *Comédie*. The editor's coda shows Tullius given again the Orphic role. This time, defying the myth, he carries Marianine back alive, now into the realm of social respectability. What is more, this resurrection is effected by a science that is now totally regulated by social usage. "Horace de Saint-Aubin" speaks as "editor," and tells of letters he found in the effects of a deceased brother that shed light on the story's aftermath. In the first letter, M. de Saint-Aubin the elder, writing to a certain James Gordon, recounts how he intercepted a man running through the streets with a girl in his arms. Like his addressee, the elder Saint-Aubin is a doctor and an adept in the science of magnetism. He tests the girl's state by placing a red-hot brass wire on her hand, to which there is no reaction. He then "awakens" her (using here the technical jargon of the practitioner), and the young man carries her off. Saint-Aubin is a modern professional; his remarks are condescending both to hypnotizers who operate outside the guild, and to the ancient sources of their métier: "You see, my dear Salvator, that we are not the only ones interested in this science, whose wonders surpass the miracles of yore." He tells of returning the next day to the spot. He learns his interlocutor was General Beringheld, and that the night before a terrible struggle occurred, with three soldiers left in the house near the catacombs to overcome a "demon." Seen through the eyes of this narrator, the Centenarian is reduced to a creature of superstition.

The second letter, from Beringheld to Saint-Aubin the elder, explains the happenings that preceded their meeting in the street. Tullius's tone is now one of polished sentimentality: "The first impulse of a man who *loves* . . . is to take hold of such an adorable and adored woman, and to take her away from all possible malign influences, from heaven knows what demons that have dogged us ever since the war in Russia." He tells of feeling a force draw him to the old man's lair. But his account itself is tame, already domesticated: "but the zeal that drove us on, and whatever spirit that flies between lovers, led me to follow in obstinate manner the right route." Smug in his role as bourgeois Orpheus, he turns his back on the Centenarian's heartrending cry: "My son, my son!" He spirits his bride off to marriage and a conventional happy end, out of the clutches of an ancestor and a science he rejects as demonic. Significantly, when Saint-Aubin returns to investigate the site of the Centenarian's lair, all that remains of the man is his huge overcoat. Two things are evident: one, the absence of a body may mean the old man has slipped into the catacombs and perhaps found a means of staying alive beneath the streets of modern Paris; two, his lack of a coat marks his isolation in relation to social world Balzac will now depict, where the clothes make the man.

Domesticating the Myth

A curious "editor's note," at the beginning of volume 4, where the old man seduces Marianine in Paris prior to her abduction, tells us that General Beringheld, when Marianine told him of the magical happenings of that strange evening, wrote down a note that proved that, at the time he wrote it down, he had already acquired all the powers the old man deployed. Maurice Bardèche remarks that this note was omitted from the 1837 reprinting of the novel.[2] A possible reason for the omission is that Balzac, in hindsight, clearly saw what he may have only dimly felt in 1822, that mastery of the Centenarian's science could only lead to another Centenarian, a figure whose radical and aggressive singularity was totally at odds with the *Comédie* and its world of social skills. The Tullius of the final pages is headed to a place and time where a being like the Centenarian is at best irrelevant, and at worst catastrophically disruptive.

The "editor," claiming to be a historian and not a matchmaker, refuses to marry his couple. Indeed, marriage will become problematic in a world where the strong-willed Marianine of the last pages is reborn as Eugénie Grandet, and where Tullius must learn to calculate in the manner of Rastignac, or De Marsay. By the same token one might think to find in Vautrin an incarnation of the Centenarian. He is called "Trompe-la-mort," and manipulates, now in openly homosexual fashion, "adopted sons" such as Rastignac and Lucien de Rubempré. But his final act, in *Splendeurs et misères des courtisanes*, is to move seamlessly from chief of outlaws to chief of police, revealing that under- and overworld obey the same set of laws. This sort of social "circulation" excludes all solitary activity, scientific or otherwise.

But the Centenarian's relation to the *Comédie* is more subtle yet. In early stories, Balzac refashions the gothic tales that inspired his Centenarian, and in doing so demythifies them. His "L'Elixir de longue vie" (1930) features Don Juan, who figured so prominently in Maturin's ending.[3] But Balzac presents here a very different context for Don Juan's activities. The don's father is the one who takes the Centenarian's role. This time, however, the old man's "science" is strangely deficient. Though he is dying, on his deathbed he has no secret to tell, and only one single, irreplaceable vial of elixir to pass on. For some odd reason he is unable to take it himself, but needs his son to anoint his body with it, and only after his death. Whereas the second ending to *The Centenarian* swerved away from Oedipal conflict between father and son, Balzac creates in the Don Juan story a double Oedipal bind. Don Juan selfishly withholds the elixir from his father. He has however a residue of "scientific" curiosity and this extends to his trying a drop of the elixir on his father's eye, which comes alive. This eye however is no longer the organ of scientific investigation, but rather an omen of bad conscience. Nor does the don, subsequently, spend his years seeking the secret of the elixir. Hoarding the bottle of elixir, he will have to depend, as his father before him, on his own son to anoint him on his deathbed. To make sure this works, his strategy becomes a purely social one: he will temper his libertine ways and become a good family man. When however the good son dutifully begins to perform the unction, rubbing it on the Don's arm, the resurrected organ again revolts, this time reaching out to grasp the son, causing the vial to fall to the ground.

In this story, Balzac has conflated two mythic figures—the defiant self-hood of Don Juan and the titanic self-centeredness of the Centenarian—and created a banal tale where the jealous son becomes a grasping father in turn. Ironically, the citizens cry "miracle" at the don's rejuvenated head and arm, and make the libertine a saint. During the canonization ceremony however, the head detaches itself from the corpse, and like Ugolino devours the head of the attending priest. The Centenarian's scientific cannibalism is transposed to a realm of farcical anticlericalism, where it is now social classes that "devour" each other. Balzac's Don Juan seeks neither knowledge nor conquest, but accepts family ties in the act of betraying them, voluntarily limiting his powers to one resurrection at best.

A later story, "Melmoth réconcilé" (1835) assimilates the Centenarian's direct ancestor, with equally grotesque results, into the world of contemporary Parisian society. Maturin's Wanderer, in this story, reappears before a bank teller about to abscond with a large sum of money. Where Maturin's wanderer found no one willing to assume the pact, Balzac's Melmoth finds an easy taker in this middle-aged Parisian, whose mistress demands endless luxury. The original wanderer got scientific knowledge in the bargain. But in this soulless age, it is easy to sell one's soul, easier yet to tire of the power the sale brings: "Les sciences furent pour Castanier ce qu'est un logogriphe pour celui qui en sait le mot" [For Castanier, the sciences meant no more than what an anagram meant to one who knows the word].[4] For Castanier, the quest for the unknown is debased to dandyism. He happens upon the funeral of Melmoth, who has died a pious man. The fickle Castanier now desires the one thing he cannot have—faith: "S'il était permis de comparer de si grandes choses aux niaiseries sociales, il [Castanier] ressemblait à ces banquiers riches de plusieurs millions à qui rien ne résiste dans la société; mais qui n'étant pas admis aux cercles de la noblesse, ont pour idée fixe de s'y agréger" [If one is permitted to compare such great things to social nonsense, Castanier was like one of those millionaire bankers who can have anything in society, but who not being admitted to the circles of nobility, become obsessed with ways of entering that world] (302). In the Parisian marketplace, Castanier finds a taker for Melmoth's wisdom, for 500,000 francs. The power is further bartered, till a final "customer" pays 10,000 francs, then uses it literally to consume himself making love. Castanier's career, from Napoleonic officer to cashier for la Maison Nucingen, could have been that of Tullius. In the Parisian world of fickle and short-lived pleasures, no one wants the Centenarian's elixir any more.

Legislating the Centenarian

In the first work that Honoré de Balzac wrote under his own name, *La Peau de Chagrin* (1831), the idea of what it means to be a centenarian undergoes significant transformation. Contemplating suicide, young Raphaël de Valentin enters an antique shop where treasures from all times and places lie about pell-mell. He encounters a strange old man (like the Centenarian a "vieillard") who imparts his secret for long life: "*Vouloir* nous brûle et *pouvoir* nous détruit; mais SAVOIR laisse notre faible organisation dans un perpétuel état de calme. Ainsi le désir ou le vouloir est mort en moi, tué par la pensée; le mouvement ou le pouvoir s'est résolu par le jeu naturel de mes organes" [*To want* burns our energy and *to be able to* destroys us; but *to know* leaves our feeble organism in a perpetual state of calm. Thus desire or will is dead in me, killed by thought; movement or the power to act has been controlled by the natural function of my organs].[5] *Savoir*, or science, for the Centenarian, is not separate from will or power; restlessly he roams the earth, desiring both knowledge and progeny, exercising power in all realms, expending energy he must replenish. But for this old man, knowledge has become disengagement from strenuous activity, the ability to remain immobile, to observe from afar. The old man offers Raphael—perversely, as if his own longevity depended on others burning their vital energy at an accelerated rate—a wild ass's skin in which will and power are united. This skin emblematizes the process that will govern the life of the impetuous Raphaël: "Le cercle de vos jours, figuré par cette Peau, se resserrera suivant la force et le nombre de vos souhaits" [The circle of your days, figured in this skin, will contract in proportion to the force and number of wishes you ask it] (42).

Raphaël proceeds to burn up his physical existence, along the way meeting examples of those who, in opposite fashion, husband their vital energy—Feodora, a woman who observes, teases, but does not commit; another centenarian, but this time one who has lived to be old by remaining immobile, refusing to desire, ultimately to move at all. In Balzac's notebook *Pensées, sujets, fragments*, he tells of a projected work, *Le Crétin*, which would offer a "contrepartie et preuve" [counterpart and proof] of his cherished Louis Lambert. The cretin lives a hundred years by not thinking, while for Lambert, in the words of Félix Davin, it is an excess of thought that "kills" the thinker, which suspends his body in a catatonic state, trapping his mind in its motionless silence.[6]

Davin's introduction to the *Études philosophiques* seeks to formulate the laws enunciated in these tales that govern human actions in stories dealing with everyday life. F. W. J. Hemmings reduces these laws to a single, infernal "dialectic . . . between the contemplative and the active values, between inertia and energy —on one hand, conservation that denies itself enjoyment; on the other, consumption that abridges existence."[7] There is a deeper level yet however, and here the central law of Balzac's world is an inverse relation between the Cartesian categories of mind and matter. In the actions of the material "will," Balzac finds the interface that joins the two poles of the duality. The laws expressed figuratively in the *peau de chagrin* are, however, extrapolated from the bodily condition of the Centenarian. He is described as immobile, statuesque, but with fiery eyes burning within the frozen skull. These latter denote passions trapped within, passions that escape in words as he articulates his self-centered vision in the Café de Foy. It is clear, from Marianine's sense of the Centenarian *physically* accompanying her as her mind journeys out of body, that thinking is already a material activity, and one that functions in an inversely proportional relationship to the length of the life of the thinker.

This is the same process later illustrated in Balzac's stories of artistic visionaries like Frenhofer ("Le Chef-d'oeuvre inconnu") or Gambara. In both cases, artistic creation expands in proportion to the contraction of material limits around it, fatally tied to expense of body and its finite amount of vital energy. Gambara's music is "heard" only in his head; when he tries to play it, others hear only cacophony. This is true for Frenhofer's "masterpiece," which the artist creates in his mind; on canvas, there is only a welter of lines. This mad Pygmalion's attempt to resurrect his vision in words literally kills him: "l'Art tuant l'artiste" [Art killing the artist].

Balzac's example of the pure thinker is Louis Lambert, who, burned out by excess of thinking, leaves behind only fragments of thought. One such, published under the title of *Ecce Homo* in 1836 in the *Chronique de Paris*, shows Balzac, through Lambert (who acts as his persona), transposing the relation between vital energy and length of physical existence that was first embodied in the Centenarian, to the realm of social law.[8] We are told that:

"la durée de la vie est en raison de la force que l'individu peut opposer à la pensée" [the duration of life is in direct proportion to the force that the individual is able to oppose to the act of thinking]. Whereas "*savoir*" is neutral, the condition of knowing, "la *pensée*," is dynamic, being the act of thinking. Thought is now linked to the "theory of energy" earlier articulated in the *Physiologie du mariage*.[9] Even more significant, "thought" is defined by Lambert in terms of a circulatory system: "Pour moi, la pensée est un fluide de la nature des impondérables qui a, en nous, son système circulatoire, ses veines et ses artères" [For me, thought is a fluid imponderable in nature, which has, within us, its own circulatory system, its own veins and arteries]. Lambert has reduced the human condition to a physical circulation of energy, now bound by a law of inverse action, where to expend energy shortens life. The Centenarian's science challenges this, for it brings external energy to bear on this internal system, promising a negative entropy situation, like that which fascinated later writers, such as Heinlein in "Waldo" or Asimov in *The Gods Themselves*, in which "stolen" energy is brought into a closed system, allowing humans to escape the iron laws of thermodynamics, a process the Centenarian's actions seem to foresee.

The Scientist as Victim

Though his body inexorably ages, the Centenarian is able to maintain a balance of sorts, taking his energy in equal proportion from his victims, a life for a life. Under the iron laws of the *Comédie humaine* however, the scientist, like Balzac's artists and thinkers of the incommunicable, must equally succumb to energy spent in overreaching. Science, literally, kills the scientist in the *étude philosophique, La Recherche de l'Absolu* (1834). The author builds his novel around Balthasar Claës, a Centenarian figure reconstituted in a precisely drawn social context, and thus forced to bear the weight of its many material constraints in a way that consumes his creative energy. The setting is Flanders, a stolidly bourgeois place, in direct opposition to suggestions of German romanticism that hover over Castle Beringheld: "La matérialité la plus exquise est empreinte dans toutes les habitudes flamandes" [A most exquisite materiality is impressed in every Flemish custom].[10] Claës, a member of an old respectable family, studies chemistry with Lavoisier in Paris, then returns home to domestic life. His passion for science is fatally reawakened by the visit of a strange Pole. This latter has the "large crâne sans cheveux" [large bald skull] of the Centenarian. More like the Arab Alquefalher, however, he is a tempter, luring the modern scientist with the possibility of completing the search for the Absolute. The goal of the search however is no longer a physical elixir, but rather an intellectual problem to be solved: "une substance commune à toutes les créations modifiée par une force unique, telle est la position du problème offert par l'Absolu et qui me semble cherchable" [a substance common to everything in creation and modified by a single force, such is the nature of the problem the Absolute offers, a problem that seems solvable by research] (534).

This "unitary chemistry" seeks a "fluide électrique, principe de toute fécondation" [electric fluid, the principle of all fertilization] (533). The "Absolute" is the principle underlying all forms; as such, it is but another name for Lambert's circulatory system, a dynamic that confines rather than extends life. Claës keeps hoping to create diamonds out of water, to get more for less, yet finds himself in the process unable to sustain a positive energy balance. Instead, his scientific quest slowly consumes the moral and material world around him. His wife sees the Pole as a devil and Balthasar's materialism as a sacrilege that would make humans into "machines électriques" (538). His science, in her eyes, is rival to her love, hence a "maladie morale" [moral disease] (538). Science for Claës is an ideal. For his family, however, it takes on a tangible, physical presence, a force that consumes the goods and money that is their inheritance: "L'idée de l'Absolu avait passé partout comme un incendie" [The idea of the Absolute passed everywhere like a conflagration] (647) Through an equal and opposite reaction, its pursuit "burns up" the scientist's physical life span. Claës increasingly looks like the Centenarian. In his wasted face, the light of his sunken eyes gradually dims. Sixty, but with the looks of an octogenarian, Claës is the Centenarian without the hope of a regenerating elixir. Like Louis Lambert or Gambara, he can extend his life only by creating an alternate, mental reality. Seeing his wife crying, he responds: "Tiens . . . j'ai décomposé les larmes. Les larmes contiennent un peu de phosphate de chaux, de chlorure de sodium, du mucus et de l'eau" [Look . . . I've analyzed the tear into its component parts. They contain a touch of calcium phosphate, some sodium chloride, mucus, and water] (536). Across hundreds of painful pages, the reader follows the agonizing spectacle of the scientist gradually wasted, stripped of power and dignity, made the grotesque fool of the social order he challenges. Only in death does Claës grasp the Absolute; but confined to a mind bounded by his wasted body, the discovery dies with him. Here the last alchemist dies; his death does no more than affirm the closed nature of Balzac's system of material law.

The Secret of the Ruggieri

The one figure in the *Comédie* who addresses the existential dilemma of the Centenarian is the alchemist Laurent Ruggieri in the historical triptych *Sur Catherine de Médicis*. Published in 1846, the work is comprised of tales whose dates of composition span a period from 1830 ("Les deux Rêves"). The middle section, "Le Secret des Ruggieri" (retitled "La Confidence des Ruggieri" in the final version) appeared in *La Revue de Paris* in 1836–1837, several years after the publication of *La Recherche de l'Absolu*. For Maurice Bardèche, "par son décor historique comme par ses idées, 'Le Secret des Ruggieri' est dans le sillage des projets de Balzac en 1828" [in its historical trappings as in its ideas, the "Secret des Ruggieri" is closely related to Balzac's projects in 1828] (340). If this is true, it is so only in the general sense that Balzac, as testified to in his letters, had problems of life extension on his mind. For the vision of science and the nature of the scientist's quest in this story is significantly different, not only from that of the Centenarian, but from that of Claës as well. Evidence that this is essentially a work of late 1836 is the fact that it seems a direct response to Claës's failure, indeed to the author's sacrifice of this anti-social scientist, last in the line of Centenarian avatars. In the *Comédie*, the lone individual who overreaches, whether scientist or artist, perishes in his singular body. In "The Secret of the Ruggieri" however, life extension, in words at least if not in deeds, is seen as the work of a consortium of scientists. We seem to move closer to the modern sense of science as a collaborative quest, a "body" of knowledge that survives because it is passed on from individual to individual. The part perishes, the whole remains. Yet, over this fine theory, the shadow of the Centenarian still hovers.

The larger narrative paints in detail the intrigues of Catherine de Médicis. Our focus in this section, however, is the episode where Charles IX tells his mistress of a nocturnal adventure on the roofs of Paris. He has discovered hidden alchemical laboratories belonging to Cosme Ruggieri (Catherine's astrologer) and his brother Laurent. At the time, alchemists were suspected of illegal dealings, such as making *sortilèges* (effigies in which pins were stuck) and poisons. Charles does not arrest the Ruggieri, but summons them to explain their activities. In a long speech, Laurent, grand master of alchemists, reveals the nature of his science.[11] On the surface, his statement seems that of the classic humanist. Because God has abandoned things human, mankind is free to deal with them—indeed, must do so. In order to master nature, the individual scientist, though he may toil in isolation, is nevertheless part of a long chain of researchers, all working for the advancement of knowledge. Laurent's "revolt" is even tempered by Cartesian prudence, for "nier l'action directe de Dieu n'est pas nier Dieu" [to deny the direct action of God is not to deny God's existence] (270). This division of realms gives him license to proclaim what appears a materialist vision of things. For if God has no part in earthly things, then there is no "soul," Socratic or otherwise, only material substance, "le mouvement subtil que nous nommons la vie" [that subtle motion we call life] (271).

Yet, for Laurent, more exists than simply matter. A Cartesian "ghost" remains, in the sense that he continues to privilege the "self" [*moi*] above all other material entities. Indeed, the scandal of this material world without God is that "tout ce qui est le moi actuel périt" [everything that constitutes the individual self perishes] (271). Subtly, Laurent's sense of the individual mind, though constituted of a wholly material form of "thought," takes the place of the soul. If God is banished, the Cartesian duality still abides, and here the self stands opposed to *res extensa*, defined as the material world without this "I." Even so, to the extent that this rational self is matter, it operates only in the realm of matter, in obedience to laws of quantity. Thus Laurent measures human superiority in terms of length of life alone. Trees live centuries because they are passive. The scientist's challenge then, for Laurent, is ultimately to find a way to give active humankind, in all other things destined to rule earth, more duration. We are back to the Centenarian's elixir.

The Ruggieri, by institutionalizing the scientist, do little more than institutionalize the existential dilemma of the Centenarian. Laurent's scientists are a *cénacle*, an elite and secret power group within society at large. They use covert (and unlawful) means to finance their efforts. Laurent therefore must justify these in the name of common good. Thus, whereas Columbus gave the world to the Spanish king, he would give "un peuple éternel pour le roi de France" [a nation of eternal subjects to the king of France] (275). Balzac's narrator however characterizes such remarks as a "pompeuse loquacité de charlatan" [the pompous drivel of a charlatan] (296). Caught in a political power play, the Ruggieri's lives depend on their seducing the king. And yet, despite the noble sentiments, were Laurent by himself to discover the elixir of long life, we imagine he would, like the Centenarian, hoard it for himself.

What is different from the early novel, and its mythical giant with seven-league boots, is the social situation of the selfish seeker. The Ruggieri live in a world of "divertissement," where endless intrigues cause them to squander energy they otherwise need in their rush to defeat time. Their science claims to be secular; indeed it bears the stigma of what Pascal calls the life of man without God. Of all figures in the *Comédie humaine*, the Ruggieri are most thrall to the dynamic Pascal describes in *Penseé 420* (the "I" here is the Cartesian *cogito* that seeks to rival God): "If he exalt himself, I humble him; if he humble himself, I exalt him, and I always contradict him, till he understands that he is an incomprehensible monster."[12] For Pascal, mankind's dilemma is that it cannot stay in a room alone for an hour. The Centenarian, on the other hand, shows us the necessity of his staying there. Whether that "room" is Descartes's stove, the Ruggieri's laboratory, or the Centenarian's body, it cannot be expanded. The only hope for these figures is to extend Pascal's hour, to stretch it in time, within a mindspace which is that of artistic or scientific creation, a realm of thought that expands in relation to the material confines of the body that contains and restricts it. One could argue that it was the challenge of the Centenarian, of his excessive, romantic search to extend the life of the body by means of science that led Balzac, in his later *Comédie humaine*, to formulate laws that regulate the relation of mind to body. It was, in a sense, the Centenarian's grotesque quest that reasserted the possibility of the Cartesian duality in a world consigned to matter, the possibility that mind could, if not separate itself from the extended world, at least achieve parity with it, and thus suspend the inexorable march of dissolution and death. It was the Centenarian who foreshortened the Cartesian equation, by reducing *res extensa* to the limits of the individual, physical body. It is this body that becomes the realm of science. In Balzac's later works, this same body becomes the curse and destruction of mind, the place where the Cartesian equation has become an inverse relation in the manner of Pascal, where expense of mind kills the body, which in turn kills mind, obviating all possibility of "science" as we know it. In the division that ensues, knowledge (as with the old man of *La Peau de Chagrin*) is of necessity severed from action and desire. If there is to be a scientific quest, it must now take place in an inner space of mind, but mind now locked away in the immobile body of a Louis Lambert, forever cut off from the world of people and events. Balzac's terrible divided world, and the iron laws that regulate them, are the legacy of the Centenarian. Banished from Balzac's world, this figure set in motion a dynamic that would have a powerful resonance across French literature and French science fiction alike for the next two centuries.

George Slusser and Danièle Chatelain

NOTES

"Balzac's Centenarian *and French Science Fiction," pp. xxi–xxvii*

1. Though Alfred North Whitehead pretends to a more cosmopolitan view of the rise of Western science (he mentions Newton, Galileo, and Descartes in the same breath), he nevertheless sees a "Cartesian apparatus" as the prime factor that launches modern science on its "triumphant career": "The whole Cartesian apparatus of Deism, substantial materialism and imposed law, in conjunction with the reduction of physical relations to the notion of correlated motions with mere spatiotemporal character, constitutes the simplified notion of Nature with which Galileo, Descartes, and Newton finally launched modern science on its triumphant career." Whitehead circumvents the key element in this process. For once Descartes separates mind from matter, the mind is free to "simplify" Nature, to reduce it to a set of mechanical relationships, as precondition for (as Descartes states) rational mind's "mastery" of res extensa (*Adventures of Ideas* [New York: New American Library, 1955], 118).

2. See Honoré de Balzac, *Correspondance*, ed. Roger Pierrot (Paris: Editions Garnier Frères, 1960), 1:197–198.

3. Charles Maturin, *Melmoth the Wanderer* (Oxford: Oxford University Press, 1972), 538.

4. Tirso's play was written in 1625; it is the first dramatic appearance of Don Juan, and a masterpiece of the late "Siglo de Oro." In the play Don Gonzalo appears to Don Juan as the "convivado de piedra," the guest of stone. Don Juan is in incessant movement, marked by endless energy, ever shifting verbal flow. In the final scene, divinity functions as a redressment of equilibrium, the balance sheet of crimes and punishments ("quien tal hace, quien tal pague"). The stone guest holds Don Juan in his embrace, rendering his life force, his power of movement, futile ("Más, ay! que me canso en vano/de tirar golpes al aire").

5. See the edition of Pierre-Georges Castex (Paris: Librairie José Corti, 1950).

6. See Harry W. Paul, *From Knowledge to Power: The Rise of the Science Empire in France, 1860–1939* (Cambridge: Cambridge University Press, 1985). As late as the 1850s, Paul says that "like anthropology, biology in France was a lusty daughter of medicine . . . Charles Robin was a professor at the Paris faculty of medicine; and over two thirds of the regular members of the Society [of Biology] in 1850–1851 were connected with medicine" (213).

7. Allen Thiher, *Fiction Rivals Science: The French Novel from Balzac to Proust* (Columbia: University of Missouri Press, 2001), 37–38.

8. Honoré de Balzac, *La Comédie humaine*, ed. Marcel Bouteron (Paris: Bibliothèque de la Pléiade, 1949), 1:4.

9. Comte's first work, his *Système de politique positive*, in which are found many ideas later to become a common "positivist" heritage for generations of French scientists, thinkers, and writers, was published in 1823, barely a year after *The Centenarian*.

10. John Stuart Mill, *Auguste Comte and Positivism* (London: Trubner, 1865), 169. Mill was originally quite favorable to Comte and positivism. In the second half of his essay, however, Mill came to a cultural divide, reasserting a tradition of experimental science, much as Claude Bernard was doing in France at the same time.

11. *Close Encounters* (Bristol and New York: Adam Hilger, 1990). The authors reproduce a marvelous still from Alec Guinness's *The Man in the White Suit*, which shows the scientist dwarfed and barely visible behind a welter of equipment: "His lonely research, amongst glass tubes and retorts, brings misery to all" (90).

12. See Steven B. Harris, "The Immortality Myth and Technology," in *Immortal Engines: Life Extension and Immortality in Science Fiction and Fantasy* (Athens: Georgia University Press, 1996), 45–67.

13. A. S. Eddington, *New Pathways of Science* (New York: Macmillan, 1935), 68.

14. Mary Shelley, *Frankenstein* (London: Collier Macmillan, 1961), 48 (text of the 1818 edition).

15. See George Slusser, "The Frankenstein Barrier," in *Fiction 2000:*

Cyberpunk and the Future of Narrative (Athens: Georgia University Press, 1992), 46–75.

16. Arthur B. Evans, "The Vehicular Utopias of Jules Verne," in *Transformations of Utopia: Changing Views of the Perfect Society* (New York: AMS Press, 1999), 99–109.

17. Jules Verne, *L'Île mystérieuse* (Lausanne: Editions Rencontre, 1966) 10:814.

18. Roland Barthes, *Mythologies* (Paris: Editions du Seuil, 1957), 80.

19. Even though Rimbaud claims that "je est un autre" [I is an other], one strongly senses the presence of a conventional self behind the visionary odyssey of his "bâteau ivre," if only in the sense that boats do not get drunk.

20. Pascal J. Thomas, "French SF and the Legacy of Philip K. Dick," *Foundation* 23 (spring 1986): 32.

21. Philippe Curval, *Cette Chère Humanité* (Paris: J'ai Lu, 1976).

22. Kurt Steiner (André Ruellan), *Le Disque rayé* (Paris: J'ai Lu, 1970), 147.

23. Michel Jeury, *Le Temps incertain* (Paris: Robert Laffont, 1973), 94.

The Centenarian

1. The poems of Ossian, who claimed to be a Scottish bard of the third century, were the creation of poet James MacPherson. Published in 1760, purportedly "translated from the Gaelic," the Ossian poems were works of great sentiment and empathy with "primitive" nature and had a strong influence on later romantic writers. An ingenious counterfeit, they were praised for their "authentic" voice.

2. The "Colline de Grammont" is situated to the south of the River Cher, on the outskirts of modern-day Tours. Grammont, which was open countryside at the time of the novel, is today the site of a park, lycée, and apartment complexes, part of thriving suburbs along the National 10, the road to Poitiers.

3. The early sections of *The Centenarian* are set in Tours. Balzac was born in Tours on May 20, 1799, where his father, Bernard-François Balzac, had exercised the function of quartermaster ("directeur de vivres") for the 22d Army Division since 1795. His family lived at 29,

rue Indre et Loire, today 52, rue Nationale, then as now the central north-south axis of Tours. The Balzac family lived in Tours till 1814, when they relocated to Paris. After this novel, throughout the *Comédie humaine*, Balzac returned to Tours and the Touraine again and again in his novels and stories. His stories and novels with a setting in Tours are "Maître Cornélius" (1831), *Le Curé de Tours* (1834); and *La Femme de trente ans* (1842). Works set in regions surrounding Tours are *La Grenadière* (1833), in St. Cyr to the north of Tours; *Le Lys dans la vallée* (1836), set in the valley of the Indre river, near Balzac's home in Saché, current site of the Balzac museum; and *L'Illustre Gaudissart* (final version 1843), a work whose first title was "L'Excellent Vin de Vouvray." There is today a statue of Gaudissart in the town square of Vouvray, located on the north bank of the Loire, opposite the Tours suburbs of La Ville-aux-dames and St. Pierre des Corps. One finds the presence of the Touraine in a number of minor, unpublished, even posthumous works of Balzac. For example, the short sketch "La Grande Bretèche, ou les Trois Vengeances," published in the original version of *Scènes de la vie de province* (1834–1837), which constituted the germ of *La Muse du département*, takes place in the park of the chateau Grossou, located on the banks of the Loire, several miles from Sancerre, well to the east of the Touraine. Or another sketch, "Les Deux Amis," published posthumously in the *Revue des Deux-Mondes*, September 15, 1917, is a "hymn to the Touraine," possibly written in 1830, at the beginning of Balzac's mature career, during his stay at La Grenadière with Madame de Berny.

4. Such "dwellings in rock" are common in the Touraine, in the banks and hillocks of this region crisscrossed by rivers—the Loire, the Cher, the Vienne, and the Indre. Here is a description taken from *La Femme de trente ans*: "Au délà du pont sur lequel la voiture était arrêtée, le voyageur aperçoit devant lui, le long de la Loire jusqu'à Tours, une chaîne de rochers qui, par une fantaisie de la nature, paraît avoir été posée pour encaisser le fleuve dont les flots minent incessamment la pierre . . . de Vouvray jusqu'à Tours . . . En plus d'un endroit il existe trois étages de maisons, creusées dans le roc et réunies par de dangereux escaliers taillés à même la pierre" [On the other side of the bridge on which the carriage had stopped, the

traveler sees before him, along the Loire as far as Tours, a series of rocky cliffs, which, by some caprice of nature, seem to have been placed there to contain the river, whose current incessantly erodes the stone banks . . . from Vouvray down to Tours . . . Moreover, in one spot, there exist three levels of dwellings hollowed out of the rock and connected by dangerous stairways carved directly into the stone] (*La Comédie humaine*, 7.686). These caves are the result of centuries of quarrying these hillocks for stone—the "craie tuffeau" or calc tuff used as common building material in Touraine—as well as of flood and erosion.

5. "Cave of Grammont" translates the French "Trou de Grammont." This place is lost today, but surely refers to a large cavern or grotto in the Hill of Grammont. The word "trou" is related to the word "troglodyte," the word commonly used in French to refer to cave dwellers in the region. A troglodyte village in the valley of the Loire, to the north of Tours, bears the name Trôo.

6. Herman Boërhaave was a Dutch chemist and physician (1668–1738). He taught at Leyden and was a partisan of iatromechanism, a "science" based on the Cartesian idea of living beings as "mechanisms." Blaise Pascal (1623–1662) was a French mathematician, physicist, and philosopher. Heinrich Cornelius Agrippa von Nettesheim (1486–1535), historiographer of Carlos V, was a famous alchemist and author of *De occulta philosophia*, a major treatise on the principles of alchemy.

7. The iron gates are the tollgate or "octroi" that controlled commerce entering the city.

8. The Place St. Etienne can be found in present-day Tours, marked by the Église St. Étienne, on the Avenue de Grammont, the major north-south axis of the city southward from city center.

9. The Cloister ("cloître") Saint-Gatien is joined to the cathedral. Opposite it is the house said to be that of Balzac's Curé de Tours, marked by a plaque.

10. Henceforth the "Substitute," a magistrate empowered to act in the name of the imperial prosecutor. As the *Petit Larousse* puts it (describing a similar position under the Republic): "Magistrat chargé de suppléer au parquet le procureur général ou le procureur de la

République" [magistrate whose responsibility is to stand in, in his functions, for the public or state prosecutor].

11. Balzac must mean here the Substitute, who returns on the scene in the paragraphs that follow. This may be a sign perhaps of more than one hand in the writing, or of the extreme haste with which these early chapters were written.

12. We see the young Balzac displaying some schoolboy history here. The Saint-Barthélemy Massacre was the slaughter of prominent Protestants in Paris, the night of August 23–24, 1572. It continued in the provinces well into October of that year. August 10, 1792, was the assault of the Tuileries and the fall of the royalty during the French Revolution. The days of September 4 and 5, 1795, marked the beginning of the Reign of Terror. The League (la Saint-Ligue) was the powerful Catholic confederation founded in 1576, active during the Wars of Religion and French internal politics leading up to the abjuration (racanting of the Protestant faith) of Henri IV.

13. Caius Julius Caesar, famous Roman general (15 BC–AD 19), who earned the nickname "Germanicus" for his victories over the Germanic tribes. His death was said to have occasioned great mourning in Rome.

14. In reference to the Beringheld "lineage," the Brabant is a historical region situated between the Meuse and Escaut rivers, today divided between Belgium (the provinces of Flemish Brabant and Walloon Brabant) and the southern Brabant province of Holland. Charlemagne (742–814) was king of the Francs and holy Roman emperor (800). These two facts account for the Germanic origin of the name "Beringheld." Balzac's location of a Germanic "source"—associated in the French romantic mind with occult sciences and powers (thus Boërhaave and Agrippa)—for his fantastic creation foreshadows his lifelong fascination with the work of Hoffmann and other German writers and artists. Philippe le Bon (1396–1467) was duke of Burgundy. Henri II, son of François I, was king of France from 1547 to 1559. Charles IX, second son of Henri II and Catherine de Médicis, ordered the massacre of Saint-Barthélemy (1572), touching off the times of continuous turbulence that Balzac refers to. Henri III was third son of Henri and Catherine, successor to Charles IX, king of

France from 1574 to 1589. Henri IV, son of Antoine de Bourbon, king from 1589 to 1610, signed the Edict of Nantes in 1598.

15. Some dates are in order here: Philippe-le-Bel [Philippe IV, king of France] (1285–1314); Charles IX (1560–1574); Henri III (1574–1589); Henri IV (1589–1610); Louis XIII (1610–1643); Louis XIV (1643–1715); Louis XV (1715–1774).

16. Beringheld Castle and the goings-on inside it offer interesting variations on (to use the narrator's term) the "romantic" gothic. The gothic setting, strictly speaking, is medieval as opposed to classic, mysterious (or supernatural) as opposed to rationally ordered. But, as C. Hugh Holman puts it, the romantic generation extended the sense of the gothic to encompass their own predilections: "it suggested whatever was medieval, natural, primitive, wild, free, authentic, romantic" (*A Handbook to Literature* [New York: Bobbs and Merrill, 1972], 243). Thus Beringheld Castle (a gift, remember, from Charlemagne) in its "boldness and vastness" vies with the highest peaks in the Alps. The Centenarian first appears in gothic fashion, in a night meeting on deserted roads with the officer from Angers: "You have traveled with a *spirit*!" The officer scoffs at the superstitious Lagradna, only to be scared off by the moving eyes of the Centenarian's portrait. The painting moves mysteriously; it cannot be taken from the wall. The force however that does all this moving is not magic, but "natural" science, the powers of "magnetism." To Holman's list, we may add Balzac's term "scientific." The Centenarian's actions prove to be as natural and primordial (his is the "authentic" *ur*-science), as those of the free and natural mountain girl Marianine.

17. Given Lagradna's pose as witch here, was Balzac thinking of Shakespeare's *Macbeth* and the witches' prophesy? If so, then an ironic subtext is created, for the Centenarian's invulnerability is equated with Macbeth's brash defiance: "Let them fly all! / Till Birnham Wood remove to Dunsinane, / I cannot taint with fear" (5.3.1–3). Somehow nature finds a way to bring the mountain to the plain.

18. The Centenarian, in this passage, reveals himself an adept at Mesmer's "animal magnetism," in which the physician taps into a universal magnetic "fluid" that flows from his hands as a healing

power. The Centenarian's visit and Tullius's conception and birth are dated 1780, exactly contemporary to Mesmer's moment of fame and shame. We notice that both here and in the conception scene there is action at a distance, a transfer of vital fluid without touching (the hands the countess feels running over her body are "icy," yet the body is somehow permeated with beneficial warmth). Mesmerism is a forerunner to modern hypnosis, and Lagradna's state—awake during the Centenarian's "operation" yet unable to move, as in a dream—is hypnotic in nature.

19. Though there was a Tullius Hostilius, third king of Rome in legendary times, Balzac surely refers to M. Tullius Cicero, born January 3, 106 BC, who founded a line of Tulliuses. Curiously, the Beringheld line now is said to reach back, not merely to the Germanic holy Roman emperor, but to Rome itself. Does not the family line then, in its divided origins (Roman = practical or technological "reason"; German = occult, mystical science, finite accomplishment vs. infinite yearning) contain the germ of the split, dramatized in the novel, between the two Beringhelds?

20. Interestingly, the journey of the Centenarian and Butmel parallels that of Christian Rosenkranz, reputed founder of Rosicrucianism. The *Fama fraternitatis*, published in 1614, tells of Rosenkranz's voyage to exotic lands, moving among a brotherhood of kindred souls (all adepts at some common mystical language). At some unspecified place, he received the ultimate wisdom, secret and inexpressible. Balzac, who benefits from more recent speculations on a common Indo-European or Aryan source, makes the final goal of this quest India—the Brahmins—and the high Himalayas. In fact, Rosenkranz's reputed life span (he too was a centenarian, living 106 years) overlaps the time of the Centenarian's birth. Rosenkranz's death is placed at 1484; the Centenarian, son of the first Count Maxime Sculdans-Beringheld, was born in 1430, traveled to China and India in search of the secret of science, only to "disappear" the day of the Saint Bartholomew Massacre (1572).

21. Young Tullius reenacts the (by now clichéd) romantic hero, "unstable," ever searching. Like Chateaubriand's René, he experiences world weariness (ennui) and the *vague des passions*, the inability to

attach himself to a single worldly pursuit. In his "historical" posturings, there is also a strong dose of Byron's Manfred, who also sought poses of refuge and solace on lonely, high mountains.

22. The young Balzac throws around knowledge in a sophomoric manner here, as befits the omnivorous prodigy he created in his own image. The Capitol is the famous temple first built by the Tarquins on Mons Capitolinus in Rome; The Forum, or Forum romanum, was the central public open space for transacting business in republican Rome; the Field of Mars, or Campus Martius, located on the Tiber on a plain north of the Capitol, was the place of martial exercises, then of public assembly, which imperial Rome covered with monuments to Rome's glory; Thermopylae is the pass in eastern Greece where the Persians defeated the Spartans in 480 BC; Cape Sunium is the promontory that forms the southernmost extremity of Attica; Orchomenus is an ancient city in Boeotia located northwest of Lake Copais; the plain of the Chersonesus probably refers to Chersonesus Thracica, the peninsula of the Dardanelles or Gallipoli.

23. Another role model for Tullius, the celebrated Athenian Themistocles was born in 528 BC. Commander of the Athenian fleet, he defeated the Persians at the Battle of Salamis. He was known for his youthful impetuousness.

24. Castle Beringheld should, by all logic, have fallen victim to the Revolution (1789–1799). Around this menace Balzac builds an intrigue, which includes Jesuits and the devoted "citizen" overseer Veryno, as well as "supernatural" intervention from the Centenarian. In his later novels, Balzac remains fascinated with machinations and power plays of this sort. The tutor of Tullius, Father de Lunada, is a Jesuit. The Society of Jesus, the renowned educators of the earlier eighteenth century, was dissolved in France in 1764, and in all Europe in 1773. It was only reinstated, as concession on the part of Napoleon, in 1814. A knowledge of "clandestine relationships" maintained by former monks would give the Centenarian important leverage during the anticlerical height of the Revolution. Veryno is the bourgeois man of feeling, of noble heart if not birth; likewise, his daughter Marianine is patterned on the "bon sauvage" of sentimental novels such as Bernardin's *Paul et Virginie*.

25. Tullius's youthful searching, bypassed by the Revolution, comes to resolution in the midst of the Directoire, the executive power instituted by the Constitution of October 26, 1795, as successor to the revolutionary Convention. The Directory was transitional between the revolutionary government and the Napoleonic period. In 1797, Bonaparte was an obscure general, about to launch his Italian campaign, which would sweep him and many of his generals to power and glory. Against Father Lunada's exhortation to seek permanent fame with discoveries in "the arts and sciences," Tullius chooses military glory, as did so many of his generation.

26. Myron, Greek sculptor, fifth century BC, known primarily from Roman copies of his *Discus Thrower*. Phidias, Athenian sculptor (ca. 490–430 BC); like Myron and Polyclitus, he is reputed to have been the student of Agleadas. Phidias's workshop sculpted the friezes of the Parthenon, most of which are in the British Museum. He is considered the creator of the classical style in Greek sculpture. The only thing to justify these allusions is the fact the marquise wears her hair "in the manner of Titus" and her dresses are styled *à la grecque*.

27. The marquise de Ravendsi (1797 is still a dangerous time for nobility in the open) is the figure of the *initiatrice*, the experienced and cynical woman who initiates the inexperienced young man into the ways of love in society (opposed here to the "natural" love of Marianine). In terms of literary sources, the marquise owes more to the libertine seductress (cf. Laclos's Madame de Merteuil and the Chevalier Danceny) than to Rousseau's Madame Warens (the "Maman" of the *Confessions*). Stendhal has yet to write *Le Rouge et le noir* (1830), but Balzac has just declared his love for Madame de Berny, who may be the inspiration for the marquise. In later novels, Balzac continues to complicate this seminal relationship between the young man entering social life, and the older, more mature and worldly woman. Félix de Vandenesse and Madame de Mortsauf in *Le Lys dans la vallée* are a prominent example.

28. Marianine the shepherdess inspires in Tullius moments of the romantic sublime, the contemplation of vast and tormented expanses

of mountain and ravine. In contrast to the worldly marquise, she is innocent, pure, and beset by conventional melancholy.

29. The reference is to the conspiracy led by L. Sergius Catilina, which came to a head during the consulship of Cicero in 63 BC, ending with Catilina's death on the battlefield. The story of this conspiracy is written by Sallust.

30. Curiously, we find a very similar set of heightened "definitions" of love, with the same formula ("Aimer, c'est . . ."), in a letter to Madame de Berny, which Roger Pierrot (*Correspondance de Balzac*, 1:170–171) dates "Jeudi, avril 1822." More interesting yet, this catalogue of love appears lifted more or less verbatim from Maturin's *Melmoth*. Pierrot invites us to compare both the letter and the corresponding passage in *The Centenarian* with pp. 412–414 of the Cohen translation (the translation Balzac read, reprinted by Éditions du Club français du livre, preface by André Breton, Paris, 1954). This is the only place in *The Centenarian* where such verbatim lifting of text or ideas occurs. It was probably too tempting for a writer balancing multiple commitments, and certainly in a hurry to complete the job.

31. Balzac is historically exact here. The battle of Rivoli, a location on the Adige River near Verona, took place on January 14. Tullius has arrived just in time for this decisive battle, in which Bonaparte defeated the Austrians.

32. Louis Alexandre Berthier (1753–1815) was above all an army man. In 1789, as general of the *garde nationale*, his task was to protect the royal family. We find him chief of staff of Bonaparte's army in 1796; he was made *maréchal* in 1804, and promoted to major general of the Grande Armée (1805–1814). In 1814, he went over to Louis XVIII. During the One Hundred Days (the period between March 20, 1915 —the date of Napoleon's return to Paris—and June 22, 1815, four days after his defeat at the battle of Waterloo), Berthier died in exile in Bavaria. André Masséna (1756–1817), the victor at Rivoli, was named *maréchal de France* in 1804 and distinguished himself at the battles of Essling and Wagram. Given command of the army of Portugal (1810), he was defeated by the British at Torres-Vedras (March 1811).

In 1814, he too went over to the Bourbons. Barthélemy Catherine Joubert (1769–1799), general in the Italian campaign, died in the battle of Novi. His death cut short Sieyès's hopes of using him in a coup d'état against the Directory; he chose Bonaparte in his place. The Treaty of Campo-Formio (1797) was signed by the French and Austrians in that Venetian town, ending the Italian campaign.

33. Bonaparte's Egyptian campaign was initially a struggle with England over trade routes to India. Bonaparte entered Cairo on July 23, 1798. On August 1, Lord Nelson sank the French fleet at the battle of the Nile, cutting off Bonaparte's escape route. Bonaparte was forced to engage the Turks, nominal rulers of Egypt, and defeated them at the battle of Mount Tabor on April 16, 1798, possibly the battle described by Balzac.

34. This passage is a good example of Balzac's technique of shifting verb tenses, as the logic of the shifts is clear and consistent here, which is not always the case. Verbs in the preceding paragraph are all in the present, which heighten the immediate, dramatic nature of the scene. In this paragraph, verb tense shifts to the imperfect in its descriptive capacity: "La lune éclairait cette scène d'une lueur que l'ombre et la présence des pyramides changeait au point de la rendre verdâtre." In the following paragraph, there is an imperfect of duration ("le vieillard achevait son quatrième voyage"), but duration of an action: he "was completing" his fourth trip. The shift back to present tense, immediate dramatic action, is marked by the phrase "at this moment." At the end of this paragraph, tense shifts back to the narrative past, in fact to the simple past, abruptly, but significantly, as if calling a sudden halt to this grammatical ballet: "et bientôt les cris cessèrent." Balzac's tense shifts are not always this logical, and the translators have, in many cases, had to opt for consistency.

35. Seeking perhaps to return to France by land, Bonaparte invaded Syria (Palestine) in February 1799, taking Jaffa (Haifa). His troops were decimated by the plague. In the famous painting of Antoine Gros, *Les pestiférés de Jaffa* (1804), surely known to Balzac, it is Bonaparte who visits the sick and dying. Balzac displaces this icon with the Centenarian, enhancing the theme of rivalry between the

great Warrior and the even greater Man of Science, who cures these soldiers.

36. Napoleon was proclaimed emperor May 18, 1804, and consecrated December 2. On May 5, 1805, the emperor, in the wake of bloody insurrection, forced the Bourbon Charles IV to abdicate in favor of Joseph Bonaparte. Balzac seems vague here, both about chronology and what battle Tullius fights. Only after the Congress of Erfurt (October 1808) did Napoleon personally intervene in the campaign. He returned to Paris January 1809, leaving Soult in charge. The historical window for Tullius's experience, then, is between October 1808 and January 1809. The "Battle of L." mentioned in the chapter title probably refers to La Coruña, where Napoleon met resistance from the British troops of Sir John Moore (October 26, 1808).

37. The allusion is strange: why a veritable Hebe? Hebe (Juventas to the Romans), daughter of Zeus and Hera, was the goddess of youth. She married Hercules after he was admitted to the company of the immortals. Her association was rather with the power to make the old young again, to rejuvenate.

38. The Gros-Caillou district ("le quartier du Gros-Caillou") is found in today's 7th arrondissement, roughly from the Champs de Mars on the west to the Hôtel des Invalides on the east. It is bounded by Avenue Rapp (west), Avenue de la Motte-Picquet (south), and Boulevard de la Tour Maubourg (east), and crisscrossed by the rue de l'Université, rue Saint-Dominique, and rue de Grenelle. The name "Gros-Caillou" originates from a large rock, now gone, located near today's intersection of rue Cler and rue Saint-Dominique. Today the Eglise St. Pierre du Gros Caillou stands at this spot. The area was, in 1811 as it is today, a "good address." The Gate of the Bons-Hommes is one of the 57 *barrières* in the Wall of the Fermiers-Généraux, customs stations built (by architect Claude Nicolas Ledoux along a perimeter around an expanded Paris) between 1784 and 1791, at which date the majority were torn down by the Revolution (today the Barrière d'Enfer stands at the Place Denfert-Rochereau). Although the edifice is gone, the name and emplacement reside in the minds of the inhabitants of Gros-Caillou in 1811. Its location is to the south of the present-day Pont de Grenelle.

39. The Council of Five Hundred ("conseil des Cinq-Cents") was the legislative assembly of elected "citizens" adopted by the Convention (September 23, 1795) during the Revolution. It was dissolved by Bonaparte in the coup of November 9, 1799, which ended the Directory.

40. By 1810, Napoleon had surrounded his empire with vassal states ruled by his relatives and other commoners in his service: Westphalia (Jerôme Bonaparte), Spain (Joseph Bonaparte), Italy (Eugène de Beauharnais, Josephine's son), Naples (Joachim Murat, his brother-in-law), and so on, all duly ennobled.

41. At the time of the story, the two wings south and north of the actual Cours du Louvre were joined at the west by the Château des Tuileries, dwelling of kings since the sixteenth century, and not destroyed until 1870 at the time of the Commune. The Arc de Triomphe du Carrousel was then located *inside* the courtyard of the Tuileries Palace. Military parades were conducted in this courtyard in Napoleon's time.

42. Napoleon's Russian campaign (June–December, 1810) was marked by a rapid advance, the entry into Moscow, and the rout and retreat of his army under the terrible conditions of the Russian winter.

43. Pierre Corneille (1606–1684), French playwright; the reference is to his Roman tragedies, such as *Horace* (1640) and *Cinna* (1640). Jacques-Louis David (1748–1825) was Napoleon's official painter; his subjects and style are neoclassical, as in his famous *Mort de Socrate* (1787).

44. Nicolas Poussin (1594–1665) is France's great classical painter. His *I Too Was in Arcadia* dates from 1650. Antonio Allegri, called Il Correggio (1489?–1534) is a painter from the Italian High Renaissance. Guido Reni (1575–1642) is a later baroque painter. Balzac has no coherent reason to lump these disparate artists together, except to name-drop.

45. In January 1814, the coalition opposing Napoleon invades France. In the ensuing French campaign, despite Napoleon's victories at Chateau-Thierry, Morment, and Montereau (in the region around Paris), the allies enter Paris on March 31. Napoleon is deposed by Talleyrand, abdicates, and goes into exile on Elba.

46. Fallen on hard times, Veryno and family have relocated in the more modest Faubourg Saint-Jacques, an area of Paris described as "peu urbanisé au début du XIXe siècle" (*Paris: Guide Bleu* [Paris: Hachette, 1994], 614). The faubourg is situated in the southern quadrant of modern Paris, in the 14th arrondissement, between metro stations Denfert-Rochereau and Port-Royal (south–north) and running west–east along the Boulevard Saint Jacques, in the direction of the Place d'Italie. The area began to take shape in the seventeenth century, around the construction of the Abbayé de Port-Royal (1626–1648). Colbert founded the Observatoire in 1667.

47. Montereau-Fauld-Yonne, a community in the department of Seine et Marne. In the battle of Montereau, Napoleon defeated the Austrian army, February 18, 1814.

48. The reference is to the daughter of the river god Peneus who, pursued by Apollo, prayed the gods, and was transformed into a laurel tree (Balzac's "magic bark").

49. The Palais-Royal denotes a group of buildings, shops, cafés, and gardens whose *Galeries de Bois*, during the later eighteenth century, became a popular place to conduct business or amorous affairs. Café discussions of the sort presented here were surely common, as attested to by the dialogues of Diderot's *Neveu de Rameau* (1774), also set in the Palais-Royal.

50. Franz Mesmer (1734–1815) was a German physician and founder of the theory of animal magnetism called mesmerism. Mesmer rose to prominence in prerevolutionary Paris. He was considered by some a scientist, by others a charlatan. "Le baquet" or "bucket" of Mesmer was a famous device used in magnetic séances. Here is a description by Bailly, head of the scientific commission that investigated Mesmer and his practices: "In the middle of a large room where curtains let in mitigated light, we find a circular recipient in oak: the famous 'bucket.' In the water that fills half the recipient there is immersed iron filings, ground glass, and other tiny objects. The cover is pierced by a certain number of holes from which iron rods protrude, coiled in rope and moveable, which patients apply to areas of the body where they suffer. In the corner of the room, a piano or harmonica is playing tunes in various cadences, especially toward

the end of the séances. Patients gather silently around the bucket, a rope tied around their waists unites them one to the other. If somebody asks for something to drink, he is given lemonade in which cream of tartar has been dissolved. In the meantime, the magnetic influence begins to be felt. Some patients remain calm and feel nothing. Others cough, spit, feel slight pain, and experience moments of sweating; others are shaken by extraordinary convulsions . . . The salons in which such scenes take place are called "hellish convulsion chambers" (quoted in www.medardus.org/Medecins/MedecinsTextes/mesmer.html).

51. Alice M. Killen, in "L'évolution de la légende du Juif Errant," in *Revue de littérature comparée* 5, no. 1 (January 1925), argues that during preceding centuries, precisely those when Balzac's Centenarian roamed the earth, the popular mind amalgamated the Rosicrucians (as secret society of scientists) and the Wandering Jew (an immortal being possibly recipient of the elixir of life) with the activity of alchemists in general. The agenda of these Rosicrucians/alchemists/wanderers (transmuting metals into gold or monetary power, extending life in order to enjoy that power) surely attracted Balzac, who easily blended it with his fascination with Swedenborgian mysticism and other "parascientific" matters. The testimony of William Godwin in 1830 (in *Lives of the Necromancers*) seems an echo of Balzac's sentiments ten years earlier. He remarks that the Rosicrucians "appear to have imbibed their notions from the Arabians, and claimed the possession of the philosopher's stone, the art of transmuting metals and the *elixir vitae*" (35).

52. Clearly here, the Centenarian practices the "science" of phrenology, much in vogue at the time. The founder of phrenology was Franz Joseph Gall (1759–1828), another German physician who, like Mesmer, achieved fame in Parisian circles after the Revolution. Phrenology is defined in the *Dictionary of the Philosophy of Mind* as a medical discipline based on the theory that "mind could be divided into separate faculties which were discretely localized in the brain, and that the exercise of or innate prominence of a faculty would enlarge the appropriate brain area that, in turn, would show up as a cranial prominence" (quoted in www.artsci.wustl.edu/~philos/MindDict

/gall.html). Phrenology became a common device for Balzac, as he perfected what he saw as the science of description in his later novels. Here is an obvious passage from *Le Père Goriot*, describing changes in Goriot's physiognomy after three years at the Pension Vauquer: "Young medical students, having noticed the sagging of the lower lip, and having measured the height of his facial angle, declared him stricken by cretinism" (*Oeuvres complètes* [Paris: Edition de la Pléiade, 1964] 2.892). Just as Mesmer's "research" led, by the path of error, to experiments in hypnosis and psychosomatic medicine by Charcot, one of the founders of modern science of the mind, so Gall's phrenology, soon discredited as a tool for reading moral "qualities" from external configurations of the skull or face, pointed the way to modern neuroscience and its maps of the brain.

53. Bernard le Bouvier de Fontenelle (1657–1757), French scientist and man of letters, was author of the *Entretiens sur la pluralité des mondes* (1686) in which he exposes the Copernican system in witty dialogues.

54. Sully (Maximillien de Béthune, baron de Rosny, duc de) (1560–1641). Of Protestant background, Sully was a brilliant finance minister under Henri IV.

55. The present-day catacombs of Paris consist of some sixty-five kilometers of galleries in a space of eleven acres, bounded by rues Rémy-Dumoncel, Hallé, d'Alembert, and René-Coty. The Faubourg Saint-Jacques is right in the middle of this area, thus the Centenarian would have at his disposal a veritable labyrinth of underground passages. A more or less contemporary poem by Pierre Lebrun ("Les catacombes de Paris," 1812) gives a sense of how the Parisian of the day saw this underworld: "Descendez, parcourez ces longues galéries / Qui sous le Luxembourg et sous les Tuileries / S'étendent, et des morts montrent de toutes parts / En long ordre, aux parois, les reliques dressées" [Go down, wander these long galleries, / Which beneath the Luxembourg and Tuileries / Stretch forth, and on all sides, along the walls aligned, / All that of the dead remain are relics, lying supine]. The Observatoire de Paris, built by Colbert along the Paris meridian (2° 20' 17" east), is (symbolically at least in Balzac's time) the "temple" of official French science.

The Centenarian's choice of the Observatoire as his entry point to his alternative scientific domain, in a sense, strikes a blow at the scientific establishment, represented by the doctors in the epilogue who revive Marianine.

56. François Ravaillac (1578–1610), assassin of Henri IV (May 14, 1610). "Jimenez" is possibly Francisco Jimenez de Cisneros (1436–1517), archbishop of Toledo (1498) and grand inquisitor of Castille (1507). He was responsible for the expulsion of the Moors (1502); at the same time he was a noted humanist and friend of Erasmus; he commissioned the Alcalá Bible. Montmorency is François de Montmorency, duc de Bouteville (1600–1627), a powerful nobleman whom Richelieu condemned to death for defying the law forbidding duelling. Armand Jean du Plessis, cardinal de Richelieu (1585–1642), was author of *Mémoires*, and a *Testament politique*. *Miramé* (1641) was written by Jean Demarets de Saint-Sorbin (1595–1676). Sixtus V (Felice Peretti, 1520–1590), 225th pope, was a supporter of Henri II and the League; he excommunicated Henri of Navarre (1585) and financed the Armada defeated by the English (1588).

57. Friedrich von Schiller (1759–1805), German poet and playwright. *Maria Stuart* (1800) figures among his mature historical dramas, along with the *Wallenstein* trilogy (1794–99) and *Die Jüngfrau von Orleans* (1801).

58. While Frankenstein's laboratory equipment is not described in Mary Shelley's book, the Centenarian's apparatus is presented in surprising detail. There is nothing like this representation of beakers, retorts, great bells, and "diabolical instruments" under black sheets until the twentieth century; it foreshadows not only such devices as Zamyatin's Bell in *We* (1921) but also the visuals of Rotwang's laboratory in Fritz Lang's *Metropolis* (1926) and James Whale's *Frankenstein* (1931).

59. The vague "metaphysics" of Beringheld's footnote gives us the occasion to comment on the "out-of-body" experiences of Marianine and their relation to what seems a similar faculty of movement in the Centenarian himself. Marianine's experiences are the more "classic." Balzac claims to have read the work of Emmanuel Swedenborg during his school years at Vendôme (1807–1813). Sweden-

borg describes how his "interior being" leaves the body to explore the organization, visible and invisible, (the "correspondences") of all things in nature. The young Balzac also had an interest in mesmerism and magnetism. The idea here, as later expounded in *Louis Lambert*, is that if one's *être intérieur* and body can part ways during sleep, why not during waking as well? In the first draft of an early Balzac novel, *Falthurne*, the "science" of magnetism, or action at a distance, is expounded ("il est une chaîne de rapports necessaires qu'on peut manier en la connaissant" [there exists a chain of necessary connections that one can manipulate if one understands it) as means of "willing" one's "being" out of places of material confinement. The Centenarian, on two occasions, apparently uses such powers to enter or leave prisons. He also possesses the power to direct the out-of-body excursions of others; in the case of Marianine, he even appears physically to accompany her "interior being" as it passes through the material spacetime of Tullius's frantic dig. What is fascinating in "General Beringheld's" account, however, is his description of a relation between space and time that seems to imply an almost modern sense of space-time (the time of a day becomes "a unit that, though much vaster, offers no more than the space of a minute"). Human thought seems capable of condensing temporal measurements into spatial units, dilating time at will around spacelike locations, much as in SF time travel stories; in the latter the benchmark "time line" is always that of the physical body, advancing second by second, while the traveler is free to "move" in vaster times, or even (as with Marianine) in alternate spacetime dimensions.

60. Some sense of the geography of Balzac's Paris is necessary here in order to get a sense of the extent of the Centenarian's underground travels. Since Gallo-Roman times, large areas beneath Paris, notably beneath the three "monts" (Montparnasse, Montsouris, Montrouge) were quarried for building stone. In 1785, the city began to use abandoned tunnels of this underground network to house human remains, relieving the clogged and unhealthy cemeteries of the city. From Balzac's description, the Centenarian is master of a vast series of subterranean tunnels that spans much of what

was then Paris. The entrance to the catacombs today is found at the Place Denfert-Rochereau, the site of the Barrière d'Enfer, one of fifty-seven tollgates, built by the architect Claude Nicolas Ledoux, that constituted the "mur des Fermiers-Généraux" that marked the limits of Paris in Balzac's time. The Observatoire is not far from today's Place Denfert-Rochereau, more or less equidistant from Montrouge to the south and Montparnasse to the West. A straight line across Paris to the north takes one to Montmartre. The Centenarian takes Marianine into the catacombs near the Observatoire. He heads due north; his passage beneath the Seine and the Louvre on the Right Bank is described. Apparently, this journey turned in an easterly direction, for the exit point presented in the text is the Hospice des Enfants-Trouvés. This orphanage (rather, the place where stray children were rounded up and housed) was constructed during the Regency (Louis XV, early and mid-eighteenth century) by the architect Boffrand. In Balzac's time it was located, in the Ile de la Cité, on the south side of Notre Dame, adjacent to the infamous Hôtel-Dieu. This hospital, built at the same time as Notre Dame, encroached on both banks of the Seine during Balzac's time. It and the Enfants-Trouvés were demolished during the radical works program of Baron Haussmann (ca. 1865). If one visits today the crypt beneath the Square of Notre Dame, one can see vestiges of the foundations of the hospice. Tullius and Marianine emerge from the catacombs then in the exact center of Paris, followed by the rest of the party. Where the Centenarian went, no one knows.

61. "Salvator" designates not only a member of the fraternal order of medical doctors, but suggests an initiate into the more occult discipline of "magnetism."

Notes to Afterword, pp. 000–000

1. See letter from Mme. Balzac to her daughter Laure, dated August 30, 1822: "*Le Centenaire* marche en même temps; Honoré veut que je te dise qu'il savait bien pourquoi il s'était dégoûté du *Centenaire* là-bas, c'est qu'il était fini, et trop grandement fini, car en étalant un peu la fin, il y aura 4 vol" [*The Centenarian* is proceeding at the same time (as the writing of *Le Vicaire des Ardennes*). Honoré wants me to

tell you that he knew why he became disgusted with *The Centenarian* when he was over there; it was because he was finished with it, and glad to be finished, for by spreading out the ending a bit, he was able to get four volumes] *Correspondance*, ed. R. Pierrot (Paris: Garnier, 1960), 1:206.

2. Maurice Bardèche, *Balzac* (Paris: Julliard, 1980), 67.

3. There are references to *Melmoth* in Balzac's *Correspondance* as late as 1826. In a letter to "Monsieur Balzac, imprimeur à Paris," publisher G.-C. Hubert offers the printer and aspiring author, for the sum of 500 francs, the "droit de réimprimer une nouvelle édition . . . de la traduction faite par M. Jean Cohen du roman anglais intitulé *Melmoth ou l'homme errant*" [right to reprint a new edition . . . of the translation of M. Jean Cohen of the English novel entitled *Melmoth, or The Wandering Man*] (1.331)

4. Balzac, "Melmoth réconcilié," *La Comédie humaine*, 9.298.

5. *Comédie humaine*, 9.40.

6. Félix Davin, "Introduction aux *Etudes philosophiques*," in *La Comédie humaine*, 11.204.

7. F. W. J. Hemmings, *Balzac: An Interpretation of La Comédie humaine* (New York: Random House, 1967), 174.

8. See Bardèche, *Balzac*, 336–337: "Que ce récit soit directement lié à *Louis Lambert*, une phrase de *La Chronique de Paris*, supprimée plus tard, nous l'indique sans ambiguïté, puisque Balzac présente cette anecdote comme un incident qui eut lieu lors de la visite qu'il fit à Tours en 1822 pour revoir Louis Lambert et qu'il la régarde, dit-il, comme 'un des faits qui complétaient l'histoire de son camarade d'enfance'" [A sentence in the *Chronique de Paris* text, later suppressed, shows without ambiguity that this story is directly linked to *Louis Lambert*; there Balzac presents this anecdote as an incident that took place during his visit to Tours to see Louis Lambert again; he considers it, in his terms, as 'one of the facts that completed the story of his childhood friend']. The date 1822, that of the writing of *Le Centenaire*, is an interesting detail in this fictional scenario.

9. Balzac published the *Physiologie du mariage* in 1826. He links here for the first time mind and physical organism, the material and moral realms. "Energie" and "volonté" [will] become synonymous, and

their quantity finite: "L'homme a une somme donnée d'énergie" [Man has a given sum of energy] (Bardeche, *Balzac*, 154).

10. *Comédie humaine*, 9.476. By this time, the "mad" scientist or artist —mad in the sense of being an isolated overreacher, who pursues a solitary and (thus for Balzac) antisocial project—was generally in France associated with Germany, and particularly E. T. A. Hoffmann. Flanders is a borderland between French society and the outlands of fantastic science. Balzac's tempter in this novel comes from Poland, farther east and more mysterious even than Germany.

11. The title of this section in the final version is "La Confidence des Ruggieri," but the original title better describes the nature of Laurent's revelation. William Crain, in his critical edition of *The Secret of the Ruggieri* (Columbia: University of Missouri Press, 1971), reveals two versions of this narrative. The focus of the first version, which Balzac intended to publish in *La Chronique*, is clearly the "confiding" scene. The embellishments, which present the complexities of court intrigue and politics, were added later, and perhaps once again display a need, on what level of consciousness, to ballast the powerful, alternate vision of Laurent, to constrain the science of life extension (however communal) in the meshes of material cause and effect.

12. Blaise Pascal, *Pensées*, intro. T. S. Eliot (New York: E. P. Dutton, 1958), 111.

The Author

Honoré de Balzac (1799–1850) is considered one of the most
talented French novelists. His more than eighty short stories and
novels, collectively known as *La Comédie humaine*, cover a wide
expanse of French life in the early nineteenth century. Balzac is
recognized as the founder of social realism in French literature.

The Translators

George Slusser is professor of comparative literature and curator
of the Eaton Collection at University of California Riverside. He has
written or edited thirty-two books dealing with SF and the relation of
science and literature. His most recent book is *Genre at the Crossroads:
The Challenge of Fantasy* (with J. P. Barricelli) (Xenos Books, 2004). For
his contributions to the field of science fiction, the Science Fiction
Research Association gave him the Pilgrim Award in 1986.

Danièle Chatelain is professor of French at the University of Redlands
and author of *Perceiving and Telling: A Study of Iterative Discourse* (San
Diego State University Press, 1997). She has published a number of
essays in collaboration with Slusser, notably "Conveying Unknown
Worlds: Patterns of Communication in Science Fiction," in *Science
Fiction Studies* (July 2002). She coedited (with Slusser) a collection of
essays, *Transformations of Utopia: Changing Views of the Perfect Society*
(AMS Press, 1999).

Library of Congress Cataloging-in-Publication Data

Balzac, Honoré de, 1799–1850.

[Centenaire. English]

The Centenarian, or The two Beringhelds / Horace de Saint-
Aubin, pseudonym of Honoré de Balzac ; translated and
annotated by Danièle Chatelain and George Slusser.

p. cm.—(The Wesleyan early classics of science fiction series)

Includes bibliographical references.

ISBN 0-8195-6797-3 (alk. paper)

I. Title: Centenarian. II. Title: The Two Beringhelds.

III. Chatelain, Danièle. IV. Slusser, George Edgar.

V. Title. VI. Series.

PQ2163.C27E5 2006

843'.7—dc22

2005056364